Wolverine's Daughter

Doranna Durgin

BAEN

WOLVERINE'S DAUGHTER

A Baen Books Original

Baen Publishing Enterprises
P.O. Box 1403
Riverdale, NY 10471

ISBN: 0-671-57847-2

Cover art by Larry Elmore

First printing, January 2000

Distributed by Simon & Schuster
1230 Avenue of the Americas
New York, NY 10020

Typeset by Brilliant Press
Printed in the United States of America

BAEN BOOKS by DORANNA DURGIN

Dun Lady's Jess
Changespell
Barrenlands

Touched by Magic
Wolf Justice

Wolverine's Daughter

Seer's Blood
(forthcoming)

Surprise . . .

Strangers! Looters! Their quick presence stunk of magic. She had to move fast.

Kelyn ran into the roundhouse, flung her satchel on top of the rough wood chest that held foodstuffs and supplies, grappled with it a moment before she got enough of a grip on it to heave it up against the dirt-and-rock wall of the house. She snatched a handful of furs and tossed them leather-side-up over the chest and, grunting with the effort, hoisted a water crock the size of her torso high up into the air so that it crashed down to soak the leathers, chest and surrounding floor.

Pounding hoofbeats marked time for her as she snatched a burning limb from the fire and dashed outside. She glanced at the waiting pyre. A signal fire was her only chance to call for help, but she'd be damned if she used her mother's glory, her pyre for the purpose. The galloping, whooping looters were in sight; she didn't have *time*. She ran back inside anyway, scooped up her mother's stiffening body and carried it to the pyre.

The looters were circling the house and grounds now, looping around the pyre and plowing through the dried stalks from last summer's garden. Kelyn made one last, desperate dive for the house as the looters mocked her, circling closer, mimicking the fear they were sure they saw.

They saw wrong.

Dedicated to the Book-Facing Legion

With thanks for help with the details to:

Lucienne, Judith, Gary (who provided Muse Amusement),
Mom, Jennifer, Steve Stirling,
and Vince at Europa Tailors.

The God Horde Territory

Chapter 1

"Hssst," Gwawl said, drawing Kelyn's attention from the bright cave entrance. He lurked in a dark nook, hunched over a sputtering, smelly fat candle.

"What?" Kelyn's voice echoed loudly in the cave. Unimpressed by his dramatics, she propped her staff against the entrance rock, but took only a single step inward. Her toes and her nose told her well enough what they'd find here. Bats. Stinky bat guano. Nothing to keep their voices limited to *hssst* and whispers. Now, if there had been small bones crunching beneath her toes, that would be something else. Rock cat, from which to run, or holed-up nightfox to stalk. Catching the fox in its lair was the easiest of the many difficult ways to obtain nightfox pelt.

"Come look," Gwawl said in normal tones, but tinged with disappointment at her unwillingness to turn the moment more exciting.

Any regret Kelyn might have felt dissipated with the substance squishing between her toes as she joined Gwawl in his nook—a set-back with an unusually flat surface for the back wall, a solid slab of upthrust rock with enough air currents playing around it to keep the candle on the verge of snuffing out.

In the wildly uneven light, Kelyn saw what had drawn Gwawl's attention. She crowded in close to him—shoulder to adolescent shoulder, thigh to thigh, unself-conscious about it as were they all. Gwawl, Iden, Mungo, Frykla, Huon . . . and Kelyn. A hunting pack, a training pack, living the mountain summers together to learn survival, to forge the bonds of trust that would carry them through life in the tremendous, craggy Keturan mountains.

"Someone's been here," Gwawl said in grand pronouncement.

Kelyn looked at the roughly sketched creature on the cave. "Grant me more of your wisdom, Gwawl."

He scowled, and gave her a far from gentle shove. Even prepared for it, Kelyn still found herself sitting in bat guano. She kept her curses silent. Gwawl would regret it . . . later. For now she was just as intrigued as he by the discovery, and she carefully climbed to her feet, wiping her hands on the rough knit of his sleeveless tunic.

He ignored her, and pointed at the creature—smeared, it seemed, in a paint made of blood and ash and charcoal. "Do you think it was him? Doesn't it look like a wolverine?"

It did. "Maybe," she said.

"It makes sense, why there's only the one. They say he hunted alone, never trusted anyone in his pack."

That's what they said. Kelyn relieved him of the candle, suddenly disinterested. Or perhaps too interested to trust herself. When it came to her father, she was never sure just which it was. "Let's go."

"No—wait—Kelyn! Let's get the others!"

Kelyn moved past the nook and deeper into the cave, having found the steep slanting passage that caused the air current. "We'll get them," she said.

"But give them a chance to find rockrabbit first, if you want evening meal. Besides . . ." she hesitated, giving her concentration over to her toes as she negotiated a sudden drop. "Besides, maybe that's not a wolverine at all. Maybe it's an ugly turtle, and we'll find what's left of the painter just down this way. Maybe it was *his* blood in the paint."

"Kelyn, that's—"

Ridiculous, he might have said, or absurd. But he didn't, because he was just as curious as she, in a land where learning every aspect of one's surroundings could mean the difference between life and death, and learning a cave meant the potential discovery of gold or silver nuggets—and an escape route if a hunt went bad at its end. So what Gwawl said was, "Wait for me!" and Kelyn—possessor of the candle—smiled. Time to explore, and never mind the wolverine.

Turtle, she reminded herself. *Ugly* turtle.

❖ ❖ ❖

Kelyn's eyes flashed open at the soft scuff of calloused foot against rock; her hand closed around the sturdy, familiar grip of her staff. With its padded grip and its securely wrapped and mildly weighted ends, it was far from the walking staff her mother had carried from Rema. Reman ironwood—nearly impervious to blade, unaffected by magic. A good weapon to have to hand when she was being stalked in the middle of the night.

The fire, some distance away, had died to a mere glow of coals at the corner of her vision, and showed her nothing. She breathed slowly and quietly—listening—and pinpointed another pair of soft footfalls; a prickle of anticipation ran down her spine. More than one creature stalked her, then, and yet left her hunting group unaware. She was on her own, at least for the first crucial heartbeats of the struggle that loomed before her.

Another step—far too close! Whooping her ululating cry of challenge, Kelyn snatched the staff and rolled away from the creature, only to run into the bony legs of another. Sweeping the staff along the ground, she tumbled the second creature from its feet and bounced up to her knees, jabbing the weapon into the dark shadow of the first creature, a glancing blow. The creature yelped, a noise that sounded far too familiar.

"Iden!" she cried, anger quickly finding its way to her voice. "What in Ketura's name are you—"

Iden, still doubled over, waved a frantic arm before him, though she'd abandoned attack posture as soon as she'd recognized him. Then two hands clamped down on her shoulders and she knew he'd been trying to wave off whoever was with him. Her anger doubled, and she shifted her grip and drove the staff back into the ribs of the boy behind her, freeing herself. His initial grunt of pain quickly turned to a cry of fear, and the sound of feet and fingers scrabbling over rock.

"Mungo!" Iden screamed. Kelyn whirled to see Mungo sliding over the rounded edge of the granite outcrop she'd chosen for her bed. *Ketura's balls!* She lunged for him, fingers barely closing around his wrist before he slipped away from the stone.

"Got him!" she shouted, then added her own short shriek as his weight dragged her forward. Iden's weight came down on her legs, stopping them all.

"Kelyn," Mungo said, a mere whisper. He hung free and clear, dangling above a drop that would kill him several times over before he reached bottom; Kelyn herself was halfway to following him, her black hair streaming down below her head to mingle with his own. In the light of the stars, his pale face shone up at her, and the look in his eyes was easy to read. *Oh, Ketura, my life depends on Kelyn the clumsy!*

"D-don't—" he stuttered, as another pair of hands joined Iden's on her legs and yet another on her ankles; they both jerked backwards, Kelyn's skin grinding against rock. "Don't d-drop—"

"Shut up!" she hissed. Assured that she no longer needed her own clawhold on the rock, she twisted, adding her other hand to her grip on his wrist. Her fingers sunk into his flesh. Mungo's face was a rictus of pain and fear as his elbow scraped up the outthrust curve of granite, and then Kelyn jerked back again, pulled to solid ground. A pair of hands left her ankle and settled instead on Mungo's arm, reaching for his shoulders, and finally, in one last concerted heave by all involved, pulled him up with a firm grip under his arms.

They sprawled together in a sweating, fear-reeking pile of bodies, ringed by the few who had kept their feet and were demanding to know what had happened. Kelyn glared meaningfully at Mungo and Iden.

"We were just—" Iden started, but the sudden, out-of-place guffaws of one of the others cut him short.

"*I* know," Gwawl said, pointing at Mungo in evident glee. "You took all that talk at the fire too seriously!"

"You tried to sneak up and *kiss* her!" Huon said, catching on. "I bet you were gonna try to—"

"Shut up!" Mungo growled, but Kelyn already knew. She shoved Mungo's leg off her own with evident disdain.

"Don't be like that," Mungo said. "You should be glad we even think of you that way, considering—"

Little Frykla snapped, "Mungo!"

But Kelyn knew what he'd been going to say, too. Everyone knew. She was a parody of her mother's beauty, her legs and arms unceasingly gangly and perfectly matching her reputation for clumsiness. Her features themselves were lovely enough—striking green eyes, so unlike the normal Keturan hazel, and only echoed in her Reman mother's own green-tinted grey. They were tilted up on the outside edges and would have been breathtaking—if only they weren't set so wide. Her mouth was her mother's as well, shapely and . . . and too wide for her face. And her nose sat in the middle, a strong nose that must have come from her father, for it was nothing like Lytha's.

The overall effect was as if someone had set perfectly nice features upon a face that was slightly too small for them, and then pulled the skin tightly back. Kelyn had seen enough pond reflections to know, and seldom bothered with the polished bronze mirror her mother owned. Combined with her tall gawkiness, it hardly made her the sort of woman men longed for.

As if it mattered. After all, which was more important—a comely face or the ability to survive in this world?

She shoved Mungo's leg again, hardly necessary since it wasn't even touching her anymore, and disentangled her staff from where the group had communally fallen on it. "Whatever you were after, I trust you've learned you'd better *ask* first." She didn't wait for a response, but got stiffly to her feet, doing her best to reinforce her point with body language. Then the staff stubbed against someone's hip as she was bringing it upright, came free with a jerk, and clunked her on the side of the face.

She turned so fierce a glare on them all that they didn't dare laugh. "Move off," she demanded. "I'm going back to sleep."

They did as they were told, muttering amongst themselves, a combination of muffled amusement and sharply aimed jibes. Frykla hung back, as though she had something to say, but in the end remained silent and trailed the others back to the fire.

Kelyn settled back into the moss-filled hollow she'd been sleeping in, her face burning and her fingers not quite ready to release their light grip on the staff beside her. The boys' stupid attempt to fondle her upset her far less than the pointedly public reminder that she could never forget herself, never be less than perfectly aware of what she was doing, no matter how distracted, or she'd pay a price for it—usually out of her own skin.

It was a message to her, as well, that things were changing in her life, a reinforcement of the thoughts she'd put herself to sleep with—far more than her usual final review of her staff's location and the defensive points of her chosen position, both of which Mungo and Iden should have considered before they started their stupid game.

Earlier, she'd settled into the mossy spot, secure in her perch despite the fact that an arm's length away, the massive granite outcrop fell away in a precipitous drop, long enough that the sparse treetops below looked like mere puffs of green and were not visible at all in the dusk. Such were the mountains of Ketura; it was what she knew. Besides, with her belly full of roasted rockrabbit and sweet roots baked to mushiness, there was little to do but think contented thoughts in a cushion of moss and darkness.

But contentment had refused to come. Not far from her, her foster cousins still sat around the fire, making it spark and crackle by tossing in bits of fat and bone. Waste of good food, Kelyn called it, but their first hunt of the season had gone so well that they certainly had plenty. She hoped it was a good omen for the summer to come, and especially for her annual harvest of rare mountain plants.

Usually Kelyn and her mother Lytha dried and sold the precious herbs—some were medicinal, some offered delicate seasoning for the most sophisticated palette—to the Orrickian traders that veered toward their tiny village at the end of each summer. This year, Kelyn thought they would set aside the larger portion for Lytha's use, for her mother had fallen ill over the winter and had never quite come out of it.

One of the boys at the fire made a loud comment, and the others responded with raucous jeers. Kelyn made a face at them through the darkness. Since she'd been old enough to walk any distance, she and her foster cousins—all boys, except for Frykla, who was several years younger than Kelyn—had been taking this summer trip into the mountains, going deeper and deeper each season, honing skills of survival common to none outside the beasts of deep Ketura. By the time they'd started the growth spurts of adolescence, they knew each other well despite the sometimes long absences over winter, and were bound together by the extremities of life and death in an unforgiving land.

Twice the group had returned home smaller than it had left. Kelyn had watched her best friend Sigre plunge to her death after setting a careless foot on a crumbling trail, and seen young Fiacre die under the vicious claws of a giant snow panther, his guts trailing the story through the late spring snow of a high peak. Kelyn herself had touched death several times, and to the wonderment of all had prevailed. For Kelyn was, she had to admit even to herself, prone to awkwardness and the worst of luck. She stumbled on clear paths and barked her shoulders on widely spaced trees; she bore more scars than any of her peers. She'd never handled a sword because her mother was afraid she'd cut off her own foot, she had to practice hunting skills more often than any of her peers, and all of the stunted trees around the village bore the marks of her Reman ironwood staff. What took nonchalant competence for her friends often took fierce concentration on her part, and it seemed all the more notable when Lytha told her—and the others—stories of Kelyn's warrior father. *Thainn*. Kelyn had heard far too much of Thainn for a man she'd never even seen. *Thainn the Wolverine*. The man who'd left Ketura young and blazed through the outer lands, leaving tall tales behind.

Leaving Kelyn's mother behind. Leaving *Kelyn* behind, to teach herself what skills she could, striving impossibly to live up to her father's reputation.

But despite it all, she survived when others did not, and she hardened into one of the most dependable members of their closely knit group. Yet . . . this year, something seemed different. Although Frykla was as stocky and girlish as ever, Kelyn had come to her woman's courses, and her body reflected the change. And since she'd joined up with the summer hunting band, she'd come to realize that the boys had changed as well. Cracking voices were the least of it, she thought with some disdain, though the boys made much of such moments among themselves. A certain . . . *witlessness* seemed to pervade them, and at the most annoying times.

She certainly had better sense than to sit noisily around a fire drawing the attention of every territorial flesh-eater in the vicinity, especially now when the creatures were insanely protective of their young.

Kelyn checked that her staff was at hand and wiggled deeper into the moss, ignoring the furtive giggles from the fire ring. Probably just another crude breast or balls joke. Not that normally she wasn't up for as much pranking as the rest of them, but this year . . . this year, all she seemed to be able to think about was her mother, and gathering the best summer harvest of plants and dried meat that she could.

Starting tomorrow. Kelyn had drifted into sleep, secure in her ability to again come instantly awake at the slightest out-of-place noise—though she'd never expected to use that skill against someone in her own hunting pack.

Now, looking back on those thoughts and the events that had followed, she knew. This year . . . things were going to be different.

Chapter 2

Kelyn ducked her head against the wind that whipped through the Keturan foothills, unchecked by anything other than a few thin stands of trees fighting to sink roots into the rocky soil. It was a familiar scourge, this wind, and served to dry her tear-touched cheeks, leaving them tight over her bones and tingling with cold. She closed her arms more securely around her load of precious wood. She thought she'd been ready—she'd certainly seen it coming—but the calm practicality that led her to gather the first of the pyre wood three years before Lytha's death had now utterly vanished.

Kelyn looked back on the summer three years earlier, the summer when the changes started, and shook her head, a minute gesture lost in the hair that lashed around her face, try as she might to keep it tied back. Oh, the summer hunting group had adapted to their fitful advance into maturity, had held together even as they grew to be different. Aside from the loss of Mungo last year, they'd remained successful and safe, and had even taken a handful of younger siblings on their easier forays. And Kelyn had continued to deal with her own clumsiness, overcoming it by hours of practice and strength of concentration, until even Mungo, right before he died, ceased to tease her about those moments she tripped over ruts no one else could even see.

Those changes meant nothing next to this. Up until now her life had revolved around this thin-soiled meager subsistence farm, set on the rocky, deeply rolling hills below the rugged peaks of Ketura. Her mountain summers were for gathering meat and plants to tide herself and Lytha over the winter, although the year had long passed since she had become capable of surviving on her own. The winters were for making the round, rock-walled home more comfortable to live in—and lately something for Kelyn to tend her mother through. And what was this farm without her mother to center it? Was it even a farm anymore? Was it still her home?

Lytha had come here a lifetime ago—Kelyn's lifetime—to birth her daughter and raise Kelyn in her father's land. A land, she'd said, more suited to raising the daughter of the Wolverine—legendary even at that young age—and for keeping Kelyn too busy with life and survival to get into the trouble for which any child of the Wolverine would no doubt have a knack. Trouble from which no one parent alone could keep her. Lytha had never expressed any expectation that Thainn would or should consider staying with her. She never seemed to mind that the burden of raising that daughter had fallen on her shoulders alone.

The early spring wind, cold and biting, lifted the edge of the fur-lined cloak Kelyn wore, and she cursed her laziness for not having slipped her arms through the looping inner straps that would have kept it closed securely around her despite the wood she carried. She trotted quickly to the emerging shape of the pyre—behind the house, where the prevailing wind would carry the flames away from the thatched roof.

Kelyn dumped the wood beneath the pyre frame, ignoring the two long-dried limbs that bounced off her foot, and hastily gathered the cloak around herself, warming her cold fingers in the luxurious fur of the snow panther she'd slain in the highest peaks of the mountains. Luxury, that is, if she'd tried to buy it in even the rudest of marketplaces, days of travel from here. Here, it was another of the furred skins mounded around the sleeping pallets, all results of Kelyn's skill with staff and knife and sling. This one, with the supple fur of the snow panther at her shoulders and waist supplemented by two rock cat skins to protect her to mid-calf, was just more striking than most.

Despite the cloak's warmth, when the next gust of wind hit, Kelyn stiffened. Wind carried noise along with cold, and now it brought her the faintest of whoops, the louder neighing cry of a horse calling to its companions. Kelyn whirled into the wind, squinting into the tears it brought to her eyes while the cloak flapped fiercely against her grip. There, just cresting the top of the barren hill opposite the farm. Riders. Three of them, hovering on the ridge itself, their horses plunging against their bits and calling out to the fourth, whose rider galloped it foolishly down the side of the hill. Kelyn sent a curse at him, wishing him the fall he deserved, but the sturdy little horse plunged onward, and after a moment, the other three followed.

Strangers. *Ketura!* They weren't here to lay offerings on her mother's pyre. Kelyn hesitated only a moment, just long enough to pick out the wavering shape of a raised sword. Looters, then, reivers—vultures who had detected the scent of death from afar—for what little this area's inhabitants owned, they clung to far too fiercely to encourage casual raids. The looters' quick presence stunk of magic.

Kelyn ran for the roundhouse, shoving aside the flapping leather doorway and leaping down three steps to the dirt floor in the same motion. She had to move fast, choose what to save. She flung her satchel on top of the rough wood chest that held foodstuffs and supplies, and grappled with the heavy chest a moment before she got enough of a grip to heave it up against the dirt-and-rock wall of the house. She snatched a handful of furs and tossed them leather-side-up over the chest, and, with a loud grunt of effort, hoisted their largest water crock, a container almost the size of her torso, high up into the air. It crashed down to soak the leathers, chest and all.

Pounding hoofbeats marked time for her, growing louder, growing closer. Kelyn moved to the strong fire, hand hovering until she spotted and snatched the coolest end of a burning limb, and then dashed outside with it, running around the house to light the entire lower edge of the thatch without even sparing a glance at the waiting pyre. A signal fire was her only chance to call for help, and she'd be damned to a Silogan hell-cave before she used her mother's glory, her pyre. A glance at the galloping, whooping looters told her she didn't have the time, but she ran back inside the house anyway, scooped up her mother's bundled, stiffening body, and carried it as carefully as possible to the pyre—though she had no time to get Lytha up on the frame, oh no, the looters were circling the house now, looping around the pyre and plowing through the dried stalks from last summer's garden. Kelyn made one last, desperate dive for the house as the looters mocked her, circling closer, mimicking the fear they were sure they saw.

They saw wrong.

As her hand closed around the staff leaning up beside the doorway, her concentrated frown turned into a fierce grin. Tugging the tie that released her cloak, she kicked it away so she couldn't trip in it, and turned to face the looters—who by now were whooping with anticipation as well, for the first time able to see that the tall, lithe young body before them offered as much as the house.

Then they saw the look on her face. For a moment, in silent accord, they halted, cruelly pulling up their horses to regard her. The wind died. Behind her, Kelyn felt the feeble heat of the strengthening flames eating at her house; before her, the four men stared at her, not sure what to do with her.

Abruptly, they grinned at one another, pleased with their anticipated take. Pointing at her defiant stance, they broke into laughter. Kelyn stood her ground, vowing to ram her staff so far down each of those throats she'd see it come out the other end. As the laughter died into silence and the only sound was the snorting of the horses and the building crackle of flame, the men exchanged a glance, their unbound hair whipping in the sudden return of the wind.

Finally one man dismounted, throwing the reins to his companion. Sword out but at his side, he walked toward her, extending his hand in a peremptory gesture, waiting for acquiescence.

Kelyn lifted a lip in silent disdain, as eloquent as any poet.

The man stopped short, surprise quickly turning to annoyance—but not as fast as Kelyn went from defender to attacker. Shifting her hands down on the staff, pivoting around one foot, she loosed her hunt cry into the midst of them, bringing the staff around to slam into the man's arm at the elbow. She couldn't hear the cracking bone above her own cry, but white bone ripped clear of the shirt. As the man screamed she reversed her direction and grip and felt the solid blow of the other end of the staff just below his ear.

His body wobbled, then fell. Kelyn leapt for his sword, unfamiliar as it was, and crouched over him, staff in one hand and his sword in the other, her back still to the flaming house.

"Barbarian bitch!" one of the men shouted at her, the first intelligible words from any of them and heavily accented at that. She spat at him, and they didn't take it any more lightly just because the wind caught it and the spittle landed on her chin. They attacked, rushing her one after the other, trying to draw her off balance with the charging intimidation of barely controlled horses. Her staff became her shield, wielded one-handed and as often as not almost torn from her grip. The sword, badly balanced and as odd to her hand as a one-ended staff, nonetheless managed to cut flesh, scoring on the leg of one man, wounding the horse of another.

But all too soon she was panting, tiring, and becoming aware that this was what their game was all about—wearing her down until she could no longer lift sword or staff to defend herself. An ill-judged dodge brought her into the shoulder of one of the horses, and Kelyn tumbled, unable to hold onto the staff. By the time she was back on her knees, the next horse was rushing her, its rider wearing a grin of delight on his dirty face.

The horse was huge in her vision, its chest as wide as the horizon itself, its sharp hooves reaching for her—Kelyn flung herself to the side, under the reaching sword of the rider, and used the strength of a two-handed grip to plow her borrowed blade right through the animal's belly, closing her eyes against the warm spray of blood.

The horse grunted, surprise more than pain, its legs

giving way with the shock, and its rider tumbled off with his momentum. Not even fully on her feet, Kelyn lunged for him as he rolled, landing on him with her knees and bringing the sword hilt down into his face just as he could see she was right *there*, his eyes widening with realization far too late to do him any good.

Kelyn staggered to her feet to find the others pulling up a distance away, watching with shock of their own, their confident expressions turning into something more grim but just as determined. For the first time she was aware of the ache in her arms, the bruises and cuts she had sustained, and the fact that her tunic was torn and pulled most of the way down her shoulder. Behind her, the roof had flared into its brightest flame and was starting to gutter, the wind turning into more hindrance than help. If no one had seen the smoke by now, they weren't going to.

One of the riders seemed to notice Lytha's body for the first time. He took his horse in a prancing, jerky trot around the pyre, and looked back at Kelyn with a leer. Kelyn stiffened. Would he—? The beast would even *consider* desecrating her mother's body?

Think, Kelyn! He just wanted to get her away from the house, get her to leave herself open on all sides so they could both attack at once.

And was she supposed to cringe there and watch this filth touch her mother? The other rider laughed as his companion dismounted, watching for Kelyn's reaction to her choice.

That Lytha herself would have certainly wished her body trampled and defiled before her daughter submitted to filth such as this was both clear as sunlight and totally irrelevant.

Kelyn's hand clenched into a white-knuckled fist around the sword hilt. She would not be helpless without it. Her staff was by her feet, and her knife still in her belt. She was an accurate throw, and could hit either man where they stood—except that a thrown weapon was a lost weapon. Clenching her teeth, Kelyn held the sword straight out from her side and dropped it, forcing her fingers to uncurl from the blood-sticky grip. Giving up. Or—at least presenting a fair semblance of a young woman giving up.

They laughed, all confidence again despite their downed comrades. Head down, hands out, Kelyn moved away from the house a few steps. The dismounted looter looked at her, his laugh turning nasty. And then he reached for Lytha's wrapped body.

"*No!*" Kelyn's outraged cry brought nothing but further laughter, and her decision was made. Out came the knife, whipping through the air to bury itself in the man's lower back, while Kelyn herself twisted and dove for her staff, knowing she had the time to grab it but not the time to bring it up—sudden hoofbeats did nothing but confirm the horseman's charge and the weary determination of her effort to be inhumanly quick—

And then Kelyn realized that the hoofbeats were too far away to be the man before her, and that they came inconsistently against the gusting wind. Rolling to her feet, she discovered a new player galloping in, coming from the direction opposite the looters, resolving into two figures clinging tightly to a sturdy, short-legged plow pony. Another blink of time and she thrust her staff defiantly into the air, renewing her hunt cry in a greeting to Iden and the still stocky, ever stronger form of Frykla behind him. They matched her cry with their own, and Frykla brandished a short sword as the pony swerved around the pyre and headed straight for the remaining horseman, making the odds a sudden three against one.

He was no fool. He turned the horse on its haunches and spanked it with the flat of his sword, pushing the astonished animal into a run for his life.

The horse barely made it up to speed before the running animals merged into one awkward shape. When they separated, Frykla was on the ground with the looter jerking out the last of his life beneath her.

That was it, then. Kelyn closed her eyes, taking a deep breath. Her knees were wobbly, her hands trembled, and her stomach roiled at the thought of these first human lives on her hands. But with another deep breath, she decided that perhaps she trembled because of the cold bite of the wind against her battle-sweaty skin, and that her knees were simply tired. She turned to find her cloak—and tangled her feet together, landing on the ground with a tired grunt.

She didn't bother to curse. From here she could see the cloak and she merely crawled to it, fastening it securely before climbing to her feet and trying to tug her tunic into some semblance of its former shape. Wiping blood and sweat off her face, she strode to the looter who was twitching next to Lytha, jerked the knife out of his lower back, and matter-of-factly drew it across his throat. She cleaned the blade on his clothes and sheathed it before dragging the body away from Lytha, dumping it well behind the house.

Of the other two, one man was already dead, and the other, his nose smashed beyond recognition along with one of his eyes, was just groping his way to his hands and knees. Kelyn kicked him down again and ran her hands over his body, wondering how anyone who wore such greasy leathers and who smelled so bad could think to call *her* barbarian. She relieved him of his knife and several flat weapons with a number of oddly shaped blades. She was turning one over in her hand when Iden and Frykla trotted back up, dropping off the pony to survey the ruins of her house with uniformly grim expressions.

"He lives?" Frykla asked, eyeing the man with distaste.

"For now," Kelyn told her, experimentally tossing one of the strange blades. "I'm of a mind to tie him to one of those horses and whip them on their way to the border." Let others of his ilk see what happened when they crossed the border with mayhem in mind.

Iden nodded once, satisfied with the idea. The looters' horses stood around in uncertain poses, not quite willing to leave each other or Iden's pony. Even the one who had been chased off with the last bandit was slowly meandering back toward the house. "I don't understand," Iden said, gradually taking in the sight of her mother's prepared body. "We all knew Lytha was ill, but not . . . we would not have left you alone in your time of mourning. That these men knew you were in a vulnerable time—"

"Maybe this has something to do with it," Frykla said, lifting her hand. A sharp, black-dyed bone needle, far too thick for sewing, dangled from a long thong, glittering impossibly.

"Sorcery." Iden made a face.

Kelyn reached for the needle. "I thought I smelled magic in this." She held it by its thong, careful not to touch the bone itself. "Rika might know what it is."

"Destroy it," Iden grunted, and Frykla nodded quick agreement.

"How? Crush it and release Ketura knows *what* into my body?" Kelyn leaned over the man beside them, who had managed to crawl several feet away, as if he'd hoped they wouldn't notice. "Save your effort," she whispered harshly into his ear. "You'll need it, soon enough." She jerked a pouch from his belt and dumped its meager contents on top of him, replacing them with the needle and stuffing it all into one of her cloak pockets.

Frykla moved to what had been the door to the house and was now a gaping hole in the circular rock wall. "What of your house?"

Kelyn joined her there. Burning thatch had fallen inside to ignite anything that was flammable; the air was redolent with the lingering odor of burnt fur and charred leather, while cinders still swirled aimlessly in the currents that the wind, gusting over the rock walls above, created on the floor of the dug-out circle. Against the wall, a steaming leather mound marred by random scorch marks was the only object not made of rock that seemed reasonably whole.

Ignoring the cinders, Kelyn hopped down into the room and strode over to the chest, throwing off the furs to find the satchel and chest untouched. Iden and Frykla made no comment as she rummaged through the contents of the chest, adding *this* to her satchel, putting *that* aside. When she stood, the satchel was full. She rolled up the still-damp furs and tied them that way, then tossed the bundle over the rock wall. "Take whatever's left for yourselves," she told her friends.

"But, Kelyn—" Frykla started, glancing up at Iden.

"Come stay with us," Iden told her. "We'll build you a new house when the ground thaws enough for the digging."

Kelyn looked at them, imagining herself the third person in the small home of the newly handfasted couple, and shook her head.

"Then talk to Gwawl. You know he wants you. And he's started his own home, not far from ours—"

Kelyn shook her head again, more firmly this time. "I'll take no one who wants me out of pity," she said. "And . . . I've a craving lately . . . To see things. To know more than this land can teach me." She couldn't leave while her mother had still lived, and even then, the house had exerted a pull on her. Now both were gone. She looked at Frykla and Iden and shrugged. "The gods seem to have given me a shove."

"All gods should be like Ketura, and stay out of our business," Iden muttered. "Gwawl has no pity in him, Kelyn, you should know that. Nor do you need it."

"Kelyn—" Frykla started again, and again her protest died in her throat, this time at Kelyn's expression.

"Come," Kelyn said. "Lytha waits. Do me the honor of standing by while I light the pyre."

❖ ❖ ❖

"Move, you son of a donkey," Kelyn muttered hours later, tugging on the reins of the horse she led. It didn't know her, it didn't trust her, and as far as she could tell, it was only half tame, anyway. She began to have second thoughts about gifting it to Rika, but she supposed if anyone could handle the beast, it would be Auntie Rika. Rika, nobody's relative yet everybody's aunt. She had midwifed Kelyn, treated Lytha's illness, and provided everyone in the area with charms and wards for years beyond memory, although she only rarely dealt in curses.

Her attention on the horse, Kelyn stumbled over something in the rough path and nearly fell, losing her satchel and staff in the process. At least neither had fallen into any of the numerous muddy patches around her. The path wound along the hillsides, over rocky outcrops and through thin patches of lower Ketura's stunted little hardwoods and stocky pines; the track was never any good at this time of year, and yesterday's sleety rain hadn't helped any. Kelyn scooped the satchel up without pausing, and the horse chose that moment to stop short, snorting suspiciously and almost jerking Kelyn's arm out of its socket.

Kelyn closed her eyes and gathered the shredded remnants of her temper around her. When she opened them, it was to glare at the horse. "You could be drying in someone's smokehouse right now," she told it in a dangerously quiet voice. "It could still happen."

"Now, now, child," came a voice from the small stand of trees ahead of her. Kelyn started, even though she'd already recognized Rika's warm, creaky voice. And she berated herself for being taken by surprise, even though no one ever saw Rika before Rika was ready to be seen.

"Aunt," Kelyn said. "I was coming to see you." She hesitated, then blurted out all at once, "I—this horse—Lytha's dead—"

"Yes, I know," Rika said, her voice tinged with sadness. She stepped out of the trees, an elderly woman barely bowed, like a fine straight piece of wood made only stronger with age. Her hair was long and wild, and often looked about to spring free from the thong that held it. But her impossibly wrinkled skin, as usual, nearly masked her expression. She murmured again, "I know."

Kelyn thought about asking just which of those things the old woman had known, and thought better of it. "I brought you this horse. I thought you might be able to do something with it. If not," she said, and shrugged, "you can always fatten it up over the summer."

Rika held her hand out. "You've had a long day, I see. Give me the horse, and we'll go sup together."

Kelyn hesitated, thinking how much harder it would be for the old woman to lead this fractious creature along the muddy path. Then again, she'd never seen Rika trip over her own feet. She handed over the reins.

"There, there," Rika murmured to the horse. "Wouldn't you like to be in a nice little shed, with plenty of hay for your supper?"

Rema's Blessing, the creature's ears perked forward and then actually *drooped* in contentment! Kelyn kept her disgruntled noises to herself, and wondered again that if Rika could accomplish such things, surely it wouldn't be too much to ask for a little charm against clumsiness. . . .

She followed the now-placid horse to its new home, keeping a cautious distance from its heels all the same.

Rika put the horse in the tiny outbuilding that held her goat and had Kelyn carry its gear into her roundhouse, where the oil lamp would offer better light than growing dusk. After a great deal of *tsking* at the dry, unmaintained leather, she allowed that it would fix up to be a nice kit, and she would likely get a good price for it if she decided to butcher the horse for winter. Then, while Kelyn sat in numb fatigue, she fried sweet root and flour cakes at the fire, slathered butter on them, and handed Kelyn a share any growing boy would be challenged to put away.

Kelyn did it handily, without pausing. She chased it down with goat milk and sat, glaze-eyed, before Rika's fire. Rika finished her own meal in a more refined fashion, seated on the rock bench that curved against the wall of the house, then pulled her short milking stool up next to Kelyn and sat. "Thainn is a loner; he was always so. He trusted no one, not truly. But he touched Lytha, and she, I think, touched him, for she was a remarkable woman. I knew so when I first saw her, so far from home, carrying little more than your staff, a sturdy knife, and a tinder bag with only the remnants of an old mouse nest. And coins. A handful of gold, traded—"

"For the ruby Thainn gave her." Kelyn didn't bother to hide her flat disinterest, even in the startling news that Rika had known her father. Everyone knew how she felt about Thainn.

"Her journey here alone made for a tale as stirring

as any of Thainn's," Rika said gently. "You gave her a proper send-off?"

Kelyn blinked. "Yes," she said. "A huge pyre. Iden and Frykla were there."

"She would have been proud of how you handled yourself this afternoon," Rika said. At Kelyn's sharp look, she chuckled and said, "No, child, the details are your own. I felt the magic and scryed out the men just as they reached you. And now I see you here with one of their horses. I can come to my own conclusions from there."

Kelyn thought there was probably more to it, but her attention was elsewhere, and abruptly so. She reached for her set-aside cloak and pawed through it, looking for the right pocket. Ah—there! She thrust the newly acquired pouch and its contents at Rika. "What can you tell me of this?"

Rika upended the pouch and shook the bone needle into her hand, heedless of Kelyn's wince. "It can't hurt me, child," she said. "Nor you." Kelyn gave her a skeptical eye, but Rika ignored that, too. "Here is the magic I felt. It's a nasty thing, not something I would deal with."

"They rode upon us before anyone else knew of Lytha's death," Kelyn said, and then amended that to, "Anyone else besides you, I suppose."

"Yes, I felt her pass," Rika murmured. "After working so long together to fight her malaise, we had some small connection. As I have with you, and every other child I have helped to birth." She held the needle up, turning it to display the glitter of its cold beauty in the firelight. "Think of it as a kind of vulture, Kelyn. Something that points to folk who are in mourning and vulnerable, or who live alone and in death have left their treasures, whatever they might be, unguarded and free for the taking."

Kelyn snorted. "And what would they have found

at our home that would be worth even the bother of riding out there?"

Rika smiled at her. "You alone would be worth twice whatever distance they rode," she said, her wrinkle-enclosed eyes filled with affection. When Kelyn snorted at that, too, Rika merely said, "Your cloak, then. Used as the lining for luxuriously fine cloth, it would fetch much more than you imagine at market."

Kelyn had nothing to say to that. She thought the cloak meant much more to her, who had faced and slain the creature, than it would mean to someone who had the money to buy it. But then, she was not one of the city dwellers, who were, from what little she had seen, bent on cluttering their lives with objects. She had what she needed to live, and she wanted nothing else.

"Shall I destroy it for you?" Rika said, and nodded at the needle.

Kelyn shook her head, though she could not have said why. What she *wanted* to say she suddenly found awkward in her mouth, and she wished that, of all things, this would be one of those things that old Auntie Rika knew before she ought. But then, maybe some things were meant to be said, though the words might have been more carefully chosen than those she blurted out. "I'm leaving."

Rika's eyes might have widened a little, but it was brief and looked not at all like surprise. "Perhaps it is time."

"What's that supposed to mean?" Kelyn scowled at her, forgetting for an instant the respect and awe this woman commanded in her.

"It means that you are alone in the world, and it is time to find your self."

That brought nothing but another frown. "I know who I am."

Rika turned brusque. "Like everyone else, you think you do." She handed the needle back to Kelyn. "Let this be your guide. Follow it to your self, and to your father. When you find your father, you will find you."

So shocked that she could not do so much as reach out for the spelled needle, Kelyn found herself staring opened-mouthed. "My *father*," she sputtered finally. "I need nothing from him! He's nothing but a—" *cocker!* "—a witless warrior!"

"I don't recall your mother ever speaking such about him," Rika said, and there was something in her voice that shamed Kelyn. She looked steadfastly at her own feet, at the ends of those too-long crossed legs, her hands curled in her lap. Finally, Rika leaned over and gently dropped the needle into Kelyn's grasp. "Stay the night here, child. And in the morning, go looking for your self. Your path will end at your father."

Chapter 3

Kelyn set out for Orrick, the needle tucked safely away at the bottom of her satchel—something often thought of, and never touched. Perhaps she would become used to the idea of dealing with such magic, though she would never use it the way those looters had. Rika had said to use it as a guide to find her self, but Kelyn knew well enough that she wanted to make her way through Atlia, so what was the point of consulting it before then?

Any excuse to avoid the thing.

Travel through Orrick's land was not a hard thing. She hadn't known what to expect—only that the gods shaped their lands as they would. Ketura had chosen craggy, jutting mountains and cold, sparsely vegetated foothills, and had made a strong, large people to populate them. Orrick, it seemed, favored trees, and she found the people here to be distinctly shorter than her own. And she'd heard that other gods marked their lands with stranger environs: Rema, a land of herbs, forests, and simple folk—her mother's land; and Dryden, where there was nothing but sand

and snakes and lizards; and Siloga, from whence came the darkest mages, and a slight people with handsome features and nut-brown skin.

She'd *heard*.

Now she was going to see for herself.

She didn't have the coin to stay at the travelers' houses along the road, but no one kicked her out for quietly warming herself by the fire as she passed through. She spent time at the little inns if the keepers found work for her, usually carrying heavy loads or cleaning noxious stalls and pits—though she quickly learned the hazards of that duty if she let her concentration slip.

Pit farming, feh. Not for the occasionally clumsy.

But the woods provided plenty of shelter themselves, as well as much more kindling and game than Kelyn was used to having at her disposal. Even when the trees thinned to day-wide areas of rolling plains, Kelyn slept out under the stars, always finding enough of a hollow in the tough, stalky grasses that the wind whistled over her as she slept. The wind was never as cold as that which swept through her foothills, anyway, and she was just as content making her own fire and roasting her own kill as sharing someone else's of either.

She took her time, lingering where she had a chance to pick up the language—for almost everyone disdained to know hers—or to study the people. She practiced with the strange knives she'd taken from the looter, and soon learned to flick them into targets as she would skip a stone across a pond. By the time she neared the Atlian border, the winds were turning warm and less insistent, and she slept where she would, oiled and waxed cloak pulled over her head against the frequent, gentle spring rains.

It was in one such rain that she found herself sprawled on her stomach at the top of a slight rise, cloak hood drooping over her forehead as she chewed on the stem of one of last year's grasses and considered the town before her. The huddle of buildings rose cleanly from the cleared ground around it, and the path leading into them was wider than any of the meandering traders' roads that Kelyn had followed so far. There were even the beginnings of a stout wood wall around it.

She had the feeling that this town would teach her more—or provide her with more challenges—than had any of the little way stations and trading spots she'd hesitated in before. She also figured it would take coin if she wanted to stay there long, and so faced a decision that would only become more imperative as she moved away from Ketura: finding a way to earn that coin. The skills she had were things that anyone might be good at, but she knew she didn't want to spend much more time doing the things no one else wanted to do . . . like cleaning pits.

Kelyn made a face and spit out the grass stalk. What was the point of gathering people together in such populations that their food had to be carried in, their shelters all crammed together, and their waste carried out? Why, when the wind shifted, she could smell the town from here!

Perhaps she'd just stay out in Orrick's mild lands for a while, and walk into the town each day to learn what she could. That plan seemed most sensible. Kelyn climbed to her feet and scouted a wide circle around the town, taking note of gaps in the wall and finding an area downwind of the garbage heap where she definitely wouldn't choose to sleep. She found a spot that satisfied her just inside the nearest tree line—too close, but all right for tonight—and turned toward one of the gaps, not hesitating until she arrived at the wall. Inside, the buildings crowded close; they were square-built things of timber, wattle, daub, and whitewash, their roofs as much shingled as thatched.

Kelyn took a deep breath, noted that the wall workers weren't paying the least attention to her, and moved into the town with the same long, easy strides that had carried her across Atlia.

That was her first mistake. Fine for the outskirts of the town, such a pace was nearly impossible once she was among the people in the marketplace—to her eyes, a huge, impossibly crowded area where no person could possibly sift out and locate the specific goods they wanted, especially not amidst the bright canvas tenting the tops and sides of the stalls. After stepping on a number of heels and barely rescuing her own toes from the solid wooden wheels of an oxcart, Kelyn choked back her strides. These people must not really have anywhere to go, to meander as they did.

Then again, neither did she.

She paused to look at a vendor's collection of nuts, none of which she had ever seen before, and her grumbling stomach convinced her that when she finally earned some coin, this place would be the first at which to spend it. Why, she could try a different type every day and take half a moon going through them!

The vendor eyed her expectantly, and she spread her empty hands at him; he promptly ignored her. It was his intense gaze on something behind Kelyn that prompted her to turn. Through the stream of people passing by, she deciphered the form of a short woman and the man who was dragging her down the street by her arm. Her face was streaked with tears, and she kept tripping on her long tunic-dress, resisting him every stride.

"Why does that man drag her?" Kelyn asked the nut

vendor, careful with the new language. He eyed her, assessing her accent and reassessing her appearance, and then shrugged. Kelyn tried again. "If she doesn't want to go with him, why doesn't she fight him?"

At that, he grunted, pointedly looking up and down her tall frame, her rough, untailored tunic and simple pants. "*She's* no savage, you. What's her strength to his?"

Kelyn traded her stare between the vendor and the altercation edging its way down the street. A particularly strong yank dragged the woman through a pile of baskets, and she shrieked, almost falling, while the owner of the baskets picked up her own cry of protest. The man shouted something back, not hesitating in his progress. And the nut vendor watched, obviously interested, but just as obviously not about to move.

"Why doesn't anyone help her?" Kelyn asked. "Is she being punished?"

He gave her a hard look. "Because we know how to mind our own business. You do the same, you want to get along in these lands."

Baffled, Kelyn just looked at him. Would she stand by and let one of her companions be mauled by a rock cat, or gored by one of the territorial mountain goats? Survival of the fittest was the rule of the mountains, but everyone got into trouble sometimes. Where would she herself be now, if Iden and Frykla hadn't come to her aid at the house? With a scowl for the nut vendor, she flicked her cloak back over her shoulder and went after the couple, going past the man to stop behind him and stand squarely in his path.

He backed right into her, gave her a startled glance, and quickly turned it into a frown. "Outta the way," he grunted, as the woman, seeing opportunity, redoubled her efforts to escape. He merely reestablished his grip and moved on—only to bounce off Kelyn again. This time he rounded on her, but with his mouth open and ready to spout rudeness; he suddenly seemed to realize that he was looking *up* at her.

"She doesn't want to go with you," Kelyn said. "But you probably can't see that, considering you've just walked into me twice."

"Mind yer own," the man snapped, recovered from his surprise. "She committed to me."

"No!" the woman said. "My father did that, and it was before either of us knew what a black-hearted bastard you are. My father would never hand me over to a man who beat me!"

"And I say he would," the man sneered, a quick gesture with his fist making the woman cringe. "Since he's dead, I guess we'll just have to take my word on it, won't we?"

"No, we won't." Kelyn thought she sounded quite reasonable. Of course, she couldn't help tightening the grip on her staff, wishing it was his throat, but if one didn't notice, perhaps she would *look* reasonable, too.

"No one's going to stop me, you can see that," the man said, his eye gleaming as he indicated the marketplace with a sweep of his arm. "I'll do as I please with this worthless trash." He gave a little laugh, and as if to prove his point, balled up his fist and turned on the woman.

Kelyn instantly tapped him on the shin with her staff, knowing from hard experience that it took little effort to create excruciating pain along the edge of the bone.

It got his attention, all right. He threw the woman against the building beside them and turned on Kelyn, aiming that same fist right at her face. But the reflexes that could handle the lightning-swift moves of a rock cat had no problem with this supposedly civilized human. She knocked his hand out of the way with the upper end of the staff and hit him on the shin again with the lower. She couldn't follow the torrent of ugly words that came from his mouth then, but she got the meaning well enough, especially when he came at her again—this time with the glint of metal in his hand, slashing for her arm. Idiot.

Without stepping back, Kelyn knocked him aside and whacked the other shin, putting some force behind it. He went down, bellowing outrage, but came right back up again, still clutching the knife. Definitely an idiot. Kelyn stepped back into guard, whirling the staff before her. While he was still evaluating his chances of getting through it, she tapped him on the shoulder, the flank, beside his knee, his elbow—the knife went flying at that one—and then, without quite the force to ruin him, brought the ironwood up between his legs.

Already staggering, he dropped with a screech and made no attempt to rise. Kelyn set the staff against the ground and regarded him with one hand on her hip, frowning. The people in the market walked around them, muttering and scowling, but doing no more to help the man than they had the woman. Kelyn had a sudden strong urge to return to Ketura, where people behaved in a reasonable manner . . . but that would end this journey before it had really started. She was not one to ignore Rika's words, besides.

She leaned over the man, impartially watching his gyrations of pain. When she couldn't get his attention, she resettled the staff from the ground to his stomach. He blinked up at her, panting, tears leaking from his eyes. She said, "Protect this woman well, cocker, or—Rema curse you—I will come for you." She looked over at the woman, who still cowered against the building, seemingly unable to comprehend how quickly the fates had turned on her tormenter. "I'll be around."

And she was, at least for a while. Oblivious of the stir her actions had caused, over the next few days Kelyn found several establishments willing to pay her for fresh meat. While dawn and dusk found her stalking game on the plains, perfecting her newly acquired skills of hunting in this environment, during the day she strolled the town, learning the ways of people outside Ketura. She discovered a small population of ragged, independent children who were as adept with their tongues as they were with their thieving fingers, and from them she learned the most. They were, she thought, much like her own hunting pack—only their territory was here in this civilized world—and she accorded them respect for it. In turn they fed her gossip, told her stories, explained who was who, and what they did for the town . . . or *to* it.

The oldest child's name was Aktel, and one day as she put down her coin and contemplated which of the nut vendor's wares to sample next—for he had been scrupulously polite to her since that first day—he came running to her. The vendor started at his sudden arrival and instantly snapped, "Here, you! Get away from my nuts!"

Kelyn said, "He is here to talk to me. Your *nuts* are safe." At her scowl, he backed up, his hands reflexively moving to protect himself. She turned to the boy. "Aktel, what?"

"The lady," Aktel said, his face serious beneath its accustomed smear of dirt. "The one you helped. Busted Balls has her in the tavern, and—"

That was enough. She tossed him a nut, one of the biggest—the man had said it came from some jungle so far south that the people there were all black, but she didn't believe it herself—and ran for the tavern on feet that no longer stepped on other people's heels nor rarely tripped over themselves, for she was accustomed to the sounds, sights, and smells of the town now, and didn't find them such a distraction.

But she would never grow accustomed to the thick smells of the tavern. She wrinkled her nose as she stepped into the already open doorway, Aktel at her heels no matter how many times she waved him off. The place was noisy, and overcrowded, and always too warm; the occupants moved in an extemporaneous dance of customers, serving wenches, and the ever-changing number of scantily clad women who were always thrusting their personal wares in some man's face.

As soon as her eyes grew used to the squat building's dim light, Kelyn saw what she was there to see. The man she'd already dealt with once, loud and laughing, sat with his back to her and his face to the half-score of friends seated around a rough round table and laughing along with him. The woman, her face bruised, one arm cradled protectively close to her side, sat on the filthy, ale-and-worse soaked floor by his feet, where she'd evidently been commanded to stay.

Busted Balls, Aktel had called him—she *ought* to have, too. But that would still have left him the ability to hit this woman and any other. . . .

Kelyn stalked through the tavern, half aware of the hasty shifting and dodging that cleared her path. The expression on his friends' faces must have warned the man, for he turned to see Kelyn coming, his hands on the table to steady himself after who knew how many tankers of the thick ale this place served.

"I *told you*," Kelyn said, and brought her staff down hard on both his hands.

❖ ❖ ❖

Kelyn sat on a stool in the corner of the small, dim office, not bothering to hide her impatience. The windows were high and much too small for a body to fit through, even if the shutters weren't in the way. The door was thick, solid wood—and locked. There was a fireplace, but the tiny chimney offered no escape. Kelyn drew her cloak closed and scowled around the room.

Finally, the lock made a few grating noises and the wiry little man who had escorted her here came in. Evidently he wasn't too worried about her, for he didn't bother to lock the door when he closed it. He dumped a roll of parchment on the rickety little desk up against the wall and fumbled for the inkwell, finding the proper place in the roll at the same time. "What's yer name again?"

"Kelyn. And I want my staff back."

"Not so fast, not so fast," he muttered, carefully scratching a notation on the roll. "From Ketura, I take it? I've seen yer like before. Not all that often, no, the savages stay where it suits their ways, but I know what I see. . . ." Mumble, scratch, mumble. Kelyn, unseen, rolled her eyes.

A huge man barged through the door, talking even before it was all the way open. "Gort, there's one dead down in the pit, dammit, I told ya that scrawny one wouldn't last—" On catching sight of Kelyn, he stopped short, and Kelyn found herself slowly rising to her feet, almost as if accepting a challenge.

"Eh, leave off," the wiry man grumbled, still not looking up. "She ain't given me any trouble."

"Knew she'd end up here sooner or later," the big man grunted. "Fer what?"

"Broke a fellow's hands to bits," the other said shortly. "Whole tavern of witnesses, unprovoked assault." He finished his notations and set the quill and ink aside, holding the parchment open with one hand so it could dry. For the first time since returning, he glanced at Kelyn, but she couldn't read him at all.

"He deserved it," she said, shifting warily, unhappy to be caught in the corner with both of them in this small room. "He's lucky I left him his—"

"Keep your silence," the big man snarled at her.

Gort waved an imprecise hand in the air. "Neh, neh, none of that."

But Kelyn's temper, once ignited, only grew hotter. "What about that woman he beat? How can you protect him, and not her?"

"That were personal," Gort said. "It sure weren't yours to bust into. As it happens, she's got cousins from south a ways, and word is they're on their way. It'd've been handled, private like. Just can't let folks—that's *you*—go around bustin' other people up 'cause they've took offense."

Kelyn glowered at him and the big man both. "And if she hadn't had family?"

No one said anything, until the big man grunted, "Can't go around bustin' people up in this town, Keturan trash. It'll be the pit fer you."

"The pit?" Kelyn repeated. She hadn't liked the sound of the place the first time she heard of it, and now—

"The pit," Gort affirmed. "So just hand over yer cloak, now, you wouldn't want it spoilt down there."

Kelyn crossed her arms over her chest and glared at them. She'd never have simply *followed* him to this place if she'd had any idea what it was all about, and she had no intention of staying here. Gort shrugged, and gestured to the big man. "Take her, then. You've got a hand of days coming to you, Keturan. You best take those days to think about yer life. I seen more'n my share of you come down from the hills, and them that don't scurry on back spend most their days in pits one place or another, never turnin' away from trouble when it steps out in front of them. You're headed for the same, you don't wise up."

Kelyn snorted at him. "*I'm* not afraid of trouble," she said, and what she didn't say sounded just as loud through the room. *Not like you are.*

"Neh," Gort said, finally letting the parchment curl back into its roll. "None of ye are. Just look at that Thainn fellow. But ye got any brains to speak of, ye'll change yer mind. Be a shame to waste one such as you."

And what was that supposed to mean? Kelyn opened her mouth to cut through all these words and demand her staff again, but Gort had nodded at the big man, and his hand closed around her arm, fingers digging in at her initial resistance. As if she would let these two bullies throw her in some pit for doing the very thing they ought to have done themselves!

Looking at the big man's bulk filling the door, at the tiny window high on the wall, Kelyn abruptly squelched her first impulse to fight. This was not the place. She let herself be led out the door—not missing a syllable of Gort's whispered, *Get that cloak before she goes down*—and into a corridor so tiny the man had to drag her behind him, for they didn't fit abreast. They went past a series of doors, one of which was open far enough for Kelyn to get a glimpse of weapons and satchels and an odd saddle or two; she craned to see if her staff was there, but the man unheedingly jerked her onward—toward a growing stink which far outmatched that of the tavern.

Civilization.

The corridor dead-ended and there in the floor there was a rusty iron grate. *The pit.* From within came weak, pleading cries for water and freedom, and the most incredible *stench*. . . . Kelyn stared into the darkness beyond the grate, her face wrinkled into an expression of utter disgust. Beside her, the man rumbled in mean laughter and yanked the heavy grating up, leaning it against the wall. "Gimme the cloak now, sister, we've got better use for it than you."

Kelyn's eyes narrowed. As strong as she was, she had no doubt the man was stronger, and she had no staff to use on him—but there was something to be said for quickness and leverage. The floor between the other side of the pit and the wall was a mere hand and a half wide, but Kelyn had gripped narrower ledges than that with the same toes on which she now balanced. Slowly, she undid the ties to her cloak, and handed the fur over to him.

As soon as his hand closed over it, she leapt, whirling to face him, her feet landing solidly in the narrow space available and the cloak stretched between them over the stench of the pit. He was already off balance, surprised and even confused, though the confusion vanished as Kelyn gave the cloak a yank, putting all her strength into it—and he teetered forward over the gaping hole. Snatching another handful of fur, she gave another, sharper tug—and over he went, dropping the cloak in favor of grabbing the edge of the pit.

Kelyn leapt over him, snatching at the grate as soon as her feet hit the floor, tipping it back where it belonged. It hit the man's head first, settling crookedly into place on top of one of his hands. Bellowing protest and pain, he yanked the hand loose and fell.

He made a squishing noise as he landed in the filth and sprawled amidst the stunned silence of the prisoners. Then they seemed to realize their opportunity, and a rally cry of anger rang out.

Kelyn didn't wait around to hear the blows that surely followed. She turned and ran, thinking of her staff, and of freedom.

❖ ❖ ❖

Staff by her side, Kelyn sprawled on her stomach at the top of a slight rise, cloak puddled beside her as she chewed on the stem of one of this year's new, sweet green grasses and again considered the town before her. It had taught her as much as she'd expected and more—especially that wiry little man called Gort.

When you find your father, you will find you, Rika had said. And of the needle, *follow it to your self*. Kelyn smiled grimly. All the needle could do was point her at trouble, to places where people were in shock and grieving. Maybe even to scenes like the first time she'd dealt with Busted Balls, when any good looter could have made use of the distraction to snatch things from the vendors.

Never turnin' away from trouble, Gort had said about Keturans—because, like Kelyn, they didn't fear it. *Thainn the Keturan*, Kelyn thought, lifting the needle on its thong to twirl it lazily in the sun, trusting Rika's words to her. *If I follow this trouble dowser long enough, I'll find* you.

Chapter 4

When the evenly spaced stone pillars marking the border between Orrick and Atlia came into view, Kelyn turned southeast to skirt the border, paralleling the faint trade road that ran that same course. She had learned her lesson about spending too much time in towns—*for now*—and had discovered that if she approached with plenty of field-dressed game in hand, she could sell her bounty, treat herself to a good meal, and move on with a few more coins in her purse and a trinket or two in her satchel.

The outlands.

The lands themselves were no real problem; easy to learn the ways of, and easy to adapt to for one used to harsh Keturan climes. The people, now . . .

Ketura, with its seldom-breeding women—another decision of its god—left women to fill the roles that best helped them to survive. Hunter, fighter, gatherer, weaver, healer . . . as they chose and were able. But these outlands—Orrick's, at least—were fertile ones, and the men and women lived within closely defined roles.

Kelyn fit in neither. But she didn't worry overmuch for their judgment of her. Instead she stuffed her winter boots in the satchel to travel barefoot despite the disdain it garnered; disdain, after all, didn't stop them from trading for her game. She practiced the changing dialect of the language, and was relieved to learn that the basic language itself changed little until one entered the Hurstian lands beyond Atlia—or returned to Ketura.

And every morning, she found high ground. Staff in hand, the snow panther fur rippling at her shoulders and the cloak belling gently away from her legs, Kelyn stood tall, unconcerned that the rising sun limned her with light and painted her for all the world to see. She'd met nothing in this land worth hiding from. She dangled the trouble dowser high in the air, waiting for it to do something other than sway in the warming breeze, and not sure what that would be when it finally happened.

Maybe, she decided after a double handful of days, she used the needle incorrectly, or missed its subtle signs, for surely in these outer lands of men like Busted Balls and Gort, there was trouble to be found on a regular basis. Or maybe it wasn't worth anything anyway, and she should just follow her own nose for trouble and see if it led to her father.

She needn't have concerned herself. On a morning of drizzling spring rain, with the cloak's fur sticking up in spiky wet patches and her hand grateful for the leather grip on her staff, Kelyn blinked water from her lashes to double check what she thought she saw—what she *did* see. The needle strained away from her, pulling her south. Across the border and into Atlia's unknown ways. Kelyn tucked the needle away and shouldered the satchel, heading into trouble with a light in her eyes and a grin on her face.

❖ ❖ ❖

As the drizzle ceased, she struck pony tracks in the rain-soft grasses, fresh and wide-spaced, and she lengthened her own stride to match, the satchel bouncing on her shoulders, the staff skimming the grass. The undulating ground rose before her, turning harder—Atlia's land—the grass sparser, as she crested the top of a hill and stopped short, surveying the scene laid out before her—the pony, down, and two panicked children frantically tugging at it. Coming in from a slightly different angle from Kelyn, hidden from them by the sweep of the low hills, a rider cantered at them, his pace leisurely, his manner assured.

The children—a boy and a girl—gave up on their boldly spotted pony and started to run—and then, realizing the futility of it, dove back for the pony, putting it between the rider and themselves. *Split up!* Kelyn thought at them, but of course they weren't doing it, and wouldn't. Kelyn shed her cloak and pack in one swift movement and charged down the hill behind the children, the noise of her approach lost in the nearing hoofbeats. The man saw her; he leaned over his mount's neck and urged it forward, and it became a race, fleet bare feet flying downhill against four pounding hooves.

Kelyn got there first. She leapt over children and pony both, startling shrieks from the children and avoiding the pony's thrashing legs, and straightened into guard before them.

The rider pulled his horse up short, a wary but unconcerned eye on the staff. "These are mine," he said, spitting the words out in harsh syllables; he held a coil of rope in the hand with the reins, a whip in the other.

"They don't look like they want to be yours." Kelyn gave the staff a lazy turn, a promise of action.

"He's a—" one of the children cried in a thin voice,

but the name he used for the rider wasn't a word that Kelyn knew. Her face must have shown it, for the man rested his hand against his saddle pommel, and regarded her with less hostility.

It was the expression of a man who knew he could afford to be reasonable, because he expected to get his way in the end. And he looked like a man used to getting his own way, for his horse was sleek and his clothing—leather and well-tailored cloth—hardly worn. Finely made gloves protected his hands from rope and rein, and a well-oiled scabbard rode his hip.

"Slaver," she said, repeating the word. "And what is that? What are you?"

"I sell goods," he said, as if it were no matter. "The children are mine; I saw them first. Find your own if you want them."

Kelyn shifted uneasily. There was more going on here than she understood, and his casual attitude worried her. "The children belong to themselves."

"He'll take us away!" the other child said—a girl's voice, frightened into thinness. "He'll sell us!"

Sell them? Kelyn narrowed her eyes. The man only smiled at her, unpleasant—and satisfied. Not pushing her; happy enough to drag this out. "There are others," she said with sudden perception.

Agreeably, he said, "Not far behind." He hefted the whip, as if judging where best to apply its lash. "We'll be glad enough to take three instead of two. You, now—you're as much a prize as both children together. So if you're thinking of running, I wouldn't bother. I'll round them up later—after I've got you."

You alone would be worth twice the distance they rode, Rika had said to her, and Kelyn hadn't understood. Now, suddenly, she did. She spat at the horse's feet, startling it. "Then come and get me," she told the rider. "Before I get *you*."

"Kill him!" the boy child shouted.

"Take his horse!" the girl said, more sensibly.

Yes, the horse. With the horse, all three of them could get away from the slaver's friends. Kelyn showed her teeth at the man and whirled the staff in a complicated figure-eight pattern, perfected by years of practice and many barked shins.

He shook his head and lifted the reins, and Kelyn saw that he simply meant to dance out of her reach until his friends arrived. Instantly she darted forward, bringing the stout ironwood down across the horse's nose with a carefully measured blow and taking both horse and man—and children—by complete surprise.

"Don't hit the horse!" the girl screamed at her, while the creature struggled to deal with both its pain and the sudden haul on the reins as its rider tried to force it out of reach. It reared, and the man cursed—another word Kelyn didn't know, though she thought she'd learned all of those—and though Kelyn dodged out of the way of those hooves, she couldn't avoid the lash that came down on her shoulder, splitting her tunic and skin alike. The horse skittered sideways, leaving Kelyn behind despite her desperate lunge to close on it. The lash wrapped around her staff, yanking it from her grasp.

If he expected it to slow her down, he was wrong; while he jerked the whip to free it of her staff, she closed the ground between them, coming up hard against the horse's side when, still fighting the reins, it abruptly reversed its movement. She lost all the air in her lungs with a grunt, but not her purpose—digging her fingers around the man's arm and scabbard belt, she dragged him down with her as she fell.

He landed on top of her and tried to roll away, clawing for the knife on his belt, but she went with him; they tumbled and grappled and then suddenly he was sitting on top of her, his hands pinning her arms by her head and his hips wisely and quickly lowering to sit on hers, where the kick she'd already been aiming couldn't land on his most vulnerable parts. There, he grinned at her. "Nothing like a little hands-on check of the merchandise," he said, and ground his hips into hers most suggestively.

Kelyn smiled back. Before it could make him wary, she gave a quick buck of her hips and twisted beneath him, making no effort to free her arms but letting them twine and cross where they were as she flipped to her belly and kicked up and back with limber fury, stunning him with a boot between the shoulders and another, as he jerked in reaction, on the back of his neck.

And then suddenly she had help, for as she yanked herself free of his grip, the children fell upon him, and she snatched the boy's thin arm just before it rammed a knife into the man's chest. Wresting the small knife away, she jammed it up the man's nose, stopping just short of ripping through his nostril. Dazed as he was, he instantly froze, recognizing the cold sharp steel even in that totally unexpected place.

"Be good," Kelyn told him, and then turned a sensible eye on the boy's frustration. "I need the shirt," she said. "He's ruined mine."

❖ ❖ ❖

She did indeed, she decided, like the feel of fine cloth against her skin. She shrugged into the leather vest that went over it, swiftly searching the pockets and divesting herself of the man's sniffing tin, a disgustingly used piece of the thinnest leather she'd ever seen, and a yellowed tooth strung on a cracking thong. Suspecting the last to be magic of some sort, she used the butt of his knife—also now hers—to grind it into powder, ignoring his inarticulate grunt of protest.

He might have been more articulate had he not been tied and gagged, the skin on his hairy chest goose-pimpling in the resumed drizzle, but the boy had knotted him up well, and Kelyn doubted he'd free himself no matter how long it took his friends to arrive. Kelyn adjusted his wide leather belt around her hips, trying to decide if she wanted to bother with it, and finally rammed the knife home in its ornate sheath; she could always sell it if she chose. Her own lighter belt and sheath, she arranged over it.

Behind her, the boy, crying silent tears, slit his pony's throat; the creature had stepped in a hole and snapped its leg, and the boy had refused to let Kelyn see to its disposal. The girl, who was crying even harder, had nonetheless grimly set herself to the task of catching the horse and tying Kelyn's satchel to the saddle.

Kelyn discovered a hook on the side of the belt, and scooped up the whip, coiling it and settling it into place. Perhaps she could teach herself its use.

When she looked up, the girl was in the saddle and the boy stood by the horse's nose, waiting for Kelyn to mount up. From his expression—resentment and calculation—she had the feeling he'd fought with and overcome the impulse to climb up and leave her where she was; the three of them on the horse certainly might slow the animal enough to jeopardize their escape. But he waited, adjusting the bridle so the noseband didn't fall on the rising lump from Kelyn's blow, and muttering something to his crying sister that made her straighten and wipe her wrist across her nose. They were ragged children, and thin, but strong and attractive, their hair and skin and eyes all shades of golden brown. And both were covered with enough clothing to protect them from the rain—a shapeless dress for her, with skirts full enough to allow her to ride astride, and calf-length trousers for him, both topped with patched but serviceable short-waisted jackets.

Without any plan other than that of escaping the

slaver's friends—and disregarding her severe disinclination to put herself on the back of a horse for the first time—Kelyn reached for the stirrup.

The horse had other ideas. As her foot jammed at the wooden stirrup, he jumped aside; she landed on her rump on the hard ground. "Ketura's balls," she muttered. "It wasn't personal. Stand *still*." But some part of her was greatly relieved when a second attempt brought the same results.

The boy shook his head. "He's not going to allow it, mistress."

Mistress. Kelyn snorted, and let the frippery pass; the girl gave a nervous look in the direction they'd run from, clearly expecting to see slavers at any moment. "Get up," Kelyn told the boy, and at his hesitation, asked, "You can ride this horse, yes?"

He reacted as though stung by the greatest insult. "Of course!"

"Ride, then. I'll run. Do you have people? Take me to them."

He took a moment to process her staccato of directives, then grabbed the saddle and pulled himself up. "We won't leave you behind."

A generous statement, considering he'd clearly already pondered doing just that, but his determined expression was convincing enough. Kelyn's fingers settled into their familiar depressions in the padded grip of the staff, and she started them off, settling into a strong pace that surprised the children but didn't leave them behind for long. As they settled in beside her, bouncing generously but without concern at the horse's fast trot, Kelyn's stomach grumbled. She hoped that wherever they were headed, she would find breakfast.

❖ ❖ ❖

As the rain stopped for good, the children led her to a copse of stunted trees, following the shallow creek they had run across soon after leaving the slaver behind. Atlia, she had heard, was a stingy god, and so far his land proved it. The grasses were sparse, and the very same oaks that populated Orrick's land—when they somehow managed to get a roothold—grew to only half the size, their leaves just breaking out when Orrick's trees already held bright spring foliage. Even the creek was stingy, a trickle over a rocky creek bed that was lined with short, tangled nettles on either side. It made Kelyn long for Ketura, where the living was hard but the harsh beauty of the mountains made her feel alive inside.

She paced the horse until she spotted the wagons within the trees, and then fell back; the children forged ahead and soon an outcry from the camp told her they'd been spotted. Breathing deeply but easily, she shook out her arms from the run—but stopped walking outright when she saw the number of people who poured out from the copse to surround the children, all of them talking and gesturing, pointing at the horse, asking questions. In return the boy pointed at her, and as one, everyone from the camp turned to look at Kelyn. Their sudden silence was as overwhelming as their gabble of questions.

Well. Here she was, and there was nowhere else to go; while she had already learned enough not to presume on her welcome, she doubted that she was in any immediate danger from these people. She resumed her approach, wishing she hadn't handed her staff to the girl along the run, or that she'd gotten it back before they moved ahead. She did a quick mental tally of the weapons she carried—familiar and unfamiliar—took note of the fact that none of them carried a long blade, and decided that she was safe enough. Right up to the group she walked, long confident strides—careful, now more than ever, not to take one of her stumbles—that carried her to the edge of it but no closer.

The boy said something in a quick, tongue-rolling language, and then spoke so Kelyn could understand. "This one saved us. Without her, Darada and I would be gone to slavers."

She was sure he'd said as much before her arrival, but the words seemed to be a signal of sorts, for suddenly the group boiled around her, touching her on the arms, the back, her hair . . . they, like the children, were a spare people, and Kelyn topped all but the tallest of the men. Though she found their close attention bewildering, it fell short of threatening. She stood for them until someone clasped a hand on her whip-lacerated shoulder. *Ketura's balls!* Hissing, she batted the hand aside.

Again, the silence was instant, until the girl spoke quickly in their language; understanding crossed their faces—handsome faces, she thought, with deep gold hair that matched their browned complexions in a mildly startling fashion, and rounded features—rounded noses, rounded cheeks and chins—completely unlike the flatter Keturan planes Kelyn was used to seeing, or her own mix of her mother's aquiline lines and her father's Keturan features. One of the older women stepped forward and patted her arm with unnerving familiarity. "Come," she said. "I'll care for your wound."

They drew her into the copse, where she discovered that they had managed to conceal an entire camp—wagons, fire circles, a number of goats and chickens, cats that waited until she was nearly upon them and then trotted off with great purpose, right across her path . . . there was even a herd of horses on the other side of the copse, spread out to graze on the poor pasture, their bell mare hobbled in the middle of them.

It was, she concluded, more like a traveling village than a caravan, and she soon found herself sitting in the center of it, her satchel and staff by her side, the children merged into the group, the horse turned out with the others. Her seat—a leather hammock slung between two side pieces—wobbled beneath her, eliciting grins from those who still gathered around her.

There were fewer of them now; most had gone about their business. Those who remained seemed to have some purpose—an older man who received deference from all the others, the older woman who had spoken to her and now sat beside her, a young woman of Kelyn's age who brought a shallow pan of water and an intricately woven wicker basket to set at the healer's feet, the couple whom Kelyn had pegged as the children's parents, another babe clutching at their legs. . . .

It was naught to Kelyn if they stayed. She shrugged out of the vest, pulling the long shirt free of the knife belts and crossing her arms to grab the hem and pull the shirt over her head—

"Oh, no," the older woman said, hasty words. "The shirt is large; I'm certain it will pull down over your wound."

Kelyn glanced around at their shock, and at the men's carefully averted eyes, and lifted one shoulder in a shrug. "There's nothing new there," she said, nonetheless pulling the shirt ties loose so she could peel the blood-striped material from her shoulder without choking herself.

The healer gave a matter-of-fact mutter and set to work. She sponged the wound clean and salved it, and Kelyn expected that to be the end of it, but a gesture from the woman stayed her hand when she would have eased the shirt back into place. With the young woman watching, the healer laid precise strips of a soft, limp leaf along the oozing welt. She rested her fingertips on it, and nodded to the young woman, who moved up behind Kelyn to do the same; they joined hands, palm to palm, fingers laced.

Mystified, Kelyn watched without fear; even so, she couldn't help but jerk away when a sharp, painful tingle ran the length of the wound. *Rika never did* that. The woman ignored her frown, her accusing stare, and pulled the shirt up, tugging the ties closed to her satisfaction. She gave Kelyn a final pat on the knee as she rose and left, followed by the young woman.

"You're not used to healing magic," the older man said. "Leave the *alchfeth* where it is; it'll drop off in a day or two, when the wound is healed."

"It'll take longer than a day to heal this," Kelyn said with certainty.

The man made no attempt to convince her. "My name is Gergo. We owe you a great debt, more than any small healing can repay. We can offer you supplies, although our trading has been slow in this area, as ever. Or we can offer you some service. At the least, we insist on feasting you tonight. The slavers prey hard upon our people, and our children are precious to us; we will do what we can to show you so."

Kelyn shook her head. "I stopped that man because he needed to be stopped, not for any reward you might offer." *But . . . feasting?* Her stomach showed great interest, not listening to her mouth at all.

Gergo frowned, stiffening, while the couple exchanged an unreadable glance. Kelyn shifted in the hammock seat—carefully, but she almost tipped it anyway—not sure what she'd said wrong but quite sure she'd said it. Why couldn't everyone speak Keturan?

"If our goods are not to your liking, we will find

some other way," Gergo said. "We have a number of handsome young men—"

Kelyn scowled. A beauty she wasn't, but to have such implication that she needed their pity— "I find my own men!" she snapped, disregarding the fact that she hadn't ever done so.

"Are our children not worth such a gift?" the father said, bristling.

Kelyn stood, facing him, reminding him of her height. *I stopped the slaver. I can stop you.*

A low chuckle broke the tension as the healer returned to them, shaking her head. "Can't I leave you for a minute, old man? Even a Trader king cannot rule the outside as he would his people. This one, I think, is so new to this land that she knows not of us at all. How can you expect her to know our ways?"

"There are no other ways," Gergo said, but if he did so with resentment, it was also without force, and he took a step back, as did the children's father.

The healer said, "I am Lenci. I would have your name, now, child. That is important to us."

"Kelyn," Kelyn said, still wary, one hand on the hilt of the slaver's big knife, ready for any quick reversal of her hosts' mood and annoyed enough to let it show.

Lenci gestured at the hammock seat. "Kelyn. Please sit. You must know that while a Trader will bargain with you for every advantage in the marketplace, we cannot abide being on the short end of gifting. You have made us a gift by saving the children. We do insist on returning it with a bigger one."

Kelyn looked at her a moment, and then eyed the parents, who seemed to be holding their breath. She didn't see how one could offer a bigger gift than saving someone's children for them, but she suspected that was not a thing to say out loud, and thus stopped herself just in time. Finally, she nodded. "I understand," she said, "but since it is not my way, perhaps you won't mind if I just think about it for a while."

"Say, during a feast?" Lenci suggested.

Kelyn nodded. "I am," she said, trying to play the role these people wanted of her, "very hungry."

"Food now," Gergo declared, "and the feast in its time. To judge from the growl of your stomach, you might not last long enough to put this feast together!" They all had a laugh at Kelyn's expense—for her stomach had indeed been grumbling, even through the tension of their short confrontation—and then Gergo pointed at the children's mother. "Gazi, it is your place to see to the gathering of things. And Tass, it is yours to clear a place for the dancing."

Dancing. Kelyn's heart fell. Her idea of dancing was of a drum-led charge of feet, vigorous and aggressive movements that she'd quickly learned had no place in Orrick's world and, she was certain, would have no place here. And she had the strong suspicion that in order to partake properly of this feast they insisted on giving her, she would have to dance. *Then*, her feet—learning new steps—would show how well they could stumble.

Chapter 5

Dancing.

Yes, they wanted her to dance. With her belly full and grease still on her lips from the spicily sauced, sliced and fried meat that had been stuffed inside the halves of bread rounds—and just at the point when she was sure she'd have to go sleep the meal off—Kelyn found herself being drawn into a circle of activity.

The music, played on big-bellied stringed instruments and drums not unlike Ketura's despite their higher timbre, was foot-moving music, and the early dances seemed to be just that—much running about, with some subtle pattern Kelyn never figured out but was glad enough to be towed through. When the music changed, she hoped she had satisfied her hosts, but no, she was not allowed to sit. This time, all the men moved back, adding their clapping hands to the music, their faces shining with appreciation as the women, from the slenderest to the plumpest, bared their bellies and shimmied around the fire circle.

Hands divested Kelyn of her knife belts and tied up her shirt to expose her belly—normally flat, now slightly rounded with the feast—and tugged her pants down so they barely clung to her hips. The women surrounded her, showing her the dance with movements rather than words, and after a few moments of protest, Kelyn gave up and applied herself to learning the peculiar undulations. Soon enough she fell into the rhythm of it, and found herself laughing, dancing alongside Lenci with her arms raised and fingers snapping to the clapping of the men.

"You see?" Lenci said to her, showing Kelyn a particularly tricky twist that looked no less sensual for the thin, sagging skin on her aging torso. "We'll have you dancing like a Trader before we're through!"

"First fighting for our children, now dancing for our men," Gazi said from her other side, laughing as Kelyn tried and failed to execute Lenci's twist.

"Whatever your curse, it doesn't seem to hold you back," Lenci added, and Gazi nodded agreement. Kelyn found herself nodding, too, until the meaning of their words sunk in and she stopped short, standing still in the midst of their motion and garnering some disappointed noises from some of the men.

"What do you mean, my curse?" she said, though the words were lost in the noise of the dance. There seemed to be fewer women around her, she noticed—and fewer men. She tried again, louder. "*What do you mean, my curse?*"

"The curse," Lenci said, matter-of-factly. "Dance, girl! Try this—" and she moved her hips in a fast rhythm that elicited several shouts of approval from the men.

Half-heartedly, Kelyn resumed her dancing. "Tell me of this curse, Lenci!"

"How could she not know?" Gazi asked, and a

woman dancing on the other side of her nodded—and then accepted a man's arm, walking out of the dance and the conversation both.

"How can all of you *know*, when I have heard nothing of it my whole life?" Kelyn slowed her dance again, glaring at Lenci. "You're making it up."

Lenci shook her head, and nudged Kelyn, directing her attention to the young man at the edge of the dancing, the only young man left there. "That's Endre. I think he's waiting for you. He's shy. Dance over there, why don't you?"

"The curse!"

Lenci only shook her head again, and held her hand out to someone Kelyn couldn't see. "Later, child. This is for now!"

And Kelyn found herself abandoned, the music dying to one lone instrument that had picked up a slower, more thoughtful tune, while men and women paired off and disappeared into brush and wagons. *A curse? What—*

Endre interrupted her thoughts, appearing before her and standing close. "Walk with me?" he asked. She gave him an absent look—he almost of her height, with features more defined, more sharply cut than typical, and shy eyes that couldn't quite meet hers in the fading firelight . . . and decided there was nothing to gain by pursuing Lenci.

At least, not at the moment.

She nodded at Endre, and he took her hand and led her out toward the horses. There, on the edge of the copse and not far from the nearest horse, he turned to her, putting his warm hand on her chilled belly, covering the scarred claw marks from the day she had earned her fur cloak. "You dance well for a stranger to the Traders."

"My people have dance, too," Kelyn said. Dance around the fire after a good hunt, dance to warm the blood in winter. "Perhaps the Traders should try *my* ways."

"Show me your ways," Endre said. "I'll try them." His hand tightened on her belly; it was a big hand for his size, and a strong one.

She didn't think he truly referred to dancing.

"I'd need someone to play the drums," Kelyn said, just in case he was. "And bigger drums. Deeper—" she broke off as his other hand snaked around her waist and he bent to kiss her belly button. "What did I just agree to?"

"When?" he murmured, straightening, moving in close, where she discovered he was quite tall enough, thank you, and where he leaned in to kiss her.

Kelyn took a step back. "When I said I'd walk with you," she told him, but she already knew. Too slow, she'd been, to figure that one out, with her mind on curses. And not paying enough attention, for she tripped and fell backward in the still-wet grass, landing on her bottom with little grace. He didn't seem to notice; he seemed, in fact to approve, and was instantly on his knees beside her, reaching for her. "Did Gergo ask you to do this?" she demanded, and that stopped him short as her ineptitude had not.

"Did he . . . ?" Endre said, sitting back on his heels, looking both hurt and puzzled. "No, why should he?"

"Because he wants to present gifts to me for saving the children. Because he mentioned being serviced as something I might like."

"It is a gift we sometimes offer, if both parties are willing. I would have been, if he'd asked, but he didn't—"

Kelyn scowled at him, feeling big-footed and clumsy and knowing by heart the reflection her mother's bronze had shown her the last time she looked—a face as awkward as her body could be. "I don't want his pity," she said. "I don't want *your* pity." Unfortunately, she did, she realized with some surprise, want *him*.

"Pity for what?" he asked, still puzzled, and Kelyn could almost believe him. But these were, she reminded herself, a people of traders, and a good bargainer could cultivate all the sincerity he needed. He said, "I liked your dance."

"I can barely do it," she said, no hesitation.

"That's what I like about it," he said. "It's different. It's open-hearted." He caressed her belly. "What more does there need to be, besides a man and a woman and an agreement for the evening?"

Kelyn might have said something then, if he hadn't kissed her again, doing his best to prove his point. A thorough job, and a most convincing one . . . oh, if only he hadn't opened his mouth again, and for all the wrong reasons. "I like your eyes," he said. "And your mouth—what?"

"My mother had beautiful eyes," she said, pulling away from him. "I don't. Gergo sent you. Well, you can go back to him and tell him I meant what I said the first time."

"But—"

No buts. She scrambled to her feet. "Come back to me some day when you have truth on your tongue," she said, and stalked away—but her pounding heart and her trembling legs were on his side, and all but mutinied on her. "I'll get my own men," she told them, a fierce and private mutter. "*When* I want them." They remained unconvinced.

She didn't blame them.

She found her satchel at the edge of the abandoned fire circle, and considered walking away from the camp right then—but that, she knew, would be enough of an insult to make a real enemy of Gergo, which she didn't want. Not in this world about which she knew so little. She pulled her cloak from the satchel and lay down beside the fire, and could not help but wonder where Endre was doing the same.

I like your eyes.

She wished she could have at least pretended to believe him.

❖ ❖ ❖

Kelyn opened her eyes the moment the first footfall brushed against the wilted and crushed ground growth of the dance clearing—but it wasn't fast enough. Before she could stand up, brush herself off, and stuff her cloak back into her satchel, half the Trader camp was there—some of them looking sleepy and sated, and some of them bright-eyed, their faces full of question and meaning. "Where's Endre?" someone asked, though not directly to her.

Ketura's balls, were there *no* secrets in this camp?

Endre appeared at the edge of the crowd, and she couldn't decide whether his agreeable features were glowering at her or pleading with her—in the end, she decided it was both. Kelyn mustered her dignity, picked a crumpled stem out of her hair, and said, as if it made no never-mind, "It is my custom to sleep alone. You can respect that, I hope. Endre did."

It was truth, in a way. Not the truth they were hearing, but that was their problem, wasn't it?

"Of course," she muttered in a mixture of her language and theirs, as no one immediately responded, "it isn't my custom to be surrounded before breakfast and put to a silent inquisition, either."

Endre seemed to wake up, assuming the role Kelyn had left open for him. "Don't be rude," he told them all, and shooed most of them away. "Go to your breakfasts. She has danced with us, and respected our customs. It is only fair to respect hers."

They left with a few sleepy giggles, and enough yawning so that Kelyn couldn't stop a reflex yawn.

She stretched hugely, and when she opened her eyes from it, she found Endre up close, close enough to make her blink. "Two things," he said, with far too much intensity for so early in the morning. "One thing: we are not done, you and I. It was I who spoke, among all those who wanted to, and you are not to forget that. The other thing—" He glanced over his shoulder, saw he had the privacy he wanted, and said, "thank you."

She didn't pretend not to know what he was talking about. "You're welcome," she said, and then patted her stomach. "Do you know where I can get some food?"

Endre stepped back, then gave her a sudden grin, nodding. "Were our women as straight-roaded as you! Yes, come with me. I'll see that you're fed."

"And the curse! Lenci said something about a curse!" Kelyn scrubbed her fingers through her hair to comb it as best she could, hastily following him.

"I cursed plenty, last night," he said, low-voiced, and then looked back to see if she'd heard; she caught a gleam of humor in his eye and grinned back at him.

He took her first to a small washing area, where she washed her face and slicked back her hair, fastening it at the back of her neck with a bronze pin that he provided. He showed her the curtained-off toilet area and then casually wandered away so she could use it. And then he led her to break her fast at the small fire circle in front of Lenci's wagon.

Unlike the other wagons, which were painted in bright red and white combinations and festooned along the sides with fabric banners, Lenci's wagon bore subdued green colors, and the trim was covered with scrolling vine patterns. The healer, identified to all. Did it, Kelyn wondered, protect her in case of attack? Gergo was just leaving, but there were a number of others gathered here—mostly women and a few small children. Darada's mother, Gazi, was at the kettlebox under the back of the wagon, clattering around with sooty pots and pans, while three other women huddled with great intensity at a small side fire over which they had placed a stout stick, now burned almost all the way through. As Kelyn watched, the youngest woman dipped her fingers into a small bowl and pinched up the contents—sugar? flour?—sprinkling it along the length of the stick. Flames flared high, and the woman looked at her companions with shy delight.

Kelyn looked at Endre, who shrugged. "Women's magic."

Lenci smiled, and waved her in to sit at one of the hammocks, and Kelyn did so, accepting the plate that someone thrust at her. Leftovers from the evening before, which suited her fine. "Bold Endre, welcome," someone murmured, and Kelyn thought it was Lenci's assistant, Anci, the quiet girl from whom she'd heard nothing until now. She decided she'd prefer to eat than to follow Endre's response, and eat she did, until she put the plate aside and looked straight at Lenci.

"Tell me about the curse," she said.

"Truly, you know nothing of it?" Anci again, apparently over whatever reticence she'd had the day before.

"Nothing. And how do *you* know so much?" Kelyn leaned forward, propping her elbows on her knees, and waited.

"Why," Lenci said, "we are many of us witches, of course."

"*Witches?*" A whole camp full of Auntie Rikas?

Except—Auntie Rika, she *knew*. Rika's magics were quiet things, and she kept them mostly to herself. These people, she did not know. Not really, no matter how kind they had been—for she had also seen that they could bristle and anger as easily as any she'd met.

"Yes, *witches*," Lenci said, and without so much as a by-your-leave, pulled Kelyn's shirt down at the shoulder. The limp *alchfeth* clung there yet, and Lenci ripped them off with a twitch of her hand, startling Kelyn—but not, as she'd expected, hurting her. There was no scab beneath to tear open; nothing but a clean pink line. "Think you any healer could have done this? Think you just any healer would have bothered?"

Kelyn shook her head. But to be in a camp full of women who so casually perceived a curse of which she knew nothing! It . . . embarrassed her. As though she'd been caught in bright torchlight during one of her clumsiest moments. "Please," she said. "You said you owed me a gift—then make it the gift of knowledge. Tell me about the curse, tell me *everything* about it."

Lenci pursed her lined lips and exchanged glances with her assistant; they said nothing, but Kelyn could see the unspoken words between them. She didn't give them a chance to say those words. "Can't you?" she asked.

"We can tell you a little," the younger woman said. "It is a physical thing, this curse. And it is old, very old. It has been with you a long time."

"A physical thing?" Endre said, snorting. "Darada and Nea know how well she fights. We all saw how quickly—how *well*—she learned our dance."

"We see what we see, Endre." Lenci shrugged.

"But what exactly does it *do*?" Kelyn demanded, unable to settle for what little they offered. "Where did it come from?"

Where did it come from—

Where else *could it have come from?*

From home. From the sparsely populated Keturan

foothills. From the very woman of whom she'd been thinking so fondly, only moments before. "*Rika*!" she muttered, standing up in her shock and denial—and forgetting herself, forgetting the hammock seat, tangling with it to stumble backwards, heading for a hard fall—had not Endre caught her, grunting as her solid length landed against him.

"Ah," Lenci said, as if that explained everything. "Does that happen often?"

"I—" Kelyn said, too dazed by events to think much about her words in this other language, keeping them simple "—I do this, yes."

Lenci gave her a smile, a small and sympathetic one. "There is your curse, Kelyn of Ketura. These moments."

Kelyn just stared at her, open-mouthed, hardly aware that Endre had propped her back up on her feet and was removing the collapsed hammock seat that wrapped around her foot. *All those years of bruises, of humiliation, the extra work—none of it* me! *But why*—Why had Rika done this thing to her? This betrayal? How had she watched Kelyn struggle from year to year, saying nothing, doing nothing?

Later. Deal with that later. The important thing—the *only* thing—was to know how to get rid of the curse *now*. "I want it off," she told Lenci, a grim demand. "I want it *gone*. Tell me how!"

The three women looked up from their separate fire, surprise on their faces, protest—unspoken—obvious on their lips. Anci shook her head, as if to herself. And Endre, in her ear, said, "That's not how it works. No one knows, Kelyn, but the one who put the curse on you."

Rika. Unconsciously, Kelyn looked back toward Ketura. Rika was the one who had blessed her journey into the outer lands. *And does that mean anything? Can you trust the blessing of one who cursed you?*

But no. Rika had done more than just send Kelyn on her way. She'd sent Kelyn looking for Thainn, the father she had never known—though far too many people had heard of *him*. She'd sent her with purpose. She'd sent Kelyn to *find her self*.

"Rika," Kelyn said under her breath, "I will trust you one last time."

And if Kelyn's search for Thainn went nowhere, if this lifelong curse never lifted, then Rika had better wish herself to a Silogan hell-cave before Kelyn found her way back to Ketura.

Chapter 6

Kelyn sat at the edge of the copse, watching the horses graze. Baffling creatures, horses. She could understand their usefulness in certain situations, and they were edible enough, but the Traders seemed to base much of their lives around the creatures—which to her, seemed less than practical. They were too unpredictable, and too delicate. She frowned at them.

Not that she was out here to think about horses. In fact, she was trying not to think at all—and especially not to think about her curse. How could Rika have done such a thing to her? Had Lytha known? Had her *own mother* known, and said nothing? All those years of stumbling, of bruises and humiliation . . .

Without the curse, what was she *really* like? Who would she have been?

She stared down at the long legs stretched before her. She'd still be gawky, that's what. She'd still have a face that didn't fit itself. She'd still be Thainn's daughter. She sighed again, deep and deliberate, and dug the trouble dowser from its pouch, letting it dangle in the sunlight. It gave her no direction.

Someone approached from behind, making no effort to quiet his progress through the weedy groundcover. When he stood beside her, Kelyn glanced up. Gergo.

"You should keep that to yourself," he said, frowning a little, nodding at the needle when she frowned back in puzzlement. "It's not safe."

"Rika told me it was," she said, lowering her hand anyway. At the moment, Rika's words were suspect. "She said it couldn't hurt me."

"It can't. But the Atlian soldiers can." He moved out a little further, far enough so he could turn and face her and she didn't have to crane her neck to look at him. He had been working this morning, as had they all; they'd been packing up camp. Kelyn's attempts to assist only got her shooed away, and she soon saw that they had a refined system with which she'd only interfere. Stationing herself at the edge of the copse seemed to be the best way to help. Now Gergo wiped his forehead and straightened his shirt, and said, "Our debt is not yet paid. Let us offer you a place among us as we travel into Atlia."

Kelyn said nothing, knowing she could get along fine on her own.

Gergo must have read it on her face. He gestured expansively around himself, indicating the whole of Atlia. "You know nothing of this world, Keturan girl. Why do you think I told you to put the needle away—which I note you have not yet done?"

She looked down at her lap, where the needle rested on its pouch, glinting despite the fact that it was in her shadow. "I think you don't like it."

"You would be right. Traders, even Trader witches, do not deal in such objects—not even the god-touched objects so many covet. But that's not the reason I had to stop myself from slapping it out of your hand when I came upon you with it."

That's not the reason you had to stop yourself from trying. "Tell me, then."

"Atlia's lord of this region is called Abendar. He is a *sashec*, a—" Gergo stopped, searching for words in their common tongue. "He makes himself big by stepping on others. At the moment, he is stepping on witches."

"I'm no witch," Kelyn snorted.

"It's not necessary to *be* a witch to be arrested as one," Gergo shot back without hesitation.

Kelyn looked at her lap, and slowly replaced the needle in its pouch. No flaunting this little magic, then. Not that she'd been doing any such thing, but she understood well enough the practice of maintaining good habits even under circumstances when they were temporarily unnecessary.

She understood, too, what he was telling her: what she didn't know *could* hurt her. As the land became more populated, it would be harder to bluff her way through the same tricky situations that it would also become increasingly easy to blunder into. She tucked the pouch into a vest pocket. "I'd like to come with you for a while," she said. "Until I learn more about these people." *Until I leave to find my father.*

Gergo nodded, satisfied at the transaction and already walking back into the copse. "We leave soon," he said. "You can ride in one of the wagons, or borrow a horse."

Not long afterward, Endre approached, leading a horse. She had watched him remove it from the herd moments after Gergo left, followed by others who called up their own, bits of harness in hand. She had assumed he was getting the cart horse for the wagon he and his family—father, younger brother, and uncle—lived in.

Apparently not.

"For you," he said. "So you don't have to walk."

Kelyn stared at the beast. She was certain it eyed her with equal antipathy. "I'm good at walking." She had never shared Frykla's enthusiasm for riding; indeed, she had always found herself to be quite busy any time Frykla tried to get her atop one of her ponies. She stood, and shook out her whip. "I was planning to practice as we move. I can't do that from horseback."

Endre stared at her, his expression shifting subtly as he considered whether she meant offense, or spoke the truth. Then his eyes widened. "You're afraid."

"I am not." Afraid? Of an animal that wouldn't eat her? She snorted.

"He's a good horse," Endre said. "He's old. He'll just follow the horse I ride."

Kelyn twitched the whip, wiggling the end of it in the weeds. The horse moved uneasily. She narrowed her eyes at it. "No, thank you."

"You *are* afraid."

She glared at him. "I'm not." Just sensible, surely. A Keturan had to be able to rely on her legs.

Surely.

Endre looked at her in incomprehension, and indecision—mouth hesitating on his next words. No doubt sure he could convince her . . . and wisely not certain it was the best course.

"I trust my legs," Kelyn said, cutting him off. *Trust*. In Ketura, it meant being willing to put your life in someone else's hands. She did not trust this horse. When it came to that, she didn't even trust the Traders. Not in the way the Keturan meant when they spoke of such things. "I'll walk."

And walk she did, to Endre's clear bemusement, as well as trot along when they made speed, and felt herself in luxury for not having to carry the satchel as she did so. The Traders placed little emphasis on covering ground quickly, and Kelyn found it easy to wander from them and then wander back again, without any worry of being left behind—not that she couldn't have tracked them if she were.

But just as often, she found herself hunkering on the edge of this circle or that, as the Traders stopped for a spontaneous communal meal gathering, or chose to camp for a day or two following significant trading, so they could sort and examine their new stock.

The goods, she gathered, belonged to them all. Aside from their horses and wagons, only Gergo seemed to own personal property of any significance—a wagon which he seemed to occupy on his own, as well as a huge laundry and bath tub that traveled in a goods wagon, and a fancy fire cookframe. Which, Gergo's or not, everyone else seemed to use as they would.

Despite their welcome the evening she had arrived—and their apparent enjoyment in including her in communal activities—Kelyn discovered that the women, when gathered for their duties or the little charm circles they often formed, didn't quite seem to know what to do with her. The men, deferring to Endre's unspoken claim—or perhaps spoken, for all she knew—stopped to talk to her readily enough, but after a few moments they'd glance at Endre or take a look from one of the women, and they'd move on.

Kelyn took to wandering through camp, moving from one circle to another when they ran out of things to say to her, or—as she was now—fumbling away at a new skill or practicing an old, never quite joining the Traders in their duties.

Snap! The whip came alive in her hands, briefly turning from an awkward, unwieldy length to a weightless thing that danced at her command. Kelyn grinned, recoiled it, and snapped it out again, making one of her rock targets jump. In the next moment, of course, the braided leather wrapped itself around her ankle, of its own mind again.

Atlia's pits. She didn't know whether to blame the thing's behavior on her curse or its innate unwieldiness, but she knew she'd had enough for the day. After just one more good snap, something she could keep in her mind to try for the next time she practiced . . . *there.* Kelyn sighed, shook out her arms, and carefully coiled the braided leather, not bothering to secure it at her belt as she strode through the almost-trampled weeds—by tomorrow morning they'd be flattened—to the goods wagon where the women gathered. For while the men transacted Trader business, it fell to the women to sort and value it.

Lenci's assistant, Anci, greeted her there. "Look at these furs," she said, holding up a supple, dramatically marked skin and stroking it. "When we get closer to Hurst, we'll be able to sell these to a rich man for a rich price."

Kelyn touched the fur. "Nightfox," she said, as Anci lifted the skin to run its fur across her cheek. "Hard to catch. I only snared . . ." she hesitated, and spread her fingers. "This many, last winter." And sold such prizes the moment the old fur man had pushed his way through the melting snows. She grinned at them. "I wonder if this is one of mine?"

Anci lowered the soft skin, and Kelyn realized that they'd all stopped talking, that they had turned to her with . . . *something* on their faces. Mystification? Distaste? She couldn't be sure.

She knew it made her uncomfortable.

Anci looked around, catching their gazes with a quick glare; immediately, the others turned back to their work, limiting their attention to sidelong glances.

Anci cleared her throat. "Your life . . . was much different from ours."

Was much different? Did they think she would change, simply because she was in their company for a while? "Ketura takes what it will from you, and demands much."

"But surely," Anci said, looking at the whip, "surely now that you're here, there is little need for taking the man's role."

Which men? Not even the Trader men paid as much attention to their surroundings as they ought, or seemed bothered to learn how to protect themselves properly from predators, human or animal. And yet they seemed safe . . . perhaps their constant charm-working had something to do with that, although of late they had ceased gathering in their circles. Kelyn frowned at the young healer. "I live how I know to live. Not a *man's* way . . . just a different way."

"But—"

"My ways keep me alive, wherever I am." Keen observation. Quick reaction. The heart to fight, the tenacity to keep fighting when she was down. And as for trouble . . . a willingness to learn how to avoid it. Though she was half certain the Keturan reputation came not from looking for trouble, but from refusing to run from it when it came one's way. "If you were in Ketura, you could not say the same."

"You may not find that as true as you think," Anci said, but didn't push. Instead she brought out another fur and asked Kelyn's opinion as the women tried to value it and gauge where on their route they might find the best trade.

❖ ❖ ❖

They traversed the sparsely populated edges of Atlia, slowly swinging eastward into an area of rough little farms and small copper mines. To Gergo's suppressed consternation, Kelyn did not take the arrangement of traveling with them to mean always traveling *with* them. When they were at a settlement, interacting with people, Kelyn stayed close, watching . . . learning. But otherwise . . . she moved off to hunt, to explore, to practice with the whip and skipping-stone knives . . . and sometimes, after private, huddled consultation with the dowser, she moved off toward trouble. Once, she freed a miner trapped under his laden ore cart. Another time, when the dowser stirred only slightly, she discovered a youth surrounded by his peers, bullying him . . . and did nothing. She had learned from that first Orrickian town, and knew that such situations would only repeat themselves until the victim—or someone else from the settlement, someone who could stay to watch the situation—did something about it. If the boy's life had been in danger . . .

But it wasn't, and she left it at that.

"What do you do, on your own?" Endre asked her from atop his stout little horse. His legs fell below the creature's belly, but his pride in his mount was such that Kelyn kept her opinions to herself; she supposed it was well-muscled and obedient enough, at that. Endre could drop its reins and count on it to walk quietly enough beside her, which is what he now did, stretching in the padded saddle and looking down at her when she didn't answer right away, too busy watching the way he moved with the horse—casual, graceful—even when he was all but slopping around on its back.

"Be on my own," Kelyn told him. She enjoyed these people, but they weren't *her* people, and there were far too many of them, constantly talking and calling back and forth, from one end of the line to the other. When he frowned at her, not understanding, she tried again. "I lived only with my mother, and spent summers with"—she ticked them off on her fingers, and displayed them for him; she'd known only a few numbers even in Keturan, after all—"this many. You are too many for me to stay with all the time." Language. She was getting better, but . . .

Endre stared at her for a moment of disbelief, and then laughed. "Then you're traveling in the wrong direction, because this land is going to get a lot more crowded before it spreads out again."

Kelyn gave a little squirm inside, and reminded herself that she had managed in Orrick, ignoring the prodding voice that said she had also spent much of her time outside that town, hunting. Reminding herself that she had to find her father. Out loud, she said only, "So I would be foolish to ignore my chances until then."

"Gergo worries."

For her, or that she'd bring trouble down on the Traders? But Kelyn didn't ask the question out loud. Instead, she thought of how, for the past several days, Endre and his pony had always been within sight of her, that he didn't spend the time with his family's wagon that he might. She'd rather been hoping he might tell her her eyes were beautiful again, though she doubted she'd believe it this time, either. "He's told you to watch me."

Endre shrugged, not looking the least abashed. "He was going to have someone do it. I asked that it be me."

"Better you than some," Kelyn said, matter-of-fact. Not that she intended to make it easy for him. Hunting went better without a noisy horse along, and she wasn't about to show him the dowser, not after Gergo's reaction.

But she wasn't thinking about Endre the next day, when the trouble dowser nearly jerked itself out of her hand with the strength of its reaction. Hunkered behind a wagon wheel, her stomach rumbling for supper and the scent of it cooking strong in her nose, she immediately resigned herself to cold leavings. She snatched up her staff from where it leaned against the wagon beside her, settled the double arrangement of belts on her hips, and left the camp—another copse by another stream, this one not far from a reasonably large settlement, she had been told—in a long-strided walk. As soon as she felt she was beyond notice, she broke into a run.

Not long after, she heard hooves against the hard ground, a pattern of easy speed; she didn't look up as Endre came up beside her and slowed his horse to match her pace. "You're nice," she said, "but don't get in my way."

"Not my plan," he agreed, cheerfully enough. No doubt he was pleased with himself.

"Your people are not fighters," Kelyn said.

That did not please him as much, she could tell by his silence. "I can hold my own," he said eventually. "Why do you bring it up?"

Kelyn slowed to a walk, a swift and ground-covering pace. "You have strength in numbers. You have wagons to hide behind, and horses to run with. You use just your fists when you fight." She had noted it early on, that the Traders would put up a scrap on the spot only if provoked—and even then, that they faded away from any armed confrontation. It served them well, and kept attention away from their traveling village. But at the moment it served her to speak of it without acknowledgment of its usefulness as a strategy. "I've seen you in towns. All of you, you run before you'll fight."

Or perhaps not so useful, for though his voice tightened, he said, "And this matters now because . . . ?"

They were, after all, Traders. Better at verbal fighting than she would ever be. "I don't want you hurt. Go away."

"I can take care of myself."

"I don't want you to get *me* hurt. Go away." She

picked up a run again, starting up a slight rise, her progress hindered by the weedy brush. It couldn't be far, not with the dowser so emphatic.

"What makes you think—"

The scream was faint, but not so faint that Endre didn't hear it over his own words. He put his heels to his horse and surged ahead, while Kelyn cursed him for a fool and kicked in some speed of her own, topping the rise.

Dugout house. Scattered chickens, open cowshed, barking dog—

Three men grappled with a woman and a young boy, while a fourth was chasing down the cow. They had the woman shoved up against a stone-sided well house, her clothing half ripped off, her wild struggles not hindering them. Endre, riding at full tilt, had overshot the scene and was wheeling his horse around; the air was full of the men's grunts and curses and the woman's panting cries, overlaid with a non-stop, piercing scream from the boy.

The man by the cow stopped, eyed Endre and Kelyn, and headed for Kelyn; the two others stepped between Endre and the well. The remaining man flipped the woman over and bent her over the well, snatching at her skirts, raising them, unconcerned at witnesses or interruption.

Kelyn went for him.

The cow man intercepted her. "You should have stayed out of it," he said, but seemed happy that she hadn't.

"You'll wish I had," she said, her voice a low snarl and half her attention on the man by the well, the one she had only moments to stop. Her foe had approached with two blades—long curving knives with wavy-edged blades. He whirled them with an expert's touch, fancy moves that were meant to intimidate and dazzle and give him the chance for a lightning strike.

If Kelyn had had a sword, they might even have stopped her. Instead she blocked a quick cut, and then another; the metal bounced off her ironwood, and then her staff bounced off his helmet, staggering him. Her return sweep from the lower quarter took out his knee, and she bounded past him, heading for the well. Beyond, Endre was down from the horse but scrambling to his feet, his horse trotting away with its head held high, issuing alarmed rolling snorts.

She'd warned him. Grimly, she drove in for the rapist, while the others realized too late that their friend had not stopped her. She gave the staff a little toss on the move, caught it in the lower third of its length and, with the drive of her legs behind her, slammed it across the small of the man's back even as he half-turned to realize his danger, his over-confidence changed abruptly to alarm.

His legs collapsed beneath him as his weight drove the woman forward. Kelyn dove to grab her; the staff clattered to the ground as she yanked the woman upright.

"Kelyn!" Endre bellowed, and she caught a flash of movement in the corner of her eye, just enough warning that she was able to whirl and duck the weighted cudgel heading for her head; it skimmed down her arm, ripping cloth. She snatched her knife even as she drove her hand for his stomach, blade down and out; a backhanded swipe parted the layers of the last man's padded leather tabard. The would-be rapist leapt back, suddenly more cautious, and Kelyn moved away from the well, out into the open.

They assessed one another then, he hefting his cudgel, she wishing for her staff and glad to have not just one knife, but two. She was reaching for the second when she saw that Endre had run out of luck, and was brandishing only his own knife up against a long blade. He'd retreated until he was backed against the house, and though he looked determined to fight it out, Kelyn saw in an instant that he didn't have a chance. She dipped into her vest pocket, feinted at her opponent, and took advantage of his dodge to flip out one of the flat skipping-stone knives. It buried itself between the shoulder blades of Endre's foe. Not deeply enough to do any real damage, but certainly a distraction, and one that Endre took advantage of.

Kelyn's man leapt back, his gaze darting around to see that he was the only one of his crew left standing. He took another, wary step back from her as Endre, panting and disheveled, approached.

"You don't have to die," Kelyn told him. "It's up to you. Put down your weapon and you can see to your friends."

He scowled at her, and Kelyn gave a disgusted sigh, jamming her knife home in its sheath. "Put it down," she said. "Ketura's balls, I've got other things to do. Endre, you might want to catch that horse."

And leave you here alone against him? Endre's expression protested as clearly as words. She raised an eyebrow at him, gave a meaningful glance at the downed men. He cleared his throat, quietly sheathed his knife, and backed a few steps, his eye on their enemy, before turning to do as suggested. Kelyn suspected that the fact that the horse was jigging unhappily around the yard, its eye on Endre and its shoulders turning for home, did as much to convince the Trader as her request.

Kelyn, too, backed a step, nodding at the cudgel. "Toss that thing into the cow pen and I've no more business with you."

After only a moment, the man did just that. He still had a knife, but Kelyn left him that; she suspected he might need it for a mercy stroke or two.

A quick look at the man by the well confirmed that fact; though his fingers scrabbled to pull him away from her as she approached, his legs flopped uselessly in his wake, and she knew she'd hit him hard enough to make him piss blood for at least a week; enough so he'd probably not survive that long even if he *could* walk. She sidestepped him and the fear in his eyes, and found the woman huddled against the well, doing her best to hold her torn clothes closed while one arm curled protectively against the boy. Now silent, he stared open-mouthed at the downed man not so far from him.

Kelyn reversed track, not liking the blank fixation on the boy's face, the way it bordered on childish madness. Ignoring the man's protests—his grasping blows against her legs, his curses—she grabbed his shirt behind his neck and summarily dragged him out around the well, out of the boy's sight. When she returned, the child's face was already coming alive again, contorted for impending sobs.

"Are you all right?" Kelyn said, crouching by the woman with a suddenly heightened awareness of how strange she must be to this Atlian wife and mother, of how awkwardly her tongue still curled around the language. "Do you have someone?"

Dazed, the woman at first did nothing but rearrange her grip on her clothes, trying to cover her breast as Endre approached, her gaze going from the wounded men to Kelyn to the enemy who had just dispatched his friend by the house. Finally she said, "Paitre. He's at the mine. He'll be home soon . . . they've wanted the mine, they've been after us for months."

"I don't think they want it any more." Kelyn sat back on her heels and lifted her arm, peering down the length of it to see what actual damage had been done. Little but for the shirt, as far as she could tell, and perhaps one of the Traders would have the needle and thread that she lacked, and even a patch. She looked up to find Endre off to the side and waiting, and the man helping one of the others to his feet, the first one she'd taken on, and hadn't had time to do more than stop. His leg didn't seem to work properly and his expression was thoroughly dazed, but he, at least, would live. "You!" she called, getting the unwounded man's wary attention. "I'll be around. I knew what you were up to this time, and I'll know if you come back. So *don't*."

"Are you a witch?" the woman whispered, clutching the boy a little more tightly, just as Endre shook his head and said, "You cannot say such things, Kelyn."

"Of course I'm not a witch," Kelyn said. "Do you think I'd have fought them off by hand if I had any magic on me?" She snorted and stood, snagging the staff on the way up. "I probably won't be around, either, but it put a fear into them, didn't it?"

After a moment, the woman nodded. "Yes."

"Good. Now take your boy into the house, take care of yourself. We'll be out here for a while." Burying bodies, or at least hauling them off. At least, that was her intention. But as the woman gathered up the boy and made her unsteady way into the small dwelling, Endre put a hand on Kelyn's arm, a grip he didn't release even when Kelyn made as if to move away.

"How did you know?" he said, his eyes intent on hers. *I will not be put off*, they said.

"Know what?" she said, trying it anyway.

"Don't," he said, his expression hard; there was no trace of the Endre who'd pulled her from the dance circle, or taken her in hand the morning afterward.

Kelyn took it for what it was, a sudden reminder that his people were alien to her, and that she couldn't assume his reaction to anything. She retreated into her Keturan ways—blunt, unapologetic, willing to back up her words with action—but today—*now*—she wasn't on the attack, either. Just telling him the way of it. "I have a trouble dowser," she said. "I'm using it to find my father . . . and to keep men like these"—she nodded at the body by the house—"from having their way with those who aren't as strong."

"A trouble dowser," he said, flatly . . . not pleased, for all that he didn't seem to know exactly what that was. "It sounds like magic."

"Yes." She touched the pouch without thinking; his gaze darted to it, and back to her face. "Not magic it takes a witch to use."

"Atlia's pits," Endre said, taking a step toward her, one that looked like a threat. "I know Gergo told you about Abendar's witch-hunt—don't tell me you've been using this thing while you've been traveling with us!"

She took the threat for what it was, and didn't take kindly to it, either. She settled from her hipshot stance to something more balanced, and shifted her grip on the staff—her own subtle rejoinder. "Yes. I've been careful; no one's seen me. Gergo knows I have it."

"Of course no one's *seen* you. But for days the witches have thought someone might be using magic, though none of us should have been so foolish, this close to Abendar's land—we're not even doing minor charms anymore, and *no* one can feel that. Only no one told Gergo, because his anger would be so great—" He spat a word in his language, one that was surely a curse. "We should have told him. He'd have known it was you—"

"Stop," Kelyn said, as a hint of foreboding tightened in her stomach. "What are you upset about? What are you saying?"

His abrupt, impatient arm wave startled the horse backward, although Endre paid it no heed—and that alone, told Kelyn that he was upset, indeed. "Those who know magic don't need to *see* it, Kelyn. They *feel* it. And Abendar has plenty of pet witches who have saved their hides by going over to his side!"

"They can track that magic to your wagons?" Kelyn's foreboding swelled to alarm.

"*Yes!*" he said, nearly shouting, still incredulously impatient at her ignorance. "Of course they can! They specialize in it! Where my people might only suspect it, his can pinpoint it from miles away!"

Rema bless. Dread hit her, a dead weight in her chest. "Then we have to warn them. *Now*."

"*Finally*," he said, turning his anger toward sarcasm.

"No—wait," she said as he turned to the horse. "We can check on them from here." Quickly, she fished the dowser from its pouch, glancing at him only long enough to say, "If they come here to check on the magic, she can say it belonged to the claim-jumpers."

"Yes," he said after a moment. "Do it."

With some trepidation, Kelyn held up the needle. For an instant, it swung aimlessly at the end of the thong; for an instant, she allowed herself to feel relief.

The needle gave a tug, and stretched back toward the way they'd come. "Snakeshit," Kelyn breathed. Abendar's witch-hunters or not, the Traders had trouble.

"Let's go." Endre turned for the horse as Kelyn shoved the needle back home. But when she picked up her staff, prepared to take off on foot—the woman's husband would have to deal with the bodies—he stopped her short. "No. You ride with me, or get left behind. I'm not waiting."

All of Kelyn's certainty, her momentum, withered away. "Ride?"

"Behind me." When she hesitated, he gathered his reins and mounted up. "Trust me, and do it now, or get left behind. Thanks to you, my people are in trouble. I'm leaving." He took his foot from the stirrup so she could mount, a tacit invitation.

Kelyn hesitated. What would be so bad about being left behind? She'd catch up eventually—but she needed to be with them *now*, to help them face what she'd brought down upon them.

Endre had given up; he wheeled the horse around.

"No! Wait! I'll . . . I'll ride."

Wordlessly, he put out a hand; she took it, stuck her foot in the stirrup, and clumsily swung her leg over the horse's rump, rapping herself in the head with the staff. He took it from her; she didn't resist. "Use both hands," he said. "Hold on tight. You won't fall unless I do, and I won't."

She wasn't so sure she couldn't take him down with her by accident, but she did as she was told, pressing herself up against him and glad for the solid feel of his confidence. Her legs, too, tightened, and over Endre's shoulders she saw the horse pin its ears, felt the hump of its back.

"Not with your legs!" He turned his head, enough so she could see his impatient anger. "Hold on to me, move with him." And with those snapped instructions, he put the horse into a walk only long enough to see that her flinch didn't turn into a panic. Then suddenly they were running, with the horse's loins coiling and stretching beneath her, her arms wrapped tightly around Endre—tightly enough to feel his ribs, the wrinkles in his clothing, the lumps of the seams—and her heart racing at the fact that she had absolutely no control. The landscape flew toward them at a frightening speed; Kelyn squinched her eyes shut—*no, mistake!*—and instantly opened them again. She realized that she was shaking, she who had faced rock cats and reivers and hunger and the heights of the mountains, and willed herself to quit.

She didn't, of course.

She had completely lost her bearings by the time they stopped—how could things look so different from up here?—and when the horse plunged to a halt, she almost lost her seat as well.

"We walk from here," Endre said, his voice low, when she didn't release her still-shaking grip. "Get down now, Kelyn."

Abashed, she unclenched her fingers from her own wrists, untwined her arms, and slid off the horse's rump, finding her knees as unreliable as her arms. As Endre quickly dismounted and extended the staff to her, she looked at her shaking hands and frowned.

"Here," he said, shoving the staff at her again, taking no note of her reaction. "We're almost to the wagons; I want to go on foot from here, keep those trees between us."

Kelyn nodded, regaining some of her equilibrium, and struck off ahead of him. Endre led the horse for a while, then left it loosely tied to a tree. They moved more quickly after that, more quietly, getting first just a glimpse of the wagons, then finding enough of a gap in the trees that they stopped to take a good look.

"They're not moving," Kelyn said.

"No," Endre responded shortly. They stayed a moment longer, but the wagons hid the Traders from sight, and Kelyn took the lead, moving from tree to tree, and then—when the copse petered out—went to her hands and knees, and then her belly. Endre crept along at her heels.

At last they could see around the lead wagon to the confusing activity on the other side. It took several moments of watching before Kelyn was able to sort out the strangers from the two groups of Traders they were organizing, and not gently. Endre made a hissing noise through his teeth. "The witches," he said. "They've found them, they're pulling them out from the others."

All right then. Kelyn settled down on the hard soil, chin resting on the back of her hand, to think.

The worst had happened.

Abendar's men were here, and had felt the magic, intended to take the witches in—and had even identified those Traders who *were* witches. And while Kelyn's first impulse was to rush in and rescue them, she wasn't about to take on those odds—not all those soldiers, not with only fistfighters to back her up, and plenty of vulnerable children and oldsters nearby, just waiting to take a blade. Not without thinking it through.

Perhaps it would be better to wait, to trail the soldiers, and catch them with their guard down.

She inched backward to where Endre was thinking his own thoughts; she'd put her head with his, see if he'd go along with her forming plan . . .

Among the Traders, someone stumbled in the hands of a soldier; a woman shrieked. There was a flurry of activity, cries of dismay and fear. Endre shot to his feet, ignoring Kelyn's protest, and went charging for the soldiers.

Ketura's balls—the idiot. Halfway to following, she forced herself down. *Loyal* idiot. It was still a plan. It could still work.

She didn't want to watch; she wanted to duck her head and press her nose to the ground until the chaos subsided. But she forced herself to look up, peering through the weeds, as Endre was tackled and clubbed and taken down. So she saw the moment he looked back her way, a little expectant, a little surprised she hadn't been on his heels. She saw the soldiers take note, too. Immediately, she started inching backwards.

They didn't even bother to come look for her. One of them grabbed a child and tossed it to the front of the group, where another soldier caught it and dangled it—a little girl, Kelyn thought, too far away to tell for sure—all accomplished before the Traders even had time to protest. Practiced.

Shaking the child slightly, the man in possession of her bellowed something in Kelyn's general direction. The distance too far, his accent too great to decipher, Kelyn nonetheless understood the threat. Slowly, she stood; he beckoned for her to approach. She did that, too.

The closer she got, the bigger the scowl on the man's face grew. When she stood before him, he lowered the girl to the ground and ignored her as she scurried for her family. He turned his scowl on Endre—still in the grip of a soldier, bleeding from a spot or two and bruised in a number of others but back on his feet—and said, "What is this?"

"A friend," Endre said. "Someone who is traveling with us. She's fresh from Ketura—a savage. She knows nothing."

Shocked, Kelyn glared at him. He met her gaze square on, with no shame at his words and such intensity that she blinked and looked away; when she looked back, he was still watching her. Trying to tell her something, she thought, with no idea what it might be.

The confusion on her face apparently only reinforced his story, for the soldier grunted, relaxing a fraction. "Obviously she knows nothing, or she wouldn't be traveling with *you*." Unaware that Kelyn was at that moment searching his plated leather armor for weak points—the multitude of small dents in the pitted metal helmet made it a likely candidate for her staff—he eyed her and demanded, "Do you even speak a civilized language?"

Endre's head moved the merest fraction to the side and back again. Kelyn hesitated. Did he *want* her to play the coarse barbarian? She'd rather knock some sense into this stupid man. She might even create enough of a disruption for the Traders to join her, to overcome this ridiculous hunting party. She tightened her grip on her staff, on the edge of—

Endre's eyes widened dramatically, as much of a plea as he dared to make. Kelyn looked to the witches, huddled together and ringed by soldiers; there she found Lenci.

And Lenci nodded. Backing Endre.

No! cried the defiant and angry Keturan within her. *I won't!*

But she did. This situation was her fault. She gritted her teeth, and, realizing it, deliberately relaxed her jaw. That, too, was defiance, and the soldiers would see it. The one in front of her had given up on her, and called back to his fellows, "Dumb as the rocks she comes from."

"Bet she's warm at night," one of them suggested, inciting sniggers.

I'll bet you're sorry for that before we part ways. But not now. Kelyn said in a low voice, "I speak some," and made her tongue clumsy on the words.

Some of the threat must have leaked through despite her efforts, for the soldier turned back to her, his eyes narrowed, his moment of amusement over. "Good. Then listen up. Your friends have been harboring witches. We've found them, and we're taking them in to Abendar's town." He stepped back from her, turning to address the Traders as well. "We've no use for the rest of you. If you're smart, you'll go on your way. But since you people are never smart, you'll probably want to eat our dust all the way to Abendar's, figuring you'll make some daring raid and rescue your witches." He snorted. "*That* won't happen. We know your kind too well. You want to follow along, you'll give up all your weapons. Couple of my men will travel with you, and the rest'll be guarding your witches. You start any trouble—

you so much as frown at one of us—and the witches start dying."

Gergo moved through the Traders, pushing to the front to stand by Endre. He, too, bore signs of his struggles against the soldiers, and his puffed lower lip fumbled his words. "What can they expect from Abendar?" he said, still every bit a man speaking for his people. "What justice does the lord have in place?"

"Justice?" The man gave a short laugh. "What they deserve, is what they can expect. They'll be questioned and punished according to the crimes they confess." He rested a hand on his sword, making his meaning more than clear. Kelyn's arm twitched, aching for action; she stilled it. "My name is Atelic," the man told them all. "I don't care about yours. In fact, you'd better hope I don't care enough to learn it, because it'll only mean trouble for you."

No one said anything. The Traders' faces, normally open and emotive, were so blanked of emotion that Kelyn realized how little she really knew of them. Were they as cowed as they seemed? Did they have some plan? She had no idea what they were really thinking—and neither, she was sure, did the soldiers.

Not that it seemed to bother the soldiers in the least. Atelic said, "Get them moving. Weapons first, then separate out a wagon for the witches." He glanced at the size of the group in custody and said, "Make it two. We've got us a good haul this time. Good work, Thyra."

A woman's lazy voice came from the edge of the gathering, a drawling and disdainful voice. "Easy enough to find 'em when they're so stupid about their magic."

Kelyn winced, and looked away from the Traders, unable to bear the thought of meeting Gergo's eye. But Atelic's men were in action again, demanding the

Traders' knives right down to their little eating tools, shoving people around to suit them, sending three of the young men to reorganize the wagons while the others sorted themselves into new travel units. Atelic turned back to Kelyn—who did her best to look vaguely puzzled about the proceedings. "Not me," she said, in her stupid barbarian voice, indicating the Traders. "I can go?"

He tilted his head, as though he might actually consider the request. Then he smiled a nasty smile and said, "I think I'd rather keep an eye on you. No, you'll stay with us. I'll need your weapons now."

As if she would simply hand them over to him. But Endre broke away from the man who had been hanging on to him and stepped forward. "Do it, Kelyn. It's best this way. We'll appeal to Abendar when we get to his fortress."

"You're her handler, then? Suits me. Keep her in line; she's in civilized country now." Atelic reached for her staff, pulling it from Kelyn's reluctant grip—or trying to.

"Kelyn—" Endre said, and Kelyn heard nothing else, for Atelic's powerful backhanded blow came from nowhere, knocking her from her feet. While she shook her head clear, her body racing through reactions that her mind managed to stop just in time, Atelic grabbed the staff from the ground and slid her knives from the sheaths, running his free hand up and down her body several times until she couldn't stand it anymore and spat out in Keturan, "I don't keep any blades in my breasts, you pig-cocker!"

He grinned at her, gave a breast one last squeeze, and stood up, having either failed to recognize the outline of the round skipping-stone knives, or missing them because of his interest elsewhere. She dug her fingers into the stringy plants beneath her, restraining herself, as—with one last tug at her belt—

he took the whip. She spat at his back as he walked away, tossing words over his shoulder to Endre, "Get her with the rest of your kind, and make sure she minds her place. My men would be more than pleased to teach her a lesson."

Kelyn touched her cheek where it burned from his blow, and took the hand Endre offered her as she climbed to her feet. "Be careful," he muttered to her. "You're an unexpected opportunity for them—they won't touch our women; they never do. They're afraid it'll curse them."

"Will it?" Kelyn said, still scowling at Atelic. She dusted herself off, trying to brush away the sensation of the soldier's fingers on her skin, slapping at her clothes with more enthusiasm than was necessary.

"That," Endre said shortly, letting her know she was unforgiven, "is something that only the Traders will ever know." He glanced anxiously at the soldiers, and took her arm. "We need to join the others, Kelyn. Stay with us at all times. And always keep one of us between you and any soldier."

Kelyn snorted at the thought—hiding behind fistfighters!

Endre's fingers tightened on her arm. "I mean it."

She shook herself free and glared at him. "I didn't hit that Atlian rock slime for touching me so. You might not be so lucky."

Endre's face darkened under its bruises; he brushed back his disheveled hair, bronze Trader hair, and his words came out in a snarl of sudden anger. "Haven't you caused us enough trouble? Get over with the others and stay out of the soldiers' sight!"

Bold enough against rock cats and Atlians, Kelyn shrank before her guilt. Astonished and mortified to feel her chin quiver as his words hit home, she spun away from him and stalked the distance to the Trader wagons. The two witch wagons were already loaded and on their way, surrounded by soldiers on foot; a number of women looked out the back of the second wagon, silently watching as they drew away from their families.

Several soldiers hovered around the remaining wagons, prodding the Traders along, shoving someone every time they got close enough to do it. Kelyn felt their eyes on her and did as Endre asked, circling to keep herself as far from the soldiers as possible.

Endre had said nothing about his horse and she soon saw why; they'd barely started the wagons moving before the creature trotted into sight, trailing his neck rope and letting out an anxious neigh at his herdmates. This inspired a spate of responses from the wagon horses, and made conversation impossible.

Just as well. No one was saying anything anyway, and they especially weren't saying it to her. Gergo must have guessed what had happened, or else Endre had managed to get word to him, and to the others. She might as well have been invisible.

Kelyn sunk into the misery of her guilt. It was poor company, but at least it was company.

After a short distance, they came upon a soldier and supply wagon; the man saluted smartly at Atelic and moved to the head of the line. Kelyn could see little of it from her place at the back of the caravan, but that the soldiers had a supply wagon at all implied that they were more than a day's march from Abendar's.

And that meant she had at least one more day to make things right.

Chapter 7

Kelyn walked in silence, slightly separated from the rest of the Traders as they started their second day under their erstwhile escort. While not included in the Trader conversations, she was ever on the fringes of them, and had heard that they wouldn't enter Abendar's town before the next day was over.

Good. She needed that time, for until now she had seen no way to free the witches, and the Traders—not a single one of them—dared not stray as long as Atelic could punish the witches for it. She was under intense scrutiny from both soldiers and Traders alike, and at night had been wordlessly directed to and tucked away in one of the wagons—where she had slept not a wink, surrounded by the disapproving anger of her wagonmates.

And yet they did their best to keep her from the soldiers' attention.

Waiting until they got to Abendar's, as the Traders seemed to be willing to do, struck Kelyn as worse than hopeless. She'd been in a jail; she'd seen the pit. She understood the civilized notion of justice, and had no intention of waiting around to watch it enacted. Not when there were little more than a double handful of soldiers to watch over them all.

During the night she could have crept to the soldiers' wagon, retrieved her weapons, and given the Traders a fighting chance at escape by freeing the witches. For as long as the witches were held against the Traders' good behavior, no one was free to act.

But her guilt twitched at her, and made her think twice about making decisions for these people. What if she retrieved her weapons, damaging soldiers in the process, and the Traders didn't trust her, didn't move fast enough to take advantage of the chance she offered? What if her effort to help only made things worse?

There were consequences to dealing with other people's fates, it seemed.

She'd have to ask Endre. Or at least see how he reacted to her intentions.

Endre, however, didn't seem inclined to cooperate with this plan. He had placed himself between the three watch soldiers—who walked a large half-circle in front of the wagons, as much as the mildly varying terrain allowed—and the rest of the Traders, along with others of the unpartnered Trader men, Rago and Tierde. They were the barrier—quiet, nonthreatening, but definite—between the enemy and the sundered Trader families. And Kelyn, having felt the force of each soldier's gaze at one time or another in the past day, was not inclined to disregard Endre's instructions to stay away from them. She had, at times, wished herself shorter, less easy to spot at a glance. Instead she stood a head taller than the others, a difference she felt more acutely now that they made no effort to draw her into their world.

Most of the women and children traveled in the

wagons, behind which the saddle horses were tied; the men had been forbidden to ride. Every now and then a child's face would peep out at Kelyn from one of the wagons, only to be drawn back by an adult hand. The men seemed to have assigned themselves to certain wagons and rarely strayed from them, just as Endre and his fellows kept themselves up front. But Gergo moved from wagon to wagon, Trader to Trader, easing from place to place in the procession as he talked to his people.

Gergo. If she couldn't talk to Endre, Kelyn would talk to Gergo, and convince him of the merits of her plan. Throughout the long afternoon, with her empty hand aching for her staff and her feet resenting the hard Atlian soil, Kelyn waited for Gergo to drift, if not *her* way, toward the Traders she was nearest. Never had she found travel so tedious, with no break for hunting, no chance to explore the interesting sights along the way. She was thirsty and afraid to drink, knowing the difficulties involved in arranging to relieve herself—and once she thought of it, the niggling need to do just that created a constant ache in her bladder. She set her teeth against the irritation and waited for Gergo to move her way.

Quite suddenly, he obliged her, walking beside her with a tension in his shoulders that made her hesitate to speak. He didn't look at her; his gold-brown eyes were lined with worry. With his bruised temple and the fatigue on his face, the grim set of his mouth, it all made him look a generation older than he had just days ago. *I'm sorry*, Kelyn wanted to say, but was afraid to, was afraid of how vehemently he would agree that this was all her fault.

She hunted for the words to talk of escape, instead.

Gergo cut the effort short. "Our debt," he said, "is paid." And walked away from her.

Kelyn watched his retreating back and muttered, "I know."

Hers wasn't.

❖ ❖ ❖

Why hunt witches? The question ran through Kelyn's mind, as it had done since the Atlians had seized the Trader witches. Were witches only women? Were there no men with the same talents? And what could a witch do, besides the minor curses and cures that Rika had offered, and the multitudes of charms the Traders worked? For even Kelyn's curse, as annoying as it was, as much as it had changed and formed her life, was not a thing of great power.

She was surrounded by people who knew the answers to her questions, she was sure . . . if only they were talking to her. Somehow, as now, a plate of food always found its way before her at mealtimes, although her efforts to help prepare or clean up met silent yet effective blocks. No room around the wash basin, or hands swooping in to appropriate whatever task she reached for. The one time she had found a pile of tubers to scrub, they had literally disappeared from before her when she'd paused to narrow her eyes at one of the soldiers as he approached, leered at, and passed by a Trader woman.

So Kelyn quit annoying both the Traders and herself by trying, and simply ate the food that came her way, leaving the plate where she'd found it. But her acceptance of their unspoken rules did nothing to stop her mind from wandering, and wondering.

Why chase after witches who, as far as she could tell, affected nothing but their own community? She slipped her hand inside her shirt and ran her fingers down the barely discernable line of whip lash Lenci had cured. Why stop anyone from doing *this*?

She scooped the last of the fried pea paste from her plate and left the plate on the ground beside the hammock chair as she stood—carefully—taking the lamb leg bone with her to gnaw as she slowly circled the wagons to a spot where she could sit and watch the soldiers. Where she could watch the one who had been called Thyra, for it was Thyra who had felt her dowser magic, and Thyra who had led Atelic to the Trader witches.

If the woman noticed her as Kelyn settled into the scratchy weeds, if she felt Kelyn's scrutiny, she gave no sign of it. She ate with the soldiers, and though she was an attractive woman—if not sturdy enough by Keturan standards—the men kept a respectful distance, and offered none of the rude comments or gestures they so often sent Kelyn's way.

Atelic sat with her, and they put their heads together for a conference of some length; when they drew apart again, Atelic jabbed a finger at two of his men. "Go get the witches," he said, and then gave Thyra a self-satisfied nod. "Soften them up well enough, Thyra, and Abendar will be well pleased. It's past time he saw my worth above that cocker mercenary."

Thyra gave him an amused glance, but Kelyn saw the disdain it hid. "Abendar will also know which of us made the difference, Atelic."

He gave a little nod that was supposed to have been acknowledgment, but Kelyn somehow doubted it was any more than appeasement. These Atlians, she thought, would perish in her own world, where truth was truth and was spoken as such.

Herding the witches like sheep, Atelic's men brought them to the cluster of fires around which the soldiers ate; the men—still seated, still chewing and spitting and gulping beer—seemed to know no more than the Traders what to expect from this development; they simply shifted for a better view. Kelyn inched closer as dusk darkened already cloudy skies, aware of Endre's injuncture to stay away from the soldiers, but too curious—and alarmed—to miss the details of what was happening. A glance behind her told her that the Traders had noticed the new activity, and that several of the men had drifted closer—but none so close as she, sitting down in the weeds, unmoving, unnoticed.

Atelic had said the witches would remain unharmed, as long as the Traders remained on good behavior. One look at them told Kelyn the witches themselves held no stock in such assurances. All of a kind, with their deeply gold hair—brown, in the fading light—and rounded features, with their generous curves, not quite hidden by their loose, layered clothing. It was a good thing for the Trader women, Kelyn thought, that these soldiers were conditioned into fear of Trader curses. Odd that they seemed to have no regard for such things when it came to causing harm other than that powered by their lust. For there was no fear on Atelic's face, only anticipation—while Thyra only looked bored. Kelyn frowned, trying to read the woman.

Wiping his hands on his thighs, Atelic stood, resting his palm on the hilt of his short sword. "Abendar has forbidden witchery in his lands," he announced, importance lacing his voice.

Still seated, Thyra said, "Unsanctioned witchery." Kelyn had trouble making out Atelic's expression, though she thought it was probably annoyance; she inched closer. No one seemed to notice, not even the Trader men who had done the same. Soon they would all be hidden in the darkness, and the nightly sentries would walk the length of the wagons with their torches. Discovery at that point was less likely, but more dangerous—the Traders were forbidden to be away from their wagons after dark.

"Unsanctioned witchery," Atelic repeated, and there was definitely annoyance in his voice. "Your freedom is lost because you break that rule." *They hadn't. Kelyn had.* But Atelic wouldn't free them, now that he had them, even if he knew the truth—and the Traders knew it, or they would have given her up. "Your only hope is Abendar's mercy."

"Abendar is not known for his mercy," Thyra said, apparently getting into the spirit of Atelic's game.

"Your only true chance is to earn it." Atelic shifted back as one of the soldiers replenished the dying fire, darkening it even further until with a sudden snap of sparks, the new wood caught and the flames danced high enough to illuminate them all. "If you want to see your freedom again," he repeated, unnecessarily driving the point home, "you'll have to earn Abendar's mercy."

Kelyn snorted silently, making a sour face in the darkness. Mercy was cutting the throat of a wounded animal. Mercy was holding back the blow that would kill your enemy. It was what she had given Busted Balls in the border town, by letting him walk away that first time. It was *not* threatening those who were already in your power until they gave you something you wanted in an effort to earn the freedom that should have been theirs already. These Atlians had a way of twisting truths both spoken *and* unspoken.

The witches had said nothing, none of them. They held each others' hands in silence, the mature women on the fringes of the group, the youngest and oldest in the protected center, with Lenci centermost and barely visible at all.

"Tell me," Atelic said, too casually after the lengthy silence, "what do you know of god-touched talismans?"

Silence. Several of the witches flinched as he took a sudden step forward. "Traders are not known for using them, or having them—but your kind have your noses into everything. Always asking questions, always passing secrets—everyone knows it." He leaned toward one of the witches, tilting her chin up with one finger to stare long into her eyes. Then he pushed her away, letting her friends catch her as he turned back to Thyra.

"We're asking you," Thyra said, sounding bored. Kelyn was beginning to think that this was not necessarily a good sign. "We're giving you a chance to help yourselves. *Abendar* will be bothered with no such niceties. He is pleased enough to use magic when it suits his purposes."

She held a gem out high before her, nestled in her upturned fingers. Kelyn hissed and threw herself back on her hands, unable to stop the reaction or, as she regained her balance and sat upright on her still-crossed legs again, the warding sign she made, two fingers drawn across her eyes. For the gem glowed with an unearthly illumination, the sickly yellow-brown color of something long dead. Too intense to look at directly, it yet somehow failed to cast any light.

The witches drew tightly together; Kelyn thought she saw a faint greenish haze settling around them, and realized she was seeing the first true signs of magic from the Traders, magic that even she could perceive. Thyra, concentrating on the gem, didn't appear to notice or care; she spoke a harsh word, and a spark leapt out, trailing an umbilicus of light. All the soldiers in the area drew back, and two of them suddenly remembered they were on guard duty; they snatched torches, thrust them into the fire, and trotted away in unseemly haste. The spark hovered a moment, and then floated purposefully toward the witches.

Kelyn averted her eyes, warding herself again. And then blinked, her eye caught by movement that seemed to disappear when she looked directly at it. Quickly she corrected herself, aiming her gaze to the side, looking with her peripheral night vision. Barely, she found the movement again—a snake of dark green glow oozing quickly across the ground toward Thyra from the witches, from the center of the group where she was sure Lenci still hid. Moving swiftly, so dark it nearly blended with the ground, the glow snake reached Thyra's toe—which sucked it in with such force Kelyn fancied she could hear the sound of it. No one, Thyra most of all, marked the glow-snake's passing. The spark commanded their attention, floating over the heads of the witches, dipping now and then as if it was particularly tempted by something—or someone.

"It will go in through your eye," Thyra said, and the boredom in her voice no longer masked her anticipation, "and that eye will melt down your cheek. It will burn down the back of your throat, and you'll never swallow again. And it will find your heart, where it will lodge . . . and feed. Making my soul-gem ever more powerful . . . making *me* ever more powerful." She shrugged, making the gem's brilliance bob in the night, and added matter-of-factly, "Eventually you'll die, of course."

Atelic broke in; after a startled moment, Kelyn identified the harsh note in his voice as fear. Uncertain of Thyra, was he? "This is nothing compared to what Abendar is willing to do to get this same information from you. You will not be blamed for knowing where such magics reside. Speaking of them can only ease your fate."

Kelyn couldn't see who responded; it might as well have been all of them, using a single voice. "We know nothing of magics so strong. We stay away from them."

"Of course you do," Atelic said, waving away the protest with an irritable gesture. "But you *hear* about them. We want them destroyed," he added suddenly, which was what Kelyn had assumed until he said it—

and then she realized that Abendar hadn't destroyed Thyra's gem, had he?

The hovering spark gave a sudden dip; the witches cringed from it as it easily penetrated and dissipated their misty green protection. Kelyn stiffened, wondering if she should—if she *could*—she heard a rustle behind her, the reaction of the watching Traders.

Then Thyra sagged, catching herself. The spark disappeared with a smacking *pop* as Thyra drew the gem back, curling her hand over it to clasp it protectively to her chest. Atelic gave her a startled glance, and she snarled weakly at him, "I'm going to kill your Siloga-cursed cook!"

Atelic looked down at himself, an obvious self-check, and found himself fine enough. "You ate too much."

Thyra's face twisted in pain, and she doubled over—at the same time rising to make a hasty departure from the fire circle.

No, not this *direction!*

Of course, this direction. Kelyn heard the abrupt departure of the lurking Traders, and didn't dare move herself, not in the wake of the noise they'd made. She ducked her head and let her thick black hair hide the pale flash of her face—not that Thyra was likely to notice, or that anyone had bothered to follow her from the circle. Kelyn didn't blame them—she didn't want to be anywhere near Thyra when the inevitable happened, either. But here she was—

And there Thyra went, only a man's length from Kelyn. Down on her knees, trying to get her pants down, not succeeding as she folded over and spewed from both ends. The stench was immediate and overwhelming; from the fire circle, someone made a crude comment. Atelic had turned to the witches, confrontational, both hands balled at his fists.

And that was when another of the men ran hunched

from the circle, more successful in his attempt to distance himself before the ragged noises of his misery came through the darkness.

"Find the cook!" Atelic snapped. "Bury the food! And you—fool! *Stop eating!*"

But Kelyn knew better. Even as a third man ran from the circle, she knew better. Lenci was simply too clever; she'd magicked more than one of them, pointing Atelic's suspicions at the poor cook. Even now, Atelic bellowed something about a beating.

She wasn't safe out here, no matter how unlikely was Thyra's notice. If this kept up, the men would run out of separate directions, and another one would come this way soon. She got to her hands and knees, intending to creep away before rising to slink back to her assigned wagon. Instead, she found herself eyeing Thyra, watching the men as they hurried the witches back to their wagons. Thyra, convulsing with illness, fell to the ground, fainting in her own filth.

Moving carefully, guiding her path by her sense of smell as much as anything else, Kelyn made it to Thyra's side and gingerly rolled her over, patting down her bony sides and around her cowpat-flat breasts until she hit upon the hard round gem. She quickly smothered her triumphant grin—teeth gleamed white in the darkness—and tore Thyra's shirt open to snatch the leather pouch. The thong must have been charmed—it wouldn't break at her tug, and Thyra stirred weakly in protest. Kelyn dug in her vest for the round skipping knife Atelic had missed in his eagerness to fondle her, slashing open the pouch itself, and then tearing a jagged section from the hem of her shirt with which to pick up the gem gingerly. Thyra had held it in her bare hands, but Kelyn was no witch, and she doubted that the gem was as harmless as the dowser had turned out to be.

Booty in hand, she crept away, moving as fast as she dared.

The men were otherwise occupied.

❖ ❖ ❖

By the time she made it to her assigned wagon, she thought that the exodus from the fire circle had stopped—though she could see only vague movement from this distance, even against the firelight. Surely Lenci had not been able to send out enough spells to sicken them all. Kelyn would have seen at least one other glowsnake, if so. Wouldn't she? Unless they had been weaker spells, invisible ones . . .

She stopped her useless speculation. Her own curse was enough magic to carry around; she wasn't going to waste time on Lenci's. Or on Thyra's. She hadn't taken the soul-gem for herself, but to keep it out of Thyra's hands—or, if she died, Atelic's; he'd no doubt simply find another witch to do his bidding.

The question was, what to do with it now.

The others from her wagon were already inside; their fire had shrunk to the mere suggestion of flame among glowing hot coals. Kelyn gave it a speculative eye, hefting the gem in her hand within the cloth that bound it. Then, before she could think too much about it, she tossed it into the depth of the coals and danced back to crouch beside the wagon.

Moments passed.

Nothing happened.

Of course, she thought, feeling foolish. A magic gem would be a sturdy thing, probably forged in fire. Now she'd have to fish the thing out and think of something else to try. Maybe even hang on to the hell-touched gem until she could talk to a Trader witch, find out just how to destroy it—

The fire flared in sudden, violent light, instantly blinding her. She threw herself back, aiming for under the wagon and clunking her head against the kettlebox on the way. Burying her head in her arms did no good; the light seemed to seep through her very flesh, all the more eerie for its silence—even the normal hiss and crackle of the fire had stopped. *Stupid, stupid, stupid,* she chided herself, while the pounding of her heart did its best to fill in the unnatural hush and she wondered if the light would grow to consume them all. *Stupid Keturan,* always *finding trouble . . .*

The glare faded. Kelyn dared to peek, her night vision in ruins but not needed to see the intense sparks of light—handfuls and handfuls of them—hovering in confusion over the fire, mingling and dancing and swirling and then simultaneously fading away. Cautiously, she raised her head.

Above her, those within the wagon shifted it with their movement, their murmurs coming to her through the floorboard. Further away and less concerned about being heard, the soldiers shouted at one another, still absorbed in the aftermath of Lenci's clandestine spell, and the cook's punishment. But someone had seen . . . someone *had* to have seen.

She couldn't be found out here. Blindly, Kelyn crawled out from under the wagon, groping for the door in the back. It was already cracked—no doubt by the wary Traders trying to understand the light that had probably seeped through wood as easily as it had seeped through her own flesh—and she yanked it the rest of the way open, hurling herself through to claim her sleeping spot.

Even at this startling intrusion, the Traders said nothing to her. Tonight, she didn't care. As long as they also said nothing to the soldiers who pounded toward them—and toward what was now a perfectly normal fire.

❖ ❖ ❖

Kelyn sat in the wagon, her knees drawn up and her arms looped around them, waiting to see if any of her wagonmates would stir at her movement, still relieved that the two soldiers who'd stood at the end of the wagon, pondering the light they'd seen, had neither figured it out or decided to draw Atelic's attention to it. Sooner or later, someone would miss the soul-gem. Sooner or later, they would connect it to the flare of light, and possibly to her. But by then—she'd be gone. And she'd do her best to take the Traders with her.

Her wagonmates slept on, oblivious—a mother and her child in one of the hard narrow beds at the side of the wagon, a young couple impossibly intertwined to fit in another. In a woven hammock stretched from one side to the other at the head of the wagon, a young woman whose sisters and mother now rode in the witch wagons curled in a miserable ball; Kelyn had heard her cry herself to sleep. An old man slept in the single bed across from the mother and child. Nea the older, Vencel, Rez, Chapa, Dente, and little Chiya. All of them quietly uncomfortable with the unusual makeup of the displaced occupants in the wagon that belonged to Rez and Chapa, the young couple. None of them speaking to Kelyn, who slept on the floor by default and had no complaints about it. Her satchel was a good pillow and the cloak kept her warm enough.

She moved to the end of the wagon and crouched there, waiting. Patient. If the whisper-slight noises she made were enough to disturb any of them, she'd be sure to give them plenty of time to settle in between. After a good long moment in which none of them moved, she opened the door in tiny increments, glad for the well-greased hinges, not so pleased about the cool night breeze that rushed in. It was as likely as noise to disturb someone. She opened the door only wide enough to slip through it sideways, one long leg searching for the ground. Finding it, she eased herself through, taking her weight carefully so as not to come down hard on any rock that might disrupt her balance and the fluidity of her movement. Intense, concentrating to overcome the potential clumsiness she now knew to be Rika's curse, she opened the door a smidgen wider to accommodate her belt buckles, offset to either side of center.

Finally, she stood on the other side of the door, stilled to listen for any response from inside. Someone shifted, sighed, and settled again, and then there was silence. Carefully, Kelyn closed the door.

Unlike their normal habits, none of the Traders slept under the stars; she at least had no worries of stepping on someone in the dark—though under this cloudy, starless night, with all these horses around, she was bound to step on *something* she didn't like. Endre, she had seen, was in the first wagon, the one closest to the soldiers. Kelyn, of course, was assigned to the last.

She started the long, slow process of creeping forward, throwing herself under a wagon when one of the soldiers strolled by, weak and flickering torch in hand. Useless thing, she thought, protecting her eyes against it. She'd much rather move in what little light the night offered with all her senses alert than blind herself with flames that illuminated little, or fill her ears with their crackle and her nose with a torch's stink of pitch.

This night, the torch worked for her; the soldier noticed nothing of her. He looked for his companion, and after he passed, she heard him call out. "Sef! We found Thyra—she's dead!"

Kelyn hesitated, long enough to wonder which had killed the woman—Lenci's spell or the destruction of the gem—and then shrugged. If ever a witch *did* need killing . . .

She moved more quickly after that, knowing both guards were behind her somewhere. Outside the door of the head wagon, she hesitated, not knowing where Endre was located within.

Finally, with no better idea and no intention of wasting more time out in the open, she cracked the door open and hissed, "Endre!" There was no response, and she drummed her fingers lightly against the door. "Endre!"

Close to the door, someone gave a grunt of surprise and stirred. "Endre?" Kelyn said, more quietly this time.

"Atlia's arse," said whoever it was—definitely not Endre's voice. "What trouble are you causing now?"

"I need to talk to Endre."

"Do it tomorrow!"

"*Now*," Kelyn said, opting for brevity of spoken word, though there were plenty on the tip of her tongue. As though Endre would talk to her tomorrow any more than he'd done so today.

With a mutter in the Traders' tongue that could only be a curse, the man heaved himself off the bed; Kelyn heard muffled movement and a snatch of murmuring, and then Endre crouched by the cracked door, a blanket pulled around his shoulders and what she could discern of his face set in wary caution. "What?" he said, sounding tired. No doubt he was, the way he was taking events upon himself. He was, after all, the one who was supposed to have been watching her; he was the one who should have noticed what she was up to. She felt like telling him that no one could have done any better, not if she hadn't wanted them to, but decided against it. Not now.

Perhaps later, if things worked out.

"This is our last night before we reach Abendar's town," she said, putting her head close to his so she could all but mouth the words. The wagon rocked again; the other man settling, she presumed. "I can reach the front wagons, Endre. I can get my blades back, my staff. I can keep the witches safe while the rest of you go for the soldiers, if you're quiet enough about it to start."

"Ketura's balls," Endre said with surprising force for all its silence, a phrase he'd picked up from Kelyn. "Can't you just stay out of it?"

"Stay out of it?" Kelyn blinked at him in the darkness. "How can I *stay out of it* when *it* is my fault to begin with?"

"Because we don't want your help!" Endre paused, taking a deep breath; those last words had gotten louder. When he spoke again, it was in safer tones. "We aren't going to leave our witches, or even take the chance one might be left behind. We have friends in Abendar's town, Kelyn. We are not all like you, wandering alone in a land we know nothing about, stirring up trouble for other people. We don't need your rescue—despite what you may think of us, we can take care of ourselves!"

"But—" Kelyn said, trying to assimilate his words, feeling unaccountably hurt and equally stubborn. "But once we're in the town, it'll be so much harder—"

"No!" he said. "Enough! Get back to your wagon before—"

Too late.

Footsteps pounded toward them from the front of the wagon; Kelyn stiffened, suddenly recalling the shifting of the wagon, knowing it was the man she'd awakened—not settling, but going for the soldiers. *Run.* If the Traders wouldn't accept her help, then there was no reason to stay here. *Run.*

Run she did, angling away from the Traders, one arm before her to protect her face as she sped into the darkness. "There she goes!" cried one of the soldiers, his Atlian accent harsh in her ears. And then she heard Atelic's returning shout.

"Leave her! She's not worth bothering with." He made a derisive sound loud enough for her to hear as she slowed. "Just a Keturan, and a woman at that; we'll never see her again. Get back to your posts!"

Hidden in the darkness, Kelyn eased down from her run, angered beyond all expectation. She wasn't worth bothering with, was she? Just a Keturan, was she? Just wait—

She stumbled, her step landing heavily in a dip in the ground; her other foot snagged on stringy tangled ground growth, and she landed on her knees, her teeth clicking together at the impact. *Ketura's balls!*

Well. Enough to sit here for the moment, once more brought back to reality by her curse. She crawled around to face the Trader caravan, watching the soldiers' torches sputter and bob as the minor chaos caused by her departure subsided. The faint sound of a baby's cry carried through the still air, then faded away. No one was coming her way; they probably thought her long gone.

They probably wanted her that way. She thought again of the Trader who'd tattled on her, and felt an unexpected pang at the betrayal. Not that she could blame him. Not after what she had brought down on the community.

I only wanted a chance to make it right.

She wondered, suddenly, if sometimes there *was* no making it right.

Perhaps. But not this time. Whether they wanted her help or not.

Chapter 8

Even as she approached the fringes of Abendar's town, Kelyn realized it was bigger than the border town she had found so crowded, bigger than any settlement she had ever imagined. Shacks and tents and greasy cookfire smoke trails smudging the horizon were the first signs of what the Atlians liked to call civilization. At first they were nestled in among the weedy growth and sparse copses so typical of this mildly rolling land, but even as she passed the first of them, Kelyn saw that ahead, the weeds had been tromped into dust and the trees thinned.

After a morning of following the wide trail left by the Trader caravan, she now walked a true road, with stone markers set just close enough so you could see one from the other. Her satchel bumped against her back; her staff fit comfortably in her hand. The first she had found at the back of the wagon she'd been sleeping in, tucked behind the back wheel. Someone, it seemed, had thought she might come back for it. The staff—along with her knives and the whip—had required more stealth, but men sleep hardest in those hours right before dawn, and she'd only had to help one of them along. She hoped she hadn't hit him too hard.

Imagining Atelic's reaction when her weapons were discovered missing had kept a grim little smile on Kelyn's face all morning.

She had no plan. She didn't, she realized as she passed a smelly pen of pigs just as the dirt road turned to cobblestones, *know* enough to have a plan. And after her experience in the border town, and with the Traders, she knew better than to rush into this new place with the same enthusiasm. No doubt there were strange customs lurking here, too, the things everyone took for granted and thus didn't bother to mention.

Kelyn stopped to examine the squalid neighborhood ringing Abendar's town, realizing it would be hard enough to blend in even if she did nothing wrong. The women here seemed much like those in the border town. Petite, covered in loose skirts and tunics with a single long piece of material wrapped in a complex pattern over it all, these women looked at the ground instead of making close observation of what was around them. No one had hair as dark as hers, or matched her length of limb. No one of them walked with purpose, but instead seemed to wander from place to place.

It would, she decided, draw more attention if she made some feeble attempt to disguise herself. She would simply go in as what she was, a Keturan, and do what had worked with Atelic—she would fulfill their expectations of what that meant. It *was* a big town . . . as long as she did nothing truly outrageous, there was no reason for Atelic to learn she was here. Atelic was a witch-hunter, and would probably go right back out to hunt for more.

As long as she did nothing truly outrageous . . .

as if she'd *know*. Kelyn bounced the staff gently on the top of her foot. This wasn't a plan, it was speculation. She had learned young in Ketura's mountains, speculation meant failure, and failure usually meant death.

This time, it was the best she could do.

Or . . . maybe not. She watched a child dart across the street, returning to its mother's skirts. In the border town, she had found allies in the children, who seemed pleased enough when an adult took them seriously. And they talked to her, instead of turning their noses up at her. Children, it seemed, were children everywhere. She'd find some. Maybe it would work . . . maybe it wouldn't. Now was a good time to find out.

As Kelyn passed from the outskirts of town into its depths, the buildings grew larger, and older, squeezing tighter and blocking out the low sun. At one point, standing at a main intersection, she could look down the road to the entrance of Abendar's fortress. The flat, open, surrounding grounds meant no one could approach unseen, and from here it looked like she would have to pass through two gates to get inside.

Well, inside wasn't where she wanted to go, not now. Nor did she want the clean streets and freshly whitewashed shops and homes of the area around the fortress. Kelyn looked in the opposite direction, where the street looked narrower, dirtier . . . darker. That's where she'd find children like Aktel.

Walking down that street, feeling the clamminess of the ground work up between her toes, for the first time she found herself considering boots in warm weather. Her own were in her satchel, with hard, waxed rawhide soles and fur lining. If it got worse . . . Kelyn stuck to the middle of the street, avoiding the run-off ditched to either side.

With the fortress out of sight and her sense of direction challenged by the winding little street, Kelyn finally stopped outside a dark tavern with a faded and unreadable symbol painted over its door. It, like the streets around her, seemed abandoned, and she had the sudden feeling that this section was not at all like the border town, and that she had made a serious error in coming this way. The marketplace, that's what she needed, although it was surely closing down, this late in the day.

Next best thing—something to eat. But not here. She turned to retrace her steps, and discovered them—silent, watching. Three children, observing her with eyes that belonged in older faces. Finally. They could help her; if nothing else, they could point her to a safe place to eat and spend the night. For though Kelyn had utter confidence in her ability to take care of herself, that, too, she had learned, would draw attention.

They must have seen the relief in her face; they came to her, tugging each other along, their chatter loud after the unwelcoming silence of the street. She greeted them, turning a circle to keep track of them when they split up to move around her, touching her cloak, wrapping grimy fingers around her staff only to release it before she could object. Children, being children—curious, fingering anything within reach. "I'm looking for the market," she said. "And something to eat. Can you help me?"

"Easy done," said the oldest child, who Kelyn thought might be a boy. His hair was long, and so dirty that the little braids that kept it out of his eyes seemed glued in place; there were certainly no ties to keep it that way. "Guide you for a bit of copper."

Kelyn shook her head. "Don't have it." She did, in fact—leftover from her hunting—but intended to spend it on food. "Just tell me."

"Why should we?" said a shorter child, one whose hair was just as dirty and who had a definite smell. "Find it yourself, you don't want to pay."

The older child made a sudden gesture, and the smelly one flinched. "Don't mind him," the boy said. "We'll tell you, 'cause we like the looks of you." Still they moved around her, the smallest one bumping the back of her legs, a finger landing on her knife sheath and then dropping away, the smelly one at her side, trading places with the oldest child so one was always at her side and one before her. Without thinking about it, she stepped to the side, to give herself more space. They followed, taking on the oldest one's helpful expression.

"Tell me, then," she said, feeling a hint of annoyance at whatever game they were playing. The street wasn't so abandoned any more; several lanterns burned beside doorways, and the tavern door had been propped open; a woman stood in it, watching Kelyn with her arms crossed.

"Got to go back the way you came," said the smelly child. "At Six Corners, turn out-town—"

But Kelyn knew better; that was the way she'd come. The oldest boy slapped the smelly one's arm. "Don't be a cocker. Head for the fortress, that's what you want. Food for a nice lady like you there, 'long the Rim."

Suddenly she didn't believe any of it. "Thank you," she said, as if she had. Play the stupid barbarian, even for the children . . . That was when she noticed that she'd been herded almost to the chimney-narrow opening between the tavern and its neighbor—and a sound from within its dark recesses turned it decidedly unwelcoming. She took a decisive step away from it, startling the children and nearly bowling the smallest over. "Thank you," she said again. "I'll go do that."

Another step, the slightest of tugs at her side—her hand shot out, clamping down on the head of the smelly one, who to all appearances was simply skittering to get out of her way. He yelped as she jerked him back, snatching her pilfered whip from his hands—and then hissed at the sudden sting in her arm, the glimpse of metal in the hands of the oldest—

He'd cut her! Another prick at her leg, and she whirled to find the youngest at work. And then they weren't children, but enemies, and she sent the youngest one flying with a kick that she somehow managed to pull, unable truly to hurt the little menace. The oldest came flying at her as the tavern woman gave a shout, and she jumped back, whacking the coiled whip across his chest even as she used the staff to shove the smelly one away. And then she had them all at a distance, the staff before her, the whip uncoiled and ready, as she backed a step away from them.

A handful of men rushed to crowd the door of the tavern, and the woman pointed an accusing finger. "She been shoving my kids around!"

Kelyn backed another step, suddenly noting a shadowed form in the gap between the buildings, and more doors opening along the street—good Rema, how many of them were there? All on the brink of action, working up into a collective growl of gleeful resentment—they'd tear her apart like a pack of wolves!

Even a Keturan knows when the odds are against her. Kelyn gave them a sudden grin, a piercing rendition of her battle cry—making them hesitate just from the surprise of it, the noise of it in this closed-in street. And then she turned tail and ran.

They chased her a ways, pounding after her as she ran on silent bare feet, not wasting breath or motion, but running lean and hard. As they fell back, their speed quickly spent, others took up the hunt, and the street echoed with shouts and threats and promises, inspiring a blaze of lanterns up ahead. Soon enough someone would jump out before her, and delay her just enough. . . .

Panting now, Kelyn felt the street grow drier beneath her feet, felt cobblestones here and there, and then more often—and someone did appear in the darkness before her, a man, his arms spread wide and his stance eager, expecting to stop her simply with his presence.

She lowered her shoulder, jutted out her elbow, and took the staff in both hands so it protruded just beyond her elbow—and jammed it into his midriff, jumping over his legs as he went down.

In another couple of strides, she found herself in the middle of the main street, cobbles beneath her feet, shouts behind her, and a number of lanterns beckoning to her right. Maybe the brat had told her right, then; the place to go was between town and fortress, what Smelly had called the Rim. The place to go *now*. Without so much as a glance at her pursuit—their noise alone told her how close they were—Kelyn sprinted for the Rim.

Weaving her way between the small groups of people walking the street wasn't hard, but her pursuit engendered angry shouts and protest. She heard them fall behind, and eased her pace. By the time she hit the mouth of the marketplace, she'd fallen into an easy walk, and neither heard nor saw any sign of the dark street denizens.

She stepped aside, out of the trickle of foot traffic, to survey the Rim. While not crowded—none of the meager shops in the semicircle facing the fortress showed signs of occupancy—it held a number of cramped buildings with open doors and people spilling out onto the cobbles for argument and jest. Taverns, she guessed, although their lantern-lit signs were identified with symbols she couldn't read, and with rough carved caricatures she was too far away to recognize. Only two of the establishments seemed to cater to a mixed clientele—both men and women, but rarely a woman without a man—while the others boasted rowdy men, half of them already drunk by the looks of it.

Civilization.

She caught the eye of a man who stared as he passed by, and glared him into being interested elsewhere. *The cloak*, she realized suddenly. That's why the brats had taken such an interest in her—at first, anyway. The others had simply fallen into howling mob mentality, stirred to trouble by the mere scent of it. *Too conspicuous.* Her hand went to the ties at her chest, then hesitated. Atelic had not seen this cloak; he wouldn't recognize her from afar in it, nor think of her if anyone mentioned it.

Besides, the fickle spring night had turned cool, and she had no desire to shiver in the darkness.

Or to let her belly continue to growl in hunger. She picked out the more modest looking eatery, and regarded it warily, wondering what pitfalls she would find within. As she scowled off the stare of another passer-by, she'd suddenly had enough of Atlia, of places with streets and soldiers and so many people she didn't know. Until she had left her home, had there ever been a time when she was faced with someone she didn't already know? A trader here, perhaps, a misguided pilgrim to Ketura there . . .

And now, the only person she knew was herself—and after what she'd learned about the curse, she wasn't all too sure even of that.

A particularly loud rumble of hunger brought her thoughts out of that place, a pitfall as surely as anything else she had run into here. She'd get herself a meal, find a place to curl up, and go looking for Traders—or, at least, information—in the morning. So, with another lesson learned—*not even children are untouched by Atlian ways*—Kelyn shifted her grip on her satchel and went to hunt some food.

❖ ❖ ❖

"What *are* you?"

Kelyn blinked into daylight and blew a stem of hay off her nose. The door to the barn was wide open, and the bright sunlight outside turned the small figure between Kelyn and the door into a black blob. "You can't be in here," it said solemnly, and climbed the rest of the way up the short ladder to join her in the hayloft.

"I *am* in here." Kelyn sat up, drew her satchel closer, checked her knives. In the daylight, the small pole barn turned out to be sturdy enough, with a row of standing stalls down the wall she could see from here; the shuffling activity below her made her think that there was probably nothing more than a communal pen there. The structure itself had large gaps in the narrow wall logs, but the roof loomed dark and tight, and the thatching seemed fresh. She'd managed to find a place at the edge of the Rim, and what she now saw reassured her that she hadn't inadvertently put herself into the hands of more like Smelly's kin. Still . . . "You stay back there," she told the smudge-faced girl, who had released the security of the ladder to move into the loft.

"I have to throw down hay," the girl said. "I'll get in trouble if I don't. And it's *my* loft."

Kelyn couldn't argue with that. She grabbed the satchel and dragged it with her, moving on her hands and knees to get to her feet under the roof peak, where she could almost stand, ducking only her head to avoid brushing it among the spiders of the rushes.

Ignoring her, the girl set about her task—shoving hay down the holes in the loft floor meant for that purpose, and then shoving it over the front edge to land behind the occupied standing stalls. The horses—scrubby things, not even worth eating—moved restlessly in the stalls, jerking at their ties.

"You should help," the girl said. "You'll be in less trouble when they find you, if you help." She frowned up at Kelyn, keeping her distance, but not so much wary as responding to Kelyn's earlier directive. "What *are* you? You're big. And you dress funny. Can I touch that fur?"

"If you try anything, I'll throw you off the loft," Kelyn said, but the girl only made a derisive face as if to indicate *who would be stupid enough to try?* Kelyn took hold of the cloak and held it out so the girl could touch it without coming too close, and the child surprised her by putting not her fingers, but her cheek to the fur.

"Mmmm," she said. "Nice. Did you steal it?"

"No," Kelyn said, startled. "I killed it."

The girl lifted her face to give Kelyn a skeptical eye. "No you didn't."

"I did *too.*" Kelyn pulled the cloak back in affront. "I come from Ketura, where the beasts live. And I saved a friend's life when I killed it."

"Then what are you doing here?"

A very good question. Arguing with a child with no more than two hands of age on her, and losing. Discovering the problems of sleeping in the coarse Atlian hay, which had scratched her face and neck and found its way down her shirt, where it now tickled for her attention. Realizing that she didn't have enough money left for another meal, that she didn't know where the Traders were, that she had lost too much time already in her quest to help the witches. "Looking for help," she told the girl. "And not the kind I got from the ratlings down that slime-covered street last night."

"You went into the Darks at night?" the girl said, surprise on her open face. "That's stupid!"

"Yes, and so is arguing with you in this loft. If I help you with chores around this barn, can I get something to eat?"

"If you do my chores, *I* won't eat." The girl frowned at her, and then looked down at the stalls. "But Ikla hasn't cleaned in a week. You can do his work, and I bet you can get two meals out of it."

Kelyn peered over the edge of the loft. Back to this, was she? Well . . . it wasn't as bad as pit farming. But she thought it might be time to find something to put on her feet.

❖ ❖ ❖

Kelyn gulped down the entire mug and held it out for a refill of milk before the old woman had finished pouring Kila's serving. Kila—the girl—grinned at her; the old woman made a less pleasing face as she refilled the mug and clomped away, leaving them each with a bowl of steaming boiled grains. Kelyn had already asked for another. Kila, using a not-very-discreet whisper, said, "I bet you wouldn't have gotten two meals if she'd known how much you eat!"

Kelyn grinned back at her. "With what I mucked today, they're getting a bargain."

They sat at a rough-hewn board balanced on top of a stump. Kila fit the makeshift table perfectly, sitting primly on her knees; Kelyn scrunched cross-legged before it. The barn bordered one side of the small yard, and the back of an inn the other; between, there was a rickety fence with gaps, and a garden with early greens and several prowling fowl. Kelyn ignored the chicken that pecked at nonexistent insects to work itself closer, hoping for some sensible human to offer it seed, and gestured to the fortress, the top of which peeked over the roof of the inn. "I'm curious about the witches," she said. "I hear Abendar is rounding them up. Are there so many of them here in your land?"

Kila hesitated, her mouth open, and then abruptly shoveled porridge into it instead of responding. Kelyn wrinkled her nose at the girl, and, after fumbling with the broad scooped eating implement, joined her. After a moment, the girl mumbled, "I don't hear much about that."

She wasn't a good enough liar to pull it off, but Kelyn didn't push. Especially not with the old lady making her way out the creaky back door of the inn to plop another bowl down before Kelyn. "That'll be it," she announced with a scowl, turning her back on them before Kelyn could say anything else.

As soon as the door closed behind her, a boy scooted in from one of the gaps and settled in beside Kila, dipping his fingers into her bowl to help himself. At Kila's complete lack of reaction, Kelyn decided this must be an arrangement they had. The boy was of Kila's age and size, and looked much like her, save for his dirtier face and scruffier clothes—while they both wore tunics with no sign of any other clothing beneath, his was ripped at the neck and had him constantly tugging to keep it from falling off his shoulder. "Who's she?" he asked Kila, as if Kelyn couldn't hear.

"She was in the loft," Kila said. "Mucked out the barn. She killed the beast she wears, she said. Did you get anything from the shops this morning?"

He held up a coin, tucking it away again before Kelyn could even see the metal of it. The whole while he stared at her in a frown of thought. Then his face lightened. "You must be the one," he said. "The one who got out of the Darks last night. Are you? How'd you do it? Why'd you go down there?"

Kelyn dropped a glob of porridge right down the front of her shirt.

Ketura's balls. She didn't answer until she'd fished it out, and even then, it wasn't an answer. "You must be related—the questions spew out of her just as fast. But she doesn't answer them well."

"We're twins," the boy said proudly. And then, not so proudly, "Killed our ma to have us. And Dadda got in the way of a witch-hunt last season. But we can look for ourselves. We," he said pointedly, "don't go down to the Darks, not even in the day."

"Why is it called that?"

" 'Cause it always seems dark there," he said. "How'd you get away?"

Kelyn caught the rhythm of it. Answer for answer. "I run fast," she said. "And I don't give up. Does Abendar have a problem with witches?"

"He didn't used to. Then that Silogan got here." He smirked. "Penis-sanji."

"*Petissanji*," Kila said, rolling her eyes.

The boy shrugged. "My way's better. Why'd you go down there?"

"I was lost. What does Abendar do with the witches once he catches them?"

"Kills 'em," the boy said. "Pulls 'em apart and then kills 'em. Dumps the bodies in the fortress trash. I seen 'em myself," he added, forestalling any objection. But Kelyn had none. It was not the news she hoped for, but it seemed no less reasonable than hunting the witches in the first place. She'd seen what they could do—what Lenci *had* done—but she'd also seen it only under duress, and in response to a much more wicked threat from Thyra.

The boy reclaimed her attention, reaching for her cloak, taking his turn at questions. "I never seen any woman that looked like you. Where you from?"

"Ketura," Kelyn said, waving in the approximate

direction of her homeland. "The other side of Orrick. Where we don't hunt anything but food and furs. I'm looking for some Traders. Have you heard anything of them?"

For the first time, the boy didn't respond. He looked at Kila, who said, "You talk too much." He eyed Kelyn, then, daring, snagged her almost empty bowl and cleaned out every last softened grain.

When he reached for the second one, Kelyn caught his wrist, a fast snatch that startled him. "Tell me."

His gaze skittered over her cloak, her knives, the staff on the ground beside her; a sudden faint tremble passed through his bony arm and into Kelyn's fingers. "No one talks of them," he said. "If you do them harm, you're cursed."

"It's true," Kila said, grabbing Kelyn's hand and trying to pry loose her fingers. "Let him go!"

Kelyn ignored the wash of shame in her chest. *Bully*. "I've been with them. We were separated outside this town, and now I need to find them again. We're friends." She doubted Gergo would say as much. "You won't be cursed for helping a friend to find them."

"What do you know? You're the one who went into the Darks at night," Kila said, scorn not hiding the way her voice thinned with fear. She hammered a small fist against Kelyn's thumb. "Let him go!"

"I mean well by them," Kelyn said, capturing Kila's arm before Kila thought to do anything truly annoying with it. "I swear it by gentle Rema."

"Swear it by Siloga," the boy said, abruptly ceasing his tug-of-war over his own arm.

Kelyn made a face. "I would rather honor Rema," she said.

"If you lie, Rema won't do near as much to you as Siloga will," the boy said. "Siloga will make your hair fall out, and your eyes turn white, and your privy parts crack and bleed." Kelyn gave him a startled look, and he nodded vigorously. "It's true, I've seen it. If you really mean your words, swear them by Siloga!"

Kelyn cast through those words, and found nothing with even the taint of falsehood. She'd always *meant* the Traders well . . . "I swear by Siloga," she said firmly. "I mean well by the Traders."

The children exchanged a glance and ceased to struggle with her; cautiously, Kelyn released Kila. But the boy she held, until he said, "Out past the Darks. On the other side. Abendar lets 'em stay out there because they bring in good trade. Sometimes you see them in center town, but they never stay long." He rubbed his wrist, his expression sliding into a pout.

"You aren't hurt," Kelyn said, nonetheless shoving what was left of her breakfast his way. "If I wanted to hurt you, you'd know it."

He applied his attention to the bowl without responding to her.

Kelyn eyed the fortress. It wouldn't do to go to the Traders without a plan. And she couldn't plan without scouting things out. The boy, over his sulks, said, "I wouldn't go in there. Abendar has a big warrior helping him."

"He catches more witches than all of Abendar's men," Kila said, real enthusiasm coming into her voice. Kelyn didn't think it had anything to do with the witches; she gave Kila a frown, and Kila responded with dramatic offense. "It's true! I've seen him! He's bigger than anyone in Atlia, and he doesn't like witches *at all*. He's killed mighty sorcerers *all by himself*."

Well, he had certainly gotten Atelic worried about his place with Abendar, if nothing else.

Kelyn sighed, shaking her head—an unspoken comment on she wasn't sure what. Abendar, bothering witches in the first place. Traders who wouldn't trust her to help even if they knew she was going to try. Warriors who hired on to help kill those who had done them no harm. Out of the murk of that tangle came one clear realization—she couldn't do this their way. Her own thoughts could never wind themselves around that kind of twisted reasoning. And that meant that *they* probably couldn't do it her way, wouldn't know a head-on approach if they saw it coming at them.

"Who goes into the fortress?" she asked.

"Lots of people," the boy said. "They bring food, and haul out garbage, and half the people who work in there live out here. I've been in there, myself."

"Zeffe!" Kila said, giving Kelyn a first chance at the boy's name. "Don't you go there!"

"They don't care," the boy scoffed. "They only care that the work's getting done, and if you look like you're doing something, they leave you alone. I got that half loaf there, and weren't you glad to have that?"

Kelyn reached for her staff and stood, startling them both. "Tell the old woman I'll be back for my other meal," she instructed Kila. "I'm going to check out the market."

Kila looked doubtful, but Zeffe wasn't fooled for a minute. "Just look like you're doing something important," he said. "And don't wear that cloak. Someone important will want it if they see it."

Let them try to take it. But no—she stopped that line of thought right there. Just the sort of thing that would get her in *real* trouble. So after she had visited the stinking hole that served as the inn staff's privy, she ducked into the barn to stuff her cloak into the satchel, and then to stuff the satchel into the rafters where inquisitive and acquisitive young hands couldn't reach it. She left her whip as well; she'd seen few others carrying one, and that, too, could make her stand out.

But plenty of people had walking staffs. And plenty of them carried knives.

And so, with her skin goosebumping a bit—from today's cool breeze, she told herself, and not from anticipation—she walked into the midmorning market and aimed herself at the fortress.

Chapter 9

Zeffe, Kelyn found, had been quite right. The traffic through the gates seemed steady enough in both directions, and the guard at the first gate let his gaze linger on her, but his interest seemed purely personal. The guard at the second was busy arguing with an officious-looking man; as far as Kelyn could tell, they disagreed about exactly where he had chosen to take up his post. It looked to her like he had crept away from the actual gate to stand in the sunshine, and she found herself taking his side as she strode past.

Once inside, she would have hesitated to let her eyes adjust to the gloom—for the windows were high and narrow, and the torches in place but unlit—but that would have given her away as someone new to this place. So she followed on the heels of the woman in front of her, shortening her stride to suit and waiting until the woman paused to shift her load of rushes. She'd barely gotten her mouth open when the woman cut her off.

"What're you about, following me? See to your own work!"

"I took a wrong turn," Kelyn said, wincing inwardly at the unnatural way the words came out. *Lies, all lies* . . . "I . . . have a message to deliver to those guarding the witches."

The woman stared at her an instant, and snorted. "As you say. Go back the way we came and turn right. After that, every chance you get to go down, take it. Now be on your way—I've work to do, don't want to know any more about you."

Kelyn touched her breastbone with her knuckles, the Keturan gesture indicating thanks, and reversed her course, bemused by the woman's response. She had obviously seen Kelyn's lie . . . and just as obviously hadn't cared. Strange.

Doing her best not to betray her unfamiliarity with the fortress, she found the turn and took it. After that it was more difficult, for she had to check every doorway to see if it went up or down, and, certain of impending discovery, she tingled from her nape all the way down to the backs of her knees—but she quickly realized that most of the people she passed were dull of expression, and though they noted her and her strangeness, they didn't react. They didn't care.

Two levels down, where the traffic was thinner, she passed an armed man whose gaze lit on her and stayed, marking her difference. She nodded briskly as she'd seen him do to someone else just moments earlier. His return nod was grudging, but he let her go. Kelyn couldn't imagine seeing a stranger at home and not at least asking his business, but perhaps a town like this was so large that seeing a stranger simply wasn't all that unusual, even within the fortress.

Until you know, a little voice in her head said, *you can't gauge your danger*.

Wise words, but not words that did her any good

now. She would just trust the prickling down her back, which had served her well enough in Ketura, and for now at least no longer extended all the way down to her legs.

At the end of that hall, she found a substantial door on well-oiled hinges, with a thick metal handle worn smooth with use. Without looking back to see if she was being watched—as much as she wanted to, with the memory of that man's sharp eyes—and without allowing herself the hesitation she felt, Kelyn opened the door and headed down the stone block steps. At the bottom was another door, and at this one she paused, trying to hear what might lie beyond it.

If anyone was there, they were quiet about it. She cracked the door just enough to put her ear to it, and waited. The noise came to her ears in bits and pieces, creeping in as unrecognizable until suddenly she had enough to put it all together—mutters and mumblings and hushed whispers, rustling straw, a choked-off moan, the jingle of metal and the sharp curse of an Atlian tongue.

This was it. *Abendar's justice.*

None of the activity approached Kelyn's door, and she slipped through it into the hall. This level had a different feel to it; she knew she was far below ground, and the way the walls seemed to close in around her only reinforced that awareness. The air, clammy and still, stung her nose with the sharp tang of rancid oil from the lamps lining the soot-stained walls, and the floor was cold against her feet. Slowly, she moved down the hall, hanging tight to the wall and wishing there were shadows to lose herself in—but the lamps, feeble as their light was, were too close-set for such luxuries.

Unlike the previous levels, the hall in this one curved. She hid along the inside arc of it as she approached an inset archway without a door, the sides of which were just under two handspans' width and seemed a good place to stop and listen. From there, she tried to discern how many of Abendar's men watched the witches. But the moments gave her no clues; if there was more than one guard, they weren't talking to each other.

Kelyn took a deep breath and peered around the side edge of the archway. Along the inner edge of the curve, she discovered thick wooden doors, set fairly close together; the hall curled out of sight before revealing anything else. She took another deep breath at her sudden impatience; sooner or later, someone would come up behind her, and then she *would* be in trouble. And she had still heard nothing to indicate that there might be more than one guard.

Her feet made the decision for her. They carried her through the archway and down the hall, along the doors as they gave way to larger areas closed off by rusting, close-spaced bars. The occupants of these areas were uniformly miserable, some bleeding, some she suspected as dead. But others noticed her, and then one of them recognized her, rousing up to point, mouth open—

Kelyn hastily shushed the woman, one of the Traders who had taught her to dance; it was too late to stem the cry, but the woman turned it into a cough that fit right into the other miserable noises of this place, and Kelyn stalked on down the corridor—doing just that, now, stalking—her ire up, her prickles lost in the snarl waiting to be unleashed on the unwary guard.

She forgot that this foray had started with only the intent to examine her options.

The corridor ended in a large, low-ceilinged, round room cluttered with benches and braziers and stacks of metal contraptions, and at the doorway slouched the guard. He appeared to be sucking at a knuckle, picking at it in an absorbed way. Scab or splinter, Kelyn didn't care; it kept him from looking up until she was upon him, and her staff descended on his helmeted head hard enough to echo down the corridor.

Her second helmet, and this one somewhat sturdier than the first; the man was as dazed by her presence as he was by the blow. If she'd wanted to kill him then, she could have, but it would have been too cold-hearted. Her hesitation gave him the chance to stagger away from her, grabbing at his sword.

No, couldn't have that. She leapt after him, slamming the staff down on his arm. The sword dropped from his numbed grip, and he launched himself at her, driving her up against the wall and into the dangling chains there. She grappled with him, the chains grinding into her back as the staff clattered away, too close to land a telling blow; his hands closed around her throat.

Tugging ineffectively at his arms, she brought her knee up into his groin—and met cold hard metal. *Air. Air would be nice.* She jammed her thumb at his eye; he turned his head to block it with his helmet and her yelp of pain became a harsh squeak with no breath behind it. Kelyn scrabbled for a grip on him, an opening in his armor, some tender point she could impact; she went for a knife and he realized it, using his throat grip to bang her against the wall.

Kelyn's greying world exploded in sparks, and the chain clattered by her ear. *Chain.* She grabbed at it, moving blindly, feeling the length of it swing below her grip, and as her legs went useless beneath her, wrapped it around the guard's neck—once, twice—and yanked.

The first yank got her some air, and she sucked it in on her way down, twisting to throw her weight on the chain before she lost her grip. Sprawling, Kelyn pivoted on her hip, her vision returning just in time for her to take aim behind his knees with her foot. She hit him with her shin instead, but it did the trick, taking him down.

Or partway down, and occupied enough with his own problems that she was able to crawl away from him, coughing and wheezing and intent on filling her lungs, groping automatically for her staff. The clamor in her head, she was beginning to realize, was no longer the buzz of suffocation, but the excited cries of the witches.

"Be quiet!" she said, more panicked at their noise than she'd been at the prospect of running into guards in the corridor. "You'll bring someone down on us!" Whirling back around to the guard, ignoring the one woman who continued to wail in a babble of Trader tongue despite her companions' attempts to hush her, Kelyn set herself to face the man.

And found him dangling there.

Lack of air or broken neck, she didn't know. Or care. She walked up to him and gave him a shove, physical derision. "I didn't intend to kill you, you stupid ass," she said. "You should have gone down when you had the chance."

Bold words for someone who had been choking her life out moments before. Ignoring the tremble in her fingers, Kelyn snagged the keys at the man's belt and sifted through them, eyeing the lock on the first enclosure. She dropped the ring in a jangling clatter and started again, thinking of speed, thinking of the noise the witches had made—

"Let me try." A firm voice from within the pen. Lenci.

Kelyn looked up at her, cheeks burning with humiliation. "I've never—" she started, and let it hang unfinished as Lenci nodded. *Never seen so many keys.*

Never worked a lock. What need had she for locks, in her rock-and-earth-walled roundhouse? Or on the mountains?

She handed the keys to Lenci.

With firm surety, Lenci fitted the correct key to the lock and swung open the door. Moving with no apparent haste but faster than Kelyn would have credited her with, she herded the cell's occupants out into the corridor and went for the second door. Kelyn moved on her heels, *feeling* their luck running out, their time rushing away—

Lenci looked up at her—bent, aged Lenci, older today by years than she had been just a handful of days earlier, and said—"My inner eyes tell me there's a way out, if you keep going *down*."

—their chance at freedom, cut short. Screams came from the corridor as Lenci opened the door to the second pen, and she waded through the fleeing occupants—not all Trader witches, by far—and headed for the first of the stone-enclosed rooms.

"Go!" Kelyn called to her. "Just go!"

Lenci laughed. "What makes you think I can make it out of here with these old bones?" she said, shouting above the cries and concatenation from the corridor. "These others, now *they* have a chance!"

The ruthlessly practical Keturan in Kelyn knew Lenci was right . . . but her Reman mother had instilled deeper levels to her soul. The others had run; she closed in on Lenci. "Then open the doors, dammit. I'll stay with you. I'll get you out."

"Child—"

And time ran out. A handful of prisoners skittered back down the corridor, followed by three warriors—the first, ducking and dodging and hopeless, the second grim and snarling, weapons drawn.

Kelyn intercepted one guard and soon found herself fighting two of them. "Will you *run*?" she screamed to the two prisoners huddled beside a gruesomely encrusted contraption leaning against the circular wall. In her native Keturan, of course. And they didn't—of course—but then she had no more attention to give them, blocking knife and sword, dealing savage blows with her staff—reluctant to kill men doing what they thought was duty, but breaking bones—that one down with a badly damaged leg, still reaching for the sword he'd dropped, the next nursing a useless wrist and determined to square off with his weapon in his off hand. The third abandoning efforts to round up accused witches and charging down the corridor to this dead-end room where Kelyn fought, her swiftness catching him by surprise as he threw himself out of the way of her first attack and went back to dealing with the off-handed man.

No slip-ups now, not against this many well-armed, well-fought opponents, no matter that she'd wounded two of them. There would be more on the way; there were too many people in this fortress for it to be otherwise.

Duck! Skipping backwards, Kelyn hit the wall.

Block! The blade hit her ironwood at eye level, a finger's width away; she engaged with a brief battle of brute strength against the man and almost laughed at his expression when she won, flinging him away.

Break away! Somewhere, metal clattered—instruments falling to the floor. The broken-legged man had crawled over to take her down at the knees, and she jammed the end of the staff into his face.

They stood back from her, the two that could still stand, taking an instant to catch their breath while Kelyn panted back at them, a slow smile shaping as she saw Lenci, the last of the escapees, scurry out of sight.

Time to go. They had left an opening between

them, big enough for a young woman used to squeezing between rocks; Kelyn looked at them both, directly at them, and gave sudden tongue to her ululating fight cry. Took that space, going into top speed, elbowing them and their astonishment aside. And, beyond them, tangled her feet in toppled instruments of torture. Falling hard, losing the staff.

And rolling, grabbing the staff on the way, feeling a soldier's blade bite stone in her wake. Rolling, expecting a wall to stop her, and grunting in astonishment when the stone hit her at midback and her hips and legs kept going, scrabbling for purchase and to make some sense of the tumble as it happened.

What—?

Dust billowed around her, a musty, stinking dust; something grated beneath her, crunching a little.

What—?

Outside this tiny place, this low-ceilinged bolt hole at the juncture of floor and wall, the soldiers' moment of blank reaction had ended, and they—or at least, those that were able, and there seemed to be a number of them out there now—started laughing. Snickering. Someone bent down, blocking what little light came in through the mouth of this strange hole. "Think you want to stay there?" he said. "Think again!"

"Come out," said another. "You're safe enough—for now." And then he added thoughtfully, "Unless you start up again."

Kelyn gave them an equally thoughtful—if anatomically impossible—suggestion, and then squeaked with surprise when the man at the mouth of the hole thrust his sword in at her—not once but a number of times, aiming randomly, forcing her to roll and shrink and writhe around on whatever it was beneath—

Bones. They were bones, and decaying, bug-riddled clothes, and no little amount of mortifying tendon and stringy muscle. "Holy Rema!" she said, more of a gasp than anything else, and enough of a distraction that the sword nicked skin at its next thrust, inspiring an angrier curse aimed out the hole.

Their response—mean laughter, men in anticipation of baiting a trapped animal—cut suddenly short. Cautiously, Kelyn raised her head to peer out the hole; for her trouble she got a noseful of the dust her gyrations had raised, and she sneezed loudly. When she looked up again, there was a huge hand coming for her with far too much assurance; she sunk her teeth into it, squirming to reach one of her knives and finding her hands caught in a tangle of ribs and cloth.

It ignored her teeth. It kept coming, the arm in up to the shoulder, huge to match the hand, straining to reach her; she had to release her tooth-hold or break her own neck with the angle his movement had created. Still struggling to get her hands on a knife, Kelyn clamped her teeth back down on the bulge of muscle just this side of his elbow.

He gathered a handful of shirt and vest and pulled her out, withdrawing her smoothly and effortlessly from the hole. A ragged piece of cloth hung from her foot, trailing several small bones that dropped to the floor, the light, hollow bounce of them the only sound in this suddenly crowded room. She found herself on the tips of her toes before this new arrival. He held her there with one arm. Her staff was in the other, and she bristled to see him hold it so casually.

Or maybe bristling wasn't the wise thing to do. Not with this one. He looked like he would bristle back, and that it wouldn't go well for her if he did. He was a mature man, with grey in his black hair and lines around his eyes—oddly clear, dark, hazel, they were, and looking straight at her with a mixture of annoyance and amusement. *Amusement?* Kelyn felt her temper flare. He was that certain of himself, was he? A man who thought well of himself, though he wasn't at all what she'd call handsome—

No, reconsider that. Handsome, perhaps not. But he had a presence about him, and maybe it was the way the wry smile lurked about the corners of his mouth as he looked at his men. "This?" he said. "*This* is what caused all the trouble down here?"

Kelyn scowled at him, abruptly closing her dropped jaw, searching for some way to look more dignified than a fish dangling at the end of a line. With the vest cutting under her arms and her toes still the only thing on the ground, she didn't have much luck. At least some of the men, seeing her under control, left the room—purpose on their faces and in their step. *Run!* she thought at the witches, hoping them all long gone.

"I saw her in the Belows," a man said from the fringes of those gathered in the room. "I should have stopped her there. But she's only a barbarian, that's obvious enough—"

"Watch it, Hann," the big man growled.

"Don't take yourself so seriously," the soldier said, apparently not intimidated. "She's fresh off the mountains, despite those clothes. What's she know or care about what goes on here? I figured she'd get bored and go away."

"Pig-cocker," Kelyn muttered viciously in Keturan. The big man's mouth twitched; it might have been the edges of amusement. It didn't last long. In the Atlian tongue, Kelyn said, "Too bad for you, this *barbarian* let all your prisoners go. You have no reason to do them such harm!"

"They're witches," her captor grunted, an eyebrow arched in surprise. He eased her down to take her own full weight, but didn't loosen his grip on her. "No witch can be trusted."

"Then don't trust them," Kelyn said, aiming her scorn at him. "Stay away from them if you're afraid of them."

"And what are they to you, little barbarian girl?"

"I'm not *little*, and my ways are more civilized than your own." Kelyn switched back to her native tongue, spitting the words at him. "You may have been Keturan once, but no more—now you fit right in with these Atlian dogs!"

Not wise. She'd forgotten her decision not to ire him, and had his other hand not held her staff, she knew she would have been slapped across the room—the anger on his face told her that much.

"Watch yourself," he said, a snarl in the words. "You live only because you earned it, but that can change as quickly as my mind. You've caused us too much trouble already."

Beyond him and in the corner of her eye, Kelyn caught sight of several weeping prisoners, roped together and shoved along by rough hands, being herded back into the first pen. The man smiled at the look on her face. "Of course we've caught them. We'll catch most of them before they make it out of this place. There is no mercy for witches, and no mercy for traitors, either."

"I betrayed no one!" Kelyn jerked against his hold. "I am true to myself, and to my friends, and owe nothing to this cruel Atlian lord. *Nothing!*" She shoved against him, sharp enough to be a blow. It got her nowhere. Although he didn't react, other than to give her a little shake, his remaining men shifted around him, uneasy at her defiance, at their incomprehension of the language and conversation.

"Just kill her," one of the men said. "She's too much trouble. Too unpredictable."

The man nodded, not with conviction and not taking his eyes from Kelyn; she glared back at him.

"Don't be sentimental," said the man who had seen her in the upper corridor and let her pass. *Hann.* "Look how much trouble you could cause when *you* were fresh from the outer land."

"Kill me or don't." Kelyn gave him her hardest grin. "Don't play with me. Or maybe you'd like to try, then—let me fight you for my freedom." She turned the expression into something more predatory. "*Or* . . . maybe you've been too long from the mountains, and don't dare." She quelled the panic in her chest at the thought that he might take her up on it—he was too big, too strong. *And probably slow.* That thought helped her calm the shaking that threatened to burst out at her knees. He'd only laugh if he noticed.

He wasn't laughing, now. Oh, she'd gotten his attention, all right. "And *you*," he said, "are so close to the mountains that you haven't learned when Keturan bravado will do you more harm than good!" And he gave her another good shake.

"Atelic's men are going to laugh themselves sick over this," one of the men grumbled. "Just take care of her, Thainn, and never mind that she's from Ketur—"

"Thainn!" Kelyn cried. Thainn, the man of her mother's legends. The mighty warrior. The one, no doubt, that Atelic had referred to so resentfully, the one he'd wanted to best.

The father Kelyn had never met.

The man who was looking at her, annoyed at her interruption, curious about her reaction. Waiting, with that eyebrow raised again.

"You're my father!" she blurted.

Utter silence.

And then the men started to snicker, and Thainn muttered some curse through clenched jaws, and Hann said, "Another one! The Wolverine, mighty of thew and *loin*!"

Kelyn flushed so hard she thought her face might catch afire.

"Do you know," Thainn said, conversationally—although Kelyn caught the edge in his voice, and didn't doubt the anger in his narrowed eyes—"how many mothers tell their children that their father is the Wolverine? More women than I've ever lain with—"

"And that's saying a lot," one of the men broke in, laughing over the last of his words.

Humiliation turned to fury. "My mother would never lie!"

"And I left Ketura long before you were ever in your mother's belly!" Thainn snapped back at her. "So think again—lie, she did!"

"*Shalka*—spawn!" Beside herself, Kelyn found words she had never dared say before, words that ought to have left her scorched. Even the soldiers flinched, and so did Thainn the mighty. "You'll not say so about my mother!" She snatched her staff from his hand, thwacking him soundly at the juncture of shoulder and neck. Tearing easily away from his loosened grip, she sprinted down the corridor, gaining a significant lead before they reacted.

She dodged through another batch of returning prisoners, leaving them in a tangle that prevented their escort from pursuing her, and blocked the hallway in her wake. She barely hesitated at the door leading up, knowing that all of the soldiers would be alert, now, and she'd never make it up all those levels—but she did yank the door open and leave it that way, just in case they were easily misled.

Keep going down, Lenci had said. Behind her, the boot-slapping stride of Thainn's men grew louder, and Kelyn took off, running as fast as she could and still keep an eye on the niches and open doorways she passed—few as they were. *Down*, she needed *down*, she needed it *now*. She bolted past a small door, realized her mistake, and almost kept going—if it wasn't *down*, then she couldn't afford the time lost to check it out—but after an instant of indecision, reversed course to snatch at the door latch.

Dark. It was dark . . . but it was *down*. After another instant's hesitation—almost enough to lose what little lead she had—Kelyn plunged into the darkness, closing the door behind her.

No running in this. The tiny stairwell closed in around her, and Kelyn ducked as she felt for the steps, unable to quell the feeling that her head would bash into the ceiling. One hand along the wall, the other aiming the staff out in front of her . . . it didn't leave anything to put in front of her face. This, she realized, her shoulders tight with the expectation that any moment someone would open the door behind her, was just the sort of situation her curse thrived on. She wouldn't hurry. *She wouldn't*. Careful, focused, she moved down the uneven steps, until the staff bumped gently into a barrier.

Not a door. Just a turn, and she made it, cursing the way the steps steepened before her. She fought the temptation to turn around and descend them backwards, on hands and knees like a child going down her first steep hill. But the flight was blessedly short, and this time, when the staff met resistance, Kelyn found wood.

Slowly, she opened the door.

The silent, low corridor beyond it spilled out before her sheathed in shadows and darkness; the low torch, of which there was only one, flickered on the edge of extinction.

The fact that it was here at all meant that someone had traversed the corridor within the morning, and Kelyn didn't let herself relax into complacency. A glance at the door showed her there was no provision for barring it—pity. The soldiers would realize she'd gone this way far too soon to suit her.

Still moving swiftly but no longer at a dead run, she trotted down the corridor. The niches, dark and ominous, went nowhere; after a few moments, she realized that they held interred remains. The corridor itself ran in only the one direction . . . and, after a few moments, it ran out.

Dead end.

So much for Lenci's inner eye. Kelyn paced to the block at the end of the corridor, sweating even in the clammy coolness of the underground air. There, she walked back and forth, running her hand along the wall. Thinking. Perhaps they wouldn't come looking for her down here. Perhaps she could just wait them out, and creep back upstairs when they weren't expecting her; she wouldn't have much of a chance of fighting her way out, but it was more of a chance than she had of doing it *now*. A cool breeze ran across her sweaty forehead; she closed her eyes—just for a moment, just long enough to catch the breeze and tilt her face to it—and then stopped in her tracks.

A breeze? Here? She licked her fingers, holding them up before her face, finding the breeze, following it . . . to the wall. To a crack between stones that was bigger than all the other cracks, and that followed a crooked path around block ends from the floor to low ceiling. Just like the caves she had explored in the mountains . . .

Only caves did as they would, and had many an unexpected air shaft and dead end. This place was human-built. Surely an air shaft would have been bigger, more purposeful, and yet a structural flaw like this one could hardly be accidental. There had to be something beyond.

But how to get there? How did these Atlians think? Kelyn leaned her staff in the corner and ran her hands along the wall, trying to put herself in an Atlian mind set. After a futile moment, she balled her fists and smacked the wall. No good. In an instant, she could put herself into the mind of a rock cat, or one of the shaggy mountain sheep. She could predict what they would do in any given situation, and get there first. But these people beyond Ketura's rugged boundaries? She'd found them unfathomable. Unpredictable.

You studied rock cats for years, she told herself. She'd been out of Ketura for far less than a season. No little wonder she didn't have it all figured out. *And little good that does you now.*

Voices bounced off the walls, indecipherable in their words but clear in their meaning. The soldiers were here. Kelyn leaned her forehead against the cold wall and took a deep breath. A fight it was, then. She reached for her staff, hefting it a few times as was her habit, settling the comforting weight of the ironwood in her grip. It bumped against the ceiling and she glanced up, acutely aware of how hampered she'd be, how careful she'd have to be with her swing—

What's that?

Her gaze settled on a depression in the ceiling, a little circle with edges. If she reached, she could have touched it with her hand, but the staff was there and without even thinking of the consequences, she poked it firmly upward.

It clicked. Nothing more. She pushed it again, and it didn't even click, and then she abandoned it to get ready for the soldiers, putting her back to the wall.

The wall shifted.

Instantly, Kelyn pushed, preferring the unknown to a fight she couldn't win. Smoothly, the wall pivoted, and as soon as the space it made was wide enough for her to scrape through, she took it, never mind that it was darkness beyond. She took it and she shoved the wall back as it had been, hearing it snick back into place as darkness closed in around her.

She found the corner and crouched in it, making herself smaller despite the fact there was no way they could see her. She found she was panting—anxiety more than effort—and stilled her breathing. And she listened, inching closer to the crack when the soldiers' words were muddled, and then flinching when someone's voice came through loud and clear. She even recognized the voice—the man who had seen her in what he had called the Belows. "I *thought* I remembered a dead end here," Hann said. "She must have gone up after all."

"Then Atelic's men will get her," another voice said, less distinctly.

"She'll fight her way right through them," Hann said, snorting audibly. "Did you see what she did to three of us? And one of Atelic's men, dead. I haven't seen the like since the first time I ran upon our Wolverine."

"Maybe she *is* his daughter."

"Yes, and maybe she is, but that's not something you're smart to say in front of him. Not if you value your hide. Not after the last three who tried to lay claim to the riches they imagined he'd plundered. Or the bratling that *was* his—and turned coward in the first melee."

"I value my hide well enough," the man grumbled.

A third voice said, "We're wasting time. I've got off-shift coming up—"

Hann gave a short guffaw; his voice came less clearly as he moved away from the wall. "You've got whore time coming up, you mean. I saw you pass a coin to that pit-faced one. I'd do better for myself than *that*, I'll tell you."

"Don't judge her bed by her face," the other said, sounding smug. "Or better yet, do it. More for me."

The third man said something in reply, short and sharp and words they all laughed at, but by then they were moving away, and Kelyn couldn't hear any more. Just as well.

She took herself back to the corner and sat there, her arms resting over her knees and the knees themselves finally finding the time to be shaky as she tilted her head back against the wall, eyes closed in the darkness . . . if just for a moment. Not much incentive to rest when she had yet to find her way out of here.

It was when she opened her eyes again that she realized all was not darkness, after all, and that she still heard murmurs of conversation. To her left the blackness held a grey cast, and when she extended a hand in that direction, groping along until she had moved to her hands and knees and was still reaching, her fingers connected with something thick and velvety. Further investigation revealed that she had found a cloth-covered doorway, and when she drew the cloth aside, the darkness brightened to yet a lighter shade of grey; she could even make out the dim form of her own arms. The conversation grew into snatches of words, and once Kelyn realized that there was yet another doorway before her—also barred by this incredibly thick, soft cloth—she decided not to go any further. Not just yet. She pulled the second cloth aside just enough to confirm that there was true light beyond, and let it fall gently back into place.

Soldiers on one side of the door—and Thainn's warriors. On this side . . . well, who knew who they were. Men she didn't want discovering her.

Nor, she realized, would they be happy to learn that she had discovered *them*. A clandestine door, these light- and sound-dampening layers of cloth . . . no, these men didn't want to be found.

Atlia's arse. From trouble to trouble, and completely without the benefit of her dowser.

Not that she needed that magical problem anymore. For apparently, she had found her father. *What now, Rika?* She'd found her curse, she'd found her father . . . but she didn't feel like she'd found her self, at all. Just . . . trouble. Trouble, and a man she didn't know, like, or trust.

Maybe because Thainn doesn't yet know he's found a daughter.

Although Kelyn wasn't sure she wanted a father who spoke of her mother as that cocker warrior had.

Whoops. The voices grew louder, more agitated; Kelyn inched away from the cloth, holding her breath.

"I'm losing my patience with you, Naz. What have we to show for all this, aside from a handful of soul-gems and the belt?" That voice was nasal, not Atlian—another accent yet shaping his words. "Word is, the Traders know of the Silver Horn of Russas. I *want* that horn. That means you, my dear, must pry the information from them."

"They die!" said the second man, this one as Atlian as the soldiers who had escorted the captured Traders. "Surely they would not continue to die, Master Petissanji, not if they knew. One of them would have spoken by now!"

"You must be more careful."

Kelyn made a face in the darkness. There was oil in that voice, and an undertone that made her feel like washing.

"Master—" Protest filled that voice, objection at the insinuation.

"You are the best at the torturing game, are you not, Naz? Prove it to me, then, lest I am inspired to obtain a new assistant."

This time, the second man's defiance had disappeared, melted away and replaced with offensive fawning. "I can do this for you, Master Petissanji. You're right, I've been so eager to produce results for you, I—I must have been overzealous with my questioning. I'll be more careful. I'll—"

"Yes, yes." Petissanji's voice dropped into boredom . . . boredom with an edge Kelyn wouldn't have cared to trust. "You will. Now. I also need you to go back to the witch Thainn brought in from the border. I need more details about where to find the orb."

"Yes, Master."

"And I want you to check the watch-eyes I set in the cell floor. Make sure they haven't been disturbed. They're all that's keeping those Trader bitches from turning their pitiful spells on you and your men, remember that."

"I checked them this morning, Mast—" The man cut himself off, and hastily amended, "As soon as I return to the cell floor, Master."

"And Naz . . . my dear, I do appreciate your earnest obsequiousness, but if you continue to call me *Master*, don't you think you'll slip in front of Thainn's men some time? And don't you think even Thainn's overmuscled grunters will figure out I'm as much—no, *more*—of a witch than those they hunt?"

A brief pause. "Yes, Lord Advisor."

"Besides," Petissanji said. "I had Abendar make that title especially for me. We should show our appreciation by using it. Remain useful to me, Naz, and I'll have him make up a title for you, too." Beat. "Fail me, and I'll start by conjuring an angry wasp into the center of your left testicle."

Ketura's—Even Kelyn winced at that one. What, she wondered, would he do to her?

Suddenly, between Thainn's men and this advisor of Abendar's, Kelyn knew whom she would prefer to face. Inching backward on hands and knees, holding her breath in the intensity of her effort to keep her curse from surfacing at just that moment—a clattering staff was the last thing she needed—she made her way back to the corner and turned her attention to the wall.

There was a way in. There had to be a way out.

Why not the same as the way in?

Kelyn got to her feet in dark silence, and found the ceiling just over her head. Fingers on the ceiling . . . she looked up in automatic reflex, then bit her tongue on a curse and jerked her head down, blinking against the debris that had fallen into her eyes. *No, curse. Not now.*

There. Her fingers had never stopped their search, and now they rested on something that felt much the same as the outside trigger had looked. She pushed up; it resisted. Another push, harder, stiffening her fingers—and it *clicked* for her.

That was when she realized it would have to swing in from this direction, and that it would not be so easy. Fingers used to clawing a handhold in steep rock dug into the crack, prying, pulling, teasing the door toward her—how long would those two discuss plans of torture?—she finally had enough width of door to push her palm against, more surface and friction at her disposal. *No one out there, at least.* They would have noticed the wall's strange behavior long before now if there had been.

That, of course, was when she had enough light to notice that there was a handle on the wall, just below the height at which it was natural for her to reach out.

Short builder. Just her luck.

But not her luck for the rest of this day, for she closed the door with neither of the secret room's occupants any the wiser, and she lurked in the deserted lower niches until Petissanji swept by and the torches died, and the rest of the fortress went to sleep. When she left, it was with only two stunned fortress dwellers behind her, and she thought that perhaps they would recover well enough, if not fast enough to raise an alarm.

From the complete lack of activity outside—even the bawdy establishments had put out their lights—she thought it might be close to dawn. So be it. The old woman at the inn still owed her a breakfast.

Chapter 10

"He *is* big," Kelyn admitted to Kila, starting in on the half loaf she had pried from the old woman for finishing the job she'd started the day before. Two bowls of porridge hadn't done near enough to fill a stomach that had spent so much of the previous day within a body fighting for its life. "But I don't like him."

"How can you *not*?" Kila said. "He's so strong! And he's protecting us all from witches."

"Don't mind witches," Zeffe allowed, casually pinching a bit of her loaf. She whacked his hand with it. "Neither did Dada."

"You see?" Kelyn said. "Would your father have died protecting a witch if it were right to harm them?"

"Maybe she spelled him," Kila said, heading for a serious sulk.

"Maybe not," Kelyn said, not caring.

"Petissanji tells Lord Abendar to get the witches," Kila said. "Why would he, if they're not bad?"

"Maybe he has his own reasons." Kelyn looked

toward the fortress, even though it meant actually looking at the inn. *And maybe the Traders need to know what those reasons are.*

❖ ❖ ❖

Defiantly, although the sun hung in its midday spot, easing her tired muscles with its warmth, Kelyn slung her cloak over her shoulders and strode into the border area of the Darks. The Traders were beyond, the twins had said. And no doubt very few bothered them there, although they themselves would have to navigate the Darks to pass any business in Abendar's town.

The street passing under her feet turned just as nastily grimy as it had the first time, and the buildings looked deserted. A small, ratty-looking dog ran out at her with much bravado and seemed to be working itself up to a dash at her ankles; Kelyn mimed a stone toss and the creature beat a hasty retreat. *If only all of them were so easy to keep off.*

But no one came out to bother her, though she heard strains of whining plucked strings—music, she supposed it to be—from one house, and a loud argument from another. Not until she reached the same area where the children had accosted her did anyone come out into the street—and then it was just the woman who had taken the part of their mother, although something in Kelyn told her they likely had no more mother than Kila and Zeffe.

The woman had a bucket of dirty water, and as she stood poised to empty it, she hesitated, first glancing at and then recognizing Kelyn. Water slopped over the edge of the bucket; the woman readjusted her grip and took a step—

"I wouldn't," Kelyn said, not pausing her stride. "I might get wet, but you'll get hurt."

The woman spat at the ground in Kelyn's direction, and emptied the bucket beside her own stubby porch. Kelyn walked on, unmolested. So much for the Darks.

Although she had no intention of coming back at night.

The outside border of the Darks became clear as she approached it; the street dribbled into nothing and gave way to a series of long, low buildings with stone walls halfway up and thin wood planks taking over from there. The thatched roofs were dark with mold and decay. Abandoned.

Kelyn looked them over a moment, seeing no signs of activity, no hint of Trader presence. Perhaps they were beyond. When those minutes of frowning inspection revealed nothing more than she'd noted upon approach, she shrugged. More of civilization that she couldn't understand—someone had gone to much effort to create this collection of strange dwellings, and now they sat wasted. Too hard to heat in the winter even with multiple fires, she thought, especially with the several doors and high, small windows that each boasted. Kelyn shook her head at the puzzle of it and wandered between two of them, glad for the tough Atlian grasses between her toes again.

But she wasn't so distracted that she didn't react instantly to the whisper of sound behind her, whirling to place her staff between herself and whoever—whatever—came at her, promptly attacking when she saw the flash of edged metal in the blur of movement before her. Down the attacker went, his legs swept out from under him, and none too quick to rise despite his effort to do so.

Not much good at this, then. And slow enough that she got a good look at him.

"Rago?" she said, stepping back but keeping the staff between them. Were the Traders so angry at her that they would come for her on sight? And with more than fists, at that.

But he stopped, halfway to his feet, and his bronzed skin flushed dark. "Kelyn!" he said. "No one ever comes in from the Darks unless they mean trouble, not even the soldiers. I didn't see it was you."

And what would he have done if it had been someone truly intent on harm?

Died, probably. And he knew it, too, from the way his fingers clenched the handle of his knife, and how eagerly he had greeted her.

"Where *is* everyone?" she asked, letting it pass. "And what is this place?"

"Next row in," he said, and then hesitated on his next words. When she spoke, she felt sure he had altered them. "These old warehouses are Abendar's. He used to stock hay and grains to get the town through the winters—though he made everyone pay well enough. Then the hay started going bad almost as soon as it got here, and Petissanji told him it had been cursed. Abendar said he wouldn't stock any more until he had cleaned the witches from this part of Atlia."

"Was it?" Kelyn asked.

"Was it what?"

"Cursed."

Rago shrugged. "We weren't here. Lenci could have told, easily enough, if we had been." He snorted. "Not that Abendar would have believed her if she'd said not. Everyone wants someone to blame their problems on." Finally he stood, brushing himself off, and nodded at the next row of buildings. "You'll find them there," he said. "Starting up a good feast to celebrate the return of the witches."

"All of them?" Kelyn said, standing straighter with the hope of it. She had seen some being returned to the cells, but perhaps all of the Traders had made it out. . . . "Lenci?"

He hesitated, and then shook his head. "Not yet," he said. "But they're still coming back. We haven't given up hope." He looked down at his knife, and sheepishly returned it to its sheath. "You'll be welcomed, I'm sure."

"I'm not," Kelyn said bluntly. "What does it matter if I freed them, when they wouldn't have been there without my mistake?"

Rago shrugged, and gestured at the buildings. "Go find out."

Welcome or not, that's where she'd been headed. Kelyn watched as Rago reclaimed his post just inside the building's gaping doorway—the door itself hung ajar, half in, half out—and picked up her stride again, pacing between the two buildings and on her way to the third.

She should have expected it. Just past the intersection, someone flew at her from the back side of the building, so quickly he—like Rago—couldn't even have had a chance to see her. Mountain-trained reflexes allowed her to twist aside, avoiding most of the impact; she threw herself upon her attacker to put an end to the tussle, pinning him and holding him down until he paused in his struggles to spit out a mouthful of her hair. Endre.

"Yes," she said, before he could. "It's me." But she didn't move, didn't relent her grip on his arms. After the way he had treated her when they last saw one another, she found that she liked having such an advantage over him. Too, she was thinking of those words Rago hadn't spoken. Warning, she'd been willing to bet, that there was a second layer of lookouts.

"How'd you get past Rago?" he asked, then answered himself. "Of course you got past Rago. But why didn't he—" and then came to the same conclusion she had. "That idiot. I could have hurt—" and he stopped again, and finished, "You could have hurt me." He wiggled uncomfortably beneath her. "You can let me up now."

"If I wanted to," she said, quite complacently, glad that they were of a size. Her hair tickled his face; she let it.

He made a face, wiggling his nose against the itch. "Kelyn . . ."

"No," she said, and told him—expecting him to make the leap in understanding, to hearken back to their last conversation—"I was trying to help. I could have kept any of them from spending time in Abendar's Belows, if you'd listened. Lenci could be with you."

"We had *our* plans," Endre said, and in remembering it, recalled his anger as well. "Did you think we'd trust our fate to you, after you defied Gergo with the dowser? And what do you think happened to those of us in the wagon once they figured out you'd been trying to talk to me there?"

"Do you think I'd have sneaked around to talk to you in the dark if anyone had been willing to talk to me when it was allowed?" Kelyn's grip on his arms tightened as her own temper flared. "Do you think I would have risked myself, if I'd known you had something in mind already?"

He glared. "Let me up."

"No." If she could have willed herself heavier, she would have. The weight of her guilt should have been enough to do it. "This way, you have to talk to me. You can't just pretend I don't exist."

"That's for sure," Endre muttered, wiggling again beneath her.

"I didn't defy Gergo," Kelyn said, almost nose to nose with him. "I thought he meant to keep the needle out of sight. I *did* that. If anyone had told me the danger to you, I wouldn't have used it. And I did my best to help afterward. It was *you* who broke cover, and *you* who gave me away to the soldiers. I could have had you all free that same night."

"*Me?*" he said, and the force of the words made his stomach bounce against her. "You think this is *my* fault?"

"I think there's blame enough to spread around." *Yes*, her guilt voice decided, grudgingly. That was true. She had not been the only one to make mistakes. "And so far, the only witches to return have done so because of my hand. What have *your* people done to help them?" And Rago had said they would feed her, so why was Endre being so difficult? "I haven't slept in a full day, and haven't eaten enough to do more than line my mouth. Rago said I'd be welcomed. He *said* you were glad to have your people back."

Endre stared steadfastly at the neatly layered stone of the warehouse beside his head, his jaw set. Stubborn. Resistant. She frowned at him; she'd seen his recognition of the truth in her words, so what was his—

Oh. She dipped her head close to his ear and said, "You were supposed to be watching me, weren't you? *You* were the one who didn't see me use the dowser."

He shrugged his shoulder at her, as much as he could, like he was trying to brush a fly from his ear. "Don't do that."

"Do what?" she said. "Speak the truth, or speak it so close to you that you can't dodge it? Hear the truth then, Trader—no man sees me when I want it not."

"No," he said. "Don't tickle my ear."

Oh. That. Kelyn drew back a touch, and quite wickedly let her hair fall across his neck.

"Kelyn . . ." Endre made a half-hearted effort to break free of her.

"Was it my fault?" She turned the words into a challenge.

He hesitated, wiggled . . . sighed. "Some of it.

Not . . . all of it. And . . . you did do your best to right it, even if you were afraid of the horse."

"I wasn't."

"You were."

She had been. But she had no inclination to play fair. She lowered her head and whispered into his ear. "Wasn't."

"Rema's grace, have mercy, Kelyn!" He shifted again beneath her, his face reddening, his discomfort, she realized, having nothing at all to do with her weight, just her presence.

How interesting. There was no pity in *this* reaction. This response, she saw, was almost against Endre's own wishes, something he would rather have hidden from her. The understanding gave Kelyn a flash of pleasure—which in turn brought her own confusion. She rolled off him and to her feet in one motion. "Come with me," she said. "Just to make sure no more of you attack me along the way."

Endre brushed his shirt off, surreptitiously adjusting the front of his trousers. "All you had to do was cluck-cluck."

"Like a chicken?" Kelyn asked in disbelief.

He snorted. "No, like you're walking up behind a horse. Tch-tch-tch-tch."

"I," Kelyn said with great dignity, "don't walk up *behind* any horse." She gestured for him to lead the way. "If there's any cluck-clucking to be done, *you* do it."

They had been upwind of the Traders, or she would have found them on her own. Inside one of the buildings, no more or less dilapidated than the others, they stirred up the same spicily sauced meat dish as they had the evening she'd rescued the children; her nose prickled with the aroma, and her mouth watered. Endre, clearly uncomfortable with her—was it because she'd sat on him, or because she'd let him up?—immediately abandoned her to discuss some intense issue with his family, leaving her to stand in the dim interior, endeavoring to pick out someone she knew. Tass, Darada and Nea's father, came up to her with a battered tin plate full of food. But he didn't stay, and she sat on the ground to eat by herself.

Their chatter filled the warehouse, along with the occasional wail as someone considered a loved one still in Abendar's hands. Maybe Lenci, she thought, trying to assess the faces she saw, trying to remember who had been taken in the first place. She met with little success and gave up to eat with concentration, intent on making up for days of too little food. When the burdened plate was empty, she barely had time to consider entering the hub of the gathering to refill it before Tass came over with another.

She lingered over the contents of that one, and was gnawing a small bone when the witches arrived—where they'd been hiding, she didn't know—and only moments after that, the first witch came over. She said nothing, but took Kelyn's hand and turned it over to press something small into her palm. Another witch followed, and another, until they had all come to her—all silent, all offering some small item, not even looking at her face to do it. When they were through, and mingled back with their families, Kelyn found herself with a lapful of trinkets. Several buttons, a ribbon, a braided thong, a painted thimble, several charm-working candles marked with Trader symbols.

She touched the thimble, turning the delicate object in her fingers—how clumsy they appeared next to it, too—and looked up at the gathering. No one even glanced at her. Well. Kelyn distributed the tokens among her vest pockets with mixed feelings, not sure yet if she were champion or pariah.

Not that it mattered. She had no ties to these

people, no reason to feel wistful that she'd been left on the edge of things. And Endre had plenty of reason to avoid her, though it was not his fault that she was taller and Keturan-born, and had so easily outmaneuvered him as he had guarded the Trader camp. She didn't even see him, now—he must have gone back out.

Not that it mattered. She pulled her cloak around herself and curled up with her satchel; for the first time in a long time she thought about Ketura, and her friends there. How after a long hunt, after the danger of an encounter with one of Ketura's well-armed carnivores, her summer pack would spend the evening around the fire boasting and reenacting the most exciting moments. How they'd squabble over the best of the carcass, but always split the truly important organs equally, without discussion. How Frykla would drum and the rest of them would dance.

She brushed her face against the rock cat fur. Who wanted to dance, anyway. She was too tired for that.

She knew when someone approached—she was never too tired for *that*—but waited until a hand touched her shoulder before she opened her eyes. Endre crouched before her, his quiet words almost swallowed in the background noise of the gathering—although the witches, she noted, were gone again.

"They were giving you tokens of themselves," he said. "It's something we sometimes do." She stared at him, saying nothing—and having nothing in particular to say. He added, "But not often."

"And tomorrow?" she said, too sleepy to think much about her words. "Tomorrow, do you take them away again, when I do something wrong? Maybe I'm better off to refuse such offerings." *Except for food*, she amended silently, far too practical about eating to do otherwise. "In Ketura, when we give a gift, we mean for it to be kept. It is doubly so with the gift of friendship." Anger was for the moment, and offenses forgotten when the sun set. Knowing it was so gave them the room to play hard, and fight hard—and to speak their minds.

His mouth twisted. "I have wondered," he said, "how things would go for me in Ketura."

Your horse would start to look like food. But no, that wasn't something she could say out loud; Endre truly cared for that beast. So Kelyn didn't answer at all, but closed her eyes and shifted her satchel so that whatever was poking her, didn't.

Endre nudged her again. When she looked at him, not bothering to hide her annoyance, he nodded to where Gergo approached them. She pushed herself off the ground but didn't bother to sit completely upright.

Gergo eyed her—she was not without bruises, and of the sort that showed even in the limited daylight from the high, small windows—and said, "Things have not gone as well as either of us would have had them."

Kelyn only shook her head. No, they hadn't. Of that, if little else, she was sure.

"Every great while," he said, choosing his words carefully and looking somewhere over her left shoulder, "a trade becomes complicated. It has too many layers, and when the traders walk away from it, they are each uncertain who made the best of the deal—but each is satisfied. Do you understand?"

She understood. Even the Traders couldn't figure out who owed whom what debt.

"I have some questions for you," he said, apparently taking her silence for affirmation. "But I see you need rest. When you wake, we'll talk."

"Will we?" Kelyn said, not willing to submit herself—again—to Trader ways she didn't understand, and by default to Gergo's word. This time, her own ways would command their Trader respect. Or she would find some other place to tuck herself for sleep. Not all of these warehouses were full of Traders—though it was nice to be in one where the spiders had already been chased away.

Gergo frowned, and to judge by the number of times his mouth opened and then closed without words, appeared to be struggling with himself.

Kelyn took pity on him. "I have some things I would like to ask," she said. "After I have slept." She shifted the satchel, preparing to settle around it, and found herself poked again. *Those boots*. Those fur-lined, winter-greased boots. She gave Gergo a sudden speculative eye. "Gergo," she said, and waited for his expression to turn from that of a man contemplating whether to take offense to a Trader showing curiosity. "When this thing happens—this complicated trade—does it prevent further trades? Simple ones?"

"It depends." Gergo gave her little resistance, but Endre had less resistance and pointed at the satchel. "What do you have?" he asked. "Or should I ask, what don't you want?"

Kelyn loosened the satchel flap and pulled out her boots. Good boots, they were, made just the winter before with the last of Lytha's loving stitches. But . . . *Sentiment is a luxury, and Keturans do not know luxury*. "I've been through the Darks twice now," she said. "And in Abendar's Belows. I've learned that my feet need covering here in Atlia's settlements far more than they ever did in Ketura's wilds. I want to trade for something. Something without fur lining. Here. Take them. Bring me back something I can use."

Gergo took a step toward her, and hesitated. Then he snatched the boots and strode away.

"Another Trader custom broken?" Annoyed, Kelyn pushed her much smaller satchel into shape and tugged it into place to use as a pillow.

"No. You've just put him in a position where he can't honorably give you anything but the best deal—there's no challenge to outdealing someone who's handed you victory." He stood. "Go to sleep satisfied, Kelyn of Ketura. You've just gotten the best of a Trader."

❖ ❖ ❖

Kelyn slept with as much intensity as she had eaten, and although she was aware of the movement and murmurs of the Traders around her, she didn't open her eyes until the next morning—a fact she determined when she went outside to tend the urgent needs of her body. The sun squinted down at her from behind a thick haze of featureless clouds, and the day had a sullen, breezeless feel to its warmth. Kelyn found the Traders' privacy screens at the far end of the building and waited in the short line there, wishing the conversation hadn't stopped at her arrival.

When she returned to the dim warehouse, she saw the new boots sitting by her satchel and bypassed the communal leftovers to examine them. Shorter than her winter boots, they had uppers of slouchy soft leather that, when she tried them on, came only to her mid-calf. The soles were thick with layers of boiled leather, and the stitching even; her toes wiggled comfortably inside. Having ascertained the fit, she pulled them off and put them in her satchel.

"Don't you like them?" Gergo asked from halfway across the warehouse. She searched the gloom and found him sitting at his own little fire, stirring a small pot of something that, when she approached, smelled like anything but food.

"I don't need them here," she told him, glancing around the nearly empty building. "Where is everyone?"

"Gone to market." Gergo lifted the spoon and turned it, watching intently as the contents oozed from it and plopped back into the pot. "We're Traders. Think you we would come here and not trade?"

Given the mood of Abendar's men, that was exactly what she'd thought, but Kelyn didn't say so. Nor did she ask what he stirred, though he paid it more attention than he seemed to pay her. At least, until her next words. "Did you know Petissanji was a witch?"

Gergo stopped stirring to stare at her, but quickly dismissed her words. "You must have misheard. Many of those helping Abendar with his hunt are witches, turned to his side to preserve themselves. Or like Thyra, because they think they can gain something. But Petissanji is in a position of some power. Abendar would never allow it. Who told you this?"

Kelyn couldn't help her smile, although she knew it wasn't kind of her. "Petissanji."

"You spoke to—! No, Keturan, not if you're standing here."

"Would you have said I could enter the fortress, free the witches, and return?" Kelyn retorted. "Petissanji spoke to someone else, not me. I overheard."

"Abendar would never allow it." Gergo said, and stirred his pot with more vigor than he probably meant to. He caught himself, checked the viscosity of the fluid once more, and moved the pot away from the fire.

"I played dumb for the soldiers because Endre thought I should, Gergo, not because I *am*."

He looked at her, having the grace to put surprise on his face. "It is easy to misunderstand when one is new to a language."

"I understand you well enough. And I understood *him*. He started this witch-hunt so he can question all Atlia's witches about objects of power, god-touched things. He wants them for his own."

Gergo stared at her, his eyes narrowing. Beginning to believe.

"He talked about soul-gems and a belt. And he's looking for the Horn of Roos."

"Russas," Gergo corrected.

She grinned at him. "So there's a horn. And you know about it. Understood that much, didn't I?"

He surprised her by standing, by pushing right up close to her—and though she bristled at first, she soon saw his urgency, and realized it was not the challenge a Keturan would have made of it. "Had anyone spoken of the Horn to him yet?"

"Not yet. They died first."

"As they are supposed to be cursed to do." Gergo nodded to himself.

Kelyn frowned. "But Petissanji said something about spell eyes. He said they kept the witches from casting spells. How could they curse themselves to silence, then?"

Gergo's gold eyes went flat. "We are all cursed in this way. It is one of the burdens of caring for the Horn."

"*You're* not silent . . . *or* dead."

Gergo waved a hand between them. "You didn't ask. I told."

Oh, *that* made a lot of sense. "What *is*—"

"That," Gergo said, not even letting her finish, "I choose *not* to tell." He ran his hands down the front of his shirt once, twice; a contemplative and absent gesture. "There are things I must take care of, now. You have done all of Atlia a service today, Keturan girl, and not just the Traders." He glanced into the cooling pot, gave a satisfied nod, and left the warehouse.

All of Atlia. And witches who would die before giving away the secrets of a power that Petissanji coveted.

What in the name of Siloga's nose hairs did this horn *do*?

And what if one of the recaptured witches hadn't had the nerve to curse herself to die?

You're a Keturan in a town of Atlians who think you're stupid, and they're right. She *was* stupid, if she thought she could do something about Petissanji, here in a town where her life was probably forfeit if Thainn should so much as glimpse her face in a crowd.

Thainn. How could Lytha have spent even a moment with that man? He had no manners, he persecuted a people who had done him no harm, he had—he had *laughed* at her. Called Lytha a liar!

Don't make friends with him. Use him.

It didn't matter that she'd been looking for a father and found a prickly Wolverine. It didn't even matter that she wanted nothing to do with him. She had seen how quickly he could take offense; she had sensed that he would follow through on his anger. She wasn't sure how safe it would be to approach him, considering their last meeting. But . . .

Imagine how he'd feel if he learned he'd been used by a witch.

Kelyn tried not to think of how good it felt to envision telling him so.

But not without breakfast. And, as she ate, becoming more and more aware that the smell she had noticed was almost as much Kelyn as it was Gergo's concoction, she decided that she couldn't put herself before the Wolverine without making herself more presentable than she had been as the young woman he'd pulled from the floor hole in Abendar's Belows. For all she knew, there was still bone dust in her hair. No wonder Endre hadn't wanted it in his face!

She had not been the only one to notice. As she finished eating, several women dragged Gergo's large tub into the warehouse, and soon there was a bucket line to fill it. When it was half full, they staggered over with several huge kettles of steaming water, and Gazi, with Darada at her side, presented herself in front of Kelyn, awkward and working nervous fingers at the ends of her long light brown hair.

Kelyn rescued her. "If that's for laundry, I hope you don't mind if I use it first."

Darada said, "No, it's for you, mistress. You smell."

"Darada!"

"I do," Kelyn agreed. "But not for long!" She'd take her clothes in with her, she decided, emptying her vest pockets and unbuckling the two belts at her hips. She would have stripped without further ado, had she not heard the collective gasp of the women. They quickly produced a blanket, and held it up for her as a privacy veil. Kelyn, wondering how these women could possibly be the same ones who had produced the gyrating coupling dance she'd learned, nonetheless ducked behind it, pulled off her clothes, and splashed into the tub.

What luxury. It held enough water so she could tuck up her knees and dunk her head; when she came up, someone thrust soap at her. She rubbed it over her clothes and let them float, and decided to wash her hair so she could rinse it before the water turned any dirtier. The women stood around the tub, holding the privacy cloth between Kelyn and the door—as if anyone could see anything from there, she thought—and talking softly in their Trader tongue. Kelyn scrubbed her fingers over her scalp and sighed; they acted more shy around her now than they had upon first meeting. Maybe things would never be right between them.

Then Darada's voice rose above the adult chatter, a few high-pitched words of alarm. They hushed instantly, and Kelyn stopped scrubbing, the better to hear to what they reacted. The nearby trill of alarm repeated twice, and then started again, more loudly—picked up by someone just outside the warehouse, and then suddenly cut short.

By then they could hear the tramp of booted feet.

"Soldiers," Kelyn guessed, and the women confirmed it with their alarmed expressions. She rose dripping from the tub and would have vaulted from it to grab her staff and knives, but Lenci's assistant, Anci, caught her arm.

"No," she said. "Do you know how badly it will go for us if there is a fight here? Even if you manage to drive them off, we'll never be safe in this town again. Abendar will change his witch-hunt to a Trader hunt!"

Kelyn hesitated, hearing the truth of it, but—"I can't let them take me!"

"Then rely on Trader wiles. Get back in the tub." She grabbed the privacy sheet and began stuffing it into the water. "Get down, I said! All the way down!"

With the approaching soldiers at the door, Kelyn had little choice. She took a deep breath and plunged back under the water, bracing herself against the sides so she was shoved up against the side closest to the soldiers; there, she'd be in shadow, and they were least likely to see her.

But she couldn't stay underwater forever.

She flinched when the surface of the water shimmered and a number of dark objects descended upon her, and was barely able to stop herself from bursting forth to do battle. But as she wavered on the edge of restraint, her legs twitching with the need to move, a number of hands entered the water as well, shoving the objects—clothes, she realized, any of the Traders' usual number of layers that they could spare—deep into the water, swishing them around.

Laundry. They were doing laundry. The water-distorted sound of harsh Atlian demands reached her ears; the women's replies came more faintly. By then her lungs were burning, and she knew she would never stay down here long enough, and that if she waited much longer, she wouldn't have the strength to fight when she *did* emerge—

Dark cloth floated above her. Carefully, she nudged it toward her head until she could rise up beneath it, face first, her nose barely out of the water. Her ears, still submerged, could hear the conversation more clearly, but not well enough to pick out anything but the occasional word. "Keturan," she heard once, and "here," and "trouble." And then, quite clearly, a woman's cry of protest.

Someone, knowing her too well in this regard if in nothing else, put a restraining hand on top of her head, momentarily pushing her back under. She came up with a cough bursting to come out of her throat, and for a few moments her entire focus was on not allowing that to happen. When she could finally spare the effort to listen again, she heard nothing but a babble; someone plucked the cloth away from her head.

Either they'd found her or they were gone. In either case, there was no point in staying down here any longer. Slowly, Kelyn pushed her head out of the water, blinking it out of her eyes.

"They're gone to search the other buildings," Anci said. "You'd best stay in there until we get an all clear."

Well. At least her hair was good and rinsed.

❖ ❖ ❖

Kelyn shivered by the fire, as cold and wrinkled as last year's apples. Her clothes were there, too, and almost dry—someone had had the foresight to take them from the tub long before she was allowed to emerge, and now, as the Traders patted her hair and shoulders dry, she struggled to pull the trousers over her still-damp skin. As soon as she had the shirt on, someone shoved a hot mug of tea in her hands, and she took it with gratitude.

"They'll be back, I'm sure of it," Anci said, shaking out Kelyn's cloak and settling it around her shoulders. Others lifted her hair up out of the way, and then set to combing it, hands moving swiftly but gently at the many snarls. Kelyn curled both hands around the mug and sipped at the warm contents, letting them tend to her. She and Frykla and Sigre used to groom each others' hair by the fire after days of hunting had loosened their braids, and the feel of someone else's hands at her scalp was strange and familiar at the same time. The Traders had a different touch, and seemed to be asking permission each time they drew a comb through.

They braided her hair back from her face, securing it with some of the gift trinkets. They braided random hanks of hair at the sides and back of her head, weaving in more of the gifts, and when they were done they brought her knives and the black leather vest, which someone had washed down and brushed off.

"They'll be back," Anci said again, handing over the knives after Kelyn had adjusted the belts to suit her. "Probably more than once. It's not safe for you to return. If you need to contact us, come to the edge of the buildings and make this noise." She demonstrated the cluck-cluck Endre had shown Kelyn. "Someone will be out to talk to you. Just make sure you're not seen!"

That meant coming through the Darks at night, something to which Kelyn did not look forward. But she had hunted the mountains at night for years . . . she could certainly stalk through the Darks without being seen if she so chose.

Even so, something made her very glad for the new boots.

Chapter 11

Dried, fed once more, and finally warm again, Kelyn thanked the women—of the men, there remained little sign—and this time, though the conversation remained limited to the few words necessary to accomplish their tasks, she felt their acceptance. They didn't yet know what to make of her, of that she was sure, but they seemed willing to let her be as she was.

That was fine. She didn't think she'd ever quite understand them, either—with their prim privacy curtains and brazen coupling dances. The realization turned her thoughts to Endre. Annoyed afresh that he'd avoided her so neatly since the previous day, she found herself equally wistful at losing the chance to talk to him before she departed.

Kelyn left the area with stalking caution, and avoided a soldier who had been posted to an uneasy watch at the border of the Darks. She entered the Darks in a new spot, avoiding the main street, and wound her way through alleys and side streets. She encountered only a handful of beggars, each of whom took one look at her—and the glower she fixed on them—and decided she wasn't worth the trouble.

Near day's end, she approached the inn from the back—there were bound to be soldiers out in the market, and even if they weren't looking for her, they'd probably be glad enough to *find* her—and spent another night in the barn. In the morning, with her belongings jammed up against the ceiling rushes, she braced the scowl of the old woman to inquire after Kila. The woman closed the door in her face. While Kelyn stared at it, scowling and wondering how hard it would be to force her way in, she reappeared, towing Kila by the ear.

"Take her out of my way," the old woman grumbled, shoving Kila out the door with that very grip on her ear. Kelyn caught the girl as she stumbled, and righted her; the door slammed in both their faces.

Kila rubbed her ear, but the tears in her eyes didn't spill down her cheeks. "She eats rat dung for breakfast, that's why she's so mean."

"Makes sense to me," Kelyn said, and didn't bother with niceties. Children didn't care if you got straight to business. "Do you want to earn a copper bit?"

"How?" Kila put grubby hands on her stick-straight hips and stared up at Kelyn, tilting her head back to squint at Kelyn's face. "What do I have to do?"

"Take a message for Thainn to the fortress gate."

Her eyes widened. "To the gate? They'll snatch me up! They'll put me to work in the smelly chandlery, or the kitchens!"

"They've already got plenty of people in their chandlery," Kelyn said, with no idea what Kila was talking about. "And if you do this right, you'll meet Thainn."

"Why don't *you* do it?"

"Why do you think? They'll lock me up before I

even get a chance to talk to him, and probably never tell him I'm there."

"*He'll* lock you up."

"Not once he hears what I have to say, he won't." Or maybe he would. But he'd certainly listen to her, first, so she'd have accomplished her goal. And then he'd have to fight his way past her staff and both knives before he laid hands on her. "It's worth a copper bit, Kila."

Kila looked down at her bare toes, wiggling them in indecision. Kelyn wasn't sure which convinced her—the chance to meet Thainn, or the copper—but when she looked up, she nodded. "Now?"

"Now."

"What do I say?"

"Say the Wolverine's daughter wants to talk to him about witches, if he dares to meet her."

"I can't say that!"

"You can. And say you'll take him to me."

"You! You're not his daughter—just because you're big and you have black hair—that doesn't count for anything."

"It doesn't matter if I am or not, if the words get him out to talk to me."

"He'll ignore you. He's too smart for that."

"But I dared him. And he's too brave not to take a dare."

That made Kila scowl down at her toes again. "He's too brave," she agreed. "But that would be tricking him."

Kelyn straightened, looking around. "Where's Zeffe? I bet he wants the copper."

"No!" Kila grabbed Kelyn's hand with both of her own, tugging as though Kelyn had been about to walk off. "I'll do it! Zeffe will say something smart to the gate guard, and I'll never see him again."

"You're sure? You'll do it?" Kelyn pulled herself

even taller, looking over the ragged back fence as though she saw someone beyond it. "Because I think I see—"

"No!" Kila hung from Kelyn's hand, her eyes big.

Kelyn relented. "Tell the gate guard to tell Thainn that the Wolverine's daughter wants to talk to him about witches, if he dares."

"The Wolverine's daughter wants to talk to Thainn about witches, if he dares," Kila repeated, her doubt still clearly evident.

"And you'll take him to me."

"And I'll take him to her."

"Say it again."

Kila rolled her eyes and *tsked* and sighed dramatically, and then repeated it twice, after which Kelyn sent her on her way. Kila trotted around the inn and out into the market; Kelyn followed as far as she dared, and then sank against the side of the inn to watch as the girl joined the short line of people waiting to get in the fortress.

The guard would have ignored her if she hadn't tugged at his breeches, and even then he tried to shoo her off. But Kila, glancing over her shoulder at the inn, returned to tug at him again—barely evading the cuff he aimed at her. *A copper bit and one of the hair trinkets from the Traders,* Kelyn decided as Kila, gesturing and insistent, finally got the man's attention. The gate guard shouted into the fortress, and eventually another man ambled out; after a few exchanged words, the second man looked down at Kila, shrugged, and returned to the fortress.

A long time went by. Kila stood just to the side of the gate guard, fidgeting, hopping back out of the way when her toes were endangered by his heels, playing some sort of game that involved twisting and counting fingers and evolved into hunkering down to examine her toes.

Thainn walked out of the gate and halted, scanning the market area. Those in line to enter the fortress flinched from him, scuttling past to the second gate, but Kelyn found herself creeping forward, her eyes narrowed and her gaze—critical and assessing—locked upon him.

He was as she remembered, though she had been too close truly to see him. Tall, and with the breadth of her Keturan cousins. His hair was as long as hers and braided into a tight tail; from here, she could not see the grey his years had brought to it. She remembered the cool hazel of his eyes, and how they'd flashed with his temper.

She hoped she was doing the right thing.

Not that she was overly impressed by him. She'd leave that for the others. *Thainn the Wolverine* . . . Atlia's pits, he couldn't even find—

There. Now, at the nod of the gate guard's head, he had finally spotted Kila, still absorbed in her toe game. He reached down and lifted her to her feet as though she were a piece of fluff, and Kelyn's eyes narrowed even further. No need to scare the girl like that.

Thainn barked a demand at her, but Kila was stuck in staring up at him, her mouth dropped open and all sign of wits fled from her face. Finally Kelyn saw her stammer something, jam a dirty finger in her mouth, and mumble what Kelyn hoped was her message. Another demand from Thainn, a curt gesture; Kila shook her head. They went through a couple of versions of this ritual before Thainn, in clear exasperation, gestured for the girl to lead him on.

Kelyn stepped back into deeper shadow, backing away until the building blocked her view of the girl and the warrior, and then turned to run back behind the inn. She would wait for him out in the open—

out where she had several potential retreats if she needed them.

Which she wouldn't, not if the Wolverine had half as much sense as he had muscle.

He left my mother. He left me.

So much for sense.

"Back here," came Kila's voice, along with the growing tread of a big man making no attempt to be quiet.

"Girl, if you've played me for a fool—" Thainn broke off as he entered the small yard and glared about it.

Kelyn didn't give him time to find her, back against the inn—though it seemed to her that he was wheeling about even before she spoke, in the words of their mutual native land. "How would she even know enough to play you for a fool if she hadn't talked to me?" She tossed Kila the coin, and the hair trinket after it. Kila gave the trinket a quick, fiercely possessive examination, grinned at Kelyn, and ran into the barn.

Thainn stared at her, looking her up and down as he might well examine a goat ready for slaughter. "If I dare," he said, repeating her words in a flat voice.

"As words go, they seem to have served me well."

"Not yet," he said. "You still have to convince me not to throw you over my shoulder and take you back to the cells—where you belong."

"To any other man, our blood tie would be reason enough. But then, any other man wouldn't leave his woman to raise their daughter alone." Left his daughter struggling to fill his shoes.

"Plenty of men do," he growled. "And I told you I was gone from Ketura before you were born."

"And I never said my mother was Keturan!" Kelyn glared at him, and he glared back.

No. This wasn't the way. And the important thing

wasn't that Thainn the Wolverine was a wretched father. It was that Thainn the Wolverine persecuted her friends.

"Leave the Traders alone," she said. "Leave *all* the witches alone. They're not the problem. They're not harming anyone!"

"All witches are a problem. If not today, tomorrow."

"Are all Keturans stupid barbarians who cannot get along in the other lands?"

"Some of them are," he said, giving her a pointed look. "Some of them cause a great deal of trouble wherever they go."

"*All* Keturans?" she repeated.

"All *witches*," he said, refusing to concede the point.

"Then why are you working with one? Why do you follow his orders?"

"Abendar?" he snorted. "*Abendar?*"

She wouldn't be cowed. Not by his rudeness, not by his size, not by the fact that he was her father, and required the same respect she'd given Lytha. *Lytha had earned it.* "Petissanji."

Thainn stared at her . . . and threw his head back and laughed. Kelyn bit her tongue and suppressed her angry retort, a restraint made easier by the realization that the livid bruise creeping out from the neckline of his lined leather tunic had her name on it. Then restraint fled, and she reached out to poke him on it, evading his snatch at her hand once she'd done it.

"Little bitch!" He scowled, rubbing ruefully at his shoulder—though not, she noticed, actually touching the bruise. It was that sore, then.

Good.

"Not so little," she said. "And not so bad at taking care of herself. Her father's daughter, one might say. With a nose for trouble. And the trouble I found led me right to your Petissanji."

This scowl was more irritation, annoyance at his lack of understanding. "What are you talking about?"

"Petissanji is a witch."

Thainn snorted, and made as if to walk away.

"He's the one behind the witch-hunts. I think he cursed those warehouses himself, and convinced Abendar to hunt out all the witches so *he* could get his hands on them."

He hadn't walked. But she saw him still weighing the decision. In the lull, behind his back, Kila came out of the barn, dragging Zeffe—who stopped dead in his tracks when he saw Thainn. "See?" Kila said, in a whisper that wasn't much of a whisper. "I *told* you I talked to him!"

Zeffe, rooted to the spot with his hero before him, gaped—but only for a moment. Then he turned and fled. If Thainn heard or understood what had gone on behind him, he gave no indication. But still he hesitated, not quite able to walk away from her outrageous words.

"Are you going to listen?" she prodded. "Or would you still like to try to throw me over your shoulder and take me back to the cells?"

Thainn shifted his sword harness; the thing's thick oval pommel weight poked out above his shoulder. "I can do *that* any time I choose. So talk. Unless that's all you have to say. *Petissanji is a witch*. I don't work for witches, girl."

"Kelyn," she said. "It's a good Keturan name, don't you think? Unlike Lytha."

He frowned, but didn't otherwise react to her mother's name—or to the fact that Zeffe and Kila were back, hissing at one another in earnest whispers, and this time not venturing past the threshold of the barn. "You put yourself in grave danger by bringing me here," he said. "Either you know something, or you think you know something—or you're crazier than you ought to be, and still fight the way you do."

Kelyn released her hold on her staff to let it rest against her shoulder, a posture of long acquaintance. She was gratified to note that his eyes marked any movement of the weapon. "Reman ironwood," she said. "It was my mother's."

"Stop playing games with me." He walked a few steps away from her, returned. "Or trying to. Or I *will* throw you over my shoulder—"

"You stay back from her!" Kila said shrilly. They both looked at her in surprise, even more surprised to discover that she clutched a rock in her tense little fist. She might not understand Thainn's exact Keturan words, but she'd clearly caught his threat. Thainn glanced back to meet Kelyn's gaze, and she was surprised to see a hint of amusement there.

"Not yet, anyway," he said. "Ketura's balls, girl, don't twitter me to death. Tell me why you brought me here."

Kelyn smiled, and gestured Kila back. The girl lowered the rock, but didn't retreat back into the barn where Zeffe still clung to the door frame. "I've told you. The Trader witches are no threat to anyone." Then she put on a thoughtful face and said, "At least, not to those who don't threaten them with stolen magic, like the soul-gem Thyra tried to use on them. How do you justify that, Wolverine? Using such evil in your own work?"

He frowned again, but it was less of an objection, and more in honest response to the question she posed. "We use witches to assist us in finding others, yes. I don't like it—there's no such thing as a trustworthy witch, no matter what they might say, only a witch who will turn on you as soon as it's to her advantage—"

"Like some men I know," Kelyn murmured.

Although that wasn't quite fair. He hadn't turned on Lytha; he'd run from her.

"—but those witches only use magic to find the others, and to defend the men if necessary. There are no soul-gems in Abendar's companies, or mine."

"Perhaps there aren't any in *yours*," Kelyn allowed him. "But I wouldn't even know what they were if I hadn't seen the soldiers with one." She crossed her arms over her stomach, the staff nestled in the crook of her elbow. "I destroyed it."

He snorted.

"If you think those words were lies, then why listen to anything I say?" Kelyn narrowed her eyes at him, resisting the urge to hit him for even considering her words a falsehood. "If I lie once, then I might lie always."

"Do you?"

"You insult my mother again, to think that she would raise me so." No, she wouldn't hit him. She wouldn't spit at his feet. She had to convince him to leave the witches alone. To do something about Petissanji, who would continue to goad Abendar into witch-hunts with or without Thainn's help. "I threw the gem into the fire and ran. Ask the witches who remain in the cells. Ask them if there was a terrible light in the middle of the night. See what they say."

"A stupid thing to do—to throw a soul-gem into a fire!"

"Even stupider to leave it in Thyra's hands! Although," Kelyn said thoughtfully, putting the face on just for him, "she was dead by then, herself, of course."

"All right," he said. "You were there. That much is obvious. And if what you say is true, then . . . it is not how I would have things. But of Petissanji, you have said nothing convincing."

"Then listen. After I got away from you, I went down another level."

"My men searched that level," Thainn interrupted, frowning. "You weren't there."

"I was, along with Abendar's dead. Which just proves that there are things about that level that you don't know."

"Things I don't know after months of service there, but which you discovered in a few moments?"

Wonderful. Now his pride was involved. Kelyn closed her eyes, took a deep breath, and pasted patience onto her face. She opened her eyes to discover his confident skepticism still staring back at her. Staring *down* at her. Not many men could do that. She had a sudden glimpse of what it might have been like to look up to her father instead of to despise him. "I went down a level," she said. "I was trapped at the east end of it. I felt a breeze, and I followed it. That wall swings open, and there are rooms beyond. I hid in the first of them—your men were on the other side, looking for me."

His eyebrow raised—just one of them, turning his skepticism into extreme disbelief. Kelyn wondered if he'd given that to her, the ability to raise just one eyebrow. If she could convince him of the truth of her words, she might even get the chance to find out.

"They were talking about some pit-faced whore that one of them thought made a good bedmate," she said. "And one of them said I fought well, and maybe I *was* your daughter, and another—Hann—said that wouldn't be smart to say in front of you."

Thainn grunted in a noncommittal manner, but Kelyn thought she'd gained some ground. She gave him a quick summary of the second conversation she had overheard, between Petissanji and his obsequious henchman. "He's using the witch-hunt to acquire objects of power," she told Thainn. "He's using *you*. You might not care about saving the witches, but you ought to care about *that*. Unless you *have* been out of Ketura too long."

"Be careful," he growled at her. "One small girl willing to throw stones at my back isn't enough to keep me from taking you in."

She shrugged. "You don't like my words? Then prove me wrong."

He hooked his thumbs into his wide, metal-studded leather belt. His wrists were encircled by the same, she noted, as was his throat. She couldn't decide if he was showing off, or if he spent so much time fighting that he wore such protection as a matter of fact. "Maybe," he said, "I'll be generous. I'll give *you* the chance to prove yourself right. Do it, and you may just avoid the cells."

Prove herself right? She could show him the hidden room, she supposed—

"You hesitate," he said, and grinned at her. She didn't think it was a very friendly expression. "Not so confident in your words, after all?"

Kelyn dropped a hand to her staff grip, and the other to the knife hanging off that hip. She shifted her weight forward so she was closer to him, looking directly at him, without ever taking a step. "I've got so many ways to prove them I simply have to decide where to start first."

Not the answer he'd expected. "Show me, then," he said, and gestured toward the market and the fortress beyond.

Kelyn wiggled her toes within her new boots, considering—he might, after all, simply take her to the fortress and toss her into a cell, grateful that she'd made it so easy for him. But . . . the man her mother had spoken of would do no such thing. In this, she would trust her mother, if not the man himself. She nodded.

"Is it true?" Kila called out, the stone forgotten in her hand, her question drawing Kelyn up short and bringing Thainn's attention back to the child. "Are you really his daughter?"

"He came, didn't he, when you gave the message?" Kelyn said, the Atlian language clumsy on her lips after her reimmersion in the Keturan tongue.

"Yes, but he might have just been mad at you for saying so," Kila said, quite sensibly.

"Look how mad he is at her *now*." Zeffe still clung to the barn, not quite brave enough to come out as far as Kila. "If he weren't her father, he would have hit her."

"I'll be back for my things," Kelyn said, leaving them to argue it out and hiding her amusement as she turned away.

She thought she caught a similar spark of humor in Thainn's eye. "Who knows," he muttered. "You're certainly as stubborn as I."

❖ ❖ ❖

Thainn led her right past the gate guards, lifting a hand in greeting to the several soldiers they passed. They encountered a pair of his own men—distinctive from Abendar's with their rougher appearance and the varieties of weapons casually sprinkled about their persons—and he said gruffly, "Go about your business," when it appeared they were going to stop and ask about her presence. One of them was Hann; she thought she saw him wink at her, but when she turned to look back at him, Thainn grabbed her arm and tugged her onward.

She jerked herself loose, making sure her elbow hit his ribs in the process.

Down the levels they went, until they hit the cramped stairs she had both times navigated in the dark. It looked none the larger for the torch Thainn now carried, and his dark bulk ahead of her nearly filled it. Not the man to get stuck behind in tight quarters.

He took her to the wall she described and stood there with his arms crossed over his substantial chest. More concerned with wiping the smirk off his face than anything else, Kelyn jabbed her staff into the ceiling depression and shoved the wall door open.

She found his dumbfounded expression to be quite satisfactory.

He pushed past her, into the little antechamber that composed her entire experience of this hidden area. Kelyn had a sudden foreboding, a prickle down her neck. "This is as far as I went," she said, meaning it to be a warning as she slid into the antechamber with him.

If he heard her tone, he ignored it. The torch illuminated the thick velvet layers hanging across the opposing archway, and he drew them back without care for who or what might be on the other side.

So this is what it's like to follow in the footsteps of a Keturan outside Ketura. Kelyn took a firm grip on her staff and peered over his shoulder at the chamber beyond—and then slowly sunk back on her heels.

Petissanji could have it to himself, if that's what he wanted.

Thainn made a noise of disgust and walked into the room, dropping the curtain behind him and leaving Kelyn with the choice of standing in the dark antechamber alone, or joining him in the witch's private chamber.

She drew the hangings aside and entered.

Under her feet, the floor went thick and cushioned; a glance showed her lumpy, layered rugs, the topmost of which was threadbare, but looked to have been of high quality. The stone walls were covered with charts and diagrams lacquered into place, some of them fresh and shiny, some starting to peel away. Most of them were incomprehensible, but one Kelyn quickly recognized as a detailed drawing of a man with his innards exposed; careful notations accompanied the depiction of each organ. "What's this for?"

Thainn left his examination of another chart and came to glance at hers. "It's in one of the southern languages. I'm not familiar with the style of penmanship . . ." He moved the torch closer, squinted at the notations, and stepped suddenly back, his eyes startled.

"What?" she demanded.

He didn't much look like he wanted to answer, and when he did, it was a mutter. "Recipes of a sort," he said, and went to the long, low table against the opposite wall, taking most of her light with him. Finding herself without much choice, she followed.

His hand hovered over the objects on the table, not quite touching any of them—a globe of glass, a wide belt woven of grasses and dipped in something that left it with an oily sheen, a knife whose blade seemed to soak up the torchlight . . . Kelyn reached to touch the last, wondering what that blade was made of, what it would feel like—

Thainn slapped her hand away.

"Ow!"

"Don't touch any of this!" he said, as fierce as any warrior could sound.

"Don't touch *me*," she snapped back him, but then realized the import of his words. "You think they're magic! You see? Petissanji wants the witches so he can find more of these things—he said something about the Horn of Russas. *He's* the one you should be after."

"You've yet to prove this has anything to do with Petissanji," Thainn said. "There's no telling how long it's been since anyone was in this room. Don't you think someone would notice if he spent time on this level?"

"Why would they? Doesn't he check on the prisoners?"

"Not that often," Thainn said, but the grudging tone in his voice meant that Petissanji did.

"And there could be other ways down here."

"Do you *see* another way?"

"Did you *see* the way we came in, until I showed it to you?"

"Stubborn," he muttered.

"I've proven one thing," she said. "I don't lie. This chamber was here, just like I said. If you've any honor left, you'll look for the truth about Petissanji."

"If I've any honor *left*—"

"Yes," Kelyn said calmly. "You lost a goodly amount of it when you abandoned my mother, and you've had many years since then to lose the rest of it."

Even in the torchlight she could see the flush that spread over his thick neck. Perhaps those had not been the wisest words, not while she was here in this fortress of Abendar's.

She didn't get the chance to ponder her headstrong folly. Thainn muttered a crackling oath, turned on his heel, and stalked to the archway. Kelyn, left at the back of the room with darkness settling around her, was the only one with a chance to see the brief glow around the archway as he yanked the hangings aside.

"Wait!"

"What? Afraid of the dark?" He let the hanging fall behind him. She heard him scrabbling at the ceiling for the inner door release. He'd even have the benefit of the handle, since he had light to see it by. He'd be leaving her on her own—

With whatever monstrous creature was coalescing into solidity before her.

Not enough room to use the whip. Barely enough to use the staff. Hardly enough light to see either, or even the creature; for that matter. She smelled its breath, heard its growl, and picked out the gleam of its eye . . . its eyes . . . its *many* eyes . . .

"Thainn!" If he heard the uncertainty in her voice and came back to mock her, all the better. He had her *light*, Ketura damn him! And were those *tentacles*? The creature poised, hissing and gurgling at her, but not attacking. Just guarding. Keeping her here. Which meant . . . someone was probably on the way. Petissanji. "Get back here with that torch! And watch out for the—"

The hangings yanked back; light flooded in. "Holy Siloga!" The room greyed toward darkness as Thainn leapt back, dropping the cloth; the creature, as surprised as Thainn, lurched back from the archway. Its warning hiss escalated into a juicy growl. Kelyn had not yet seen its mouth. She didn't care to.

An instant later, she heard the sweet *zing* of a sharp blade through taut cloth, and the velvet hangings ripped away from the archway, leaving Thainn to block out the light instead. Both hands free, the torch jammed in a holder in the antechamber, Thainn sheathed his knife and brought his sword up to a two-handed grip. Kelyn shifted her staff to a lance grip and, as Thainn stepped in to attack, launched herself at the creature.

It batted the staff from her hands with one ropey limb and raked another at Thainn, revealing a row of claws set in the underside of the tentacle. Kelyn snatched at her knives with numbed hands, peripherally aware of the twist of Thainn's body as he sought to avoid deadly claws. She couldn't close, she couldn't take it from behind—with all those eyes, it didn't *have* a behind—

Get rid of the eyes, then. As quick as the thought came to her, she flipped her knife in her hand, drew back, and whipped the blade at one of those baleful eyes. It roared in protest as the missile bounced off its head, and Kelyn jumped back in surprise at the abysmal throw; glancing down at her remaining knife. Her own, original blade. The one she thought she'd just thrown, and judged the distance for. *Damn!*

A thick stench filled the room, along with Thainn's triumphant roar; the creature reeled back, one limb slashed to uselessness—and then it leapt at Thainn with a furious snarl. Kelyn quickly flung her remaining knife. This time it sank true, to the hilt in one of those eyes. Yowling, the creature whipped its limbs around in maddened fury—just how many of them did it *have*, she wondered, ducking as it snatched the knife out of its head and hurled it back at her; it clattered off the wall behind her and onto the low table of magical objects.

And then Thainn cried out in surprise, slipping, going down so hard that his feet snapped into the air. The creature jumped on him, and Kelyn scrambled to find her knife, to leap on the thing from its new blind spot—but the table sat in shadows and she had to search by feeling, frantically running her hands over the belt, the globe, something soft and grotesquely squishy—and then they found the familiar shape of a blade. She snatched it, half aware that someone else had entered the room behind her, unable to sort out just how that had happened and not yet caring. She hefted the knife, ever aware of the futile kick of Thainn's legs from beneath the beast, and felt the balance off. *What?*

It doesn't matter—move! She found the right grip and threw herself onto the creature—someone screamed at her, a futile protest—hoping its tentacles were less effective up close, plunging the knife into its scaley hide—

It gave an ear-splitting howl, writhed beneath her—and vanished. With a grunt of surprise, Kelyn landed on Thainn—then instantly rolled off, for he was still on the attack, spitting out ichor with fury.

She thumped up against someone's boots. A clean, fancy-edged robe. She thought of the cry of protest as she'd flung the knife, realized this was no friend—*where did he* come *from*—and, spotting her knife on the floor by the table, launched herself for it, dealing herself a painful rug burn in the process. And thinking suddenly that if *this* was her knife—

"The Spellcutter! You've ruined it!"

Petissanji's voice. Furious.

And Thainn, ignoring his presence, roared in outrage as he climbed to his feet and looked at himself, then at the floor where he had slipped. "It pissed itself! Atlia's pits, it pissed on everything!"

From the outside hall came a shouting, and the noisy arrival of men at full speed. Thainn had left the stone door half open, Kelyn realized, had been on his way out when he'd heard her call. In moments, one of Abendar's men pushed his way in, looking wary and surprised, an expression which did not resolve once he took in Thainn—bleeding, coated with nastiness, and Kelyn—crouched, ready for action, and Petissanji—his face livid.

Petissanji didn't hesitate. He jammed his torch in a wall holder, stepped back, and said, "Take them!"

Nor did Thainn hesitate to respond. He scooped up Kelyn's staff, tossed it to her, and turned on the soldiers in one motion. "Make way! You have no authority over me."

Petissanji stabbed a finger at Kelyn. "She's witched him!"

"You lie!" Kelyn snarled at him, and swung the staff, connecting soundly with his shoulder, getting her first good look at his handsome features, skin so dark it couldn't be from sun, a neatly trimmed beard and mustache—and eyes filled with surprise and pain, astonishment that anyone would touch his person. He squalled on the way down—and *squall* was the only way to describe that noise.

"Thainn," said the soldier in front, looking very much like he wished he was elsewhere. "Come quietly. We'll sort this out."

"Petissanji won't let you live that long!" Kelyn plucked her second knife from the rug where it had landed after bouncing off Petissanji's creature. "Do you believe me now? Where do you think he *came* from, anyway? I was right about that second entrance." In fact . . . hefting the knife, Kelyn turned her back on the tense confrontation at the antechamber, and walked over to where Petissanji squirmed on the floor.

"Hold where you are," Thainn told the soldiers. "We'll sort this out—*my* way."

Kelyn toed the witch, and he stopped his dramatics long enough to glare at her. "I didn't hit you that hard. You want to use your magic on me, don't you? I wouldn't. The soldiers can see."

"I'll kill them and say you did it," he said, his square, handsome features not so handsome through his pained anger.

She judged that in his condition, she'd be faster with her knife than he was with his spells, and ignored the threat. Crouching next to him, she prodded the hand he held over his injured bicep. He swore at her, kicking his foot against the floor at the pain.

"Thainn!" warned the soldier.

"Kill her!" Petissanji cried. "Kill her, or die yourselves, for refusing my direct order!"

The soldiers muttered among themselves. Thainn growled, "Don't. She's my prisoner; none of you touch her."

"Kill *him*," Petissanji howled.

Kelyn hit his arm hard. "The way out!" she demanded, grabbing his chin, forcing him to look at her when he would have writhed around instead. He glared through watery eyes. "The way out! You got here somehow—" She lifted her head, glancing around the room, looking for any sign of a door such as the one that led in. She left him, and ran her hands along the walls, searching for uneven stones, her gaze on the ceiling.

She found it.

Behind her, Petissanji made it back up to his knees. He intoned a terrible word, and when she whirled, she found him pointed a trembling finger at her. *No!* Swift as a striking rock cat, she lashed out at him with the staff, knocking the hand aside with an audible crack of bone.

"Get her!" cried the soldier in the lead, ducking past Thainn.

The soldiers plunged into the room, and Kelyn leapt past Petissanji—curled over his hand in pain—to meet them. Within moments she found herself back to back with Thainn, struggling to use her staff in the low-ceilinged room, while he had barely enough room to swing his sword. There was as much pushing, punching and shoving as anything else, and the soldiers pressed in on them, overwhelming them with sheer numbers.

Thainn disappeared from behind her, yanked away; someone kicked the back of her leg, and Kelyn fell to her knees, suddenly on eye level with the flash of a sword. Limber beyond any Atlian's expectations, she dropped her shoulders flat to the floor, her thighs bent back over her own calves. As she bounced back up again, she snatched her knife from its sheath and in one swift motion, twisted to bury it in the man at her side. She yanked it free as he fell, put her hands to the floor, and whipped her legs out straight in a kick that felled the man before her.

"Ketura's balls!" Thainn bellowed, tossing a soldier against the wall. "Damn fine, girl, damn fine! I do believe you *are* one of mine!"

He believed her.

Kelyn, bouncing to her feet, struggled to find her balance as a quick tingle ripped through her, the feeling of a limb long asleep, suddenly coming awake. Frozen in the midst of the melee, she nearly took a club to the head—Thainn wrenched the weapon away and disposed of it by slinging it back at its wielder.

Kelyn shook off the feeling and sprang back into movement, scooping up a sword in time to duck below a man's guard and skewer him. Startled, she stared at the weapon—it was so light in her hand! She whirled to block another blow, having lost the staff some moments before—how easy it was to turn, to move, to force his blade aside and hold it there while she slashed the knife across the unprotected spot on his inner elbow! How agile she felt, leaping back into place behind Thainn!

Find your father. Then you will find your self.

Ketura's balls—Rika had been right, Rika had been telling her how to lift the curse! She was free, she was whole, she could feel her true strength and quickness—honed by years of concentration, of fighting unnatural clumsiness—and the delight of it coursed through her, here, in the middle of outnumbered combat, with men pressing in at them from all sides and more trying to squeeze in from the hall.

Kelyn threw her head back and laughed.

And Thainn, hearing her, jerked around to see the soldiers hesitating before his daughter; he grinned in response, and bellowed, "By Ketura!" Kelyn answered with her ululating fight cry, and took down another soldier.

No others took his place.

None seemed likely to.

Kelyn turned a quick circle, confirming that the soldiers on her side of the room were wounded or backed against the walls, not willing to throw themselves at someone they thought had gone berserker. Those on the entry side of the room hesitated, their momentum gone, trying to size up the situation. "Hold them," Kelyn told Thainn, and snagged her staff; in two swift steps she made it to the door latch, triggered it, and shoved the wall back. "Let's go!"

Thainn backed the length of the room to her, his sword at the ready, a knife in the other hand. And though the soldiers followed, pressing in on him, they all looked like they couldn't quite muster the nerve to make the first move—at least, not until Thainn stepped into the opening. Too late; with both sides and his back protected, he blocked the sword cut, slashed his blade through the air with enough energy to make them all step back, and then ducked into the space Kelyn had opened for them. She swung the door shut with a resounding boom, and plunged them both into darkness.

Where they stood, with no idea where the opening led, and no easy way to navigate it.

"Oh," Kelyn said.

From the other side of the wall came the thumps and scuffles of the soldiers trying to figure out how to open the door.

"Someone," Thainn pointed out, his voice startlingly close in the darkness, "is going to remember how you did it."

"Soon," Kelyn agreed, trying to bring to mind the little she had seen of this space before they'd lost the light. Narrow stairs, she thought. Up. "Or Petissanji will recover enough to tell them."

"By then they'll have plenty of other questions for him as well." He moved, bumped something, and grumbled.

"By then, he'll have thought of answers." Kelyn felt around with her staff, found the stairs.

"He's slick of tongue, all right."

"He could even have them there to meet us wherever this lets out." She took the first step, felt her way forward.

"If we can *find* where it lets out."

"Handles," she said succinctly. "Follow me."

Follow he did, if with a disgruntled rumble in his chest; Thainn the Wolverine was clearly used to leading. He clapped one big hand on her shoulder; from the sound of it, he had sheathed his sword, and she thought he kept the other hand at head level—a wise precaution, as it turned out, since she kept forgetting to allow for his extra height as she felt out their progress with the staff.

She checked for handles every time she came to a flat spot, finding none; they climbed steep, narrow stairs, and her eyes ached from straining against the blackness. Smells assailed her—dank stone and dust, but mostly Thainn. It was he, after all, who had fallen in the beast's stinking piss. And blood—she thought she smelled blood. But she didn't ask. She didn't want to know. They were in enough trouble already.

"We must be at the very top of the damned fortress by now," Thainn said, his words coming so suddenly, and after so much silence, that Kelyn startled. He clamped his hand more firmly upon her shoulder. "Don't get knock-kneed on me *now*."

"I'm the one who got us out of there in the first place," Kelyn said. "And I'm *not* the one who got stuck under Petissanji's beast. You don't have to worry about *me*."

"I'm not worried about you. I'm worried about me.

I wouldn't be here if it weren't for you."

"You wouldn't be here if you'd believed what I told you, instead of making me prove it."

"I was supposed to believe you, just because you claimed to be my daughter?"

"*Am* your daughter," Kelyn hissed, jerking her shoulder out from under his palm.

After a long moment, he found her again. But he said nothing.

Kelyn gritted her teeth, her chest unaccountably full of pain. He *did* believe it. He had to. The curse wouldn't have lifted if he hadn't. And it *had* lifted. She'd felt it, undeniable and exhilarating.

At that exact moment, she stubbed her toe on an uneven step, and sprawled against the flat stone beyond it, the staff flying from her grip, skinning her rug-burned palms and stubbing her fingers up against a wall. Stunned more from the contrary implications of her clumsiness than the fall, she did not instantly recover.

It was back? The curse was *back*? But—

"Are you—"

"Shut up!" The last thing she wanted was his annoyed solicitation. "Until I smell like you do, I'm just fine." At that, he had the wisdom to remain silent, and as she pulled herself to her feet against the wall, she ran into a handle.

Finally. The only question was, what would they find on the other side?

"There's a way out here." She kept her voice low, remembering how well the conversation between Thainn's men had come through to the antechamber, and felt around for the staff unsuccessfully, until he shoved it at her. Had he been standing there just holding it, letting her look—*no*. Stop it. Getting angry now wouldn't do her any good.

Voices from the other side of the stone door cut that anger short. She froze, hissing him to silence, and when the voices grew no closer, she ran her fingers along the wall, finding the crack of the door's edge, and putting her ear to it. Thainn did the same, locating the other edge.

The voices remained frustratingly indistinct—but then moved closer, and suddenly one of the voices became familiar, and its words clear enough for her to hear. Petissanji. A mite breathless, although his ascent to this level had surely been easier than their own.

"Thainn is a lost cause!"

"I don't know how that can be," someone responded, a confident voice.

"Abendar," Thainn whispered, barely audible even to Kelyn.

"Don't be overtaken by his reputation as the Wolverine," said a third man—Kelyn fought to place his voice, and had a sudden flash of Atelic, leaning over her with his hands on her body. "He's a man, like any other."

"A man who took me prisoner in your own fortress!" Petissanji said. "He came upon me in the cells, and the girl ordered him to take me. Clearly, she has control over him now."

"Then we must save him."

"Save him?" Atelic said, and snorted. "Once his soul has been sullied by a witch's hand?"

"He's been of much help to me," Abendar protested. "He's a good man."

Atelic said flatly, "He's a liability, now. I can carry on his work. I've proven that."

"I think that would be best," Petissanji said, in the convincing tone of a man without doubt. "And you should have Thainn's men rounded up, as well."

After a hesitation, Abendar said, "Most are out on a hunt."

"Then we should be ready for them when they get back," Petissanji responded, without any hesitation at all. "And we must find Thainn and the girl. She's too dangerous—even more dangerous than Thainn. The Traders, too, should be taken. They're all working together—and I have hints that the Traders are hiding something. We must redouble our efforts to interrogate them—*all* of them."

"Yes," Abendar said, regret lacing his voice. "Your counsel is wise, as usual."

"Because, as usual, I always have your best interests in my heart."

With a low growl, Thainn pushed himself away from the door. And though Kelyn would have liked to have heard more, she didn't think that they had the time for it—or that, in another moment, she would be able to restrain the Wolverine under discussion from charging into the room. She hastily took up her place in the lead, feeling her way forward.

Finally, when she reckoned that they had somehow climbed twice the height of the fortress—surely, with all these steps!—the passage ended abruptly in a wall. She ran her hands over the stone, filled with the sudden fear that the only way out had been back with Petissanji—but no. There was the handle. Kelyn reached upward, searching for the ceiling, for the release. "It's not here," she said, frustration tinging her voice.

"The latch trigger?" he whispered.

"The ceiling!"

He joined her on the landing, crowding her so closely against the door that her cheek flattened against the wall. *Oof*. What had her mother seen in this man?

"Here," he grunted. "High ceiling. I've got it—"

Click.

They both froze, wondering who might be on the other side, and how audible the noise might have been. But Kelyn heard nothing—not a murmur of conversation, no shifting, no creaking leather armor.

With some trepidation, she pulled the door back.

The dim light in the outside room reassured her. Thainn, too, apparently; he gave her a little nudge. She stepped back on his foot—hard enough so he'd know it was deliberate, quick enough that he didn't have time to protest—and slid out into the room.

Empty.

Not only empty of people, but empty of furnishings. She pushed the door open wide, and Thainn came through, a frown on his face. He went straight to one of two thick-silled arrow slots of windows, and gazed out upon the land for a moment before turning back to her. "The only rooms empty on this side of the fortress are on the upper level. And the only way out is through too many people. We'd be better off scaling the side of the fortress."

Kelyn shrugged at him. "If you can think of it, I can do it." And then she did what she should have done first; she looked out the other window herself, and assessed the climb.

It was a long way down.

But not so much different from the climbing she had done in the mountains. The wall was thicker at the base, and thus slanted out slightly; not quite a sheer climb. And the stones were rough, the mortar between them chinking away. Not to mention the various window sills, the wooden stubs of the framework for the flooring that hadn't been cut off even with the stone, and the stained patches with holes above them. The holes would do nicely for handholds. But—"What are those?" she asked, pointing.

He gave a short laugh. "Waste holes. The indoor pits empty out the side of the fortress; the waste falls below. If they haven't been cleaned recently, you'll have a soft landing if you fall."

Atlia's arse. She'd spent enough time in pits earning shelter on the way through Orrick. "I won't fall."

She pulled back inside and gave him a critical examination. The blood she had scented sheeted down one arm, the sleeve nearly torn away; she saw a handful of slashes, neat rows from the beast's claws. When he found her looking, he said, "They're shallow. Let's go. If Petissanji plays dumb, it'll take them awhile to find us. If he doesn't . . ."

"They'd already be here," she said, but wasn't half as confident as she sounded.

Nor, despite her claim, was she eager to put herself out on the wall of the fortress. If someone happened to see them . . .

"Toss the staff out," he said. "The only people working this side are the cleaners and the garbage detail."

She took another look. Yes, definitely the smelly side of the building. She sighed. "Oh, all right. Let's climb down the stupid fortress."

There was no word for *fortress* in the Keturan tongue; she had to use the Atlian word for it. Looking out again at the smeared walls and the pile of garbage beyond, she suddenly found that absence entirely fitting.

Chapter 12

By the time they reached the ground, Kelyn's arms and hands shook from fatigue; her arms felt leaden as she crossed the hard, stone-strewn ground and bent to pick up her staff. It would have helped had she not wondered the entire time just when her curse would jump back out to trip her up—or, in this case, knock her down.

But she had gone most of the way with sure, swift progress, feeling light and strong. Uncursed. Only toward the end had she faltered, and by then, Thainn was in no better shape. In worse, she thought. He had more weight to haul around than she. Now he jumped from the wall—arcing out, as had she, to avoid the distasteful matter below—and landed heavily, staggering a few steps in her direction before straightening to his normal posture.

By then, Kelyn had spotted the bodies. Thrown across the garbage heap with no regard for the people they'd once been, a hand's worth of them. Slowly, ignoring Thainn's impatient call, her nose wrinkled against the smell, she circled in on the bodies.

Yes. Lenci.

Tears stung her eyes. Blinking them away—or trying to—she moved for a better look at the others. No one she knew.

Smearing her face dry with the back of her wrist—her hands still reeked of contact with the fortress wall—she returned to Thainn. The Traders had to be told. Kelyn pointed to the Darks. "That's where we need to go. After I stop at that inn, first."

"Why, to give the children a chance to stone me?" he muttered, and then sighed loudly. "What makes you think I don't have a better plan?"

"I don't *care* if you have a better plan. Those are the things I need to do. Then we can talk about your plans."

"Let's talk *now.*"

But she had already found her boots—they, too, had come down the fast way, while Kelyn climbed down the wall with the use of her strong fingers and toes—and put them on, feeling the grit from the wall work between her toes. She immediately struck out at a walk, as confident as she could make it, eyeing the low wall that curved from the fortress around most of the outer marketplace. They'd have to get over that wall, or walk along beside it for some distance.

Over. It would be better. It would get them away from this place faster. Already there was some kind of fuss out by the gates; she could hear it if not see it.

Thainn caught up with her, followed her gaze, and said, "They'll see us if we go over. We walk around. They'll think we're garbage scavengers."

"They'll *see* us if we walk around—they're *looking* for us!"

Thainn shook his head, grinning, and Kelyn frowned

back at being left out of the joke. "How many Atlian men do you think could have come down that fortress wall? How many Atlian *women*? No, they're still looking for us inside, and blocking all the exits. It won't even cross their minds that we've made it this far."

She didn't know that she believed it. But . . . he knew them better than she. And she was reassured to see that he clung close to the wall, making use of its shadow—or what little there was, with the sun high in the sky.

Maybe he was right. Or maybe no one *did* notice them. But they made it to the inn barn without incident.

Thainn, standing by a water trough to sluice water liberally over his stained and stinking self, took one look at her expression and laughed out loud. "Don't tell me I've done something right and you can't stand it," he said, and laughed again when she scowled in response and turned her back on him—more so he couldn't read her face than in pique.

"You might as well climb into that trough and do it right," she said. "You're going to have to dump it, anyway—it's too fouled to leave for the beasts."

He didn't answer, not right away. After a moment, he said, "Here," and she turned to find his sword and harness thrust at her. She grabbed it; he was already stepping into the trough. Moments later, he came out dripping but as clean as she could hope for, and he dumped the trough without comment, immediately refilling it from the well at the corner of the yard.

Then he prowled through the barn, collecting leather oil and rags. She left him to it and climbed into the loft to retrieve her satchel; she had just closed her hand around it, stretched way up on tiptoe and teetering there, when she heard the creak of the ladder and realized that he was joining her. Just in time to see her lose her balance, tangle her feet, and stumble into a pile of hay.

Dust rose around her; she sneezed.

"Well," he said, and hesitated, minding the glare she shot at him, "at least you didn't do that down in the fortress."

"You don't know anything about it," Kelyn said, just to have said something. "Don't sit, you'll ruin the hay."

"I'm not that wet. And I'm sitting. We're going to be here a while. Until darkness gives us some cover."

"You want to go through the Darks at night," Kelyn said flatly.

"Better than going through soldiers during the day. And tell me why you want to go through the Darks in the first place?"

"Kelyn!" Kila's thin voice carried up into the loft from behind the barn, where she had evidently found the signs of Thainn's bath. "Is that you?"

Kelyn struggled up out of the hay and waded through it to the small, shuttered window above the feeding slot in the floor. When she peered out, she found Kila down below, looking up at her, fists on hips. "No," Kelyn told her. "It's not me. I'm not here. *No* one's here. Now go away before you give the idea that someone *is*!"

"Is Thainn not there, too?"

Aaiieee. "Yes," Kelyn said through gritted teeth, recognizing the signs of stubbornness in that small, dirty face. The trinket tied into her hair was bright and new and ridiculous. "Kila, if anyone finds us here, they're going to blame you, you know that."

Realization wiped away the stubborn expression. "There're customers today. They'll be out here. I can't help that! And Eddo, he's supposed to clean today."

Kelyn closed her eyes. Maybe Thainn would change his mind about staying here. "Then make sure the animals are fed well," she told Kila. "Don't give anyone any reason to come up here!"

"You'd better be really quiet," Kila warned.

Yes. Really quiet. Kelyn closed the shutter and made her way back to Thainn.

"I heard her," he said, removing his wide belt and applying oil to the underside. "We'll move to the back once I don't need the light to work. And we'll be quiet. If you want to go to the Darks now, you're on your own."

"I don't need you," Kelyn muttered, but not very loudly. It wasn't the truth, not now. If all she wanted was to run, to get away . . . that, she could accomplish on her own. But to do something about the witch-hunts . . . to stop Petissanji from going after the Horn of Russas—whatever it was, whatever it did—or worse . . . for that, she needed Thainn. He had men, once he contacted them again. He knew the Atlians.

And she wasn't ready to let him go. Not until she figured out the connection between him and her curse, and how to lift the thing once and for all.

Not until she better understood how he could have left her mother. How he could have left *her*.

She glanced over at him. His face, rugged with his years, was untroubled by deeper thoughts, by anything more significant than making sure his leather accouterments had proper treatment before they dried stiff and cracking. A face belonging to the man who had probably never even thought of her or her mother over the years.

With a snarl, she grabbed up her staff and took herself into the deep recesses of the loft, leaving him startled and uncomprehending, not caring.

Maybe she could even get some sleep before they hit the Darks.

❖ ❖ ❖

Kelyn opened her eyes to the dim light of the barn just after sunset, listening for whatever had awakened her—again, for the soldiers had been noisy in the market this day, noisy enough to make her sleep fitful. They'd even clomped through the inn and poked around the barn—a few tense moments which would have gotten worse if one of the customers hadn't gotten officious about the disturbance to his fine horses, and snorted that he'd been there all day and hadn't seen a thing.

There it was again. A loud, hollow rumbling, irregular and waxing to puzzling proportions before fading unevenly away. "Ah, you're awake," Thainn said. "It's a good thing, to be able to sleep whenever you get the chance."

"That was you?" She lifted her head to find him sitting across from her, his back to the barn wall—a large, indistinct figure in the swiftly falling darkness.

His teeth gleamed briefly at her. "I'm hungry."

"I gathered." She let her head drop back to the hay, grateful to have her cloak between herself and the itch-making stuff. The Traders hadn't wanted her back at the warehouses, but to the warehouses she had to go. They needed to know about Lenci. She wondered if Thainn would really come with her, or if he'd just hidden here with her while it had been convenient, and now would abandon her to her own devices.

"Many have come to me over the years," he said, leaving her to figure out what conversation he'd started. "Even before I was old enough to have sired a child grown. They all wanted something from me. What do *you* want, Keturan girl?"

It wasn't what she wanted. It was what she *had* wanted, all these years. "Nothing." She cleared her throat—maybe it would clear the sullenness she'd heard in her own voice. "Nothing but what I've said—

for you to help me stop Petissanji. And to get Abendar to leave the witches alone."

Not strictly true. She wanted him to admit that she was—

"Witches," Thainn snorted. He must have his belt back on; it creaked with his movement. He fell silent and she let her thoughts wander—to bounce, actually, between the prospect of telling the Traders of Lenci's death and the memories of an angry child beating her mother's staff against trees and the astonishing moment when she hung from Thainn's grip and realized she looked into the eyes of her father.

"Her name was Lytha, you said."

Now he was going to talk about her mother? Warily, Kelyn said, "Yes."

"And she was Reman. She . . . took you to Ketura?"

"I was born there. She thought it best to raise me in my father's land." Kelyn had never fully understood why, though she had thrived there. *Despite the curse*. She wondered if she'd ever understand that, either.

Or if she'd ever lose it for good.

"Lytha," he said, musing. "You have your mother's eyes, and her mouth."

He *did* believe. "Don't you say that! My mother was beautiful!"

"I remember," he said, unaffected by her anger, perhaps even amused by it.

"And yet you left her. Do you *remember* why you did that?"

She heard more than saw him shrug. "I never intended to stay. She knew that. It was her choice."

"*Her* choice? To bear a child on her own? To raise that child alone?" She sat up, crossing her legs, to glare at him through the darkness. "Do you know what I wonder? At night, when I wake up, and I realize all over again that my mother is dead? I wonder, would she have died as soon, had she not had to do the work of two parents?"

He grunted, much like he'd been hit by a fist instead of her words. "You're a fighter, all right." After a moment of silence—or near silence, through which his belly rumbled its demands—he said, "She knew I wouldn't stay. I was young; I was on my way elsewhere. I . . . was on the run. If she had you . . . she knew the herbs; she told me so."

Kelyn felt a chill run down her spine. "What are you saying?"

"I think you know. Lytha was a strong woman. She did what she chose to do. In that, *I* honor her. I'm not sure you do."

"You don't even know who she was," Kelyn spat, suddenly so enraged she could barely think. "You have no right to say such a thing! Where were *you* when I lit her funeral pyre? Where were *you* when the reivers tried to defile her body?"

"Did you want me there for her? Or for you?"

Her thoughts turned red. Kelyn reached for something—anything—to throw at him, and came up only with a handful of hay. It fluttered barely beyond her own feet. Not waiting for his reaction—his laughter, most likely—she snatched up her satchel and staff and jumped to her feet, stalking around the edges of the hay pile to search out the loft ladder in the darkness.

Losing her temper was always a mistake, was always when her clumsiness caught her. She misjudged the edge of the loft, and one foot slid on a scattering of hay to go skidding out into space. Down she went, skinning her shin on the edge of the loft right through her trouser leg, thumping down on her knee, arms windmilling, just barely able to latch one hand on the edge of the loft as she went over. She hung long enough to break the fall—the loft itself wasn't much higher than she could reach from the ground anyway—and let go, nursing splinters and a new rawness on her rug-burned palms.

Ketura's balls! Right in front of him.

At least it was dark. He couldn't possibly have seen . . . though he was no doubt wondering. *Snakeshit.* She groped around, found the satchel and staff, and shook her leg to flap the trouser leg against her shin and stop the annoying trickle of blood there. By the time she had straightened her cape—it had shifted around her shoulder far enough to half-strangle her—slung her satchel over her shoulder, and otherwise sorted herself out, he was there.

"To the Darks?" he asked.

"Through them," she said, her voice strangled with the effort of speaking to him without screaming at him. "To the Traders."

Of course he'd know they were there.

When she didn't respond, he said, "And after that?"

"And then," she said, unable to stop herself, as she turned on her heel to walk away from him, "there will be choices to make. Maybe this time you'll make the right ones."

Suddenly she found herself grabbed from behind, a good strong, two-handed grip. A grip she'd never break, not with all her Keturan strength or wiles or determination. Deep, uncertain fear trilled in her heart as he deliberately tightened his hold, clamping those big hands around her arms, pushing in so hard her own arms squeezed her ribs and her shoulders hunched up around her neck. "You," he said, "know even less of me than what you suppose I knew of your mother. You think she deserves respect? Then *you* start giving it to her. Respect her enough to allow that she could make her own choices, and that they had Ketura-damned little to do with me."

"Next you'll say *I* have little to do with you—or you, with me."

"That," he said, somehow squeezing her even harder, "remains to be seen." He released her roughly, shoving her away; Kelyn stumbled a few steps forward and stopped, her knees feeling too loose-jointed and her arms aching. Numbly, she tried to sort through the turmoil she felt . . . still angry, but frightened as well—an uncomfortably unfamiliar sensation—and fighting off regret. Should she have said those things? Would he leave her, now, before Petissanji had been dealt with? And more importantly, more selfishly, before she understood how she felt about him? Or how he felt about her?

She took a step, and discovered that her legs cooperated. She took another, and another, and found her stride. And then she found her voice. Barely turning her head to address him, she said, "The Darks are this way."

He didn't answer—but he fell into step beside her.

❖ ❖ ❖

Having a father, Kelyn began to realize, was more complicated than she'd thought. She walked the Darks with Thainn, struggling with herself . . . for walking the Darks with Thainn was nothing like going through it on her own. Where she had been wary—taking back ways, or striding through with deliberate confidence, projecting her own aura of danger—he seemed not to notice that they were in any danger at all. And she . . .

She found herself believing it. Believing him, and relieved to let him shoulder the responsibility of navigating them through the dank streets. She couldn't remember feeling this way before. Ever. *She* was the one who took care of Lytha as her mother's health failed, *she* was the one who gathered herbs for them and then turned to the more dangerous duty of gathering furs. And even when she'd been very young, she'd been aware of Lytha's worries—that they had no man to protect them from whatever came along. She had filled that role as soon as she could, her clumsy nature notwithstanding.

She hadn't even known that she was capable of letting someone else do it for her.

As if you're not ready to fight if it comes to that. She didn't need to twist herself up over it, not now. There was plenty to worry about, just with Petissanji.

Thainn took her through the Darks more quickly than she'd been before, and no one accosted them. No one even came near. It was she who slowed them, coming up on the edge of the warehouses. The Traders wouldn't want them there. They'd probably already had more visits from Abendar's men, especially since the exploits in Petissanji's secret room. They might, she realized, not even be here anymore.

It didn't matter. If they weren't, she'd find them.

She touched Thainn's arm, stopping him, and stepped forward just shy of the first building, sounding the warning call Endre had told her about. Thainn didn't question her, but waited quietly where she'd left him. After a few moments of silence, Kelyn repeated the call, slightly louder. And waited, wiggling her toes inside her boots and about ready to sit down where she was and pull the footware off.

Out in the darkness, someone approached—someone trying to be quiet, but not possessed of enough stealth to escape her ears. She called again, letting them know she heard them, and held her breath—was it a soldier, she had just pinpointed her position for him.

Whoever it was returned her soft call—a good sign, but not enough to reassure her until Endre's low voice came to her. "Kelyn?"

"Yes, and—" she said, and cut herself off, stiffening at the sound of movement from both sides of her. Endre's sharp cry of warning confirmed it, and Kelyn moved, fast and quiet, not willing to stand where she'd already been revealed. Back to Thainn she went, and found him with his sword out; he turned away, leaving his back open for her to guard, and she moved into position, flinging the cloak off to the side and feeling the heat of him behind her.

Four figures resolved in the darkness, two from either side, approaching with caution—*not enough*—and weapons drawn, the same standard issue short swords all of Abendar's men carried. "You're outnumbered," one of them said, his voice one of reason. "Stand down, and we'll take you in unharmed."

As if they'd *stay* unharmed.

"The problem is," Thainn said, just as reasonably, "everyone knows Keturans can't count."

Kelyn grinned. That, she figured, was her cue; her fight cry split the air, and she whirled the staff in a quick guard pattern, crouched and waiting—and startled to feel the tingle sweep her body, and to feel the strength course through it. The curse . . . gone again.

She'd figure it out later.

"How are your friends?" Thainn said. "The ones from the fight down Below? They thought they outnumbered us, too."

The figures hesitated, close enough now to have individual features; the two within Kelyn's field of vision exchanged a doubtful glance; one of them put his arm out before the other. "I was there," he muttered, trying not to be overheard. "I *told* Atelic that four of us weren't enough. And there's a Trader out here somewhere, too."

Thainn shifted at Kelyn's back. "Drop your swords, soldier boys, and we'll make it easy for you. We'll leave you tied and alive. Atelic might well kick your asses, but you'll be sore, not dead."

"I *told* him," the soldier said, more loudly this time.

"What makes you think there's only one of us?" Endre said, still hidden in the night.

"Atlia's arse!" The other soldier before Kelyn straightened, lowering his blade. "That's enough for me. I'm not dying out here just because Atelic didn't think they'd come this way."

"Then surrender." Thainn stepped away from Kelyn, approaching the two in front of him. "We're not leaving you to tell Atelic where we are."

Surrender they did, embarrassed and resentful and even grateful. Endre—alone, after all—provided enough rope, and a dark corner inside a warehouse in which to stash them. Someone would come looking for them . . . eventually.

Thainn crouched by the men, doing a last search for hidden knives and testing their ropes; by then they were gagged and unable to express the words that glared out through their expressions. Endre took Kelyn's arm and pulled her outside the warehouse.

"What have you been *up* to?" he demanded. "The market wasn't even worth trading in this morning, and we moved out of here at noon. The soldiers have been looking for someone all day—I bet it was you, and now I know for sure."

"You're here."

"Only because—" His reply started out heated, and then cut short; he seemed to realize he was still holding her arm, and released her. "Only because I thought you might come back. And because Gergo agreed, and for some reason he thought you might have news we cared to hear. He wanted someone to stay—I figured it might as well be me."

Oh. "Well, I'm fine," she said, as if he'd asked, and

he looked abashed at that, but said nothing. After a moment, as Thainn came up to stand with them, she said, "I do have news. And I need to talk to Gergo, too. We both do."

"We do?" Thainn said, not hiding his surprise.

"Who is this?" Endre asked, looking up at Thainn with an admirable—or foolish, Kelyn wasn't sure—amount of bluster.

"The Wolverine," she said, as if it were of no importance. "He's going to help us."

"I am?"

"He is?" Endre said, at the same time. "Who says we need his help?"

"I do." Kelyn glared at Endre. This was going to be hard enough.

"And who is this?" Thainn said, quite deliberately echoing Endre's earlier words and tone.

Men. They reminded her of the boys in her hunting pack going through their worst growing ages, always checking to see who was growing hair where. "This," she said, with enough false patience that she hoped they'd take notice, "is Endre. He's with the Traders; he can take us to them. I think they can help us deal with Petissanji."

"Petissanji is *your* problem," Endre said. "Traders ally with no one."

"He's your problem, too!" Kelyn lost that veneer of patience. "He's had Lenci killed, and he'll kill the rest of your witches if you don't help us do something!"

Endre, stunned, said nothing, and Thainn gave him that time, though he quite plainly also wanted to take Kelyn aside and straighten her out. After a moment, Endre cleared his throat. "You . . . saw her?"

"Among others," Kelyn said. "Gergo knows this, if you don't—Petissanji is questioning all the witches he can, unto their deaths. He wants to find objects of power. He thinks you know where they are—and

I *know* you have what he's looking for."

Endre, taken aback, said, "Gergo?"

"He told me." Kelyn glared at him, and then glared at Thainn. "Both of you, listen—Petissanji wants power, and he's going to keep killing witches in looking for it until there aren't any witches left to kill. You"—she pointed to Thainn—"care because you don't want him to get that power, and because you can't let him get away with fooling Thainn the Wolverine into working for a witch. You"—her finger swung to Endre—"care because so many of your people are witches, and even your famous curses aren't keeping Petissanji from going after you. And because *you* don't want Petissanji taking that which you watch over, either. You—" Thainn again, "know how to fight, and you have the men to do it with. And *you* . . . you know more about what Petissanji wants, and how to keep it from him. You're the clever ones, who can help us think our way out of this, and can provide magic to back up the fighters."

Thainn and Endre stared at one another in bemused silence.

"Now," Kelyn said. "Do you think we can get out of here, before we have to deal with more than four frightened soldiers?"

Thainn cleared his throat. "I think I'd like to talk to . . . *Gerko*."

"Gergo," said Endre. "I'll take you to him. But if you intend us harm—"

"Then he'll have to deal with me." Kelyn treated them both to a final, narrow-eyed gaze, weighing the extent of their intention to cooperate. It would do, she decided. It would at least get them as far as the next step. "Which way, Endre?"

Endre pointed vaguely west, and Kelyn struck out without giving him time to offer anything more specific. First, they'd get away from here. Then they'd figure out exactly where they were going. Besides, she was ready to leave both of them behind, and she nearly did; they scrambled to catch up, and ended up walking in her tracks.

"So," Thainn murmured, in what he probably thought was a discreet voice. "Tell me just how well you know my daughter?"

"Your *daughter*?" Endre blurted, not discreetly at all.

Kelyn wanted to hide her face in her hands. She kept walking.

Chapter 13

As they passed the perimeter of the warehouses and Abendar's town faded abruptly into nothing, Endre took the lead, trailing the horse he'd had picketed by an outer warehouse. They walked in silence, and the beaten earth turned back into the weedy grasses that composed most of Atlia, though they occasionally walked the edge of someone's damp, plowed field. Kelyn by then had removed her boots—*Rema bless!*—and fallen into step beside Thainn. So it was she who noticed when he eventually slackened his pace, although it was too dark to read his expression and make any guess about the reason. Endre walked on ahead, not realizing it when Kelyn, too, slowed; the swish of their progress through the grasses obscured the other audible details of the night. "What?" she asked, careful not to look away from where she was putting her feet. She'd already tripped—literally—onto evidence that her curse had once again returned.

"Just . . . thinking," Thainn muttered.

Is it so difficult it slows you? Kelyn stopped the

words just in time, wondering what had become of her tongue since she'd met this man. She never spoke to her mother so!

Of course, neither had Lytha spoken to *her* as Thainn was wont.

And nor had he made any further effort to explain. "What troubles you?"

"Did I say I was troubled?" Thainn responded, sounding distinctly so.

"I can track a nightfox through the Adellian Peaks. I've hunted *sorba* bats at night. I'm the one who walked into a strange fortress—never having been inside a fortress at all—and found Petissanji's room. Do you really think you need to *say* that you're troubled?"

Thainn made a disgruntled noise, but didn't deny his frame of mind a second time. After a moment, he shifted his sword harness—she'd discovered that he did so when discomfitted—and admitted, "I think there may be a problem."

He said nothing further; Kelyn tripped over a dip in the ground, regained her equilibrium, and sighed. "You're going to make me ask."

"I'd have spoken if I was sure."

"Speak anyway."

"Pushy," he grunted.

"Yes. Who do you suppose I get it from, my mother or my father?"

She could have sworn she saw a quick grin; it was still in his voice when he said, "I liked that about her."

It took a moment before she fully understood, turning to him with astonishment, quite certain she should find some way to take offense on her mother's part. But he forestalled her with words, the ones she'd been asking for in the first place. "If we're going where I think we're going, no one's going to be happy.

There's a spring about half a day's walk from town. It's where my men are to wait for me if we run into trouble. If it's where your Trader's people are camped . . . Well. How do *you* think they'll be getting along?"

"Were your men in the fortress when we fought the soldiers?"

"Not many of them. Most of them were out trailing witches. They'll hear about it before they return."

He spoke with such confidence that Kelyn could not help but question him. "How do you know?"

He glanced over at her. "Maybe you can track nightfoxes, but I'm the one who's been living in the outer lands these many years. I know because I make sure it is so. Because I know better than ever to put my fate completely in the hands of those I work for. Or in anyone's hands, for that matter."

Kelyn took those words in with some surprise. "Not even . . . not even your friends?"

He laughed outright. "Friends! Friends are a luxury. Sometimes a weakness. Listen to this well, Keturan girl, if you want to survive out here—rely only on yourself. A friend might try, but they might also fail. If you depend on them, then you fail, too."

Kelyn said nothing, thinking back to the time she had saved Mungo's life as he hung from the cliff, and the time Sigre had saved her own. The times they had relied on one another to be where they were expected in a hunt, when the prey was wary and wild. Keturan trust. For the right people . . . give it, or lose your life. "How old were you," she asked, "when you left Ketura?" She thought perhaps he had done so too young.

But Endre, hearing Thainn's laughter behind him, had stopped to let them catch up, and now he turned to them. "What's wrong?"

In the darkness, Thainn's foot landed casually close to Kelyn's, and she closed her jaw on the words in her mouth. Endre, she realized, had his horse. He could well ride off and leave them, and she knew from her own experience that he would ride in to protect his people without thinking about whether he was actually making things worse. "Nothing," she said. "I stubbed my toe. It's fine."

Endre looked between the two of them, and she didn't like his expression much. Suddenly, somehow, it looked like he had suddenly paired her with Thainn, turning her into more of an outsider than she'd already been to the Traders. To him. But he said nothing of it. Only, "It's not much further," as he turned away and moved off again.

Indeed, within moments, Kelyn got wind of campfire smoke, and of some of the spices she had come to associate with the Traders. They'd had a big meal, then—which was good, it meant they felt fairly secure. Maybe Thainn's men hadn't arrived yet, after all.

"Who's that?" Endre said, stopping short as smudges of low flame became visible against the ground.

Or maybe they had. Coming up beside him, Kelyn spotted what he'd seen, the campfire that sat way off to the side. Just one. Not many men, then.

"I'll see to it," Thainn said. He touched Kelyn's arm, waiting for her to look at him, waiting to see that she would comply. "Go to the main campfire, the big one in the center. I'll come to you."

She didn't shake off his touch, as was her first impulse. In this, his was the best way. She merely lifted her head a trifle in acknowledgment, and watched him stride off.

"Does he command you now?" Endre said, anger in his voice.

Kelyn thought it was more from the fact that Endre himself had not been consulted than anything to do with her, and kept her reply mild. "No," she said. "I make up my own mind, as I always have."

He hesitated, his hand on his horse's reins, and she didn't give him any more time to consider following Thainn; she headed for the main campfire. Not that they were likely to find anyone awake—even at the thought, she stumbled over nothing. Endre put a steadying hand on her arm.

"I'm tired," she admitted, as though it had been a question. "Any day with magic beasts in it is enough to demand sleep at the end of it, and this day ended long ago." The nap in the barn seemed far too short, and far too long ago, with too little food along the way.

"Did it?" Endre said. "Have magic beasts in it?"

Kelyn yawned as they approached the fire, finding one man sitting guard at the outer edges of its light. "Only one."

"Only one," Endre repeated, sounding bemused. "I'm not sure I'll ever understand you, Kelyn of Ketura."

Kelyn dropped her satchel by the fire and glanced at him as she followed it down, crossing her ankles and folding into a cross-legged position. "Is that understanding necessary?" she asked, hearing the wistful tone in her own voice and hating that it was there.

He looked at her as though the question had never occurred to him—and now that it had, the answer surprised him. "Perhaps not. But trust, I think . . . trust is another matter."

Not to hear Thainn talk about it. Kelyn wondered how long he'd be with his men, and if she had time to grab even a little sleep before he came back.

"Those are things to talk about later," Endre said, looking down at her with a rueful little smile. "For now . . . sleep. I have to put my horse out." When she looked up, alarmed, his smile grew. "I promise

I won't go make trouble with the Wolverine. Go to sleep."

Just at the moment, Kelyn decided she didn't care if he intended to cause trouble or not. She would let herself sleep through it.

❖ ❖ ❖

She heard the camp coming to life around her before daylight hit her eyelids, and she tuned it out. Best to rest all she could, for there was no telling when she'd get another chance. But then someone came close, too close to be doing anything but approaching her.

"Leave her." Endre, also behind her, spoke quietly but with intent. "She should sleep."

"Do you speak for her?"

"I speak as anyone would—anyone who cares. I would have thought her father among those—but then again, you're the one who took her back into the fortress to face the magic beast, aren't you?"

"She took me," Thainn said. He snorted. "She is not one of your Trader women. She is Keturan. She is . . ." he hesitated, and finished it. "She is of the best of us; she proved that yesterday."

Endre didn't say anything, though he fidgeted a little in the grass, and Kelyn, coming more awake, realized he was between Thainn and herself. Standing his ground. She ought to let them know she was awake. She should, but . . .

"Don't tell her so," Endre said. "She doesn't take to pretty words." Kelyn heard the grimace in his voice.

Thainn laughed, a low sound. "So I have discovered."

"And what are Keturans like toward one another, that she would be so convinced of her ugliness? That a man wouldn't want her?"

"That last," Thainn said, an edge to it, "is not a question to ask her father."

"If you are her father, it is newly so."

Another silence; Kelyn was wide awake, now, knowing she should speak up—and far too interested in the outcome of this conversation to do so. She heard movement, and when Thainn spoke again, his voice came from lower; he had crouched. *Looking at her.* "Her mother was beautiful," he said, thoughtful, his voice full of remembering, "but she laughed when I told her. She said she hadn't grown up so. And I . . . I was long coming to my full growth, and until then, I was an awkward thing. This daughter of ours may have experienced the same."

"And she has the curse," Endre said, suddenly understanding.

"The curse?"

Riveted by their words, all but holding her breath, Kelyn still knew the moment had come to open her eyes, to put a stop to this talk—before Thainn realized this daughter of his *was* cursed. At least until she understood how it now came and went. She stretched, deliberate at first, until her body got caught up in it and took over, stretching hugely against the aches of the previous day's fighting. Endre made a strangled noise, something between a groan and a sigh. Kelyn froze; her eyes flew open to question him.

He looked down at her, apparently unable to look anywhere else—until Thainn stood and nudged him hard enough to throw him off balance, and then nudged Kelyn to prod her into moving again; she relaxed into a normal posture. "That's better," he said dryly. "Kinder."

Kelyn frowned up at him, feeling like she ought to say something sharp to him but unable to come up with anything. She sat, taking in the quietly moving Traders, seeing unfamiliar faces and realizing that Gergo's people had indeed had friends here—

friends they'd been relying on to help them, somehow, in freeing their witches.

Witches of whom she now saw no sign. In the bright daylight, she took in the wagons of the camp, more numerous than she remembered. They were tucked in at the edge of a thick copse of trees, backed by an unusually abrupt rise of ground. The spring, marked by a gap in the trees, trickled away from the bottom edge of the hill, and women gathered around it, dipping water. Too few of them. "Where," she said to Endre, who seemed to have recovered his composure, "are the rest of you?"

Endre's gaze flew to Thainn and then returned to Kelyn. "I don't know," he said, an obvious lie.

"I've got bigger things to worry about than reclaiming escaped prisoners," Thainn growled.

"You're not the only one here," Endre said, not acknowledging any belief in the statement. He looked out past the camp, and Kelyn climbed to her feet, remembering the solo campfire apart from the Trader gathering. She saw two men hunched together, apparently in some argument—their gestures were apparent even from here.

"They don't look happy," she observed, as Gergo left the green-painted healer's wagon that had been Lenci's, looked around the camp, and headed toward them.

"They don't have to *be* happy," Thainn said. "They just have to do what they're told."

"And will they?" Gergo said, joining the conversation from some distance away.

Thainn turned to eye the older man. "Yes," he said flatly. "Do you speak for these people?"

"I am Gergo."

"Ger*go*," Endre repeated with careful pronunciation, earning a strange look from the man in question.

There was a brief, wicked gleam in Thainn's eye—*don't say it*, Kelyn thought—but it faded and the Wolverine turned to business. "Kelyn tells me that we can help one another."

Gergo evinced faint surprise; clearly he knew nothing of this. Endre cleared his throat and said, "Anci wouldn't let me speak to him last night. She said he—"

"He's fine," Gergo finished. "Anci is too protective; it is a daughter's role." He looked up at Thainn, while Kelyn gave him a narrow-eyed examination. *Anci's father*. She hadn't known that. And he *did* look tired, even a little grey. *Endre hadn't talked to him yet*.

Endre caught her eye, shook his head. "I'll talk to you later," he told Gergo. "When you're through here."

Plain enough. Endre wanted to tell Gergo about Lenci himself. She only hoped Thainn wouldn't say anything about it.

"Which may be very soon," Gergo said. "As I have no need to help those who have been persecuting us."

"You may decide differently," Thainn said, so offhandedly confident that even Kelyn bristled. Why, last night it had been she who had had to convince him to consider working with the Traders! She opened her mouth, about to tell him so, when his big hand clamped down on the back of her neck, looking for all the world like a companionable gesture; only she knew how hard he squeezed. But when he spoke again, he'd moderated his tone to something less commanding. "Petissanji drives this hunt for witches, Gergo. He does it for his own ends, to increase his powers. Powers I knew nothing about. He's got to be stopped."

"You're Abendar's man," Gergo said, giving a little shrug. "Tell him. I don't see why you need us. I don't see why we should help you. Your very presence here is an offense to us."

Kelyn stepped away from Thainn, forcing him to loosen his grip or be dragged along—but she said nothing, aside from the brief glare she turned on him. Gergo was hardly any more pleased with her, on general principles, than with Thainn. Let the Wolverine be the one to struggle with his words, looking for just the right ones to barter with this expert.

"Petissanji has turned Abendar's men against me. He—" and Thainn made a face at the very thought of such a thing— "he convinced them that Kelyn was the witch, that I have been bespelled by her. By now he will have Abendar believing it, as well. My men and I are no more safe in that fortress than are your witches."

"Then you do have a problem."

"As do you! Do you think Petissanji will give up his hunt because he's lost his best hunter? Do you think I'm the only warrior with a crew of men for hire?"

Gergo waved off Thainn's emphatic words, and glanced down, searching the area. Endre hastened to move a hammock seat into place behind him, and Gergo sank down. "You seem to be the one with a reputation for speaking out against witches."

"And which do you think will be more of a problem for you—working with me to stop the hunts, or hiding your people from whatever black-hearted crew Petissanji arranges to supplement Atelic's men this time?"

"Gergo," Kelyn said, "I've seen this man—twice now. I've seen the objects he's gathered. I *used* one of them—a knife, he called it a Spellcutter—"

Gergo's eyebrows rose. "Ah," he said. "Silogan magic. That god was ever in the mood to trump the others' magic."

"You see?" Kelyn said. "You *know* these things. I

don't . . . Thainn doesn't. We need your help. We need you to work with us."

Gergo snorted. "You expect me to trust you? You—you mean no harm, but you cause it all the same. And him—he *means* the harm he causes!"

"Gergo," Endre said, his voice low—and hesitant, as if he himself wasn't quite sure of his words. "She is not entirely to blame. She didn't understand about magic, and we knew that . . . but none of us told her enough so she could. We just expected her to abide by your words."

"As she should have—she was our guest!"

"No," Kelyn said. "I traveled with you. I did not give myself up to you."

"Keturan words." Gergo scowled his disdain.

"Atlia's pits!" Kelyn scowled back at him, hands gripping the knife hilts on both hips. "You expect else from a Keturan? Are you daft enough to think that all in this world should conform to Trader ways?"

"In my camp," he said, resolute.

"Even as you keep those ways to yourself?" She felt her temper rising; she knew it did this conversation no good. Her knuckles whitened around the knife hilts. She unwrapped her hands, let them fall to her sides, found that she needed to fill them, and clenched them around nothing.

"Kelyn . . ." Endre said, reaching for her. She hissed at him, slapped his hand away.

"You see?" Gergo said, looking at Thainn; he shrugged again. "We cannot work together. I can never trust you."

Thainn grinned, a wicked expression; the gleam was back. "And I can never trust a people full of witches. But we don't have to trust, Gerko—at least not in one another. We just have to *know* one another's nature, and that, we do. I cannot allow Petissanji to go unchallenged. You cannot allow the hunts to continue."

"Did you call me—"

"I had something stuck in my throat."

Kelyn wanted to hit him. She thought perhaps she would. But a flicker of movement in the distance, obscured by the random blots of trees, caught her eye; her head went up. Thainn saw the look, and responded to it as if he'd known her all her life; he twisted around to scan the uneven horizon. Within moments, his men had risen from their fireside to stand alert and waiting; the Traders began to sort themselves out, their conversation growing louder and more clipped, their voices full of tension. Another man came to stand next to Gergo, a slightly younger man. "Yerde," Gergo said when Thainn and Kelyn glanced at him. "He is head of those we camp with." And he and Yerde exchanged a few murmured words in their own language, revealing nothing other than their concern.

Soon enough, the movement resolved into a group of men, moving on foot and none too swiftly. One of Thainn's men was the first to respond to them; he raised an arm high in greeting, and at that, Thainn himself relaxed. "I've been expecting more men," he told Gergo. "They are no danger to you."

Gergo's light brown eyes glittered with disagreement, but he held his tongue, and silenced Yerde when the other man drew breath to speak. He made no attempt to stop the camp from preparing for trouble, and by the time the group arrived, the men were arranged behind Gergo and Yerde in a semicircle of defiance.

Ketura's balls. They were more than just Thainn's men. Among the warriors—some of whom Kelyn recognized, Hann included—was a huddle of women and one older man, all exhausted, dirt-streaked, and looking ready to collapse. They were not, she noted, bruised or injured; nor did they look like Traders—

they were Atlian, lighter of hair and skin, taller of body.

But they were, no doubt, witches. Tied, captured, and run into the ground with their captors' own flight.

Hann shook his head. "I wasn't sure I'd find you here, not after what I heard in Abendar's town." He jerked his chin in Kelyn's direction. "Did she witch you, then? Or did she kill a beast to save you? Which is it?"

Thainn hesitated, and then said with some reluctance, "She killed the beast. But I was in no danger."

Kelyn's sputter of a reaction drew a grin from Hann. But his expression darkened—easy for a face such as his, with the scar that ran from his nose and pulled down the corner of his mouth, and drooping eyes above that—as he looked at the Traders arrayed behind Gergo. "What's this, then?"

Thainn looked back at them, and drew a deep breath. "Release the witches, Hann. We have more important matters to attend."

"Release—!" Hann said, apparently unable to get any more of the protest out.

"Release them," Thainn confirmed. "We have no one to give them to, in any event. And we'll be working with the Traders, now . . ." he glanced back at Gergo again, "won't we."

"Working with—!"

"He has trouble with words when he's confounded, doesn't he?" Kelyn said, an aside in the Keturan tongue, and one which drew a quick twitch of her father's mouth. But Thainn looked again at Gergo, and Kelyn understood, then—the fate of these witches depended on Gergo's next words.

Gergo understood it too, and liked it not.

Missing the byplay completely, Hann demanded, "What'd she say?"

"Later, Hann," Thainn said, short words which

subdued his second into resentful silence. Behind Gergo, the Trader men moved forward, bunched more tightly together. They, too, understood the import of Thainn's question to their leader, and liked it no better. Kelyn couldn't blame them, though she thought them foolish, with their unspoken willingness to take on the warriors.

She stepped between Thainn and Gergo, and turned her palms, still at her side, up in subtle supplication. "Please," she said. "There is much to gain if you do, and so much to lose if you don't."

Gergo stared at her, his expression unforgiving. Until, as Thainn shifted at her back, as his men passed a mutter back and forth, he gave the slightest of nods and said to her, "You are making much better use of words."

Kelyn let out a sigh of relief, and Thainn nodded at his men. "Release them."

Hann shook his head, clearly of the mind that his commander was making a mistake, but knowing better than to argue about it. He pulled the pins on the prisoners' wrist shackles, letting one of the others follow behind to collect the shackles. The witches—more than one hand's worth, less than two—hesitated, looking to each other for guidance and finding none.

"Come with us," Yerde said. "You may eat and rest, and when you're ready, leave for your homes."

With wary glances at Thainn's men, the Atlian witches eased toward the Traders, gaining assurance with each step they took. One of the Traders led them away, while Hann came to Thainn and muttered, "Abendar's pet witch left us at the town, when we decided to come here first." He looked regretfully after the ex-prisoners. "They would have gained us good coin from Abendar once he gets over whatever snit he's in."

"He's not going to get over his snit until we do

something to see that he does," Thainn said. "Get the others. We need to talk." He glanced at Gergo and Yerde. "All of us."

Hann shook his head. "I hope you know what you're doing." Then he looked over at Kelyn, taking his gaze up and down her length, and grinning. "Dunno if she's your daughter or not, but you might as well take her on as one. Killed a sorcerous beast, did she?"

"She was lucky," Thainn growled. "Get the others, before I find something unpleasant that needs doing."

"*You*," Kelyn muttered, "were lucky."

Hann grinned at her again, and gave a little dip of his head that only made Thainn's expression grow fiercer. Then he was off, trotting across the grasses to wave the other men in, meeting them halfway.

"There is more," Gergo said.

Thainn looked at him as if he'd forgotten the older man's presence. "More to what?"

"More to our working together. As long as we're here together, you will help defend my people from any threat Abendar brings. Including our witches."

"Defend—?"

"Now you sound like your man. Yes, defend them. It is their expertise you need, not mine. In order to help, they will have to reveal themselves. I will not have them do so until I have your word that you will help protect them from any dangers this brings upon them."

"Yes," Kelyn said, knowing firsthand that the Traders would need help in any such situation. Hann, settling in behind Thainn with the other two men, dug his elbow into the ribs of one of them, nodding at her.

"No!" Thainn said, earning Gergo's dark look and giving Kelyn an exasperated look just as quick. "I meant only that the decision is not hers to make!"

Kelyn glanced at Hann, and drew confidence from the reemergence of his grin; he gave her the slightest of nods. "You owe me that one," she said. "In return for the beast—among other things." And she smiled back at Hann.

Thainn twisted to see who she responded to, but Hann's smile was gone, his face carefully sober; he shrugged with much innocence. Behind him, the other men—a good solid number, they were, twice as large as the group of witches they'd brought in—nodded in agreement. "She got the beast, Thainn," said one of them, and another added, "She's got the right of it, too. You want 'em to work with us, then do it. Otherwise, let's go."

Startlement flashed across Thainn's features, but he quickly put it aside; she saw him struggle for and find a casual mien to show them all—although he apparently couldn't help the quick, hard look he gave Kelyn. "I will abide by your terms. Now. Fetch your witches. I have some ideas, and I want to act on them quickly if your people say the witchery of it can be done."

Gergo lifted a hand without looking at the men behind him, and they quickly dispersed. All but Endre, who lingered somewhere between Gergo and Kelyn, looking, she thought, like a hovering bird trying to choose a branch to land on. She gave him a cool look; she was not his branch. Maybe he truly *did* find her appealing, despite her differences from the Trader women—tall where they were short, lean and hard-muscled where they were round and soft—and to hear Thainn talk, maybe somehow she actually *was*. And maybe he *was* kind to her eyes, with his agreeable features, and the way he made her feel when she saw him ahorse, so able to anticipate the animal's needs, to flow with its movement.

No matter. Men were cockers, all of them. Give

them a chance to prove it, and they would. As they had. Her father, holding the witches' safety over Gergo's head. Gergo, demanding that the world conform to his unstated standards. And Endre, unable to decide if she annoyed him or attracted him, if he blamed her or understood her. He definitely didn't seem to trust her.

Cockers.

❖ ❖ ❖

The witches mingled with the other Traders, suddenly where they had not been a moment before. Kelyn looked around the area in disbelief, knowing they had not been in the wagons, and not believing the trees on the hill could provide enough cover for more than one of them, never mind this number—all of those from Gergo's camp who had escaped the fortress, and a number of unfamiliar faces that must belong to Yerde's people.

Endre had finally left off his hovering, and taken advantage of the lull to crouch beside Gergo. While Thainn conferred with his men, the witches came out of hiding, Yerde gathered the Trader men to the side and issued rapid instructions, and Kelyn stood alone—watching and feeling left out of it all—Endre spoke quietly wih the older man.

His face full of reluctance, he said a few simple words in their language, glancing once at Kelyn. Gergo spoke sharply in return, and Endre shook his head, sad but firm. He put a hand on the older man's knee, while Gergo seemed to struggle for breath, his eyes brightening with tears that eventually worked their way into the seamed skin around his eyes. Endre asked a gentle question; Gergo shook his head.

At that, Kelyn turned away, not wanting to see more. If she'd been faster in the cells, or if she'd ignored Lenci, and grabbed the old woman's arm, forced her to come along . . . there hadn't been any more fighting, had there? Lenci could have hidden in that antechamber just as easily as Kelyn had. And it had been Lenci who'd told her to go down—that there was a way out. Going down had saved Kelyn's life, even if Lenci had been wrong—there'd been no way—

No. *Lenci was right*. There'd been a way out in Petissanji's room.

Kelyn clenched her fists and hid them under her crossed arms, mired in guilt—guilt, and anger, and resentment. She'd caused Lenci's death, as sure as if she'd put the old woman to her knife. *But if Endre hadn't* . . . Hadn't been so willing to shut her out, to keep the Traders' plans from her, once they'd been captured. *And if Gergo hadn't* . . . If only he'd told her *more* about the needle, about how using it could endanger them all, instead of assuming her blind obedience to someone she didn't even know. *If he'd been worth such faith, he'd have known no Keturan would ever behave so.*

"Kelyn." Endre moved to her side, sounding tired.

Kelyn struck out blindly at him, shoving him away—and missing. She didn't make another attempt. "I *tried*," she said, expecting it to come out as bold and stark as all her words, and surprised when her strained voice barely topped a whisper.

"I know," he said.

"If only someone had *told* me—you what?"

"I know."

She blinked at him. There was no blame on his face, no reproach, just the weariness she'd heard in his voice. "We *all* tried," he said. "We just got it wrong."

And still, she couldn't find anything to say. All men were cockers, she knew it. But apparently, sometimes they had their moments. Her hands fell to her sides, no longer clenched. She looked over her shoulder, to where Gergo sat by himself, blankly staring through the people around him. "Lenci was important to him."

"She was important to all of us," Endre said. "But she was Gergo's wife."

She shot a startled glance at him, and then back at Gergo. "But—"

"They didn't act it. Not around outsiders, no—he our leader, and she the healer. But think on it, Kelyn. Who knew him better than she?"

"No one," Kelyn said. "But she knew so much about everyone . . . I just thought . . ."

He nodded. "As do most others." He took a deep breath, and directed her glance at Thainn, who had noted Gergo's reaction, and moved his men back a little more, waiting for the man to recover, to talk to him. "Those two will never work together without help."

No. Probably not. And then she heard the undertone in his voice, the one that said there were other words waiting. "What are you saying?" But looking into his face, at the way he kept his eyes fixed on her, Kelyn thought she knew.

"That we must be there, to make this work. That *we* are the ones who come the closest to understanding one another, and have the most chance of catching the things that aren't said when they need to be. And . . ." he said, looking at the ground, at Gergo, at the sky . . . and finally at her again, "the better we understand each other, the better for all of us." He held out his hand.

"That is not a reason," Kelyn whispered, understanding—if nothing else—what he was *really* saying.

"No," Endre said. "We have plenty of those, don't you think? From the first time you danced . . . from the way you held me on the horse, when you were frightened and wouldn't admit it—"

"I wasn't," Kelyn said, but she grinned, a small and shy expression.

"You were," he said, but grinned back at her. "And don't interrupt. I'm telling you my reasons. I'm telling you what you do to me."

She thought of the way he'd felt beneath her, when she'd tackled him at the warehouses—the moment she'd realized he hadn't first approached her from pity, or because Gergo had instructed him to. She thought of how she'd felt that first night, when she'd liked his kiss, oh yes—and had been too proud to allow herself to act on it. "I have the best reason of all," she said, and let her grin go wicked; he raised an eyebrow, waiting for it. "Because I *want* to."

Some tension in him seemed to flow away—and at the same time, he became more intent, more focused on her. He held out his hand again. She took it. "Let them talk," he said. "Walk with me?"

This time, she knew what it meant. Her hand felt big in his, and she knew it was dirty. As was her face, and she'd lost most of the trinkets the Trader women had put in her hair; one of her front braids was half unraveled. She stood there, as tall and gawky-feeling as ever, two knife belts crossed at her hips, the slaver's vest full of weapons and trinkets, his whip at her side. She was all that she'd ever been, that she'd ever thought she'd been, in Ketura. She knew she'd probably trip before he took her . . . wherever. But that was all right, because . . . for once, she believed it—that's what he wanted. Her. Except . . . she glanced around the area—the rolling, grassy area that offered little privacy, the hill behind them with its thin copse of trees. He read her gaze, squeezed her hand. "Trust me."

Yes, she thought. This was a good place to start.

Chapter 14

"Oh," Kelyn said. "*Oh.*" She rolled to her back on the layers of blankets and stared at the low cave ceiling. The uneven rock rippled and flowed in the light of the small oil lamp, shadows flickering with the same rapid tumble as her heart. "Oh!" So *that's* what it was all about. She looked over at Endre, who lay next to her in a similar state of disarray, his clothes half removed, his hair sticking up, his eyes slightly glazed, his chest rapidly rising and falling as he tried to catch his breath.

"Oh," he said, confirming her unarticulated thought with his own.

"Let's do that again."

Kelyn was unprepared for his immediate dismay, his clear reluctance. She narrowed her eyes at him. He took it for the warning it was and said, "It—you don't understand—a man just can't—"

She hitched up on her elbow and looked down at him. "Oh," she said, and sighed in disappointment, flopping back down on the blankets. "Well, how long, then?"

He snorted in disbelief, but when she looked at him, he was grinning; he shook his head. "When I know *you're* waiting . . . maybe not all that long."

Kelyn grinned back at him, and let it grow wicked. She considered a spot on his ribs she'd discovered to be just shy of ticklish, and eyed it with intent. But a faint echo of sound from without their cave chamber made her stiffen, and though Endre clearly didn't hear it, he noted her reaction with alarm. "Gergo would never!" he said, and stopped, because another, louder echo of a voice made it clear that Gergo *had*.

Kelyn sat straight up, smacked her forehead on the ceiling, and jerked back again. "Atlia's arse!" she muttered, biting down on the volume of her curse as she realized she had no idea how well their voices would carry out to those in the larger cavern.

This area was tucked far back in the caves Endre had led her to, caves whose entrance had been so disguised by Trader glamor that she could have walked right by the entrance and never spotted it. He'd led her past the cots and bedding, past the provisions, past the portions of the cave that the witches had so clearly been using for shelter and across the trickling streams that snaked through the dripping caverns. Snagging the blankets and lighting the lamp from one of the several permanent standing lamps burning near the entrance, he'd taken her to this spot—though he'd made several wrong turns along the way—and then he'd taken—

Or maybe she'd been the one—

Or maybe it had been the two of them.

"Will they come back this far?" she whispered, rubbing her forehead.

"I don't know," he told her, clearly worried, pawing in the blankets for the loin covering he'd worn under his trousers. "I was the one who thought they wouldn't come here at all!"

Kelyn joined in the search, throwing the blanket away to hunt for her own brief undergarment, throwing off her vest to tug the shirt on—and how had she ended up with the vest *on* and the shirt *off*?—trying not to hit her head again, all while the voices grew louder. She froze with the shirt half on, her arms caught in the sleeves and her face half hidden in the neck opening. "This is ridiculous," she said. "I'm not ashamed of this. I want to do it again!"

"Kelyn," he said, his eyes fixated on her exposed chest and going glazed again, "Have a heart. Put it on!"

Kelyn rolled her eyes and jerked the shirt on. "Are you?"

"No, of course not," he said, doing an interesting wiggle to get his pants over his hips while he lay on the ground, and tightening the laces with fumbling fingers. "I've used the no-get, that's all Gergo cares about." The no-get. And where had it gone, that charmed bit of leather—? Endre stopped her search for it with his worried expression. "But Thainn—you—he's—"

"Gone all my life without having a say, and he's not about to get one now." She tried to convince them both with her certainty.

They looked at one another an instant, and turned back to dressing themselves with renewed vigor, breathless, bumping into one another, and finally grabbing the lamp to scoot from the lovers' nook and to their feet. The light of multiple lamps approached from the direction of the cave entrance, making shadows shimmy wildly over the walls. A few frantic, last-minute adjustments to each other's clothing, and they were no longer alone.

Thainn stopped short at the sight of them, holding his lamp a little higher in his disbelief. Next to him was Gergo, and then Yerde, and Anci hung close to their heels, along with a small contingent of other witches. Each and every one of them had a lamp, and each and every one of them lifted it to stare at the pair.

Endre offered them a weak smile. Kelyn, standing a little behind him in the vastly increased light, saw something stuck to his heel, and realized with a little shock of dismay that it was the leaf-thin square of leather that Endre had put between them—muttering, between his gasps and panting, something about *the rules*. Just the same as that she'd found in one of the vest pockets, she realized suddenly, and knew that if *she* recognized it, so would everyone else.

Casually, so casually, she moved up behind Endre and put her own bare foot over the exposed leather.

"We wondered where you were," Thainn said, the disbelief still on his face—though it was fast turning into a narrow-eyed expression aimed more at Endre than at Kelyn. And as she feared, Gergo was giving her an increasingly suspicious eye.

"*I* wondered where the witches had been hidden," she said. "Endre said caves and I didn't believe him."

"She doubted my word," Endre said, working up a little indignance. "So I showed her."

"Yes," Kelyn said, her thoughts irretrievably drawn back to what he'd *really* shown her. "I thought we could use this place in dealing with Petissanji. It's unexpected, and anything unexpected will give us an advantage, if we can figure out *how*. . . ."

"I thought the same, once Gergo told me of the caves," Thainn said, slowly enough that Kelyn knew they hadn't quite convinced him.

But he was distracted, and that was a start.

"Gergo told you of the caves?" Endre said, startled enough to take a step forward, truly engaging himself in the conversation. Kelyn gathered the rest of the square with her toes and planted her foot firmly on top of it.

"I guessed their existence," Thainn said dryly. "Not even Trader witches can make themselves invisible. They had to be somewhere."

"In the *front* of the caves," Gergo said, giving Endre a pointed look.

Ketura's balls, he wasn't going to let it go.

But Endre's reaction made her think she'd assumed wrong; truly startled, he shook his head once, short and strong. "I showed her nothing," he said, and fell into the Trader tongue—quick emphatic words, spoken in protest. Gergo responded in much the same vein, while the witches crowded in, looking like they wanted to get in a word or two of their own.

"Don't you think that's rude?" Kelyn asked Thainn, quite deliberately using their native language.

He looked almost as startled as Endre had, to be included in her wry humor. "Very," he said. "Now let's talk about what you're *really* doing back here."

"Let's not," she said, and smiled sweetly. "It's none of your damned business, and I'm going to do it again as soon as I get the chance."

"Watch yourself, Keturan girl. Traders won't abide their blood to be split. They'll curse you up one side of the mountain and down the other."

"Lucky for me Remans don't feel the same way."

"This isn't a jest, girl! Do you think those rumors of Trader curses spring from nowhere?"

By now Gergo and Endre had fallen silent, and stood watching father and daughter. Kelyn let her ready retort trail away, and irritably regarded the two, who seemed to be waiting for some kind of explanation. "We were just entertaining ourselves while we were left out of *your* conversation," she said. Endre winced.

Anci stepped into her mother's role, and took charge by changing the subject entirely. She looked at Kelyn and said with interest, "Your curse feels entirely different, Kelyn. What have you done?"

Kelyn groaned as Thainn's eyebrows went up. "Your *curse*? What have you been up to, Keturan girl?" He smirked at her, an insufferable expression on a face that had never had the chance to learn when daughters need kindness or encouragement, but had spent its existence in the rough company of men, walking away from women when they became inconvenient. "Maybe you were wrong, Keturan girl. Maybe the Remans *do* feel as the Traders do."

"Remans do not deal in curses," Anci said calmly, her words carrying no reflection of the glare she shot at him. "Is it true? Is he your father?"

"He sired me," Kelyn said darkly, keeping the sudden pounding of her heart to herself. *What if he was* right? But surely her mother . . . or the loving family she had spoken of—surely she wouldn't . . . her own *daughter* . . . "I begin to understand it is not the same thing."

"We don't have time for this," Thainn said, having turned sullen at Anci's judgment.

"No," Gergo said. "On this, we agree. Let me tell you, children"—and Kelyn was sure she didn't imagine his slight emphasis on that word—"what we spoke of after you wandered away."

Yerde gave a heartfelt, "*Please*," and for a moment endured the scowls they'd been turning on one another. But Gergo cleared his throat and found a lump of stone to sit on, waiting for their proper attention before continuing.

"It is evident from our own information that Abendar has been completely taken in by this Petissanji. That is why," and he directed this remark at Kelyn, "we were unable to help our witches by the means we intended. Until recently, he has been reasonable, and he liked the rare wares Yerde's extensive wanderings brought him—for these reasons, we thought we could reach out to him."

Kelyn nodded, finding herself unexpectedly flattered that he bothered to explain at all.

"Things have changed since the last time we were here," Yerde said. "My people no longer dare to go to the fortress, and would not have any influence if they did."

Kelyn looked at Thainn. "Then it is as you have said. There is no chance to reach Abendar himself, and stop these hunts. Petissanji has convinced him of so much already . . ."

"There is no chance," Gergo said. "We must eliminate Petissanji himself."

Kelyn gave her lower lip a quick chew. "It's not easy to get to him, inside that fortress. He's got that room . . . and he's got spells already set up, like ambushes."

Thainn shook his head. "It would be foolishness to try. He'll be ready for us, now."

"Yes," Gergo said. He rubbed one hand inside the other, as though both were cold. He was not happy with their plan, whatever it was, Kelyn realized. And yet he had agreed to it, anyway. He must consider Petissanji a dire threat, indeed. "We need to draw Petissanji out. Out of that fortress. We will send him a message telling him that if he releases our people, we will reveal the location of the Horn."

"No!" Endre said, the protest startled from him. He looked over at the witches. "You cannot mean to let him do this!"

Gergo said sharply, "Show respect," and ceased the slow rubbing of his hands to pin a stare on Endre. "The Horn has been moved."

"It has?" Endre looked at the witches again; finally Anci gave a little nod. "It has? Then why were you so concerned about—"

"The safety of the Horn wasn't at issue. It was your decision to bring her to it."

Kelyn said in protest, "But he didn't!" and did it emphatically enough that she almost stepped away from the damp leather she so carefully hid. *I showed her nothing.* The Horn had been here, somewhere close.

"So I understand." Gergo looked as though he might say more, but a shout from the front of the cave stopped him.

"Yerde!" The voice was a young man's, and broke in the middle of the word. "Yerde!"

Yerde turned suddenly grimmer. "That's Orto," he told Gergo, though he was kind enough to keep it in the common tongue. "I had him stationed in town—only to return if there was trouble." He turned to shout, "I'm coming!" and then nodded at Gergo. "No point in making further plans until we've learned what's happened."

Gergo stood, waiting while the witches followed Yerde back toward the mouth of the cave; Thainn, caught behind them all, chafed visibly. Endre would have moved off right on Thainn's heels, but as he stepped forward, Kelyn caught the back of his pants, and held him long enough to scoop up the thin leather square. "Keep this," she told him, stuffing it into the voluminous pocket of his trousers and patting the pocket itself. "You'll need it again."

"Are you two coming?" Thainn said, not bothering to look back at them.

Kelyn and Endre exchanged a grin and caught up to the group. By the time they trailed into the main cavern—having traversed a narrow and twisting, damp-sided tunnel—Orto was well into babbling his report to Yerde. She hadn't missed anything, at least—the youth spoke in Trader, and quickly enough that even Endre frowned, trying to unravel the words.

After a moment, Yerde put a hand on Orto's shoulder, and the youth fell into uncertain silence, silence that had a kind of misery about it. The witches, too, looked grim; one of them broke into a sudden animal wail, and Anci quickly took her hand and gave her to another tearful woman, gently directing them both outside.

When she turned back to the group, Yerde addressed them all. "Orto has been watching the town for several days. This morning, Abendar brought all of the remaining Trader witches out into the market square and had them executed. Orto says that Petissanji was there; he looked like a man full of satisfaction."

"And Abendar?" Thainn growled. "He is not a man prone to such display, as I measured him."

Orto spoke with hesitation, first looking to Yerde, and clearly not at all certain about Thainn's presence—there, in the cave, of all places. "Abendar took no joy in it. I saw him arguing with Petissanji before it was done."

"Petissanji would not have killed them unless he had no more use for them," Thainn said. "I may not have seen him for a witch, but I read his nature clearly enough—he knows what he wants, and he does only those things that move him nearer to his goals. He is not full of empty gestures."

"Maybe he was trying to scare the Traders into revealing us, once he realized we were past the warehouses," Kelyn said.

Thainn shook his head, short and certain. "No. They were tools. If he was trying to get information, every living witch would have been another chance to obtain it."

"Then . . ." Endre said, looking to see if Gergo agreed, "then he's found what he was looking for."

Anci closed her eyes in dismay. "Gertzi," she said, covering her face briefly with her hand, then letting it fall away to face Gergo. "We have been concerned about her. The death curse is a matter of honor, and even so we are partnered in it. But she . . . she has shown weakness. And her partner fell to illness this last season." Her voice fell to a whisper. "We should have been more diligent in adding her to a partnership."

"She's dead, now," Orto said roughly. "He had her killed with the others. Abendar said they'd all proven too dangerous, that they'd insisted on using magic in the Belows, breaking the spell eyes—they created a beast that attacked Petissanji and his men. They'd abused his mercy, he said, and could not be allowed to threaten his people."

"I told you Petissanji would have time to make up the answers he needed," Kelyn said, and kicked at an upside-down rock icicle growing from the cavern floor, scowling both at Petissanji and the unexpected hardness of the rock.

"As it seems he did," Thainn murmured, but his mind was elsewhere, and Gergo did not fail to note it.

Yerde sighed, rubbing his hand over his face. "Our plans won't work anymore."

"They will." Kelyn put confidence into her voice. "You were going to lure him out here. Now he's going to come on his own, and to this same place—for this is where the Horn was, didn't you say? We just have to be ready faster."

Thainn came back from his thoughts and looked at Yerde; he struck Kelyn as like a great mountain cat, ready to leap. "Do you have anyone left in town?"

Yerde nodded. "I was planning to send Orto back."

"Good. And we need to set up scout runners. Best to use your people for that, some of your young men—they're lighter and faster than any of mine, except for Chenke, and I need him for other things."

"Scout runners," Yerde repeated, his flat tone making it clear no one would be setting up to do anything until he understood and approved it.

"To sight Petissanji when he leaves—one runner brings the news to another, who brings it to the next, until they reach this spot—and in that way we know when to expect Petissanji."

Gergo nodded. "It makes good sense, Yerde. And it will keep them safe."

Thainn gave an impatient nod. "Now—can Orto gain access to the fortress?"

Yerde's response held an incredulous note; he flipped his hands out in a parody of supplication. "I've already told you it's not safe for us there!"

Thainn grinned, but there was no humor to it. "That's not what I asked you."

Endre nudged Kelyn, nodding at Gergo; the older man's face had darkened; the witches behind him frowned, glancing among themselves. The alliance, she realized, teetered at the edge of a cliff. "Don't play commander with them," she said to Thainn, Keturan words. "This is *their* cave, and *their* people you're talking about."

"I thought you considered it rude to make such asides," he growled at her.

She ignored him, switching back to Atlian. "You have something in mind," she said. "Tell us what it is and we can all decide the best way to accomplish it."

From the look in Thainn's eye, she thought she would pay for this later. He stuck his thumbs in his harness and shifted it, glaring at her. But when he turned back to the others, he seemed resigned to playing it out as she'd suggested. "Even if we handle Petissanji, there is still Abendar to deal with. He thinks you cursed his warehouses . . . he thinks Trader witches conjured a beast in his Belows. Petissanji's death will do nothing but convince him you are an even bigger problem than he thought."

"We have not said Petissanji is to be killed." Gergo wrapped one hand in the other, and though his voice was firm, Kelyn could not help but think how much older he looked than the man who had first spoken to her in the Trader camp, offering her the services of one of his men.

"What do you propose to do, slap his wrist and ask him not to misuse his powers? You might as well ask a rock cat not to slaughter goats. Any witch that powerful is a danger to us all—even to your own witches. He has proven that."

"We can discuss his fate later," Endre said, his interruption somewhat more respectful than Kelyn's had been. "Your point is that no matter how we deal with him, Abendar will not believe that he has been the problem all along. He'll continue hunting the witches. From what Orto said about what happened in the market today, I think you must be right. Until now, Gergo, would you have said Abendar would order the slaughter of women? Yerde?"

Gergo and Yerde traded glances; the look on Gergo's face was answer enough, and Yerde shook his head. Yerde said to Thainn, "You have an idea, then?"

Nodding, Thainn let out an explosive breath, as if the effort of not simply stepping in and taking over was nearly beyond him. "I need to get a message to Abendar. If I tell him to meet me here at a certain time, he will come."

"He will come to take you prisoner for what you did in the Belows!" Kelyn protested.

"What does it matter *why* he comes, as long as he comes when we want him to? If we can get a message to him immediately after Petissanji leaves town, then he'll grab a few of his best men and come after me. I'll have my men in place to delay him if he rides too quickly; we cannot have him coming upon us before we have our hands on Petissanji. It is only then that the witch is likely to reveal himself while before Abendar."

"And you will get him to reveal himself . . . how?" Anci asked, concerned doubt coming out in her frown.

Thainn grinned. "By threatening him, of course—forcing him to defend himself. The timing will be tricky; we may have to play with him some until Abendar arrives."

"Play with him!" Anci said. "The man conjures beasts! He collects god-empowered objects! You want to play with him? He is not a mouse!"

"He is far from it," Thainn said. "That's exactly why I need your help. For several reasons." He pondered the witches a moment. "Your horn is gone. It is elsewhere, and while perhaps another time I would be interested in finding it, destroying it—"

"You assume it can be destroyed," Gergo murmured, a hard light in his eye.

Thainn ignored him. "For now, it is unimportant. But believing it is here is important to Petissanji. His search for it is one way we can delay him if necessary."

"You hid the mouth of this cave by making it hard to see," Kelyn said in sudden inspiration. "Can you make something else look like the Horn?"

"My thoughts, also." Thainn glanced at her in a combination of surprise and appreciation.

The witches looked at one another, and when Anci hesitated, Kelyn felt a sudden burst of temper. "We don't care about your secrets! We need help!"

Anci sighed, giving the others one last silent consultation. "If we have an object similar to the Horn, we can disguise it, as long as he's not touching it. He'll know there's magic in use, but it shouldn't surprise him—he will assume we have taken some measures to protect the Horn."

"Good," Thainn said. "And what else can you do? Can you protect us against his spells? Can you prevent him from making them? Or counter them in any way?"

Anci shook her head. "You ask too much of us. We cannot—"

But Thainn snorted, cutting her off. "I ask very little of you. My daughter may be new to this land, but I've been out of Ketura half my life. I know what witches can do."

"If we were as powerful as you imagine, we would never have been taken by the soldiers in the first place!" Anci jammed her fists to her hips and glared at him. "*And*, if you had let me finish, you might not be so quick to judge!"

"Finish, then," Thainn muttered, without any grace. Kelyn made a face at him, and it brought a small smile to Anci's face, one that made Thainn look around to see what she reacted to. By then Kelyn was smearing her bare toe across the shallow ooze of water that traversed a depression in the cave floor.

Anci shook her hair back from her face. She was the epitome of a Trader woman, Kelyn realized suddenly, and the natural one to take Lenci's place. Without her mother's presence to shadow her, Anci seemed brighter and bolder than she had before, rounded everywhere she should be, her skin and hair and eyes all different shades of the same toasted brown color. "I was going to say, we cannot predict what we can do against Petissanji, because we don't know his strength, his repertoire of spells, or which objects of power he might have already acquired. We'll help, but it's best not to count on specific spells."

"That makes it hard to plan." Thainn frowned at her, and evidently decided against directing his frustration at those he would ask for assistance; he stuck his thumbs in his belt harness—a pose Kelyn thought reflected pure swagger, and which she had already had enough of—and sighed. "Can you see in the dark? What about spells that would light all these lamps at once"—he gestured to the multitude of lamps sitting around the cave, including the one he'd set at his own feet—"or moving a large stone?"

Anci shrugged. "We don't specialize in such spells—we can't see in the dark, although the lamp-lighting spell is simple enough—but we should be free to use spells that affect anything other than Petissanji himself."

"Good." Thainn rubbed a hand over his chin—he'd been clean-shaven when he came out of the fortress at Kila's message, but generous stubble now covered the lower half of his face—more grey than black, unlike his hair. "I need to think. I want to meet with you three"—he pointed at Gergo, Yerde, and Anci—"in a short while."

"We will make ourselves available," Gergo said dryly. "Don't think too long. We have little time to prepare, if Petissanji strikes out tomorrow morning."

"Feasting tonight," Yerde told the witches. "Spread the word. A feast before danger."

"Now that," said Thainn, "is a custom I admire."

"You and your men are invited, of course." Gergo straightened, and Kelyn realized how slumped he'd been. "Provided you can remember your manners, and will respect our ways."

Thainn's mouth twisted in dark humor. "Don't worry about that. If I didn't heed such things as curses, I wouldn't be so eager to rid the world of witches. Your women are safe—as they would be safe in any event."

Gergo snorted, disbelieving the last. "If we did not heed the ways of outsiders, we wouldn't be so careful to protect ourselves with such things as curses." He blew out his lamp, and set it near the entrance with a small collection of unused lamps. "Endre," he said, "you seem eager to visit the cave today. I will leave it to you to refill these lamps. It is my guess that Kelyn will assist you."

The witches smothered a quiet laugh or two, and added their extinguished lamps to Gergo's, leaving the cave with murmured conversation that seemed equally split between feast preparation and matters of witchery. Gergo followed, with Yerde walking carefully at his elbow, watching the older man's steps. In moments, Kelyn stood alone with Endre in the cave, her eyes adjusting to the suddenly dim lighting. "It's bigger in here without all those people."

Endre gave a bark of laughter. "*Much* bigger." He knelt before the lamps, moving the already-burning standing lamps to a safe distance. Beside them sat a huge crock, and when he removed the lid, the pungent odor of oil stung Kelyn's nose. She joined him, removing a plug from one of the lamps and holding it steady so he could fill it, carefully pouring oil from a small dipper. "This is a woman's job," he said. "Setting me to it is Gergo's way of telling me he's unhappy that I brought you here."

"But *he* brought Thainn in."

Endre glanced at her, checking to see that she truly didn't understand. "He is the head of the caravan. He is allowed to make such choices. And he's right . . . I shouldn't have brought an outsider here. Except . . . I guess I do trust you that much."

Trust again. She thought Endre might even trust her more than her own father did. Kelyn traded the full lamp for one of the empty ones and looked around the cave. This relatively large front cavern narrowed into the passage they had just traversed, and then widened to split off in several directions, only one of which she and Endre had gone into—the one that still held the blankets on which they'd made love. One of the others, she realized—now that she had the time to think about it—had held the Horn. No doubt the Traders had other things secreted about the cave—their profits, other goods, and probably more mundane things like more sleeping chambers and a toilet chamber. Thainn, she knew, intended to use this cave to his advantage—otherwise he wouldn't have asked if the witches could light these lamps.

But Thainn would reveal his plans in good time, and speculating further would only be a waste of her time. Instead, she thought of something else he'd said—about the Traders. *Traders won't abide their blood to be split.* "Why," she said, struggling with the stopper on one of the lamps, "do your people take such care with their seed?"

"What makes you think—" Endre broke off to grab the lamp as it sprang out of Kelyn's hands; the stopper flew in another direction and Kelyn snagged it out of midair. Replacing the lamp firmly in her hands, he started again. "What makes you think we do?"

"Ketura's balls, Endre, the signs are all around me. You go to great effort to protect your women—no outsider will even consider touching them, and I've seen enough in my short time outside Ketura to know there are plenty of men who grab whatever woman pleases them, whether she wants it so or not. You didn't wait for me to ask how we would avoid making a child before showing me this—" she leaned forward so she could poke his pocket, an intimate gesture she wouldn't have considered several hours earlier. "Do you think other men care so much, especially when they'll be moving on? And . . . I've heard things."

He hesitated, the dipper resting on the edge of the oil crock. "A long speech for you, Kelyn."

"Only in this tongue. And don't think you can change the subject."

He grimaced. "We choose not to talk about it."

"You trusted me with the cave. Trust me with this."

After a hesitation, he took a deep breath, his gaze pinned squarely on the spot where her knife belts crossed. "There is a country far south of here. You will not have heard of it. Many generations ago, my people ruled there. We were driven out by sorcery. Now we have no country, and we wander as Traders—it is all that most people know of us. But one day—when we have gathered the magics, and the wealth, and rebuilt our people—we will regain our rightful place. When that day comes, we cannot have throngs of people—all those who lay claim to a drop of Trader blood—demanding privileges of us."

Kelyn stared at him a moment, taking it in—at first not sure if he was truly serious, but quickly realizing that he was. "But," she said flatly, "for now, it is all right to consort with those such as me."

"For now, and probably for my lifetime," Endre said. "It has been generations . . . it will be generations more." He grinned at her, hanging the dipper on the edge of the crock to place his hands flat on the rock floor, lean over, and kiss her most thoroughly. "You asked, Kelyn. Don't let it take away from what we can enjoy in one another."

"So long as you enjoy," Kelyn said, looking straight into eyes only inches from her, "and don't *use*." And she bit his lip.

"Ow!" He sat back to rub his mouth, though she'd been gentle with her teeth. "I see your point, my Keturan. Believe me, I know better than to disregard it!"

Good. Kelyn plunked a lamp into his hands and stood. "Finish on your own. I've got things to attend outside. And later, if you get a chance, I have some things I've thought of that I'd like to try. It depends on how limber you are."

This time, it was Endre who dropped the lamp.

Chapter 15

Kelyn threw back her head to release a full-throated fight cry. Taken by surprise, the Traders startled, hesitating, falling momentarily silent. And then someone laughed, and the music started again, and so did the dancing. Renci, next to Kelyn, tried to imitate the cry—though not with much success—and then all the others had to give it a try, too.

Trader feasting on a warm evening. Full, divested of her shirt and wearing only the vest to cover her upper body, Kelyn gave a twist of her hips, only now fully understanding the move.

Recent experience had improved her dance considerably.

So what if she was the only dancer to wear trousers. The knife belts, slung a notch lower than usual, only served to accent her movement. Her arms, more muscled than any Trader woman's and bared to everyone's eyes, lacked for Trader grace but not for enthusiasm. She caught Renci's eye and they laughed together, whirling around one another.

Thainn's men shouted their spirited approval as

they clapped to the music—or tried to. They were well in their cups, drink provided by the Traders in consolation of the women they weren't likely to get, and they liked what they saw.

Except for Thainn. His face remained thunderous, and his glare fixed on Kelyn. As the women circled and she passed by him, he grabbed her wrist and tugged her out of the dancers. His men shouted disapproval at him.

"Stop," he said to her. "Look what you're doing to them. How will they look at you, after you dance like this? This is no Keturan dance!"

"As if you'd know." Kelyn easily wrenched her arm from his grip, unfazed, undisturbed. She was having fun, and she intended to have more of it. "Go sit at your own fire, if it bothers you."

"Do you want them to pester you from this day forth?" He grabbed a belt, tugged at it. "Do you want them to think of this dance when they're fighting alongside you?"

"If it makes them fight harder, that's fine with me. But you talk as though you have decided my future." Did he truly want her with him? And if so . . . *why*? She gave him a hard, quick look, and twisted his finger back from a hand still wrapped around her belt. She raised her voice above the music so there was no mistaking her words as he snatched his stung hand away. "It is moments like this that decide my future, Wolverine."

"Ha, leave her alone, Thainn!" Hann called, elbowing the man next to him and nodding at Thainn as he did so.

"Let her dance!" the man said.

"Kel-lyn!" chanted another man. "Kel-lyn!" The others joined in, chanting her name; Kelyn grinned widely at the expressions that crossed Thainn's face—outrage, and the sudden realization that he had a good-natured mutiny on his hands. She spun away from him and rejoined the circle—a circle that had started shrinking, as dancers began to pair up.

And well they all deserved this feast—and were wise to take advantage of it. Ketura knew how many of these men and women would survive the morrow, although Kelyn realized that Thainn's men were the most vulnerable, and would take the brunt of any struggle—be it magical or physical. She glanced at Gergo on her way by—looking alone in the middle of the men around him, his shoulders weighed down by the loss of Lenci and his other witches, by the impending fight with Petissanji.

Thainn intended to use the cave, as she'd thought. To lure Petissanji there, into its darkness, with his fighters positioned in its depths. To lure him back, past the point where Kelyn and Endre had spent time, back to where the Horn had until recently been hidden. And to have the witches light the lamps they'd placed during the afternoon, while assigning positions to Thainn's men. He hoped the surprise—the sudden light, the men leaping out from their positions—would all give the witches enough edge to stop whatever magic Petissanji might throw at them. At least, long enough to subdue the man, to bring him out in the open, where Abendar would be. "You," Thainn had said to Yerde, "will be the reasonable one. Do not make loud accusations at Petissanji—let Abendar do the talking. Be impressed by him."

"That won't convince him that Petissanji is a witch," Kelyn had objected. "He'll just think the witches have gone after their persecutor. He'll think you're bespelled, just as Petissanji has told him."

And Thainn had just grinned. "Leave that up to me," he'd said. "I'll prod him to it."

Kelyn had found herself relegated to wait outside

the cave, hidden with the Trader men—partially by trees, partially by magic. At her protest, Thainn's men had joined in. "We'll fight alongside her," they'd said. Thainn could not be moved on the point.

"She's unpredictable," he'd said shortly. "We have enough."

I don't need your protection. Thinking of the moment as she danced, Kelyn caught Thainn's eye and put an extra flare in her movements. One of his men whooped at her. Thainn got up and walked away, his broad back a deliberate statement in the firelight.

A pair of hands landed lightly on her hips from behind, following her motion. "If you're going to dance like *that* . . ." Endre said in her ear, and left the thought unfinished.

Kelyn took his hand and led him from the circle.

❖ ❖ ❖

Kelyn, resting on her elbow in the blankets, grinned at Endre's dazed expression. "I thought that would be good." When he didn't respond, she tickled his ear with the tip of one finger—she'd already learned he was especially vulnerable near his ears.

Endre groaned. "Have mercy, Kelyn."

"Why?" She tickled him again.

The caves were full of noise on this night; she and Endre weren't the only couple to have taken to them. Sighs and moans echoed through the chambers, along with the endlessly dripping water. A communal celebration of life before facing death.

Endre pushed half-heartedly at her hand, his breathing finally settling back to normal. She was not to be deterred; she gathered the ends of her hair together and barely brushed them along the skin of his neck; goosebumps sprang up along his arms. He gave a sudden growl and rolled on top of her, pinning her arms; Kelyn let him. She smiled up at him, having gotten what she'd wanted.

He shook his head at her, half in disbelief, half in amusement. "One thing about you Keturans," he said, eyeing her neck as he might eye a target, "when you do something, you do it with enthusiasm."

Kelyn might have agreed, had she not been distracted.

❖ ❖ ❖

Rain poured across the rolling Atlian horizon, steadily thrumming into the hard ground, greying the skies and turning Kelyn's perpetually wet hands stiff and wrinkled. Thunder rumbled occasionally, well in the distance; the Traders huddled in their remaining wagons, waiting for word of Petissanji's arrival. The rest of the wagons, filled with the women who would not be taking part in this fight and a number of older men as well, were some distance away. Safe—they hoped. Thainn's warriors hunkered beneath the wagons and took turns scouting the area. Kelyn split her time between the two, raining powerless curses upon Petissanji's head.

Hann, his back to a wagon wheel, looked at her and grinned. "Here's a lesson for you, Wolverine's daughter," he said. "You can always count on it to rain all over the day you've planned for battle."

"Petissanji may not even come out," Kelyn grumbled. "We'll have to do this all over again tomorrow."

Hann shrugged. "One day is as good as another. And if it means another feast tonight, I won't complain." He grinned at her—no, she decided, it was closer to a leer, but a good-natured one—"I wouldn't think you'd complain about *that*."

She poked him with her staff, not quite as gently as she might have; he gave an exaggerated grunt of pain, but never stopped grinning. "Thainn is right to think you'd do well with us."

"He said that to you?"

Hann hesitated, a man who's just said too much, but gave her ready staff a wary glance and shrugged. "Of all the little Wolverine cubs to come his way, you . . ." But he didn't finish, and shook his head.

I, what? Not even a prod from her staff got her that answer. "Where are the others?"

"Not here." Hann said shortly, then shrugged again.

"But he said—"

"He thinks you have promise."

Promise. Kelyn glowered at him and turned away. As if she wasn't perfectly well able to handle herself right now.

Though some part of her wondered if he knew how to handle a whip.

Thainn joined them at the side of the wagon, stooping over to look at them beneath it. Besides Kelyn and Hann, four of his men sheltered there, choosing to endure the occasional damp gust of wind rather than to wait in the caves, alone and in darkness. Thainn used a foot to nudge Kelyn's staff and said, "Try to leave my men whole for any fighting that's to be done."

She made a face at him; one of the men snickered.

"Come under," Hann suggested, as water dripped from Thainn's nose and the end of the long braid that had flopped over his shoulder. "There's no point in waiting out there—you're not a tree, to soak up the rain."

Thainn shook his head. "The runner will be here soon."

"Petissanji is waiting somewhere warm and dry," Hann said.

But even as he said it with such certainty, Kelyn knew he was wrong, and that she'd been wrong when she wondered the same thing, moments earlier. The prickle down the back of her neck told her so, and when she glanced sharply at Thainn, she saw a reflection of that awareness on his face. The instinct for danger. She said, "He's coming." It wasn't a question.

"Yes," Thainn said, clearly knowing she hadn't needed the answer.

Hann sighed, and pushed himself away from the wagon wheel. "Let's go," he said to the other men. "If he's got that look on his face, we might as well get ourselves in the cave. I just hope those witches can light the lamps when they're supposed to—d'you think magic has as much trouble as flint when it comes to the rain?"

"We'll just have to—"

Trust, Kelyn knew he'd been about to say, and was certain of it at his grimace, and the skip between his words.

"—hope they can. If mine doesn't light, my call will be the signal to attack. We'll do it by Petissanji's light."

"Of course," Hann said, not a trace of sarcasm on his face. He led the other men out to the cave, where one of the Trader men waited, lamp already lit, to distribute the lamps Kelyn and Endre had filled. Upon seeing him, Thainn's other men straggled out into the open and made their way up to the mouth of the cave.

Kelyn and Thainn eyed one another. "I can hold my own," she said steadily, knowing she had no chance to join his men.

She was assigned outside the cave, where she was likely to do nothing but wait and watch; if Abendar arrived as they planned, Gergo would be the one to speak to him, and not any Keturan girl—whom his guards would readily recognize, anyway, and who could only create trouble whether she meant to or not. Yerde was already in the cave, along with the other Traders who guarded the witches, one man for each—in many cases, the woman's husband—although

Thainn had privately expressed that this was a waste of manpower. If the witches were in trouble, nothing any single Trader could do about it would make a difference. If the witches were in trouble . . . they were *all* in trouble.

But I could hold my own.

"You can," he said, ignoring her surprise at the admission. "But you're best with that staff, and there's not enough room inside to use it well. And my men aren't used to you. They won't be able to predict your actions. They can't—"

"Trust me," she finished for him. "And neither do you."

He shrugged. "No. Not to do as I tell you. Or to know what to expect of you." He glanced up at the cave. "Stay with the Traders. If there is trouble outside, you'll be needed."

She didn't argue. She'd never intended to argue. She'd just needed to say it.

And now, with the appearance of the runner from behind the nearest copse of trees, her attention was elsewhere. She nodded at the runner, and Thainn turned to spot him as well. He blew a drop of water off the end of his nose and said, "That's it, then. Go to the wagons; get the Traders in place. I'll be with my men."

Kelyn crawled out beneath the wagon to stand with him as the runner stumbled to a halt before them, gasping for breath, bent over to lean on his knees. "He's moving fast," the youth panted. "Faster than we expected, in this rain." He looked up at Thainn, worry on his face, squinting through the rain and trying to speak through his labored breathing. "He's got—more men—than we expected, too."

"They always do," Thainn muttered. To the youth, he said, "Get to safety." And to Kelyn, "Go. Do as I've said." He didn't wait for an acknowledgment from either of them before loping off to the cave.

Do as he said. Go wait beside the cave, hidden by magic and trees, knowing that she was safe while others fought a witch's vile magic. While her *father* fought a witch's vile magic.

Not if Thainn's plan works. If Petissanji was startled, and had no time to marshal his magic before the witches clapped a spellbinding on him.

He has survived all your life in the outlands without your help, Kelyn told herself, and headed for the cave. Endre, seeing her, left his wagon, bringing the other Traders with him. Soon they would *all* be wet, standing in the rain and thankful it was a warm one.

Being first at the cave had its advantages; Kelyn chose a spot right next to the angled, concealed mouth of it, crouching in the grasses and taking the time to stroke the wet stems upright, where they did a fair job of hiding her without any help from magic. Endre settled in next to her, offering her a distracted and fleeting smile as the Traders following him found trees and scrubby shrubs to conceal themselves, grouped along the hillside. Kelyn took advantage of that distraction. "Why is the Horn such a danger in Petissanji's hands, Endre? What does it do?"

He gave her a blank and startled look, but his smooth Trader words of deflection abandoned him.

She smiled, not altogether kindly. "I'm risking my life to keep him away from it. Tell me."

"I—"

"Tell me," she said, leaning close and nudging his knee with her own. No mercy, despite the trapped look in his eye, the hint of pleading there.

"Kelyn—"

"Tell me."

He sighed mightily, his resistance—lowered by his nerves, by his jittery tension—giving way. "It does what all horns do, Kelyn. It calls. And what it calls, you'll never want to see."

"What—"

This time, it was he who cut her off, holding up a hand. "That's all I'm going to say. It's enough. Now hush; they're ready for the spell."

Kelyn subsided, satisfied to have gotten anything from him . . . and wondering where the Horn was now, and how many of the Traders themselves knew.

Not many, she hoped. For if they failed here, Petissanji would be questioning them all.

Before them, the two witches assigned to hide the Traders each held up a hand, palm to palm, and interlaced their fingers, facing the Traders. Kelyn expected them to say something, to chant or make some visible indication of their spellcasting—else how could they do it in tandem?—but they were silent, their eyes wide and unfocused. Then she saw their fingers twitch, and recalled the way they'd held hands in the firelight, facing Thyra. Looking for all the world as though they'd been comforting one another. *Clever.* Definitely clever, these Traders and their witches.

She didn't feel the magic as it swept over them all; she only knew that one moment, she was able to glance around and place all the Traders, and the next, she wasn't. They were gone; the only one she could see was Endre, and he was practically touching her. Even the rustling of their slight movements faded. When she looked around again, the witches, too, were gone, and she had no idea where—although she knew they'd been instructed to stay out here in case of need. *In case Abendar, too, brought a witch along.*

And so they waited. Kelyn settled in, staff at her feet, and easily fell into the patience of a hunt; her mind blanked and calm. Endre, bereft of her experience, had a harder time; he fidgeted, tugging at grass stems and fussing at the way the rain gathered on his brow and lashes. He was retying a sleeve cuff when Kelyn spotted the first sign of Petissanji's approach—several birds bursting from cover and out into the rain. She nudged him, and he squinted out at the faint path from Abendar's town. "Where?"

"There," she said, seeing the first signs of movement. "Several of them."

"I don't see—ah. There they are." And he tensed, his sleeve lacing forgotten, his hand on his knife.

"Easy," she murmured. "Even when they get here, you'll have no cause to use that."

He glanced at her, and seemed to take in her relaxed posture for the first time. "How can you just sit there—"

"Practice," she said, interrupting him. "Conserve your energy. You shouldn't need it, but if you do, you'll be sorry if you fretted it away here."

He looked at her again, and shook his head. "We have led different lives, you and I."

"*Now* you realize so?" Kelyn murmured, not taking her eyes from Petissanji's rapidly approaching figure.

"Now I realize it once more," Endre muttered, doing his best to emulate her calm readiness.

"Five," Kelyn murmured, finally able to count the bobbing heads of those who rode with Petissanji. They'd thought he would come alone, the better to protect his reputation—or with one or two men at the most.

Endre shifted, and though she didn't turn to look at him, she heard the frown in his voice. "They ride too fast for this footing. They'll be lucky not to lame a horse."

"Probably not what they're thinking of," Kelyn said. She put a hand on his arm; he had leaned forward without realizing it, back to his anxious tension. She kneaded his bicep gently, a wordless reminder, and he subsided again. She hoped he remembered how poorly things had gone the last time he had charged into the thick of things, when the soldiers had first accosted the Traders.

It seemed half a season ago, instead of mere days.

Petissanji led his men into the small trampled area where the Traders had been camped, jerking his horse to a stop. Both hands seemed perfectly functional despite Kelyn's clear memory of the crack of bone as her staff connected with his flesh.

Two of the men stayed by his side, their helmets dripping water, their horses standing tired and quietly steaming; the others spurred on into the camp and made several passes by the wagons, finally stopping to jerk the doors open from horseback, peering inside with some suspicion. Eventually, satisfied, they trotted back to Petissanji. "Abandoned," one of them declared. "They must have moved on."

Petissanji snorted; it was then that Kelyn noticed he was perfectly dry. No moisture on his beard, no lankly wet hair on his bare head. Instead of robes he wore loose, lightweight pants and a wide-sashed tunic—clothes not meant for any activity more strenuous than dining. His horse snorted wetly, soaked at its head and tail, and dry around its saddle area.

Now *that*, Kelyn thought, was a spell worth knowing.

"What Trader would move on and leave anything of worth behind?" he said. "No, someone was here, and we scared them off."

So confident. So wrong.

"We'll rout them out," the man said, jerking his horse around. Endre hissed through his teeth as the animal's mouth gaped open in pain.

Petissanji flung out a restraining hand. "No!" He waited impatiently while the man got his mount back under control as the creature plunged against its sharply conflicting directions. "You are not here to do as you please—you're here to do as you're told. Don't make that mistake again."

"But I thought—"

"Then don't." Petissanji glared at him. "Not if you want to make it back to the fortress in the same form in which you left it. Am I clear?"

Endre leaned close to Kelyn's ear. "Sanctimonious bastard."

She didn't know what *sanctimonious* meant, but it sounded good. She nodded ever so slightly, her gaze locked on Petissanji. "Cocker," she agreed.

Petissanji dismounted, shoving his reins at the man, who quickly got off his horse and gave the reins to a second man; in moments they were all on their feet, with one man watching the horses and the other four ranging around Petissanji—though he warned them off with a glare if they got too close. "There's a cave here," he said. "Find it."

It wouldn't take them long. The witches had removed their disguising glamor, and then increased the physical camouflage at Thainn's direction. "Make it too easy," Thainn had said, "and he'll sniff out the trap of it."

Make it too hard, and they'd stumble into the Traders before they found the entrance. She and Endre were the most at risk—something Kelyn had known when she chose the spot but Endre only now seemed to realize. She tightened her grip on his arm, feeling the muscles clench there.

But no. Even as one man came toward them, the man at his side spotted the dark slash of the cave entrance, and called, "Here!" Kelyn released her grip on Endre and patted his arm, never taking her eyes from the men and their master. These were soldiers she didn't know, hadn't seen. Not Atelic's men, and not part of the regular fortress guard.

Petissanji joined them, his blousy pants and

leather slippers a severe contrast to the wet, boiled leather plates the men wore, his precise manner a contrast to their stomp-all-comers attitudes. "Ahh," he said, pleased. "Just as she said." And he turned sideways to slip through the narrow opening. One man followed, the one who was ever closest by his side. Kelyn edged closer to the entrance, counting on Endre to know the limits of the witches' concealing spell, and to stop her before she went too far. When his hand landed on the calf of her trailing leg, she halted, pressed up against the outcrop of rock near the cave entrance. Stout-stemmed plants growing in the shallow dirt of the rock crevices tickled her face and neck, and one poked her in a particularly tender spot; she wiggled in an effort to relocate it and gave up, her attention captured by Petissanji's muffled voice.

"No, fool, I don't want a *lamp*. What makes you think I want to creep through this cave like a lighted target?"

"But no one's here," the man said, in an unfortunate tone resembling that of one he might use with an unusually dense child.

"You mean you didn't *see* anyone. That doesn't mean we're alone. The Horn is a great treasure to these people—do you really suppose they've left it completely unguarded? Keep your hand on my back. I'll lead us to the Horn."

"But—"

He can see in the dark!

"Question me once more, and I'll turn you into rock and leave you here!"

He can see in the dark, and Thainn won't be able to tell when he arrives, won't know when he's in position to be attacked.

"Yes, Master Petissanji." The sullen acknowledgment marked the end of their intelligible conversation, although Kelyn heard a few fading words she could not interpret.

Moving as quickly as she dared, she returned to Endre's side. "He's gone back," she said. "But he's got some kind of spell to see in the dark. They won't be able to tell when he reaches the fake Horn—I've got to go—"

"Kelyn, no!" Endre's furious whisper surely exceeded the noise the witches had told them the spell would conceal; he glanced away from her to see that no one had noticed, but hardly paused his words. "They'll hear him. You can't get in the cave without being seen!"

"Maybe *you* can't," she said. "And they *won't* hear him. The water drips too loudly in there!"

"Kelyn—" Failed by words, he grabbed both her arms, bringing his face close. "Your father feared just this—unpredictable, he said. Was he right not to trust you?"

She glared, making no immediate effort to free herself. "He would be right not to trust me later if I did nothing to help *now*. Let go, Endre, or it's going to hurt."

Angrily, he shoved her away—not hard, not enough to make so much movement that they were revealed. "Did you learn nothing from what happened to my people?"

Ouch. Kelyn grabbed her staff, released it—*not in the cave*—pausing to favor him with a final glare. "Didn't *you*?" *Silogan-damned Trader*. At least when *she* went charging into action, it was because she was using her wits, and not because she'd lost them! She turned her back on him, her fingers searching the ground for a rock. She found instead a hard clump of dirt, and, after a quick assessment of the remaining men—they milled before the cave mouth, looking wet and miserable and not terribly concerned about anything other than when this morning would be over—tossed it over the heads into the brush on the other side of the cave.

"They're not going to—" Endre hissed at her, stopping short when he saw that they *had*. All four of them, looking into the brush, their backs to the cave while one of them moved forward and poked around. Only for a moment—and that's all Kelyn needed. Instantly in motion, silent as if she were on a swift stalking hunt, she slipped into the cave behind them. In the periphery of her vision, she saw distant movement; only moments later, as she moved into the darkness of the narrow passage beyond the main cavern, did she realize that she'd seen the approach of Abendar and his men.

Too late to do anything about it now. The Traders would have to handle it, as they were assigned.

Her eyes adjusted quickly to the darkness, but not quickly enough. She heard the soldiers return to the cave mouth. *Trapped*. No turning back now.

She felt her way along, alert for any sign of Petissanji ahead of her. Maybe he could see, but *she* knew where she was going, while he only followed the directions of a tortured Trader witch. Maybe he could see, but *she* had the experience of a hundred night hunts behind her, and bare feet to feel her way.

She closed her eyes to keep herself from trying to see in the utter darkness, a folly which would only draw her attention away from the senses that could do her some good.

Like her sense of smell. Wet leather, stinking soldier—a gust of odor hit her nose along with the cave's natural draft. And another scent, a deliberate, incense-like scent that could only belong to Petissanji and his careful grooming.

The soldier, she could have smelled from anywhere. That there was a trace of Petissanji overlying it meant she was close. And *there*—above the dripping water, a scuff of hard leather against stone. Here, she remembered, the passage narrowed even further; she drew her arms close to her body and slid sideways, feeling the brush of a stone icicle against her hair.

The passage widened; she hung to the left, trailing her fingertips lightly against the wall so she would hit the next passage as it forked left. The soldier's soft grunt, followed by Petissanji's quiet hiss, warned her; they'd stopped at the fork while the witch considered his options. Ultimately, he chose the correct direction.

Only a little further from here; they were almost to the wide spot in front of the alcove she thought of as hers and Endre's. And the Horn was just beyond. Kelyn felt a tingle run down the back of her neck, a prescience; she would in moments be surrounded by her father's men and Trader witches, and they had no inkling of her presence . . . or of Petissanji's. That tingling feeling grew, washed over her entire body, raising chillbumps in the cool cave. *The curse. The curse lifting again*, when she really needed it to. She began to understand the pattern of it.

Careful step by step, Kelyn inched closer to the soldier, sifting through her options—how to warn Thainn without eliminating the surprise factor he counted on so heavily. The rock to her left disappeared from beneath her hand—that would be the alcove, with Endre's blankets still inside—and reappeared again. She was into unfamiliar territory now, with no inner visualization of the rock formations forming it, no memory to warn her if she was about to come upon one of the thick icicle stumps, or if she needed to duck her head. She put an arm out to protect her forehead, picking out the sounds of the soldier's movement just ahead—not an easy task, not with the increased trickle of water all around her. *The rain.* No wonder her feet were cold and wet.

A single creak of leather warned her; her nose, so full of the soldier's scent, had failed to perceive she was almost upon the man; holding her breath, she backed a step. He'd stopped short—they must be here; Petissanji must be scanning the walls for the niche in which the Traders had placed the false horn.

Yes. The witch's soft *ahhh* of discovery told her she'd been right.

Now was the time to move; *now* the witch would be at his most distracted. Kelyn marked the soldier's position, visualized it, took a long step for momentum—

And planted her foot solidly in his backside, sending him sprawling with a loud oath of surprise.

Kelyn spun and ran, one hand trailing the wall, one out before her, no longer worrying about the noise, just needing to be out of the way when—

Light flared against her closed eyes; the cave erupted into sound, loud and echoing cries that clashed against one another and confused her ears. Someone grabbed her, tried to hold her; she wrenched herself free and ran on, back to the darkness of the passage out.

Once beyond them, she stopped, turning, opening her eyes for the first time. She could see nothing but the fading edges of the light, hear nothing but the chaos of the struggle. A Trader witch cried out in surprise and fear, and Kelyn checked her immediate urge to join the fray—though not before she'd taken a handful of steps in that direction. Thainn's voice rose above it all, a shout aimed at Petissanji but too garbled by conflicting echoes to make sense to her.

He doesn't want you here. He wanted her outside—where Abendar was approaching, had perhaps already arrived. Hesitating, torn between her inclination to rush to the battle—she flinched as another Trader witch cried out—and the need to do what was expected of her, Kelyn finally spun away from the light, spitting a heartfelt oath and choosing to return to the role Thainn had given her.

With the decision made, she suddenly felt just as much urgency to be outside. No need to hide her progress, not with all the noise behind her; she moved swiftly through the passages, as swiftly as any creature *could* traverse such complicated darkness. At last the light from the entrance gave her guidance, and she aimed herself at it, stopping just short of actual daylight to give her eyes a chance, once more, to adjust—and ever wary of the possibility that Petissanji's soldiers might hear the now dim and fading sounds of the struggle within, and rush to investigate.

But no one came within. *Too distracted without?*

Squinting, Kelyn eased forward to the actual mouth of the cave, blinking through watering eyes as she peered down the gentle slope below the cave. Bright sunlight made her wince; the rain had moved on, and the sun was strong enough that light wisps of steam arose from the earth.

Large wavery dark blobs resolved into groups of men—Petissanji's men, three at the bottom of the slope, surprised and uncertain, but prepared to be belligerent, and the one holding the horses, who had his hands plenty full with the plunging beasts—all of whom reacted to the abrupt arrival of so many other horses.

Abendar sat his horse at the head of his men, a number beyond Kelyn's counting—and with Atelic at the head of them. Off to the side, the Traders stood revealed, come together below the trees where they'd been concealed. Gergo stood before them all, speaking to Abendar, gesturing at the cave and, Kelyn saw with some surprise, carrying a convincing dignity into his words. Endre stood to the other side of him, facing neither Petissanji's or Abendar's men, but angled where he could see them both.

He was, she realized, the only thing between Petissanji's men and Gergo, whose words—to judge by the growing doubt on Abendar's face—were well-aimed to harm their master. At the same time, Abendar's men stared at Petissanji's soldiers with growing hostility. It did not matter to them, she saw at once, whether Petissanji was guilty of Gergo's accusations or not.

What mattered was that Petissanji's soldiers were *supposed* to be Abendar's men, and clearly, they were not.

Abendar, sensing his men's restlessness, held up a hand to stay them, not looking away from Gergo as he shook his head. *Not convinced.* He spoke a few harsh words; Kelyn made out Thainn's name.

Thainn. If he'd been successful, he should be emerging from the cave at any moment. The longer he took, the more likely that Petissanji had gained some advantage.

She wouldn't go back in there. *She wouldn't.* She'd done what she could to help; now her place was out here, where Abendar grew increasingly angry, gesturing at Gergo in an imperative motion—no, a threatening one.

Time to get closer. To hear their words, to become a member of this particular hunt. Quietly, Kelyn moved along the rock surrounding the cave, back to where she'd left the staff. Her movement was bound to attract attention, and it did; Abendar's men, the only group directly facing her, alerted to her almost immediately.

And recognized her.

"There's the witch!" Atelic cried, putting his heels to his horse—only to have the animal blocked when the man before him turned his own mount into its path at Abendar's sharp command.

But the damage was done. Abendar's men, barely restrained, had restless horses beneath them, and Petissanji's men had spotted her. She moved in on them as though it didn't matter, keeping the staff low at her side, seeing the reservation on Abendar's face coalesce into growing resolve, and determined to get close enough to hear what was happening.

She didn't like what she heard.

"Only Traders could think to talk their way out of this," Abendar said, his lip curling and his voice going sharp. He edged his horse closer to Gergo, who took an uncertain step back. "Thainn has been turned by a witch—the very witch you harbor behind you!" Kelyn, nearly upon Petissanji's men, looked up to meet his glare with her steady gaze—her own quiet denial. "Your own people are rife with witches—it was probably you who cursed my goods to begin with, so you could have those warehouses for your own use! This time, you will *all* visit my cells—until I have the truth."

Gergo's uncertainty vanished behind anger. "You slur us beyond tolerance! Your *own* man is the one to blame for your troubles; he uses you, and you refuse to see it!"

"Watch your mouth, Trader scum!" One of Petissanji's men leapt forward, his knife raised.

Kelyn snatched at him, an arm's length short—and Petissanji's other men turned on her, triggering a roar of action.

Traders and soldiers poured together; Petissanji's man snatched her staff away as she lunged past him for the fray; she whirled to find him jabbing it at her. Jumping to the side, sucking in her stomach so the staff passed by, she grabbed it, pulling the man onward even as she pivoted and kicked back, planting her foot in his midsection.

He doubled over; she shoved off from his body, whipping the staff around to slam the second man in the back. The boiled leather kept his ribs from crumbling, but the blow staggered him; she whacked him behind the knee and he went down, losing the grip on the short sword he'd drawn. She grabbed it even as he threw himself after it, ducking the first man's return engagement while she was down there and throwing the sword aside to take her staff in two hands and face him squarely.

The second man climbed to his feet, unsteady, his expression growing mean as he realized the two of them not only stood before her, but stood between her and everyone else.

Beyond them, half of Abendar's men had been unhorsed, outwitted by barely-armed Traders on foot who knew how to manage the animals, how to provoke them and where to prod them. "No!" Abendar bellowed. "Do not harm them! I want the truth from them! No blades! No blades!"

She couldn't see Endre anywhere. And was that a glimpse of Gergo's back at the outer edge of the action, that which could only belong to a man on his knees? "Endre!" she called, knowing better, knowing he'd never hear her, wherever he was.

But Gergo did. Gergo twisted to look at her, and call out to her. *Calling for help*.

"Sorry," she muttered to the two men, with one sword between them and lumps from her staff already raising on their bodies. "I've got to go." She feinted; the swordless man, his knife now in hand, instinctively brought his arm up.

She broke it for him.

The other man dove in at her, and she blocked

his hacking cuts until he realized with some consternation that his blade had no effect on the Reman ironwood. In the instant that he faltered, she knocked the sword away and dodged around him, far more interested in reaching Gergo than in taking him down for good.

The action blurred, then—Kelyn loosed her fight cry, lunging into action. She became a wild Keturan thing, unhindered by any curse, clearing the area around Gergo and not caring whether she hit Atlian or Trader as the combatants surged back against them. The fighting was a roar in her ears, and her body moved without thought—blocking, attacking, shoving—and the roar became Abendar, his voice finally rising above all with its ceaseless cries of "Hold!"

And all at once, as if everyone had finally heard him all in the same moment, the fighting slowed, and halted. Panting, Kelyn judged the wide space she'd cleared as enough and, meeting Abendar's furious gaze, threw down her staff and turned to Gergo.

But Gergo hadn't been the one in trouble. It was Endre on the ground before him, Endre with blood spreading over his shirt and a bewildered look on his face. Gergo, on his knees, had gone down only to protect his protector.

"Who drew steel?" Abendar demanded, turning on his men and the Traders alike.

Petissanji's man, the one who had started it all, took an unthinking step away from them all.

"Take him!" Abendar commanded with a jerk of his chin, and two of his men—already unhorsed, rumpled and worse for the wear, their helmets gone and their noses bleeding, redeemed themselves by snatching the instigator's arms and holding him tight. Atelic wobbled up to them and straightened himself out, taking credit—or trying to. Abendar's gaze on him grew scornful; Atelic faded back.

Kelyn didn't care. Couldn't care. She dropped to her knees next to Endre. "Oh, Endre," she said sadly. "What made you think you could fight steel with fists?"

"He would have knifed Gergo," Endre said, as though it were the most reasonable thing in the world. Blood bubbled upward, just below his collarbone and not far from the center of his chest, spitting air bubbles as Endre, looking more confused in each passing moment, drew breath. "I should have let you take him, Keturan girl," he said, lifting his bloody hand in search of hers.

She grabbed it up, wrapping both her hands around it. "Gergo," she said, looking over at the older man, her voice full of pleading. "Surely there's some spell—"

"The best of us are in that cave," Gergo said, but he lifted his voice and called out to the hillside trees, Trader words. With some hesitation, two women detached themselves, appearing out of nowhere—*magic*—to make their way down the hard-packed slope. And as they did, while Kelyn clutched Endre's hand, Gergo looked up to Abendar on his horse and said flatly, "You will not interfere with them."

Abendar, though silent, allowed the witches to approach.

"I should have let you take him," Endre murmured, his eyes drooping.

If only I had been there.

Chapter 16

"Abendar!"

Thainn's voice rang out over the gathering, garnering all their attention. He stood before the cave entrance, his hand on the back of Petissanji's neck, holding him as he might hold a puppy. His men followed with Petissanji's soldier in tow, and behind him came the witches, some of them stumbling weakly along, supported by their fellows. Anci, squinting down at them with her hand shading her eyes, was the first to discern that they knelt around a wounded Trader; she broke into a run and left the others behind.

"Thainn," Abendar said, his face and voice grim. He looked back at his men. "Traders, move away from my men. If Thainn is indeed bewitched, if he attacks, we *will* use steel—and this time I will not have them hold back on your account." He caught Gergo's eye and added, "Were you wise, you would move out while you can. There is little chance this day will turn your way."

Gergo shook his head. "We will not leave Endre."

But he raised a hand from Endre's shoulder and gestured to the rest of the Traders. "Give them room. The rest of this fight is Thainn's. We have done what we were meant to do."

Anci, all her various layers of clothing flying about her, pounded up to them in a flat-footed run, took one glance at Endre, and pulled a short knife from her side. She marched up to the soldier who had instigated the fighting and, while all the men watched in stunned bemusement, sliced the ties to his leather bracer and yanked it off his arm. "Why do you all just stand there? Rago, get my bag of salves and *alchfeth*. They're in the second wagon. And be quick about it!" She crouched, placed the leather against the ground, and jammed the knife into it, struggling to cut off a palm-sized piece.

All the while, Thainn approached with Petissanji, propelling the much smaller man along at a quick pace that made the witch stumble as much as not. Once they were close enough to speak without shouting, Petissanji—his words uneven as he tried to catch his breath and his balance both—started talking. "Abendar, the man's witched out of his senses! As you trust my counsel, restrain him!"

Abendar, eyeing Thainn's grin of a response, said, "You seem to have become confused, indeed, Wolverine. Our agreement was not that you would attack my Advisor in my own fortress, nor lay waste to my men. I have come to speak to you, as you requested—to detain you, if necessary—and I find you once again laying hands on Petissanji. It does not incline me to listen to your words. Release him."

"After all the trouble I went through to get him?" Thainn asked. "No, I think not. The Trader witches have spelled him safe, for now—after we caught him trying to steal the god-touched object hidden here."

"Of course I came for the Horn once I learned

of its presence," Petissanji snapped, trying to wrench himself free of Thainn's grip and coming nowhere near success. "It is my job to help Abendar rid this land of witches and their magic. As long as the Horn is available to Trader witches, all of Atlia is in danger."

"Odd," Gergo said, his voice dry with disdain. "We have had the keeping of that object since before we left our homeland, and Atlia seems to have survived untouched thus far."

Kelyn moved aside so Anci could tend Endre, cutting his shirt, looking impatiently for Rago even as Rago ran back to them, a green cloth bag in hand. Kelyn gently released Endre's hand, and wiped her own against the gritty earth. When she stood, she advanced on Petissanji with purposeful strides. "You rid this land of its witches only so you can steal their magics. You tortured and killed them, and when you had what you wanted, you convinced Abendar to slay them all." She looked over at Abendar. "They had never done you any harm! They've wandered this land for years beyond counting, and they had never done you any harm!"

"You!" Petissanji said, working up to righteous ire. "You're the one who bewitched Thainn in the first place! I was there! You had the power to slay the beast the witches conjured to rampage the Belows!"

"*Your* power, *your* beast," Kelyn said. "Using *your* magic knife."

"Cease this!" Abendar said. "Do you think your quarreling is going to convince me that either of you is in the right?"

"No," Thainn said promptly. "I never thought mere words would convince you of anything, when you had them coming at you from all sides." He shook Petissanji, much like a dog with a rat; Kelyn stepped back uncertainly, seeing intent in his eyes and not at all sure she wanted to be within range—and at the same time, trying to keep an eye on Endre. Anci had smeared a generous dollop of salve across the small stab wound, slapped a handful of precious *alchfeth* across it, and covered it all with the slab of leather. Salve oozed out from around the edges, creating a seal.

Thainn had his knife out—when had that happened?—and suddenly pressed it against the side of Petissanji's neck. "I thought a demonstration might serve." And he nodded at the witches still gathered behind them. They linked hands, giving Petissanji a moment of intense concentration; then the oldest of them, a woman who seemed to serve as Anci's second, nodded back at him.

But as the sharp knife parted the first layers of Petissanji's skin, Petissanji only froze, his eyes rolling at Abendar. "Please," he said, hoarse and strained, his handsome, refined features gone ugly in fear, "let this go no further!"

"Thainn!" Abendar said, a command all in itself. "An' he begins to bleed, you are a dead man!"

Kelyn wasn't sure if she saw or just imagined the instant of consternation on Thainn's face; then the Wolverine leaned over Petissanji's ear like a man whispering to his lover. "How deep will you let me cut, before you save yourself?"

"Thainn!"

"Abendar, *please*—" Petissanji was truly pale now—as well he might be, Kelyn thought, forced to choose between death and revealing himself. If he thought any of Abendar's men could move fast enough to stop Thainn—

"Thainn, release him!"

"Be quiet!" Anci looked up to glare at them all, equally. "I can't work with this nonsense going on. And I need something to bind this dressing down, *now*." She glanced around, her eyes skipping over each of the soldiers, as though they represented only potential supplies.

But Kelyn was looking in another direction, and she saw what she needed. Petissanji's sash. As quick as the thought came to her, her knife was out, slicing cleanly through the sash next to the knot as Petissanji jerked in surprise. It was double-wound, as she thought, and she tugged it from his body, turning to triumphantly present it to Anci—

And not at all expecting the astonishment on Anci's face, slack-jawed and horrified astonishment, her busy hands gone suddenly still. At the collective gasp of the witches behind Thainn, Kelyn whirled around again, discovering they'd backed away from Thainn and Petissanji, their faces full of stark fear.

The soldiers looked only as Kelyn felt—baffled. But Abendar narrowed his eyes at the witches and looked back to Petissanji, and it was then that Kelyn realized he wore another belt, one that had been hidden under the sash. In another blink she recognized it as the belt she'd seen in his secret room, the woven, unevenly decorated belt that she hadn't been inclined to touch.

"The Matrogian Belt," Anci said, her voice calmer than she looked. She took the sash Kelyn had thrust at her and addressed Abendar over her shoulder as she worked, her voice touched by dry disrespect and sounding no little like Gergo's. "Think you on that, Abendar. No man but a witch would dare to wear that belt. No man but a witch would live through the doing of it."

Thainn only then seemed to realize exactly what everyone was looking at; his expression, as he looked down at Petissanji's waist—his eyes widening, jaw dropping as he tried to suck himself inward, away from Petissanji without relinquishing his hold on the man—was one Kelyn thought she would laugh at, later.

If there *was* a later. From the reactions around her, she wasn't so sure there would be.

Petissanji, all signs of fear erased from his face, fastened his eyes on Kelyn with a cold black stare, unmindful of the knife at his throat. "For the crude, ignorant thing that you are, you have caused me an amazing amount of inconvenience. Another time, you would rue that fact. Another time, perhaps you will." He slid his gaze to the very corners of his eyes, looking at Thainn with disdain as the Wolverine tried—and failed—to press his blade home. "You should have killed me while you thought you still had the chance."

"Petissanji," Abendar said, in the tone of a man who's about to make a demand—and finds himself cut short. His hand went to his throat, massaging it, trying to choke out another word. He made only a croak.

"Too late for you, too," Petissanji said. "I'm not inclined to stand here making explanations to you. They're right. I'm a witch, and you're a fool." He made a short, sharp gesture with his closed fist, and Thainn bounced away from him as though shoved hard, stumbling back to land on his bottom with a grunt.

Petissanji ran for the cave.

Kelyn, instantly prepared to charge after him—already caught up to him in her mind, measuring her long strides against his short, flailing steps—stopped short as Anci spoke sharply; even Thainn, jumping back to his feet, stopped to listen, and Abendar—his mouth open to issue orders—waited.

"Know what he can do before you rush after him!" Anci said. "Once he begins to invoke the belt's powers, he can use no other spell—you must wait for that moment. But once he invokes the spell, the danger is great for you."

"What does it *do*?" Kelyn said, taking a step toward the cave, then two, her eyes upon Petissanji's uneven progress—in another step, he'd reach the cave.

Gergo eased Endre to the ground and stood. "With it, he can pass through any natural substance—rock, wood, water—living and breathing."

Thainn scoffed.

"It's true," Anci said, tying off the sash into a tight knot directly over Endre's wound and its packing. Endre had long since passed out, but Kelyn was reassured by the lack of haste in Anci's movements. Even now, she gave him an unthinking pat, a *you'll be all right* pat. "And you *are* a fool if you take it lightly. Once he touches you, he can take you with him. You must get him—you must *kill* him—after he starts to invoke its powers and *before* he uses them. Once invoked, the belt will be active until no longer touched by human hand."

"It will take him some moments to prepare," Gergo said. "He will be vulnerable; it is why he has run." And though Abendar had a hand up, ready to gesture his men forward, it was to Kelyn and Thainn that the Traders looked.

Abendar let his hand drop. "Go," he said to Thainn, including Kelyn in his glance. "If you cannot do this, no number of my men can help."

Kelyn sprang forward, sprinting up the gentle slope, her age and lighter weight giving her an advantage of speed that surprised Thainn, her intensity triggering a wave of cheers from Thainn's men. No curse to burden her, not now. *Gone again*. She ducked inside the cave—Petissanji was nowhere in sight, though the noise of his movement bounced back from the passages, as did the faint glow of his lamp. *He can't see in the dark anymore*. Had he been smart he'd have blown out the standing lamp and left his pursuit to navigate in the dark—but he hadn't. Kelyn went for the lamps, lighting two of them—and ready to hand one to Thainn when he came pounding up.

"Good," he said briefly, making an effort to hide his

disgruntled expression as he took the lamp. *Thainn the Wolverine . . . not used to being second in anything.*

Thainn moved to the front and they hurried through the passage, making no attempt to be silent—if Petissanji knew they were on his heels, he'd take no time for spells like the one that could make him see in the dark. Or—

"Can he conjure one of those beasts here?" Kelyn wondered out loud.

"Let us hope not," Thainn muttered with a fervent tone that made Kelyn grin at his back, though she held her commentary. For now, they needed to work together.

She'd hoped for some lingering traces of light once they exited the twisting, narrow passage and spilled out into the larger cavern beyond . . . for here, there were any number of choices to make; without the light, there was no indication of which direction he'd taken.

But there was nothing.

She covered the stout flame of her lamp with her hand; Thainn did likewise at the same moment, and glanced at her in surprised approval.

Not that it did either of them any good. Petissanji's light was beyond seeing.

"Shh," Kelyn said, sinking to her haunches, closing her eyes. Listening. Hearing Petissanji's movement, the scuff and scrape of his slippered feet against stone, the brush of his shirt against rock. She tilted her head, differentiating between the sound, trying to decipher the twisted bounce of the noises she heard. Right. He had gone right.

She opened her eyes to find Thainn conducting his own survey of sound, and stood. The slight noise of it alerted him. He looked at her. "Left."

"Right," she said at the same moment. They frowned at one another.

"Right," she said. "Young ears hear more clearly."

"Left," he said. "My ears have had more time to learn the ways of the world."

"Fine," she said, and struck out to the right.

"Kelyn!" he said sharply.

"Petissanji puts more distance between us in each breath that passes," she said over her shoulder. "I don't want to meet him alone, but I don't want him to get away, either."

Besides, she'd moved first.

"Atlia's arse!" Thainn said, and followed her. She sped through the unfamiliar passages, ducking and twisting through the narrow spots, moving with more swift agility than Petissanji could hope to attain, he who spent his days hidden in dark, secret rooms and plotting with his mind while his muscles languished.

More swift agility than her larger father, it seemed—for when she caught the first sight of Petissanji's light, Thainn was some distance behind her. She stopped, dimming her lamp, setting it down when it became clear that Petissanji's was no longer moving. When Thainn caught up with her, his sword pulled from its scabbard so he could negotiate the last tight spot, he came on with a scowl and his mouth ready to deliver lashing words. But before Kelyn could gesture him to silence, he took in the import of her lamp, saw that their quarry had stopped.

No doubt to invoke the belt.

Slowly, Thainn lowered his own lamp; only then did Kelyn inch forward, peering around a strange, faintly reflective rock flow that appeared to have oozed down in smooth, thick layers and frozen halfway down the more porous walls of the cave.

Petissanji, both hands clasping the belt in a strange, almost prayerful posture, stood with his head flung back, his eyes closed tightly in concentration, his lips moving in a constant chant. His lamp, the wick turned too high, burned in a high, flickering flame, igniting the curving walls of the small chamber into brightness—walls made of that same strange flowing rock, the upper layers of which were raised in ridges like the flow of wax down a candle.

Petissanji's feet were sunk to the ankles in stone.

Stop him! Kelyn started forward, well-trained to immediate action, to moving *now* before someone died in the mountains—and stopped herself. Here, in the outlands, when the foe as often as not seemed to be human, she lacked the experience for such instant judgment. She stepped back, making room for Thainn to join her.

Thainn instantly charged into the chamber, releasing a great roar of intent.

"*I* could have done that!" Kelyn cried, and leapt in after him, only to discover he'd pulled up after all, and that Petissanji, far from being alarmed by their arrival, pulled his teeth from his lips for an almost feverish laugh of triumph.

In those few moments, he'd sunk all the way to his crotch.

Thainn snarled at him, and brought his sword back in a two-handed grip, the windup to a blow that would take the witch's head off. Petissanji watched without fear.

Without fear.

"No!" Kelyn shouted, blocking Thainn's blade with her staff, seeing again the chant Petissanji had been finishing when he arrived, and the way his feet were already immersed in stone. "He *wants* you to attack him—he's made some kind of spell—" and then, rather than trying to explain, she pulled out one of the skipping-stone knives and flipped it at Petissanji. *Petissanji, up to his chest in stone—*

The knife bounced off the air a hand's width in front of Petissanji's eyes, rebounding sharply away;

sparks of brilliant light raced along each of its complex edges. When it landed, blackened, against the wall of the cave, it singed the rock all the way down to the ground.

"Ketura," Thainn breathed, looking from the knife to Petissanji and tossing the sword aside.

"You oaf," Petissanji said. "Count yourself lucky if you come out of this alive—you never had a chance of stopping me."

"I had you, moments ago." Thainn, his features set in the fierce scowl they formed so well, eased toward the witch, studying him, looking for some way to get to him. "You would be dead already, were it not for Abendar."

"You never would have had me, were it not for the fact that I became aware of Abendar's arrival. It was worth the risk, that chance at maintaining my position with him, and of seeing you put to death officially—Thainn, the great Wolverine, executed in Atlia—it has a nice sound to it, don't you think?"

"Grab him," Kelyn said, unable to get past Thainn to do it herself. "With your bare hands, grab him!"

Thainn looked at her as though she'd lost her wits. "The Traders said—"

"I heard them!" *Petissanji, up to his neck, one arm totally immersed, the other still free.* Too confident, now. Too close to winning. Kelyn gave Thainn a shove. "Grab him, get the belt!"

"Only a witch can navigate through solids with the belt," Petissanji said. *Up to his chin.* "You'd starve to death, lost in the rock."

"Do it!" Kelyn said. "He's getting away!" *Up to his eyes, eyes that scorned them.* "Ketura's balls, Wolverine, *trust me*—"

He turned to give her a hard, quick glare, the threat of what he would do to her if his trust was misplaced—*up to his brow, moving forward in the stone like a plow through the ground*—and dove for Petissanji's head, clamping his fingers into the man's hair.

Within seconds his arms were gone to the elbows, and even as he turned another warning on Kelyn, his head sunk into stone; Kelyn's stomach roiled at the impossible sight. Thainn's body, lying full length upon the ground, moved forward even as it merged downward, and the movement of his legs—a kick, a twist, reflecting the underground struggle—assured Kelyn that he was indeed still live.

But not for long. Not if she didn't live up to that moment of trust he had given her. She flung herself upon him, wrapping her fingers around the back of his thick leather belt, the other hand clamped around the staff—and the first she realized that she, too, had entered the stone was when she tried to brace her toes against the ground and felt no more resistance than that of cool water.

KeturaKeturaKetura—vain cries to a god who had forged his people with harsh conditions and a deaf ear to their pleas for help.

Kelyn gulped one last lungful of air as her head sunk below the ground, squinching her eyes closed against the sight of grey stone about to wash against them. Thainn's foot landed painfully against her thigh; his efforts to reach the belt made his body flex and twist beneath her hand, nearly ripping his own belt from her grasp a number of times.

Lungs bursting, must have air, must get out of here!

But to let go was death.

To be here *is death!*

Thainn's foot landed squarely in her stomach.

Kelyn lost her little remaining air; her eyes flew open—and in that moment, the staff hit the surface of the ground above her, jerking her progress to a halt. *Reman ironwood, deaf to all magics*—she took a great lungful of . . .

Best not to think what.

Thainn pulled her onward, stretching her arms, thrashing in her grip—she could see him, as though he swam before her in a thick grey lake, Petissanji an even dimmer figure beyond him—as he clawed his way down Petissanji's body, inexorably working his way toward the belt while Petissanji's magic pulled him onward and Kelyn's shoulders creaked—

—and strained—

—and screamed with pain—

She gritted her teeth and pulled back, squeezing her eyes closed against the agony of muscle and tendon stretched beyond bearing. And beneath her hand, Thainn gave a mighty jerk. Petissanji's howl, eerily filtered, filled the stone with sound—and then ceased, cut off as sharply as the edge of Thainn's blade. The pull on Kelyn's shoulders eased—until Thainn started flopping around like a fish out of water.

She gave his belt a sharp jerk—a warning—and when he stilled, she took a deep . . . *breath* . . . and tried to pull herself back toward the staff, her abused muscles protesting . . .

Failing her.

No. He'd trusted her.

She tried again. Slowly. Agonizing progress, measured in finger widths. And then suddenly her eyes rose above stone, and found her whitened knuckles, wrapped around the staff, right before her face.

She threw her elbow over it, pulling, bringing Thainn up until his head broke stone, and he, too, saw the staff, realized how she'd brought them back. He brought one arm up—*the belt*—and jammed the woven grass between his teeth so he, too, could grasp the staff, using the other hand to clamp onto her wrist—still at his waist—finally allowing her to uncrimp her fingers from the leather.

"Ketura's balls!" he said, panting, holding himself in place and helping to steady her as she slowly, carefully, pulled herself up to balance on the staff itself, no part of her touching stone. "That was a first even for me!"

"Even for you," she agreed dryly, making sure every bit of her was free of stone before pulling herself from his grip and jumping away, landing on stone that was pleasantly, wonderfully hard against her soles. In a few moments, Thainn had climbed free, balancing on the staff as she had done before him. He threw the belt away and stepped onto the ground.

Wordlessly, she picked up his sword and presented it to him, one eyebrow raised.

He took it, regarding her for a moment as the sword rested in both their hands. "Wolverine's daughter," he said, and nodded.

Chapter 17

Kelyn contemplated her satchel, laid out on one side of the small campfire she'd called her own. Flat and empty, its wide leather strap showing wear, it mirrored a pile of goods on the other. The latter clearly exceeded the capacity of the former.

But to leave any of it behind would be an insult to those who had gifted her.

She sighed, sat down cross-legged, and stuck her chin on her hand. Behind her, activity bordering on chaos filled the Trader camp, once again swollen to a complete complement of wagons for both caravans. There were squabbles and packing and sorting—and, of course, trading. Plenty of trading. Thainn's men mixed in with it all, poking through the goods and admiring this and that and making outrageously low offers on it all.

Thainn himself was . . . Kelyn didn't know where. In Abendar's town, she thought, arguing a few last details with Abendar before the Traders—and their witches—were allowed to move on. Or before *she* was allowed to move on, for that matter—although

Abendar had already pardoned her for the havoc in the cells and Belows, and had even rewarded her for her role in discovering and dealing with Petissanji.

She had never had more than one gold coin at a time before.

And she discovered a certain security in knowing that here, in this land where so many places were farmed and claimed, she had a way to secure food if she couldn't find a place to hunt. It was, she decided, a most un-Keturanlike feeling.

The coin, at least, fit easily into the satchel. Kelyn reached over and pulled the small pouch from the pile of goods, starting a pile for those things she would definitely take. And her cloak, of course—a shame the weather had warmed so thoroughly in these lower climes that she most certainly couldn't wear it during the day.

The boots. A goat-stomach bota—she could sling that over her shoulder separately. A fancy tortoise-shell comb she'd taken a liking to, with prongs much longer than her old carved bone comb. A colorful sash—much like Petissanji's—that she could wrap around one of her knife belts.

She smiled to herself, thinking of the image she would present—the slaver's loose, undyed shirt, woven of fine threads; his leather vest, black and tailored and possessed of many discreet pockets; her staff, whip, and crossed knife belts, one of which would soon be wrapped with bright finery.

Added to her stature and coloring—and her sex, for none of the cultures she had run into so far let women fill the role she had taken—no one would know what to make of her upon first sight.

That, she decided, was not necessarily a bad thing. Let them wonder. Kelyn picked out a hair trinket from the pile and considered it, musing whether or not to keep the randomly placed plaits the Trader women had given her several days earlier. And next to it . . . another item she wasn't sure if she would take with her, but one she was glad to have had, even for a short time.

A mirror.

A mirror that showed her that Endre had not been lying, nor had her father. Beaten and highly polished metal, slightly wavery, needing just the right kind of daylight in order to reflect her image with any consistency, it still told her plenty. There she was, her face grown into itself, her wide mouth no longer outsized, but pleasant above her clefted chin. Her eyes, no longer looking pulled to the sides of her face, but large and bright, tilted upward in an unusual but strangely appealing way. And when she held the mirror out at arm's length and flashed it down the length of her body, she discovered that although she was lanky and muscled, her hands and feet now suited her in size, and that, in fact, there was an unusual grace about them.

She set the mirror aside, in the pile she wouldn't take. She'd seen what she needed to see; she could carry it with her in her head.

Behind her, one of the camp conversations picked itself out of the general muddle and moved closer; she twisted, legs still crossed, to see who approached.

Anci, carrying a small bag, and Gazi. Kelyn felt no little alarm—*more* gifts to fit into her rapidly overwhelmed satchel?

Anci laughed. "You should see the look on your face," she said. "You'd never make a Trader!"

"I never thought I could," Kelyn said, making it a humble statement instead of the challenge it could have been. That much, she had learned. She indicated for the women to sit, but Anci shook her head, so Kelyn stood, instead—coming to her feet with one swift motion that should have been automatic, but instead got tangled and almost landed her in the fire.

Sighing, she righted herself, and caught Anci with her hand over her mouth, suppressing a smile.

Kelyn frowned down at herself. "I wish you could tell me more."

"About the curse?" Anci shook her head. "You know we would if we could."

"It's so . . . so . . ." at a loss for words, Kelyn threw up her hands. "All my life, my clumsiness ruled me. I worked so much harder than the others—not only to survive, but just to keep from doing myself an injury! And finally, in finding my father—or, in the moment *he* found *me*—the curse lifted. I felt it! It was so easy to move, to fight—! To think of all those years . . ."

"Ah," Anci said. "Perhaps that was the point all along."

Kelyn favored her with a skeptical expression. The woman sounded entirely too much like Rika. "To spend all those years in miserable clumsiness?"

Anci gave a sympathetic laugh. "To spend all those years working hard, so that when the curse was lifted, you had the strength and ability to protect yourself."

But it's not lifted, not for good. She had just proven that. And she'd proved it each time she had found danger since Thainn's declaration had first released her, when the tingling ran through her body and her limbs grew light and strong and faster than even she had thought possible.

Training. Continued training.

And still, the thought of all those years . . . not knowing why she broke every pot they owned more than once, or why she cut herself every time she got her hands on a sharp edge. All the tears she'd swallowed, and the teasing . . . it all burst out of her at once. "But *who*—Who would do such a thing?"

She hadn't really expected an answer, especially not from Darada's mother. But the woman didn't hesitate. "Someone who loved you," she said. "Someone who wanted to be sure you could take care of yourself when she couldn't."

Lytha. Thainn had intimated as much, once, though it had been nothing more than a jibe. Perhaps closer to the truth than he knew. *Lytha and Rika, together.* A Reman woman trying her best to prepare her fatherless Keturan child for adulthood.

"She could have told me," Kelyn muttered, annoyed at the tears stinging her eyes. She blinked them away and gestured at Anci's bag. "What have you?"

Anci held out the bag, and lifted it in a little gesture when Kelyn didn't immediately take it.

At that, take it she did, and loosened the ties at the top to peer inside. She found several candles and a few odds and ends beneath them, none of which made any sense to her; she gave Anci a quizzical look.

"Endre asked that we bring him these things, and see if you would come to his family's wagon. We thought it easier to give them to you and send you along with them."

She looked at the candles again. They were new, two white candles and one red. Charm candles. "And how does one have anything to do with the other?"

"It is something our people do when there have been misunderstandings between them."

Ah. Now that made sense, given the number of times she and Endre had gone crossways at one another, right up until the last moment. *I was supposed to have been there.* He wouldn't have been hurt. He wouldn't have gone down trying to protect Gergo. "Now?" she asked, glancing at her unsorted belongings. "He wants me to come, now?"

"Now," Anci agreed. "While he is awake. The magic helps, but his healing will still take time."

Now. Charms and misunderstandings. Kelyn sighed, left her things where they were, and headed for Endre's wagon—the one he once again shared with his father, younger brother, and uncle. A man's wagon, undecorated, utilitarian, the only fanciful thing on it the carvings on the kettlebox underneath the back end. Which, she was given to understand, had come from another wagon, long ago.

Endre's father, Verdo, sat on a hammock chair by the back, where the door hung wide open, facing the sun. Endre's brother, Derno, stood with him, arguing over some bit of something in his hand, some good over which they disagreed about the value. Upon seeing her approach, Derno's arguments stuttered to a stop; the youth had been tongue-tied around her since he had realized that Endre had taken her to the caves, and for what.

Verdo stood and gestured for her to enter the wagon, at the same time folding up his chair, making it clear he would take this conversation with Derno elsewhere. "Endre," he said into the wagon, adding a few quick words in Trader tongue. He took Derno by the arm and led him—forcibly at first—away.

"I'm coming in," Kelyn called into the wagon, ignoring the little fold-down steps and making one giant step up straight into the wagon itself.

Endre lay on the bottom bed along the side—for there were two beds to each side of the wagon, one atop the other and barely enough room to sit up in between—well propped up on pillows, looking sleepy but content. They had given him something for the pain, Kelyn deduced, and was sure of it when he smiled at her—a gentle smile, and just a shade too relaxed. Strips of cloth crisscrossed his chest in an attempt to keep the dressing snug over his wound, the sash among them.

He saw her looking at it. "I thought it fitting."

"It seems so to me." Kelyn put the bag by his side, and gestured at it. "A charm?"

"Yes," he said seriously—overly so, Kelyn thought, smiling a little. When he would have protested that smile—she knew him that well, now, to see it coming—she licked her thumb and reached over to wipe a smear of something—meat sauce?—from his upper lip as she sat on the edge of his narrow bed, nudging his hip over. That distracted him plenty; he stared at her in a bemused way while she repeated the gesture—never mind that the smear was long gone—and then traced his lower lip, letting her hand come to rest alongside his face.

"That—" he said, "that's not fair."

"Why?" she asked. "Because the door is open, or because you're hurt, or because I'm leaving?"

He gave her a cross look. "All of those."

"Do you want me to go sit on the other bed?"

"No," he said, too quickly, and then sent her another cross look when she laughed and he realized he'd been set up. "Just empty the bag, Kelyn."

She upended it, dumping the brief contents between her thigh and his side, where they wouldn't bounce to the floor. Two white candles. One red. A silver coin, and a wax-splattered dish with three candle holes in it. "A charm for misunderstandings."

"Yes," he said. "We have much of good between us, you and I. And just as much of misunderstandings. I asked too much of you . . . I judged you too harshly when you did things outside our ways."

She looked down at the candles rather than meet his flecked brown eyes. "But you were sometimes right. If I had been out where I was supposed to be, I would have been between you and the man who stabbed you. You wouldn't have been hurt. And if I hadn't used the dowser when Gergo told me to keep it hidden, your people never would have been caught by Atelic."

"No, and if we'd brought our witches openly into Abendar's town, maybe Petissanji would have found some other way to arrest them. If we'd told you more about magic, maybe you wouldn't have used the dowser. *And*—Anci told me that without your warning in the cave, they never would have overcome Petissanji. Even in taking him by surprise, they almost lost two witches to him."

"Nothing ever seems clear enough," Kelyn said. "If I never know whether I've done wrong or right, how will I ever make the right choice the next time?"

Endre looked surprised. "The same way all of us choose," he said. "We just do the best we can."

She looked at him a long moment. "I will always wonder if I'm right to walk away from you."

"We travel different paths," he said. "Maybe they'll intersect again one day." Then he grinned, and if it was affected by the witches' spells and herbs, this time she couldn't tell. "Besides, I know you. You won't be walking away. You'll be running . . . *toward* something. The next adventure."

She grinned back, slightly self-deprecating, knowing the truth of it.

"Light the candles," he said, gesturing at the standing lamp, the low-burning always flame shared among the wagons—here, no doubt, in deference to the work of the witches still in watching over Endre's healing. "All three of them. And stick them in the bowl."

There was no room for the bowl on the bed, so Kelyn balanced it on her knees, giving Endre fair warning with her glance. *Kelyn the clumsy*—still. He only nodded at her, so she lit the candles and stuck them in place. Too wobbly to suit her, but . . .

"Now give me your hands," he said, and when she held them out, he crossed his and took them; they held right in right and left in left. He looked into her eyes, long enough to make it significant, and said,

"I'm sorry. I was wrong to judge you so." Then he nudged one hand and added, "You say, *I care for you. I forgive you.*"

I feel silly, Kelyn wanted to say instead, but she didn't. "I care for you. I forgive you." Uncertain in the silence following her words, but full of the sense that he was waiting, she ventured, "I'm sorry. I didn't try hard enough to understand the reasons behind some of your ways."

"I care for you," he said. "I forgive you." He released her hands to fish out the silver coin that still sat between her leg and his side, and set it in the center of the bowl. Then he took one of the white candles and tipped it, letting wax run onto the coin. Hesitantly, she reached for the other white candle, and he gave her a smile of encouragement, so she did the same.

"Now," he murmured, replacing the white candle and picking up the red, "hold this one with me."

Together, they let red wax run over the coin. Following his lead, Kelyn blew out all three candles with him; he set the bowl between them, perched on his stomach, and said quietly, "Now we meet over the coin and candles."

She needed no prompting for this one. She leaned over and kissed him—and though she understood it not, she felt a wash of emotion—relief, and tenderness, and sadness that they were now parting. Startlingly strong, it brought forth tears—two of them, from she who had already fought them once this day and seldom even thought of tears—that rolled down her cheeks and onto his, until it was no longer possible to tell where they came from.

"Good." Endre put his arms around her. "We did well. It was a strong charm." His murmured words, so serious, tickled her ear.

She couldn't help it. She blew gently back into his own.

❖ ❖ ❖

Kelyn looped her satchel strap over her head and across her shoulder, shrugging it into a comfortable position. Definitely too full; she already had plans to trade some of the items for food.

After she was beyond reach of the Traders. No need for them to know which gifts she had chosen not to keep. She patted the pouch that held the trouble dowser. She'd wait on using it, too—at least until she was far enough away that such a small magic wouldn't be recognizable.

She hoped.

She bent over—awkward under the weight of the satchel—and snagged her staff from the ground, standing with it to look over the camp.

Typical Trader camp—active, holding plenty of laughter and many a shrewd glance. No signs here that anything had been amiss, aside from a number of wagons with black symbols painted over their doors—the wagons of the witches killed by Petissanji. Gergo sat within one, along with Lenci's aging sister. Both had been deeply affected by her loss, as well as the camp entire; Anci had years to go before she could fulfill her mother's role. And Gergo . . . Kelyn would find herself surprised if he lasted through the next winter. He was smaller, older—and, despite his boldness in bracing Abendar, not as much as he had been when Kelyn had met him.

Thainn's men no longer mingled among them as they had, these past days—for only Thainn seemed to have deep personal aversion to witches; when it came to good food, good company, and the chance to barter on a favored piece of goods, his men were hardly deterred by the stigma they had previously assigned to the witches. And so they had stayed here, enjoying themselves, while Thainn dealt with Abendar.

Now, though—now they were gone. Called back to Abendar's town, and to their next paying job—to help Abendar keep the peace in town while he purged his own ranks of those loyal to Petissanji. And Kelyn had sent Hann back with a mission—to find the two wayward children at the inn, give them a piece of her gold, and find them work—*good* work—within the fortress. Something to set them up for better lives.

Hann tried to extract from her the price of a kiss. She smacked him alongside the head instead; he only grinned and bowed as if he'd gotten the very thing he'd expected, and was playing with her in some sort of game. All of Thainn's men did that, to some degree . . . prodding her, poking her, teasing her into reaction—though usually at someone else's expense.

It was far too similar to her memories of the hunting pack for her truly to mind their games.

So.

Time to move on.

Even if Thainn had not bothered to speak to her since the day of Petissanji's grim fate. Not to ask her to stay, not to tell her she should leave. Until she'd gone from hurt to furious, and realized she needed to go, just to take possession of the decision. She'd sort out other feelings along the way.

Somehow.

All her other good-byes were said, and that would have to be enough. Kelyn put her back to the camp and struck off west. Soon she'd angle south, where she should meet the road Endre had told her of—the road that would take her into Rema. It was time to see something of her mother's land.

She walked on, long enough to loosen her muscles and to discover a newly hatched Atlian pest, swarms of large gnats that hung in miniature clouds over the land, oblivious to her presence no matter how wildly she waved her arms to shoo them away. No, the only way to get through one of those swarms was to squinch her eyes nearly closed, seal her mouth, hold her breath, and charge through, being certain to exhale forcefully through the nose upon clearing the gnats—for there was sure to be several up her nose.

Way up her nose. Kelyn doubled over for a fit of gnat-induced sneezing—once, twice, and then, just as she cautiously straightened, a surprising and thunderous third time.

Staggering to regain her balance under the satchel, she jammed the staff into the ground and took a deep, chest-lifting breath.

"I told you to stay out of that cave."

Startling as strongly as a Keturan rock goat, Kelyn whirled, staff flying, even as she recognized the voice. By the time she faced him, her startlement had changed to anger. "Ketura's balls! What are—" She stopped, blinking, and took a step back. "You have a horse!"

"I do," he said. "And glad of it, today. I had not intended to let those long legs of yours get such a start on me."

"No? You don't like the idea of the *daughter* leaving the *father*? I see some justice in it, myself."

"You're pouting," he said, bringing the horse—one of the largest she'd seen, no doubt to carry his size—up beside her.

She started walking. "I don't pout."

"You're pouting, because I had to go back to the fortress and deal with things there instead of staying with you and your Trader friends. Endre will be fine, you know."

"I don't need *you* to tell me that. And if I'd stayed out of that cave, you never would have known when Petissanji was there. You'd have given yourselves away before you moved on him, and failed to surprise him. Failed, altogether."

"True." He said the one word and nothing further,

and when she frowned up at him she found him smiling, anticipating and enjoying her reaction to the statement.

"*True?* Then why did you come up behind me and—" she stopped short, abruptly turning away from him. "Whatever game you're playing with me, I'm not. I won't."

"Then I'll have to think of another."

That earned him another sharp glance. "What do you mean?"

"If we're to travel together, we must find *something* to talk about."

"Traveling together," Kelyn said flatly.

"We need to get you a horse."

"No, we don't. No horse. *Traveling together*, you said. Don't try to run from that."

"The Wolverine never runs from anything," Thainn said, theatrically enough so she knew that he didn't, at least, take *everything* about his reputation seriously. "My men are busy at Abendar's town, but they hardly need me to oversee such work. I thought it would be best if I came with you for a while."

"You thought it would be best . . ." she repeated, and jabbed him in the thigh with her staff. "Be *best*? You don't think I can take care of myself? You don't think I'm ready to explore the outlands?" She jabbed him again. "I don't need your protection!"

"Ow!" he said, and rubbed the spot dramatically. She glared up at him, suspecting—and finding—the broad grin on his face. "*You*," he said, "are ready for anything. But the outlands . . ." He shook his head. "No, I think perhaps the outlands are not ready for *you*, and I must protect *them*." He grinned again. "*Wolverine's daughter*."

Doranna's Backstory....

Doranna Durgin spent her childhood filling notebooks first with stories and art, and then with novels. After obtaining a degree in wildlife illustration and environmental education, she spent a number of years deep in the Appalachian Mountains. When she emerged, it was as a writer who found herself irrevocably tied to the natural world and its creatures.

Doranna, who won the Compton Crook Award with first novel *Dun Lady's Jess*, lives in upstate New York with two irrepressible Cardigan Welsh Corgis—Kacey & Jean-Luc Picardigan—and a Lipizzan gelding who thinks too much. You can contact her at:

dmd@doranna.net

or

PO Box 26207
Rochester, NY 14626
(SASE please)

or visit *http://www.doranna.net*

Join the Book-Facing Legion at:
http://www.doranna.net/legion.html